THE
JESTER

THE
JESTER

JAMES PATTERSON
& ANDREW GROSS

WARNER BOOKS

NEW YORK   BOSTON

WARNER BOOKS EDITION

Copyright © 2003 by James Patterson
All rights reserved. No part of this book may be reproduced in any form or by any electronic or mechanical means, including information storage and retrieval systems, without permission in writing from the publisher, except by a reviewer who may quote brief passages in a review.

This book is an abridged version of the original hardcover.

Cover illustration by Theo Rudnack
Hand lettering by James Montalbano

Warner Vision is a registered trademark of Warner Books, Inc.

Warner Books, Inc.
1271 Avenue of the Americas
New York, NY 10020

Visit our Web site at www.twbookmark.com

An AOL Time Warner Company

Printed in the United States of America

Originally published in hardcover by Little, Brown and Company
First International Paperback Printing: December 2003
First United States Paperback Printing: February 2004

10 9 8 7 6 5 4 3 2 1

THE
JESTER

Prologue

THE FIND

WEARING A BROWN TWEED SUIT and his customary dark tortoiseshell sunglasses, Dr. Alberto Mazzini pushed through the crowd of loud and agitated reporters.

"Can you tell us about the artifact? Is it real? Is that why you're here?" a woman pressed, shoving a microphone marked CNN in his face. "Have tests been performed on the DNA?"

Dr. Mazzini was already annoyed. How had the press jackals been alerted? Nothing had even been confirmed about the find. He waved off the reporters and camera operators.

A tiny dark-haired woman in a black pantsuit was waiting for Mazzini inside the museum. She looked to be in her mid-forties and appeared to almost curtsy in the presence of this prestigious guest.

"Thank you for coming. I am Renée Lacaze, the director of the museum. I tried to control the press, but . . ." She shrugged. "They smell a big story. It is as if we've found an atom bomb."

As the national director of the Vatican Museum, Alberto Mazzini had lent the weight of his authority to every important find of religious significance that had been unearthed over the past thirty years. He had also been involved in the investigation of every hoax, hundreds of them.

Renée Lacaze led Mazzini along the narrow fifteenth-century hall inlaid with heraldic tile.

"You say the relic was unearthed in a grave?" Mazzini asked.

"A shopping mall . . ." Lacaze smiled. "Even in downtown Borée, the construction goes night and day. The bulldozers dug up what must have once been a crypt."

Ms. Lacaze escorted her important guest into a small elevator and then up to the third floor. "The grave belonged to some long-forgotten duke who died in 1098. At first we wondered, why would a precious relic from a thousand years earlier, *and half the world away,* be buried in an eleventh-century grave?"

"And what did you find?" Mazzini asked.

"It seems our duke actually went to fight in the Crusades. We know he sought after relics from the time of Christ." They finally arrived at her office. "I advise you to take a breath. You are about to behold something extraordinary."

The artifact lay on a plain white sheet on an examiner's table.

Mazzini finally removed his sunglasses. He didn't have to hold his breath. It was completely taken away. *My God, this is an atom bomb!*

"Look closely. There is an inscription on it."

The Vatican director bent over it. *Yes, it could be.* It had all the right markings. There was an inscription. In Latin. He squinted close to read. *"Acre, Galilee . . ."* He examined the artifact from end to end. The age fit. The markings. Yet how did it come to be buried here? "All this, it does not really prove anything."

"That's true, of course." Renée Lacaze shrugged. "But Docteur . . . I am from here. My father is from the valley, my father's father, and his. There have been stories here for hundreds of years, long before this grave tumbled open. Stories every schoolchild in Borée was raised on. That this holy relic was here, *in Borée,* nine hundred years ago."

Mazzini had seen a hundred purported relics like this, but the tremendous power of this one gripped and unnerved him. A reverent force gave him the urge to kneel on the stone floor.

Finally, that's what he did — as if he were in the presence of Jesus Christ.

Alberto Mazzini couldn't take his eyes off the incredible artifact on the plain white sheet. This was more than just the crowning moment of his career. It was a miracle.

"There's just one more thing," said Ms. Lacaze.

"What?" Mazzini mumbled. "What one more thing?"

"The local lore, it always said a precious relic was here. Just never that it belonged to a duke. But to a man of far more humble origins."

"What sort of lowborn man would come into such a prize? A priest? Perhaps a thief?"

"No." Renée Lacaze's brown eyes widened. "Actually, a jester."

Part One

THE ORIGINS OF COMEDY

Chapter 1

Veille du Père, a village in southern France, 1096

The church bells were ringing.

Loud, quickening peals — echoing through town in the middle of the day.

Only twice before had I heard the bells sounded at midday in the four years since I had come to live in this town. Once, when word reached us that the King's son had died. And the second, when a raiding party from our lord's rival in Digne swept through town during the wars, leaving eight dead and burning almost every house to the ground.

What was going on?

I rushed to the second-floor window of the inn I looked after with my wife, Sophie. People were running into the square, still carrying their tools. *"What's going on? Who needs help?"* they shouted.

Then Antoine, who farmed a plot by the river, galloped over the bridge aboard his mule, pointing back toward the road. "They're coming! They're almost here!"

From the east, I heard the loudest chorus of voices, seemingly raised as one. I squinted through the trees and felt my jaw drop. *"Jesus, I'm dreaming,"* I said to myself. A peddler with a cart was considered an event here. I blinked at the sight, not once but twice.

It was the greatest multitude I had ever seen! Jammed along the narrow road into town, stretching out as far as the eye could see.

"Sophie, come quick, *now,*" I yelled. "You're not going to believe this."

My wife of three years hurried to the window, her yellow hair pinned up for the workday under a white cap. "Mother of God, Hugh . . ."

"It's an army," I muttered, barely able to believe my eyes. "The Army of the Crusade."

Chapter 2

EVEN IN VEILLE DU PÈRE, word had reached us of the Pope's call. We had heard that masses of men were leaving their families, taking the Cross, as nearby as Avignon. And here they were . . . *the army of Crusaders, marching through Veille du Père!*

But *what* an army! More of a rabble. Men, women, children, carrying clubs and tools straight from home. And it was vast — thousands of them! Not fitted out with armor or uniforms, but shabbily, with red crosses either painted or sewn onto plain tunics.

And at the head of this assemblage . . . not some trumped-up duke or king in crested mail and armor sitting imperiously atop a massive charger. But a little man in a homespun monk's robe, barefoot, bald, with a thatched crown, plopped atop a simple mule.

"It is their awful singing the Turks will turn and run from," I said, shaking my head, "not their swords."

Everyone in town stood and stared. Children ran out and

danced around the approaching monk. No one had ever seen anything like it before. *Nothing ever happened here!*

Below us, the vast column wound into the main square and the queer monk at its head tugged his mule to a stop. A bearded knight helped him slide off. Father Leo, the town's priest, went up to greet him. The singing stopped, weapons and packs were laid down. Everyone in our town was pressed around the tiny square. To listen.

"I am called Peter the Hermit," the monk said in a surprisingly strong voice, "urged by His Holiness Urban to lead an army of believers to the Holy Land to free the holy sepulchre from the heathen hordes. *Are there any believers here?*"

He was pale and long nosed, resembling his mount, and his brown robes had holes in them, threadbare. Yet as he spoke, he seemed to grow, his voice rising in power and conviction.

"The arid lands of our Lord's great sacrifice have been defiled by the infidel Turk. Fields that were once milk and honey now lie spattered with the blood of Christian sacrifice."

"Join us," many from the ranks called out loudly. "Kill the pagans and sit with the Lord in Heaven."

"For those who come," the monk named Peter went on, "for those who put aside their earthly possessions and join our Crusade, His Holiness Urban promises unimaginable rewards. Riches, spoils, and honor in battle. His protection for your families who dutifully remain behind. An eternity in Heaven at the feet of our grateful Lord. And, most of all, freedom. Freedom from all servitude upon your return. Who will come, brave souls?"

Shouts of acclamation rose throughout the square. People I had known for years shouted, "*I . . . I will come!*"

My own blood surged. What a glorious adventure

awaited. Riches and spoils picked up along the way. A chance to change my destiny in a single stroke. I felt my soul spring alive. I thought of gaining our freedom, and the treasures I might find on the Crusade. For a moment I almost raised my hand and called out, *"I will come! I will take the Cross."*

But then I felt Sophie's hand pressing on mine. I lost my tongue.

Then the procession started up again. The ranks of farmers, masons, bakers, maids, whores, jongleurs, and outlaws hoisting their sacks and makeshift weapons, swelling in song.

I watched them with a yearning I thought had long been put behind me. I had traveled in my youth. I'd been brought up by goliards, students and scholars who entertained from town to town. And there was something that I missed from those days.

I missed being free, and even more than that, I wanted freedom for Sophie and the children we would have one day.

Chapter 3

TWO DAYS LATER, other visitors came through our town. There was a ground-shaking rumble from the west, followed by a cloud of gravel and dust. Horsemen were coming in at a full gallop!

There was a shriek, and then a shout. Children playing ball in the square dived out of the way. Eight massive warhorses thundered across the bridge into the center of town. On their huge mounts, I saw knights wearing the purple-and-white colors of Baldwin of Treille, our liege lord.

The party of horsemen pulled to a stop in the square. I recognized the knight in charge as Norcross, our liege lord's chatelain, his military chief. He scanned our village from atop his mount and remarked loudly, "This is Veille du Père?"

"It must be, my lord," a companion knight replied with an exaggerated sniff. "We were told to ride east until the smell of shit, then head directly for it."

Their presence here could only signal harm. I began to

make my way slowly toward the square with my heart pounding. Anything might happen. *Where was Sophie?*

Norcross dismounted and the others did the same, their chargers snorting heavily. The chatelain had dark, hooded eyes that flashed only a sliver of light, like an eighth-moon. A trace of a thin, dark beard.

"I bring greetings from your lord, Baldwin," he said for all to hear, stepping into the center of the square. "Word has reached him that a *rabble* passed through here a day ago."

As he spoke, his knights began to fan out through town. They pushed aside women and children, sticking their heads into houses as if they owned them. Their haughty faces read, *Get out of my way, pieces of shit.*

Now I realized what Norcross and his men were doing here. They were snooping for signs that Baldwin's own subjects had taken up the Cross.

Norcross strutted around the square, his small eyes moving from person to person. "It is your lord, Baldwin, who demands your service, not some moth-eaten hermit. It is pledged and honor bound to *him*. Next to his, the Pope's protection is worthless."

I finally caught sight of Sophie, hurrying from the well with her bucket. Beside her was the miller's wife, Marie, and their daughter, Aimée.

Father Leo spoke up. "On the fate of your soul, knight," the priest said, stepping toward him, "do not defame those who now fight for God's glory."

Frantic shouts rang out. Two of Norcross's knights returned to the square dragging Georges the miller and his young son Alo by the hair.

Chapter 4

OUR POWERLESSNESS WAS SO OBVIOUS it was shameful to me. Norcross's sword jangled as he made his way to the frightened miller. "On my word, miller." Norcross smiled. "Only last week did you not have *two* sons?"

"My son Matt has gone to Vaucluse," Georges said, and looked toward me. "To study the metal trade."

"The metal trade . . ." Norcross nodded, bunching his lips. "And with your stronger son gone," Norcross pressed on, "how will you continue to pay your tax to the duke, your labor now depleted by a third?"

Georges's eyes darted about. "It will be made easily, my lord. I will work that much harder."

"That is good." Norcross nodded, stepping over to the boy. "In that case, you won't be missing *this* one too much, will you?" In a flash, he hoisted the nine-year-old lad up like a sack of hay.

He carried Alo, kicking and screaming, toward the mill.

As Norcross passed the miller's cowering daughter, he winked at his men. "Feel free to help yourselves to some of the miller's lovely grain." They grinned and dragged poor Aimée, screaming wildly, inside the mill.

Norcross took a hemp rope and, with the help of a cohort, lashed Alo to the staves of the mill's large wheel, which dipped deep beneath the surface of the river.

Georges threw himself at the chatelain's feet. "Haven't I always been true to our lord, Baldwin? Haven't I done what was expected?"

"Feel free to take your appeal to His Holiness." Norcross laughed, lashing the boy's wrists and ankles tightly to the water wheel.

"Father, father . . ." the terrified Alo cried.

Norcross began to turn the wheel. To Georges and Marie's frantic shrieks, Alo went under. Norcross held it for a moment, then slowly raised the wheel. The child appeared, wildly gasping for air.

The despicable knight laughed at our priest. "What do you say, Father? Is this what you expect from the Pope's protection?" He lowered the wheel again and the small boy disappeared.

I counted to thirty. "Please," Marie begged on her knees. "He's just a boy."

Norcross finally began to raise the wheel. Alo was gagging and coughing water out of his lungs. I could scarcely breathe myself. I had to do something — even if it sealed my own fate.

"Sir." I stepped forward, toward Norcross. "*I* will help the miller increase his tax by a third."

"And who are *you,* carrot-top?" The glowering knight turned, fixed on my shock of bright red hair.

"Carrots too, if my lord wants." I took another step. I was prepared to say anything, whatever gibberish might divert him. "We'll throw in two bushels of carrots!"

I was about to go on — a joke, nonsense, anything that came into my head — when one of the henchmen rushed up to me. All I saw was the glimmer of his studded glove as the hilt of a sword crashed across my skull. In the next breath I was on the ground.

"Hugh, Hugh," I heard Sophie scream.

"Carrot-top here must be keen on the miller," Norcross jeered. "Or the miller's wife. By a third more, you say. Well, in my lord's name, I accept your offer. Consider your tax raised."

At the same time, he lowered the wheel again. I heard a struggling, choking Alo go under one more time.

Norcross shouted, "If it's a fight you want, then fight for the glory of your liege when called upon. If it's riches, then attend harder to your work."

Norcross leaned against the wheel for the longest time. An anguished plea rose from the crowd, *"Please . . . let the boy up. Let him up."* I clenched my fist, counting the beats that Alo remained under. *Twenty . . . thirty . . . forty.*

Then Norcross's face split into an amused smile. "Goodness . . . do I forget the time?"

He slowly raised the wheel. When Alo broke the surface, the boy's face was bloated and wide-eyed. His small jaw hung open, lifeless.

"What a shame." Norcross sighed, leaving the wheel aloft and Alo's lifeless body suspended high. "It seems he wasn't cut out for the miller's life after all."

A silence ensued, a terrible moment that was empty and gnawing. It was broken only by Aimée's whimpers as she emerged weak-kneed from the mill.

"Let us go." Norcross gathered his knights. "I think the duke's point is adequately driven home."

As he made his way back across the square, he stopped over me where I still lay and hovered. Then he pressed his heavy boot into my neck. "Do not forget your pledge, carrot-top. I will be looking especially for *your* tax payment."

Chapter 5

THAT TERRIBLE AFTERNOON changed my life. That night, as Sophie and I lay in bed, I couldn't hold back the truth from her. She and I had always shared everything, good and bad. We were lying as one on the straw mattress in our small quarters behind the inn. I gently stroked her long blond hair, which fell all the way down her back.

It was love at first sight for us. *At ten!*

I had spent my youth traveling with a band of itinerant goliards, given to them at a young age when my mother died. They raised me as one of their own, taught me Latin, grammar, logic, how to read and write. But most of all, they taught me how to perform. We traveled the large cathedral towns, Nîmes, Cluny, Le Puy, reciting our irreverent songs, tumbling, and juggling for the crowds. Each summer, we passed through Veille du Père. I saw Sophie there at her father's inn, her shy blue eyes unable to hide from mine. And later, I noticed her peeking at a rehearsal. I was sure, *at me* . . . I swiped a sunflower and went up to her. "What goes in all stiff and stout, but when it comes out it's flopping about?"

She widened her eyes and blushed. "How could anyone but a devil have such bright red hair?" she said. Then she ran away.

A cabbage, I was about to say.

Each year when we returned, I came bearing a sunflower, until Sophie had grown from a gangly girl into the most beautiful woman I had ever seen. She had a song for me, a teasing rhyme:

> *A maiden met a wandering man*
> *In the light of the moon's pure cheer,*
> *And though they fell in love at that first sight,*
> *It was a love that was born for tears.*

I called her my princess, and she said that I probably had one in every town. But in truth, I did not. Each year I promised I would come back, and I always did. One year, I stayed.

The three years we'd been married had been the happiest I had known. I felt connected for the first time in my life.

But as I held Sophie that night, something told me I could no longer live like this. The rage that burned in my heart from the day's horror was killing me. There would always be another Norcross, another tax levied upon us.

Until we were free.

"Sophie, I have something important to talk to you about." I snuggled into the smooth curve of her back.

She had nearly drifted off to sleep. "Can't it wait, Hugh?"

I swallowed. "Raymond of Toulouse is forming an army. They leave for the Holy Land in a few days."

Sophie turned in my arms and faced me with a blank, unsure look.

"I have to go," I said.

Sophie sat up, almost dumbfounded. "You want to take the Cross?"

"Not the Cross. I wouldn't fight for that. But Raymond has promised freedom to anyone who joins. *Freedom*, Sophie . . . You saw what happened today."

"You're leaving," she said, turning her eyes from me, "because I have not given you a child."

"I am not! I love you more than anything. When I see you each day, working around the inn, or even amid the grease and smoke of the kitchen, I thank God for how lucky I am. I'll be back before you know it."

She nodded, unconvinced. "You are no soldier, Hugh. You could die."

"I'm strong. And agile. No one around can do the tricks I do."

"No one wants to hear your silly jokes, Hugh." Sophie sniffed. "Except me."

"Then I'll scare the infidels off with my bright red hair."

I saw the outline of a smile from her. I held her by the shoulders and looked into her eyes. "I will be back. I swear it. Just like when we were children. I always told you I'd return. I always did."

She nodded, a bit reluctantly. I could see that she was scared, but so was I. I held her and stroked her hair.

Sophie lifted her head and kissed me, a mixture of ardor and tears.

"You'll come back, Hugh?" Her eyes locked on mine.

"I swear." I reached and wiped a glistening tear from her eye. "Who knows?" I smiled. "Maybe I'll come back a knight. With untold treasure and fame."

"My knight," she whispered. "And I, your queen . . ."

Chapter 6

THE MORNING OF THE DAY I was to leave was bright and clear. I rose early, even before the sun. The town had bid me godspeed with a festive roast the night before. All the toasts had been made and farewells said.

All but one.

In the doorway of the inn, Sophie handed me my pouch. In it was a change of clothes, bread to eat, a hazel twig to clean my teeth. "It may be cold," she said. "You have to cross the mountains. Let me get your skin."

I stopped her. "Sophie, it's summer. I'll need it more when I come back."

"Then I should pack some more food for you."

"I'll find food." I pumped out my chest. "People will be eager to feed a Crusader."

She stopped and smiled at my plain flax tunic and calf-skin vest. "You don't look like much of a Crusader."

I stood before her, ready to leave, and smiled too.

"There's one more thing," Sophie said with a start. She hurried to the table by the hearth. She came back a moment later with her treasured comb, a thin band of beech wood painted with flowers. It had belonged to her mother. Other than the inn, I knew she valued it more than anything in her life. "Take this with you, Hugh."

"Thanks," I tried to joke, "but where I'm headed a woman's comb may be looked at strangely."

"Where you're headed, my love, you will need it all the more."

To my surprise, she snapped her prized comb in two. She handed half to me. Then she held her half out and we touched the jagged edges together, neatly fitting it back into a whole.

"I never thought I would ever say good-bye to you," she whispered, doing her best not to cry. "I thought we would live out our lives together."

"We will," I said. *"See?"* One more time, we fitted the comb's halves together and made a whole.

I drew Sophie close and kissed her. I felt her thin body tremble in my arms. I knew she was trying to be brave. There was nothing more to say.

"So . . ." I took a breath and smiled.

We looked at each other for a long while, then I remembered my own gift. From my vest pocket I took out a small sunflower. I had gone into the hills to pick it early that morning. "I'll be back, Sophie, to pick sunflowers for you."

She took it. Her bright blue eyes were moist with tears.

I threw my pouch over my shoulder and tried to drink in the last sight of her beautiful, glistening eyes. "I love you, Sophie."

"I love you too, Hugh. I can't wait for my next sunflower."

I started toward the road. West, to Toulouse. At the stone bridge on the edge of town, I turned and took a long last look at the inn. It had been my home for the past three years. The happiest days of my life.

I gave a last wave to Sophie. She stood there, holding the sunflower, and reached out the jagged edge of her comb one last time.

Then I did a little hop, like a jig, to break the mood, and started to walk, spinning around a final time to catch her laugh.

Her golden hair down to her waist. That brave smile. Her tinkling little-girl laugh.

It was the image I carried for the next two years.

Chapter 7

A year later, somewhere in Macedonia

The heavy-bearded knight reared his mount over us on the steep ridge. "March, you princesses, or the only Turkish blood you'll see will be at the end of a mop."

March... We had been *marching* for months now. Months so long and grueling, so lacking in all provision, I could mark them only by the sores oozing on my feet, or the lice crawling in my beard.

We had marched across Europe and through the Alps. At first in tight formation, cheered in every town we passed, our tunics clean, with bright red crosses, helmets gleaming in the sun.

Then, into the craggy mountains of Serbia — each step slow and treacherous, every ridge ripe with ambush. I watched as many a loyal soul, eager to fight for the glory of God, was swept screaming into vast crevices or dropped in his tracks by Serb or Magyar arrows a thousand miles before the first sign of a Turk.

All along we were told that Peter's army was months ahead of us, slaughtering infidels and hoarding all the spoils, while our nobles fought and bickered among themselves, and the rest of us trudged like beaten livestock in the blistering heat and bargained for what little food there was.

I'll be back in a year, I had promised Sophie. Now that was just a mocking refrain in my dreams. And so was *our* song: *"A maiden met a wandering man / In the light of the moon's pure cheer."*

Along the way, I had made a lasting friend. Nicodemus, an old Greek, was schooled in the sciences and languages. He managed to keep up his steady stride despite a satchel heavy with tracts of Aristotle, Euclid, and Boethius. *Professor,* we called him. Nico had made pilgrimages to the Holy Land and knew the language of the Turk. He spent many hours on the march teaching it to me. He had joined the quest as a translator, and because of his white beard and moth-eaten robe, he had the reputation of being a bit of a soothsayer too. But every time a soldier moaned, "Where the hell are we, Professor?" and the old Greek muttered only, *"Near . . . ,"* his reputation as a seer suffered.

It was late summer when we finally came out of the mountains.

"Where are we, Hugh?" someone moaned, as another interminable valley loomed before our eyes.

"By my calculations . . ." I tried to sound cheerful. "A left at the next ridge and we should see *Rome.* Isn't that right, Nico? This was the pilgrimage to St. Peter's we signed up for, wasn't it? Or, shit, was it the Crusade?"

A ripple of tired laughter snaked through the exhausted ranks.

Nicodemus started to answer, but everyone shouted him

down. "We know, Professor, we're *near,* right?" taunted Mouse, a diminutive Spaniard with a large hooked nose.

Suddenly I heard shouting from up ahead. Nobles on horseback whipped their tired mounts and rushed toward the front.

All at once, my legs seemed ready to comply. I grabbed my shield and ran forward. Ahead of us was a wide gulf in the mountains. Hundreds of men were gathered there, knights and soldiers.

For once, they were not defending themselves. They were shouting, slapping one another on the back, thrusting their swords toward Heaven and hurling their helmets into the air.

Nico and I pushed our way through the crowd and peered out over the edge of the gulf.

Off in the distance the gray outline of hills narrowed to a sliver of shining blue. *"The Bosporus,"* people shouted. *The Bosporus . . . !*

"Son of Mary," I muttered. We were here!

A jubilant roar went up. Everyone pointed at a walled city nestled into the isthmus's edge. *Constantinople.* It took my breath away, like nothing I had ever seen before. It seemed to stretch out forever, glinting through the haze.

Many knights sank to their knees in prayer. Others, too exhausted to celebrate, simply bowed their heads and wept.

"What's going on?" Nico looked around.

"What's going on . . . ?" I repeated. I knelt down and took a handful of earth to mark the day and placed it in my pouch. "You see those hills over there?" I pointed across the channel.

He nodded.

"Sharpen your knife, my friend. . . . Those are Turk!"

Chapter 8

FOR TWO WEEKS we rested outside the gates of Constantinople.

Such a city I had never seen before in all my life, with its huge glittering domes, hundreds of tall towers, Roman ruins and temples, and streets paved with polished stone. Ten of Paris could have fit within its walls.

And the people . . . crowding the massive walls, roaring with cheers. Clad in colorful, lightweight cottons and silks, in hues of crimson and purple I had never seen. Every race was represented. European, black slaves from Africa, yellows from China. And people of no stench. Who bathed and smelled of perfume, dressed up in ornate robes.

Even the men!

I had traveled across Europe in my youth and had played most of the large cathedral towns, but never had I seen a place like this! Gold was like tin here. Stalls and markets were crammed with the most exotic goods. I traded for a gilded perfume box to take back home for Sophie. "A relic already!" Nico laughed. New aromas en-

tranced me, cumin and ginger, and there were fruits I had
never tasted before: oranges and figs.

I savored every exotic image, thinking of how I would
describe it all to Sophie. We were hailed as heroes and we
had fought almost no one. If this was how it would be, I
would return both sweet smelling *and* free!

Then the knights and nobles rallied us. *"Crusaders, you
are here for God's work, not for silver and soap."* We said
good-bye to Constantinople, crossing the Bosporus on
wooden pontoons.

At last we stood in the land of the dreaded Turk!

The first fortresses we encountered were empty and
abandoned, towns scorched and plundered dry.

"The pagan is a coward," the soldiers mocked. "He
hides in his hole like a squirrel."

We spotted red crosses painted everywhere, pagan
towns now consecrated in the name of God. All signs that
Peter's army had been through.

The nobles pushed us hard. "Hurry, you lazy louts, or
the little hermit will take all the spoils."

And we did hurry, though our new enemy became the
blistering heat and thirst. We baked like hogs, sucking our
water skins dry. The pious among us dreamed of their holy
mission; the nobles, no doubt, of relics and glory; the innocent of finally proving their worth.

Outside Civetot we had our first taste of the enemy. A
few straggly horsemen, turbaned and cloaked in robes,
ringed our ranks, lofting some harmless arrows at us, then
fled into the hills like children hurling stones.

Civetot seemed deserted, an enclave of stone dwellings
on the edge of a dense wood. No one wanted to delay in
our rush to catch up with the army of Peter, but we needed
water badly, so we decided to enter the town.

On the outskirts, a grim odor pressed at my nostrils.

Nicodemus glanced at me. "You smell it, don't you, Hugh?"

I nodded. I knew the stench, from burying the dead. But this was magnified a thousand times. At first I thought it was just slaughtered livestock, or offal, but as we got closer, I saw that Civetot was smoking like burning cinders.

As we entered the town there were corpses everywhere. A sea of body parts. Heads severed and gawking, limbs cut off and piled like wood, blood drenching the parched earth. It was a slaughter. Red crosses smeared all over the walls — *in blood*.

"What has happened here?" a soldier muttered. Some puked and turned away. My stomach felt as empty as a bottomless pit.

From out of the trees, a few stragglers appeared. Their clothing was charred and tattered, their skin dark with blood and filth. They all bore the wide-eyed, hollow look of men who have seen the worst atrocities and somehow lived. It was impossible to tell if they were Christian or Turk.

"Peter's army has crushed the infidels," someone called out. "They've gone ahead to Antioch."

But not a man among us cheered.

"This *is* Peter's army," Nicodemus said grimly. "What remains of it."

Chapter 9

WE BURIED THE DEAD for six days straight. Then our dispirited army headed farther south.

In Caesarea, we joined forces with Count Robert of Flanders and Bohemond of Antioch, a heralded fighter. They had recently taken Nicaea. Our spirits were bolstered by the tales of Turks fleeing at full run, their towns now under Christian flags. Our once fledgling troop was now an army *forty thousand strong*.

Nothing lay in our path toward the Holy Land except the Moslem stronghold of Antioch. There, it was said, believers were being nailed to the city's walls, and the most precious relics in all of Christendom, a shroud stained by the tears of Mary and the very lance that had pierced the Savior's side on the cross, were being held for ransom.

Yet nothing so far could prepare us for the hell we were about to face.

First it was the heat, the most hostile I had ever felt in my life.

The sun became a raging, red-eyed demon that, never sheltered, we grew to hate and curse. Hardened knights, praised for valor in battle, howled in anguish, literally roasting in their armor, their skin blistered from the touch of the metal. Men simply dropped as they marched, overcome, and were left, uncared for, where they fell.

And the thirst . . . Each town we got to was scorched and empty, run dry of provision by the Turks themselves. What little water we carried we consumed like drunken fools. I saw men clearly over the edge guzzle their own urine as if it were ale.

"If this is the Holy Land," the Spaniard Mouse remarked, "God can keep it."

"Hold your tears," Nico warned, keeping up with his shuffling stride. "When we hit the mountains, you will think *this* was Paradise."

Nico was right. Jagged mountains appeared in our path, chillingly steep and dry of all life. Narrow passes, barely wide enough for a cart and a horse, cut through the rising peaks. At first we were glad to leave the inferno behind, but as we climbed, a new hell awaited.

The higher we got, the slower and more treacherous every step became. Sheep, horses, carts overladen with supplies, had to be dragged single file up the steep way. A mere stumble, a sudden rock slide, and a man disappeared over the edge, sometimes dragging a companion along with him.

"Press on," the nobles urged. "In Antioch, God will reward you."

But every summit we surmounted brought the sight of a new peak, trails more nerve wracking than the last. Once-proud knights trudged humbly, their chargers useless, dragging their armor, alongside foot soldiers like Nico and me.

Yet still we climbed, one step at a time, sweltering in our tunics and armor, knowing that on the other side lay Antioch.

And beyond that, the Holy Land. Jerusalem!

Chapter 10

"TELL US A STORY, Hugh?" Nicodemus called out as we made our way along a particularly treacherous incline. "The more *blasphemous* the better."

The trail seemed cut out of the mountain's edge, teetering over an immense chasm. One false step would mean a grisly death. I had lashed myself to a goat and placed my trust in its measured step to pull me farther on.

"There is the one about the convent and the whorehouse," I said, delving back to my days as an innkeeper. "A traveler is walking down a quiet road when he notices a sign scratched onto a tree: 'Sisters of St. Brigit Convent, House of Prostitution, two miles.'"

"Yes, I saw it myself," a soldier exclaimed. "A ways back on that last ridge." The peril of the climb was broken by a few welcome laughs.

"The traveler assumes it is a joke," I resumed, "and continues along. Soon he comes to another sign. 'Sisters of St. Brigit, House of Prostitution, one mile.' Now his curiosity is piqued. A ways ahead, there is a third sign. This time: 'Convent, Brothel, next right.'

"'Why not?' the traveler thinks, and turns down the road until he arrives at an old stone church marked *St. Brigit*. He steps up and rings the bell, and an abbess answers. 'What may we do for you, my son?'

"'I saw your signs along the road,' the traveler says. 'Very well, my son,' the abbess replies. 'Please, follow me.'

"She leads him through a series of dark, winding passages where he sees many beautiful young nuns who smile at him."

"Where are these nuns when *I* am in need?" a soldier behind me moaned.

"At last the abbess stops at a door," I went on. "The traveler goes in and is greeted by another comely nun, who instructs him, 'Place a gold coin in the cup.' He empties his pockets excitedly. 'Good enough,' she says. 'Now, just go through that door.'

"Aroused, the traveler hurries through the door, but he finds himself back outside, at the entrance, facing another sign. 'Go in peace,' it reads, 'and consider yourself properly screwed!'"

Laughter broke out from all around.

For a few moments, our burden had seemed bearable. All I wanted was to get off this ridge.

Suddenly I heard a rumble from above. A slide of rock and gravel hurtled down at us. I gripped the sheer stone as huge rocks crashed around me, missing me by the width of a blade, bouncing over the edge into oblivion.

I sighed with relief, realizing how close I had come to death.

Then I heard a mule bray from behind, and Nicodemus

trying to settle it. "Whoa . . ." The falling rocks must have spooked it.

"Steady that animal," an officer barked from behind. "It carries your food for the next two weeks."

Nicodemus grasped for the rope. The animal's hind legs spun, trying to catch hold on the trail.

I lunged for the harness around its neck, but the mule bucked again and stumbled. Its feet were unable to hold the trail. Its frightened eyes showed that the animal was aware of the danger, but the stone gave way. With a hideous bray, the poor mule toppled over the edge and fell into the void.

As it did, it caused a terrible reaction, pulling along the animal behind it to which it was tied.

I saw disaster looming. *"Nico,"* I shouted.

But the old Greek was too slow and laden with gear to get out of the way. My eyes locked helplessly on him as he stumbled in his long robe.

"Nico," I screamed, seeing the old man slipping off the edge. I lunged toward him, grabbing for his arm.

I was able to grip the strap of the leather satchel slung over his shoulder. It was all that kept him from plunging to his death.

The old man looked up at me and shook his head. "You must let go, Hugh. If you don't, we'll both fall."

"I won't. Reach up your other hand," I begged. A crowd of others had formed behind me. "Give me your hand, Nico."

I searched his eyes for panic, but they were clear and sure. I wanted to say, *Hold on, Professor. Jerusalem is near.*

But the satchel slid out of my grasp. Nicodemus, his white hair and beard billowing in the draft, fell away from me.

"No!" I lunged, grasping, calling his name.

In a flash he was gone. We had marched together for a thousand miles, but for him it was never far, always *near* . . . I didn't remember my father, but the grief emptying from me showed that Nicodemus was as close to one as I'd ever had.

A knight pushed up the trail, grumbling about what the hell was going on. I recognized him as Guillaume, a vassal of Bohemond, one of the nobles in charge.

He peered over the edge and swallowed. "A soothsayer who couldn't even predict his own death?" he spat. "No great loss."

Chapter 11

FOR DAYS TO COME, the loss of my friend weighed greatly upon me. We continued to climb, but each step, all I saw in my path was the wise Greek's face.

Without my noticing it at first, the trails began to widen. I realized we were marching through valleys now, not over peaks. We were heading down. Our pace quickened, and the mood in the ranks brightened with anticipation of what lay ahead.

"I've heard from the Spaniard there are Christians chained to the city's walls," someone said as we marched. "The sooner we get there, the sooner we can set our brothers free."

From behind came the clatter of a warhorse galloping toward us. "Make way!"

We scattered off the trail and turned to see Guillaume, the same arrogant bastard who'd mocked Nico after his death, in full armor astride his large charger. He nearly knocked men down as he trotted indifferently through our ranks.

"That's who we fight for, eh?" I bowed sarcastically with an exaggerated flourish.

We soon came to a wide clearing between mountains. A good-sized river, perhaps sixty yards wide, lay in the column's path.

Up ahead, I heard nobles disagreeing on the proper spot to ford the river. Raymond, our commander, insisted that the scouts and maps suggested a point to the south. Others, eager to show our face to the Turks, the stubborn Bohemond among them, argued why lose a day.

Finally, I saw that same knight, Guillaume, shoot from the crowd. "I will make you a map," he shouted to Raymond. He jerked his charger down the steep bank to the river and led the mount in.

Guillaume's horse waded in, bearing the knight in full chain mail. Men lined the shore, either cheering or laughing at his attempt to show off in front of royalty.

Thirty yards out, the water was still no higher than the horse's ankles. Guillaume turned around and waved, a vain smile visible under his mustache. "Even my mother's mother could cross here," he called. "Are the mapmakers taking notes?"

"I never knew that a peacock would so take to water," I remarked to my friends.

Suddenly, in the middle of the river, Guillaume's mount seemed to stumble. The knight did his best, but in his full battle gear and on unsteady footing he couldn't hold the mount. He fell from the horse, face first into the river.

The troops along the riverbank burst into laughter. Jeers, catcalls, mock waving. "Oh, *mapmakers* . . ." I laughed above the din. "Are you taking notes?"

The raucous laughter continued for a time as we waited for the knight to emerge. But he did not.

"He stays under out of shame," someone commented.

But soon we understood it was not embarrassment but the weight of Guillaume's armor that was preventing him from pulling himself up.

As this became clear, the hooting ceased. Another knight galloped into the water and waded out to the spot. A full minute passed before the new rider was able to reach the area. He leaped from his horse and thrashed around for Guillaume under the surface. Then, raising the knight's heavy torso, he shouted back, "He is drowned, my lord."

A gasp escaped from those on shore. Men bowed their heads and crossed themselves.

Just a few days before, the same Guillaume had stood behind me after Nicodemus was swept off the rocky cliff to his death.

I looked at Mouse, who shrugged with a thin smile. "No great loss," he said.

Chapter 12

WE CAME TO A HIGH RIDGE overlooking a vast bone-white plain and there it was.

Antioch.

A massive walled fortress, seemingly built into a solid mound of rock. Larger and more formidable than any castle I had ever seen back home.

The sight sent a chill shooting through my bones.

It was built on a sharp rise. Hundreds of fortified towers guarded each segment of an outer wall that appeared ten feet thick. We had no siege engines to break such walls, no ladders that could even scale their height. *It seemed impregnable.*

Knights took off their helmets and surveyed the city in awe. I know the same sobering thought pounded through each of our minds. *We had to take this place.*

One by one, we continued along the ridge and down the narrow trail. There was a feeling that the worst was over. That whatever God had in store for us, surely the coming battles could test us no more than what we had already faced. The talk, again, was of treasure and glory.

Stumbling on a ledge, I noticed a glimmer coming from under a rock. I bent down to pick up the shiny object and could not believe it.

It was a scabbard, for some kind of dagger. Very old, I was sure. It looked like bronze, with some inlaid writing that I could not understand. I wished Nico were here. I knew he would be able to interpret it.

I placed the scabbard in my pouch, which was starting to fill up. I felt like a man who had just claimed the richest dowry. I couldn't wait to show it to Sophie! Back home, a prize like this could buy us food for a winter.

I couldn't believe my good luck.

"Up here, the relics fall out of trees," Mouse grumbled from behind, "if there *were* any fucking trees."

The trail we walked was flat and manageable. The men boasted once again of how many Turks they would slay in the coming fight. After my discovery, thoughts of treasure and spoils seemed alive and real. Maybe I *would* be rich.

Suddenly, up ahead, the column came to a halt. Then — eerie silence.

As far as the eye could see, the trail ahead was lined with large white rocks, spaced at intervals equal to a man's arm span. Each rock was painted with a bright red cross.

"The bastards are welcoming us," someone said. *Mocking* us was more like it. The rows of red crosses sent a shiver right through me.

Mouse ran ahead to hurl one of the rocks toward the walls, but as he got close, the boy stopped in his tracks. Other soldiers who had reached the rocks crossed themselves.

They were not rocks at all — but skulls.

Thousands of them.

Chapter 13

THERE WERE FOOLS among us who believed that Antioch would fall in a day. On that first morning we lined up, many thousand strong. A sea of white tunics and red crosses.

Then all at once a chilling roar rose up from behind the city walls. The Turks, taunting and mocking us. I fixed on a face above the main gate. Then the trumpet sounded again. We were at a run.

From behind, I heard the *whoosh* from a wave of arrows shooting across the sky, but they fell against the massive walls like harmless sticks, clattering to the ground.

A hundred yards . . . A volley of arrows shot back from the towers in return. I held my shield as they ripped into us, thudding and clanging into shields and armor all around. Men fell, clutching at their heads and throats.

It was a slaughter. Men who had traveled so far, endured so much — God's call resounding in their hearts — were cut down like grain in a field. I saw poor Mouse, an arrow piercing his throat so completely his hands gripped it on both sides, drop to his knees. Others fell over him. I felt sure I would soon die too.

Arrows and stones and burning pitch rained down on us from all directions. It was only luck to avoid death at any point. All around us, our ranks were being shredded. Soldiers fell to their knees and moaned. Battering rams were tossed aside and abandoned.

Suddenly the assault turned into a rout. Men, hearing the alarm, turned and fled from the walls. Arrows and spears followed them, dropping them as they ran.

As we fled, the mighty fortress gate opened, and from within, horsemen appeared, dozens of turbaned riders flashing long, curved swords. They swept toward us like hunters chasing a hare, yelping mad cries that I recognized as *"Allahu Akbar."* God is great.

In spite of our being totally outnumbered, there was no option but to stand and fight. I drew my sword, resolved that any breath might be my last, and hacked away at the first wave of horsemen.

Before this day I had never taken a life, but now I hacked and slashed at anything that moved as if I had been bred solely for it.

Every instant, more horsemen stormed out from the gates. They swept down on our fleeing troops and hacked them where they stood. Blood and gore soaked the ground everywhere. A wave of our own cavalry went out to meet them, only to be overcome by the sheer numbers they faced. It seemed as if our whole army was being slaughtered.

For the first time, I noticed that my own tunic and arms were smeared with blood, whose I did not know. And my legs stung from the spray of molten pitch. Though I had seen many men fall, in a way I was proud. I had fought bravely.

Chapter 14

IT HAPPENED JUST THAT WAY nearly every day.

Assault upon assault.

Death after meaningless death.

The siege took months. For a while, it seemed as if our glorious Crusade would end in Antioch, not Jerusalem.

Our catapults flung giant missiles of fiery rock, yet they barely dented the massive walls. Wave after wave of frontal attacks only increased the death toll.

Finally, we constructed enormous siege engines, as tall as the highest towers. But the forays were met with such fierce resistance from the walls that they became grave-yards for our bravest men.

The longer Antioch survived, the lower our spirits fell. Food was down to nothing. All the cattle and oxen had been butchered; even the dogs had been eaten. Water was as scarce as wine.

At intervals, Turk warriors made forays outside the city walls. They charged our ranks as if on a holy mission, yelping and hacking at those who met them, only to be surrounded and chopped to bits. They were unafraid, even heroic. It made us realize even more that they would not easily give in.

Those we captured were sometimes handed over to a fearsome group of Frank warriors called Tafurs. Barefoot, covered in filth and sores, the Tafurs were distinguished by the ragged sackcloth they wore as uniforms and by the ferocious savagery with which they fought. Everyone was afraid of them. Even us.

In battle, these Tafurs fought like possessed devils, wielding leaded clubs and axes, gnashing their teeth as if they wanted to devour the enemy alive. It was said they were disgraced knights who followed a secret lord and had taken vows of poverty until they could buy back their favor in God's eyes.

These Tafurs reported to no lord among us, and to most of us, it seemed, no god either. They were marked by a cross burned into their necks, which attested not so much to their religious fervor as to their urge to inflict pain.

The longer the horrible siege went on, the farther away I felt from anything I knew. It was now eighteen months I'd been gone. I dreamed about Sophie every night, and often during the day: that last image of her, watching me go off, her brave smile as I hopped down the road.

Chapter 15

THE WORD SPREAD like fire from battalion to battalion. "Get ready.... Full battle gear. We're going in, *tonight!*"

"Tonight, another charge?" Weary and frightened soldiers around me moaned in disbelief. "Do they think we can see at night what we cannot even shoot during the day?"

The camp sprang alive. There was a traitor inside Antioch. He would give up the city. Antioch would finally fall. Not from its walls crumbling but from treachery and greed.

Raymond ordered the army to break camp, giving the appearance that we were headed for a raid elsewhere. We pulled back two miles, as far as the river Orontes. Then we held until close to dawn. The signal was spread. *Everyone be ready....*

Under the shield of darkness, we quietly crept back within sight of the city walls. A sliver of orange light was just breaking over the hills to the east. My blood was surging. Today, Antioch would fall. Then it was on to Jerusalem. *Freedom.*

A torch waved over the north tower. That was it! Our men were inside. *"Let's go!"* the nobles shouted. *"Attack!"*

Our army charged, Frank, Norman, Tafur, side by side, with one purpose, one mind. "Show them whose God is One," the leaders cried.

Our battalions headed toward the north tower, where ladders were hoisted against the walls and wave after wave of men climbed over. The sound of shouts and vicious fighting erupted from inside. Then, all at once, the big gate opened. *Right in front of our eyes.* But instead of attacking Moslem horsemen streaking out, our own conquering army spilled in.

We made our way helter-skelter through the city. Buildings were torched. Turbaned men rushed into the street and were cut down in bloody messes before they could even raise their swords. Cries of "Death to the pagans" and *"Dei leveult,"* God wills it, echoed everywhere.

In front of us a young woman ran out of a burning house, screaming. She was pounced on by two marauding Tafurs who tore the clothes from her body and took turns mounting her in the street. When they were done, they ripped a bronze bracelet from her wrist and bludgeoned her lifeless.

I stared in horror at her bloody shape. In her clutched fist, I saw a cross. *Good Lord, she was Christian.*

Something snapped in me. Whatever I thought I was fighting for, whatever dream of freedom or wealth had brought me here, burst. And there was nothing in its place. I did not care about Antioch. Or freeing Jerusalem. Or freeing myself. I only wanted to go home. To see Sophie once more. To tell her I loved her. I could deal with the harshness of laws and taxes and the wrath of our lord, if only I could hold her one more time. I had come here to set myself free. *Now I was free.* Free of my illusions.

My regiment went on, but I stayed behind, consumed with grief and rage. I did not know where I would go, just that I could no longer fight in their ranks. I staggered around, wandering among burning buildings, passing from horror to horror. Carnage and screams were everywhere. The streets ran ankle deep with blood.

I came upon a Christian church. *Sanctum Christi . . . St. Paul's . . .* It almost seemed funny to me: *this . . .* this old tomb was what we were fighting for. This empty block of stone was what we had come to set free.

I wanted to lash at the church with my sword. It was a host of lies. I finally staggered up the steep stone steps in a fit of rage.

"God wills *this?*" I screamed. "God wills this *murder?*"

Chapter 16

I HAD NO SOONER STEPPED INSIDE the dark, cool nave of the church than I heard a cry of anguish coming from the front. *This madness just wouldn't stop!*

On the steps of the altar, two black-robed Turks hovered over a priest, pummeling him with kicks, cursing him in their tongue, while the fearful cleric did his best to defend himself with a rough wooden staff.

I ran with my sword drawn and a loud cry, just as one of the attackers thrust a dagger into the belly of the priest. The other infidel turned, and I leaped upon him. The blade of my sword penetrated his side. The Turk let out a chilling howl.

The other assailant rose and faced me, wielding the dagger that was still covered with the priest's blood. He lunged, spitting words I recognized, *"Ibn Kan . . ."* Son of Cain.

I pivoted aside and brought my sword over the back of his head. It sheared through his neck as if it were a weak limb of a tree. The Turk fell to his knees, his head rolling away from him. Then he toppled forward, landing on what would have been his face.

I stood, transfixed by the awful corpses of the Turks. I no longer knew what was inside of me. *What was I doing here? What had I become?*

I went over to the fallen priest, to help if I could. As I knelt beside him his eyes grew cloudy. He exhaled a final breath. The useless wooden staff fell from his hand.

Too late . . . I was no hero, only a fool.

Just then, I heard a rustling behind me. I spun to see a third attacker, this one bare chested and monstrous, the size of two men. Seeing his comrades slain, he rushed toward me, his sword poised for attack.

In that instant I saw my helplessness. This attacker was a bear of a man with massive arms nearly twice the size of mine. I could no more hold him off than I could a tornado. As he charged, I raised my sword, but the Turk's stroke was so strong it knocked me backward over the dead priest. He charged at me once more, his eyes focused and fierce. This time, my sword flew out of my hands, clattering across the church's floor. I lunged after it, but the Turk intercepted me with a vicious kick, sucking the air out of my belly.

I was going to die. . . . I knew it. There was no way to defeat this horrible monster. In a last effort, I reached for the priest's wooden staff. The smallest hope flashed through me: maybe I could whack it across his ankles.

But my attacker merely took a giant step, pinning the staff uselessly under his sandal. I peered into the bastard's black eyes. I was out of tricks. Above me, his blade caught the glint of a torch. *I was about to die. . . .*

What profound images filled my mind as I tensed, waiting for the blade to fall? It did not occur to me to pray, to ask God for the forgiveness of my sins. No, God had taken me where I belonged. I bade farewell to my sweet Sophie. I felt I had shamed myself, to leave her this way. She would never know how I died, why, or where, or that I was thinking of her at the end.

What did flash through my brain was the incredible irony of it all. Here I was, dying in front of an altar of Christ, on a holy crusade that I never really believed in.

I didn't believe. . . . Yet I was dying for this cause anyway.

As I looked at my murderer, my fear left me. So did my urge to resist. I peered into the Turk's eyes. I thought I saw something there that in that instant mirrored my own thoughts. The strangest urge overcame me. I could not hold it back.

I didn't pray, or close my eyes, or even beg for my life. *Instead, I began to laugh.*

Chapter 17

THE TURK'S SWORD hovered over me. At any second he would strike the final blow. Yet all I could do was laugh.

At what I was dying for. At the total ridiculousness of it all. At the precious *freedom* I was about to be granted at last.

I looked into his hooded eyes, and though I knew it was probably my last breath, I simply could not hold back. *I just laughed. . . .*

My attacker hesitated, his sword poised above my head. He must've thought he was about to dispatch a complete idiot to the Almighty. He blinked at me, his brows arched, confused.

I searched my mind for something to say in his tongue, which Nicodemus had taught me. Anything at all.

"This is your last warning," I said to him. "Are you ready to give up?"

Then I burst out laughing once again.

The massive Turk, his eyes like fiery coals, loomed over

me. I waited for the death blow. Then I saw his expression relax into the slightest inkling of a smile.

Choking back the laughter, I stammered, "Th-the thing is . . . I'm not even a believer."

The giant man hesitated. I didn't know if he would speak or strike. His mouth curved into a sheepish grin. "Nor am I."

His sword still quivered menacingly over my head. I knew any moment could be my last. I raised myself to my elbows, looked him in the eye, and said, "Then, one non-believer to another, you must kill me in the name of what we do *not* embrace."

Slowly, almost inexplicably, I saw the hostility on his face fade. To my utter amazement, the Turk lowered his sword. "We're too few as it is," he said. "No reason to make one less."

Was this possible? Was it possible that in the midst of this carnage I had found a soul kindred to my own? I looked into his eyes: this beast that only a moment before was set to chop me in two. I saw something there that this whole bloody night I had not seen: virtue, humor, a human soul . . . I couldn't believe it. *Please, God,* I finally prayed, don't let this be some kind of cruel trick.

"Is this real? You're going to let me go?" My fingers slowly relaxed from the priest's staff.

The Turk took a measuring look at me, then he nodded.

"You probably thought you were ridding the world of a complete madman," I said.

"The thought occurred." He grinned.

Then my mind fixed on the danger of the moment. "You'd better go. Our forces are all around. You are at risk."

"Go . . . ?" The Turk seemed to sigh. *"Go where?"*

There was something in his face, no longer hatred or even amusement. It was more like resignation.

At that moment, loud footsteps burst through the outer door. I heard voices. Soldiers stormed into the church. They were not wearing crosses but filthy robes. *Tafurs.*

"Get out of here," I urged the Turk. "These men will show you no mercy."

He took a look at his assailants. Then he merely winked at me. He started to laugh himself, then turned to face their charge.

The Tafurs came upon him with their swords and awful clubs.

"No . . ." I screamed. "Spare this man. Spare him!"

He managed to kill the first one with a mighty sweep of his sword. But then he was overwhelmed, consumed by heavy blows and disemboweling slashes, never once crying out, until his powerful body resembled some hideous slab of meat and not the noble soul he was.

The lead Tafur delivered one more blow to the bloody mound, then he delved through the Turk's robes, looking for something of value. Finding nothing, he shrugged to his comrades. "Let's find the fucking crypt."

It took everything I had not to leap on the Tafurs myself, but these savages would surely kill me.

They passed by me on their way to loot the church. I was trembling with horror.

The lead vermin ran the blade of his sword across my chest, as if he were evaluating whether to leave me in the same condition as the Turk. Then he sneered, amused, and said, "Don't look so sad, redhead. You are free!"

Chapter 18

I WAS *FREE*, the Tafur had said. *Free!*

I started to laugh once more. The irony was bursting through my sides. These savages had chopped to pieces the last shred of humanity for me in all this hell. Now . . . they were setting me free!

If the Turk had not hesitated just a moment ago, I'd have been dead myself. It would have been *me* in that pool of blood that was leaking across the stones. Yet he'd spared me. In all this madness I had found a moment of clarity and truth with this Turk, whose name I did not even know. We'd touched souls.

I struggled to my feet. I stepped over to the body of the man who had spared me and looked, horrified, at his bloody corpse. I knelt down and touched his hand.

Why did you spare me? I looked into the Turk's dull, still eyes. *What did you see?*

It was laughter that had saved me. Laughter that had somehow touched the Turk. I was only a breath away from death and yet instead of panic and fear, laughter had entered my soul. Amid all this fighting, I had simply made him smile. Now he was gone and I was here. A calm came over me. *You are right, Tafur. . . . I am finally free.*

I had to get out of here. I knew I could no longer fight. I was a different man. Different from a moment ago. This cross on my tunic meant nothing to me. I stripped it from my chest. I had to go back. I had to see Sophie again. What else could matter? I was a fool to have left her.

I wanted to take something from the church with me. Something from this moment that I would have for the rest of my life. I leaned over the dead Turk. The poor warrior was empty of anything: a ring, a memento.

I heard voices outside. It could be anybody. Infidels, raiders, more Tafurs hunting for spoils. I looked around. *Please, something.*

I went back to the priest. I lifted the staff that had been in my hands when the Turk spared my life. It was a rough, gnarled stick of wood, maybe four feet long, and thin. But it seemed strong. It would be my friend when I crossed the mountains again, my companion. I vowed to carry it with me wherever I went for the rest of my life.

I looked at the fallen Turk and whispered good-bye. "You're right, my friend; we are too few as it is."

I gave him a wink.

Looking up, I noticed a small crucifix on the altar. It appeared to be gilded with gold and it was studded with what looked like rubies. I took it down and stuffed it into my pouch. I had earned this much. A golden cross.

The cries of men dying hit me as I stepped outside. Mayhem was still rampant in the streets. The conquering throng had gone deeper into Antioch, cleansing the city of anything Moslem.

I heard awful cries of death farther up the hill, but I

wasn't going there. I put the priest's staff to the ground and took a step — the other way.

I would never see Jerusalem in this lifetime.

I was heading home to Sophie.

Part Two

BLACK CROSS

Chapter 19

IT TOOK SIX MONTHS for me to find my way home.

From Antioch, I headed west, toward the coast. I wanted to get as far away from my murderous battalion as I could. I stripped out of my bloody clothing and donned the robes of a pilgrim whose corpse I had stumbled upon. I was a deserter. All promises of freedom made by Raymond of Toulouse were now revoked.

I traveled by night, crossing the barren mountains to St. Simeon, a port held in Christian hands. There, I slept on the docks like a beggar until I managed to convince a Greek captain to let me hitch a ride aboard his ship to Malta. From there, I traded my way onto a Venetian cargo ship carrying sugar and spun cloth back to Europe. *Venice* . . . It was still the trek of a lifetime from my little village.

I earned my passage recalling my days as a jongleur with the goliards, reciting tales from *La Chanson de Roland* and entertaining the crew at their meals with raucous jokes. No doubt the crew had their suspicions of me.

Deserters were everywhere, and why else would an able, penniless man be running from the Holy Land?

Every night I had dreams of Sophie, of bringing something precious back to her. Of her blond braids, her delicate, happy laugh. I kept my eyes fixed on the western horizon, her image like a soft trade wind bringing me home.

When we reached Venice, my heart leaped to set foot on European soil. The same soil that led to Veille du Père.

But I was thrown in jail, turned in by the suspicious captain for a fee. I barely had the time to hide my pouch of valuables on the quay before I was tossed in a narrow, stinking hole filled with thieves and smugglers of all nationalities.

The guards all called me Jeremiah, a crazed-looking man in a tattered robe who clung to his staff. I did my best to keep my good humor and pleaded with my jailers that I was only trying to get home to my wife. They laughed. "A lice-filled beast like you has a wife?"

But luck had not run out for me yet. A few weeks later, a local noble paid for the release of ten prisoners as expiation for an offense. One died during the night, so they chose the affable, crazy Jeremiah to round out the number. "Go back to your wife, Frenchie," the bailiff said as they handed me my staff. "But first, I advise you to find a bath."

That very night, I found the pouch with my valuables where I had hidden it and began to walk. West across the marshy road to the mainland. *Toward home.*

I headed across Italy. Every town I came to, I told tales at the local inn for a meal of bread and ale. Farmers and drunks listened spellbound to the siege of Antioch, the ferocity of the Turks, and my friend Nicodemus's untimely end.

I climbed through the smaller hills and then the Alps.

The winds there blew cold and strong. It took a full month to cross them. But finally, as I descended from the peaks, the language that greeted me was French. *French!* My heart leaped, knowing I was near my home.

The towns became familiar. Digne, Avignon, Nîmes . . . Veille du Père was only days away. *And Sophie.*

I started to worry about how it would be. Would she even recognize the haggard mess I had turned into? So often, I pictured her face as I would stand in front of her for that first time. She would be heating soup or making butter, wearing her pretty patterned smock, her blond braids peeking through her white cap. *"Hugh,"* she would gasp, too stunned to move. Just *Hugh,* not another word. Then she would leap into my arms and I would squeeze her as if I had never left.

It was in a damp rain that I finally reached the outskirts of Veille du Père. I went down on my knees.

Chapter 20

THOSE LAST MILES, I almost ran the entire distance. I began to recognize roads I had traveled, sights I was familiar and comfortable with. I tried to put aside everything bad that had happened to me. *Nico, Robert, Civetot, Antioch.* All of the misery seemed so distant now, unconnected. I was home.

My plight was over. I had arrived, no knight or squire, not even a free man. Yet I felt like the wealthiest noble in the world.

I spotted the familiar bubbly stream and the stone wall that bordered it, which led to town. Gilles's barley field came into view. Then a bend I knew so well, and the stone bridge up ahead.

Veille du Père . . .

I stood there, like a beggar over a feast, just a few moments to take it in. I was filled with everything that had happened, the horrors I had put behind me, the many miles and months I had traveled, dreaming only of Sophie's face, her touch, her smile.

How I wished it were July and I could walk into town bearing a sunflower. I searched out the square. Familiar faces, doing their work. It all seemed just as I remembered. My old friends Odo the smith and Georges the miller . . . Father Leo's church . . .

Our inn . . .

Our inn! I fixed on it in horror. *No, it cannot be.* . . .

In the blink of an eye, I knew that everything had changed.

Chapter 21

I BOLTED TOWARD the village square, the pallor of a ghost upon my face.

Children stared at me, then ran toward their houses. "*It is Hugh.* Hugh De Luc. He's back from the war," they shouted.

All that could have seemed familiar about me was my mane of red hair. People rushed up to me, neighbors I recognized, whom I had not set eyes upon in two years, their faces caught between shock and joy. "Hugh, praise God, it is you."

But I pushed past, barely acknowledging them. I was drawn on a direct path to our inn.

Our home . . . My heart sank as I came to the spot.

A burned-out hole was left where our inn had once been.

Among the cinders stood a single charred support post that had once held up a two-story structure, built by the hands of my wife's father.

Our inn had been burned to the ground.

"Where is Sophie?" I muttered, first to the charred ruins of the inn, then to faces in the gathered crowd.

I went from person to person, sure that any moment I would spot her coming back from the well. But everyone stood silently.

My heart began to beat insanely. *"Where is Sophie?"* I shouted. "Where is my wife?"

Sophie's older brother, Matthew, finally pushed out of the crowd. When he saw me, his expression shifted — from surprise to a look of deep concern. He stepped forward, hurling his arms around me. "Hugh, I can't believe it. Thank God you've come back."

I knew the worst had happened. I searched his eyes. "What's happened, Matthew? Tell me, where is my wife?"

A look of deep sorrow came onto his face. *Oh, God . . . I almost did not want him to tell me the rest.* He led me by the arm to the remains of our home. "There were riders, Hugh. Ten, twelve . . . They swept in, in the dead of night, like devils, burning everything they could. Black crosses on their chests. They wore no colors. We had no hint of who they were. Just the crosses."

"Riders . . . ?" My blood was frozen with dread. "What riders, Matthew? What did they do to Sophie?"

He placed a hand gently upon my shoulder. "They burned three dwellings in their path. Paul the carter, Sam, old Gilles, their wives and children, killed as they fled. Then they came to the inn. I tried to stop them, Hugh, I did," he cried.

I seized him by the shoulders. *"And Sophie?"* I knew the worst had happened. *No, this could not be. Not now . . .*

"She's gone, Hugh." Matthew shook his head.

"Gone?"

"She tried to run, but the men took her inside. They beat her, Hugh. . . ." He pursed his lips and bowed his head.

"They did worse. I heard her screams. They held me as they beat and raped her. Knights tore up the place, ripping it post by post. Then they dragged her out. She was like a lifeless thing, barely alive. I was sure they would leave her to die, but the leader threw her over his horse while the others released their torches. It was then that . . ."

I could barely hear him. A distant voice was echoing, *No, this cannot be!* My eyes welled up with tears. "It was then that *what,* Matthew?"

He bowed his head. "They dragged her away, Hugh. I know she is dead."

All strength drained from my legs. I sank to my knees. *Oh, God, how could this have happened? How could I have left her to this fate? My Sophie gone. . . .* I gazed upon the charred ruins of my former life.

"Norcross did this, didn't he? *Baldwin . . . ?*"

"We do not know for certain." Matthew shook his head. "If I did, I would go after them myself. They were beasts, but faceless ones. They wore no crests. Their visors were down. Everyone ran to the woods for cover. Yours was the only house they entered. It was as if they came for you."

For me . . . Those bastards. I had fought two years for Baldwin's own liege. I had marched across half the world and seen the worst things. And still, they took from me the one thing I loved.

I grabbed some dust from the rubble and let it slip through my fists. "My poor Sophie . . ."

Matthew knelt down beside me. "Hugh, there's more. . . ."

"*More?* What could be more?" I looked into his eyes.

He put a hand on my face. "After you left, Sophie had a son."

Chapter 22

MATTHEW'S WORDS HIT ME like a stone wall, collapsing over me. *A son* . . .

For three years Sophie and I had tried to conceive, to no result. We had wanted a child more than anything. We even spoke of it that last night we were together. *I had left her, and never even knew I had a son.*

I turned toward Matthew, a flicker of hope alive in my heart.

"He is *dead,* Hugh. He wasn't even a year old. The bastards killed him that same night. They tore him from Sophie's arms as she tried to flee."

A wall of tears rushed at my eyes. *A son* . . . A son I would never know or hold. I had been through the fiercest battles, the worst of all horrors. But nothing could have prepared me for this.

"How?" I muttered. "How did my son die?"

"I can't even say it." Matthew's face was ashen. "Just believe me when I say that he is dead."

I repeated my question, this time fixed upon his eyes. *"How?"*

His voice was so quiet. "As they threw Sophie's lifeless body over his mount, the leader said, 'We have no room for such a toy. Toss him in the flames.'"

I felt a pressure building up, an anger clawing at me as if my insides were ripping through my skin. God had smiled on us after all that time. He had blessed us with a son. Now He spat at me with the sharpest mockery.

How could I have left them? How could I still be alive if they were dead?

I looked at Matthew and asked, "What was his name?"

Matthew swallowed. "She named him Phillipe."

I felt a lump catch in my throat. Phillipe was the name of the goliard who had raised me. It was her tribute to me. *Sweet Sophie, you are gone. My son too . . .* I felt the urge to die right there amid the charred ash, the ruins of my old life.

"Hugh," Matthew said, lifting me up, "you have to come." He led me up the trail to a knoll where I had just stood over the town. A small slate stone marked my son's grave.

I sat down under a shroud of tall poplars. "Phillipe De Luc, son of Hugh and Sophie," was scratched into the stone. "Year of our Lord MXCVIII."

I laid my head on the earth and wept. For my sweet Phillipe, whom I would never see, not even once in my life. For my wife, who was surely dead.

Was this why I was spared? Was this why the Turk had not swung his murderous sword? So I would live to see all that I loved lost? Was this why the laughter had saved me? So God could laugh at me now?

I took off the pouch that contained the things I had brought back for Sophie: a perfume box, some ancient coins, the scabbard, the golden cross — and I dug a hole next to my baby's grave. I gently placed my "treasures" in it. They were worthless to me now. "They belong to you," I whispered to Phillipe. *My sweet baby.*

I smoothed out the earth and once more laid my head on the ground. *I'm so sorry, Phillipe and Sophie.* Slowly my grief began to harden into rage. I knew Baldwin had ordered this. And Norcross had carried it out. But why? Why?

I'm just an innkeeper, I thought. I am nothing. Just a serf.

But a serf who will see you dead.

Chapter 23

A CROWD GATHERED around us as Matthew and I came back into town. Father Leo, Odo, my other friends . . . Everyone wanted to comfort and bless me. And hear of my two years in the war.

But I pushed past them. I had to go to the inn. Its ruins . . . I sifted through the charred wood and ash, searching for anything that breathed of her, my Sophie — a piece of cloth, a dish, a last memento of what I had lost.

"She spoke of you all the time, Hugh," Matthew told me. "She missed you terribly. We all thought you were lost in the war. But not Sophie."

"You are certain, brother, that she is dead?"

"I am." Matthew shrugged. "When they took her she was already more dead than alive."

"But you did not actually see her die? You don't know for sure?"

"Not for sure. But I beg you, brother, not to cling to false hope. I'm her flesh and blood. And I damn well pray she *was* dead as they dragged her out of here."

I met his eyes. "So she may *not* be dead, Matthew?"

He looked at me quizzically. "You must accept it, Hugh. If she was not then, I'm certain she was soon. Her body could have been left somewhere along the road."

"So you searched the road? And did you find her? Has anyone traveling from the west come upon her remains?"

"No. No one."

"Then there's a chance. You say she never doubted me. That she knew I would return. Well, *I do the same for her.*"

I found myself in the part of the inn where our living space had been. Everything was cinder. Our bed, a chest of drawers . . . On the floor, I noticed something reflecting light.

I dropped to my knees, swept away ash. My heart almost exploded with joy. Tears welled in my eyes.

It was Sophie's comb. Her half of the one she'd placed in my hand the day I left. It was charred, broken; it almost crumbled in my hand. But in my blood, I felt her!

I held it up, and from my pouch hastily removed the other half. I fitted them together as best I could. In that moment, Sophie came alive to me — her eyes, her laugh — as vibrantly as when I had last seen her.

"These knights, Matthew, they didn't leave her to die in the same flames as my son. They took her for a reason." I looked up at him, holding the comb aloft. "Perhaps it is not such false hope after all."

Outside, my old friends Odo and Georges the miller were waiting.

"Give us the word, Hugh," Georges said. "We will hunt the bastards with you. We've all suffered. We know who is responsible. They deserve to die."

"I know." I put my hand on the miller's shoulder. "But first I must find Sophie."

"Sophie lives as my own Alo lives," the miller said. "In Heaven."

"For you, Georges, but not for me. Sophie still lives on this earth. I know it. I can feel her."

I picked up my staff and pouch and slung a skin of water around my neck. I headed toward the stone bridge.

"What are you going to do, Hugh, jab them with that stick?" Odo hurried to my side. "You are just one man. With no armor or sword."

"I'm going to find her, Odo. I promise, I'll find Sophie."

"Let me get you some food," Odo pleaded. "Or some ale. You still drink ale, don't you, Hugh? The army didn't cure you of that? Next I'll hear you've been going to church on Sundays."

From his guarded look, it was clear he thought he would never see me again.

"I will bring her back, Odo. You'll see."

I took my stick and headed into the woods.

Toward Treille.

Chapter 24

I RAN IN A BLIND HAZE in the direction I had come. Toward my liege's castle at Treille.

Grief tore at me like wild dogs. *My son had died because of me. Because of my stupid folly. Because of my foolishness and pride.*

As I ran, a swell of bitterness surged inside. The thought of that bastard Norcross, or any of his henchmen, having my poor Sophie . . .

I had fought for these so-called nobles in the Holy Land while they raped and slaughtered in the name of God. I had marched and killed and followed the Pope's call. And this was my wage. Not freedom, not a changed life, but misery and scorn. I had been a fool to trust the rich.

I ran until my legs gave out. Then, exhausted and blind with rage, I fell to the ground, covering my sores in dirt.

I had to find Sophie. *I know you are alive. I'll make you well. I know how you've suffered.*

At every turn, I prayed I would not stumble over her

body. Every time I didn't, it gave me hope that she was alive.

After a day of traveling, I looked around and didn't know where I was. I had no food and had run out of water. All that pushed me on was rage. I checked the sun. Was I heading east or north? I had no idea.

From deep in the woods, I heard the rushing water of a stream. I clawed my way off the road and into the woods, following the sound.

Suddenly I lost my footing. I grasped for a bush, but my hand slipped. I started to tumble. I clawed for anything to hold, a vine, a branch. The ground disappeared beneath me.

Jesus . . . I was falling.

Let it come. I deserve it. I will die out here in the night.

I called to Sophie as I hurtled out of control down the ravine.

My head smacked against something hard. I felt a warm and viscous fluid fill my mouth. "I'm coming," I said one more time.

To Sophie.

To the howling darkness . . .

Then the world went black on me, and that was much better, thank you, Lord.

Chapter 25

I CAME TO — not to the rush of water, or anything heavenly, but to a low, dangerous, rumbling sound.

I opened my eyes. It was still night. I had fallen into a deep ravine, far below the level of the road. My back was twisted against a tree and I could barely move. A wound ached horribly on the side of my head.

Again, I heard the deep rumbling from the woods.

"Who's there?" I called. "Who is it?"

There was no reply. I focused on the spot in the darkness, trying to make out any shape. Who would be out here in the night? Not anyone I wanted to meet.

Then, I focused on a set of eyes. Eyes not human at all, but large as prayer stones: yellow, narrow, fuming. My blood froze.

Then it moved! I heard the brush crunch under its feet. The thing took a step out of the forest and came clear.

Dark, hairy . . .

Blessed Jesus Christ! It was a boar! Not twenty paces away.

Its yellow eyes were trained on me, inspecting me as if I were its next meal. I heard a snort. Then it was deathly still.

The thing was about to charge! I was certain of it.

I tried to clear my head. I could not possibly fight such a beast. *With what?* Its breadth alone was twice mine. It could slash me to pieces with its razory tusks.

My heart was pounding, the only sound I heard other than the beast's low growl. It took another step toward me. The boar's murderous eyes never left my own, deliberate and tracking.

God help me, what could I do? I couldn't flee. It would run me down in my first steps. There was no one to shout to for help.

I searched for a strong tree to climb, but I didn't want to move, to set it off. The beast seemed to study me, bucking its head, snorting its deadly intent. I could smell its fierce, hot breaths, the blood from past conflicts matted in its hair.

I grabbed the knife at my belt. I didn't know if it would snap against the beast's hide.

The boar snorted twice and flashed its teeth at me, its jowls red and dripping. I did not want to die. Not like this . . . *Please, God, do not make me fight this thing.*

I felt so incredibly alone.

Then, with a last deep snort, the beast seemed to understand that — and it charged.

All I could do was leap behind a tree, barely escaping the first violent gnash of its fearsome teeth.

I stabbed wildly at it with my knife, tearing at its face and neck, doing everything I could to repel its snarling jaws. The beast lunged viciously. It came again and again. I clawed with my knife, backing around the tree. The boar's jaws ripped into my thigh and I cried out. The air emptied from my lungs.

Good Lord, I was pierced.

I had no time to inspect the wound. The beast slammed into me again, this time goring my abdomen. I screamed in pain.

I kicked at it and slashed my blade. It backed and lunged. Its teeth clamped on my thigh and it shook its head as if to tear my leg out of its socket.

I kicked myself away from the boar. I tried to run, but my legs had no strength. Blood was spattered everywhere.

Somehow I limped across the clearing, my strength nearly sapped. My abdomen felt as if it were on fire. I was done here. I fell to my side and backed myself against another tree, waiting for the end to come.

Beside the tree, I saw my staff. It must have toppled there in my fall. I reached for it, though it wasn't much of a weapon.

I stared at the angry, snorting boar. "Come at me, offal. *Come at me!* Finish what you started."

My mind flashed to the Turk who had spared me, a world away. This time, no laughter would save the day. I held the staff like a spear. *"Come at me,"* I shouted at the boar again. "Do me in. I am ready. *Do me in.*"

As if to oblige, the beast made another charge.

My breath was still. I offered no defense except to raise the staff at the shape flying toward me. Harnessing all my remaining strength, I thrust the rod with all my might at its eyes.

The beast let out a blood-chilling cry. I'd actually hurt it. The staff stuck in one eye. The boar staggered and shook its head madly, trying to rid itself of the staff.

I grabbed my knife and with whatever strength I had, stabbed at its throat and face, at anything I could strike.

Blood seeped out of its fur, each knife thrust striking home. Its growls diminished. It stumbled, still swinging its head to free the rod, while I continued to slash, tearing at its coat.

The beast's blood mixed with my own. Finally its hind legs crumpled. I took the staff and forced it deep into the boar's skull. A dying snarl came out of its awful tooth-filled mouth.

With a crash, the monster fell on its side. I just knelt there, depleted of strength. And amazed. I let out an exhausted shout.

I had won!

But I was badly wounded. Blood ran freely from my stomach and thigh. I had to make it out of the ravine or I knew I would die here.

Sophie's face appeared in my mind. I know I smiled; I reached out to touch her. *"Here is the way,"* she whispered. *"Come to me now."*

Chapter 26

IT WAS QUIET, like any sleeping town. The dark riders brought their panting mounts close to the edge. A few thatched cottages with post fences, animals sleeping in their sheds. That was all there was.

This would be easy, mere sport for such men. The leader sniffed, shutting his visor. His helmet bore a black Byzantine cross. He had chosen only men who killed for pleasure, who hunted for spoils as others hunted for meat. They wore only the darkened armor of battle, no crests, visors down. No one knew who they were. They strapped on their weapons — war swords, axes, and maces. They looked at him, eager, thirsty, ready.

"Have your fun," Black Cross said, a bit of laughter coming through his command. "Just let us not forget why we are here. Whoever finds the relic will be a rich man. Now, ride!"

The night was split asunder by the explosion of charging hooves.

The clang of a warning bell sounded. Too late! The first

thatched dwellings went up in flames. The sleeping town came alive.

Women screamed and ran to cover their children. Aroused townspeople struggled out of their homes to protect themselves, only to be struck down by swords or trampled in the melee as the riders stormed by.

Fire and mayhem raging, Black Cross trotted unconcerned through the street to the large stone home, the best in the town. Five of his riders followed.

Panicked sounds came from inside — a woman screaming, children being roused from bed.

"Break it in." Black Cross nodded to a cohort. A single ax blow shattered the door.

A man in a white-and-blue shawl appeared in the doorway. He had long gray hair and a heavy beard. "What do you want here?" the cowering man asked. "We've done no harm."

"Get out of my way, Jew," Black Cross barked.

The man's wife, in a wool sleeping shawl, rushed out and spoke fearlessly. "We are peaceful people," she said. "We will give you whatever you want."

Black Cross pinned the woman by her throat to the wall. "Show me where it is," he demanded. "Show me, if you have any regard for his life."

"Please, the money is in the courtyard," the panicked husband whined. "In a chest under the cistern. Have it. Take what you will."

"Search the house," Black Cross screamed at his men. "Rip down every wall. Just find it."

"*But the money* . . . I told you . . ."

"We did not come for money, filth." Black Cross leered. "We are here for the jewel. Christendom's precious relic."

His henchmen stormed inside. They found an old man,

his arms around a boy, perhaps sixteen, already with the locks of his race.

"What do you mean?" The father crawled on his knees. "I am a merchant. We have no jewels. No relics."

Piece by piece, the house was torn apart. The raiders smashed their swords into walls, dug with axes at stone, broke into chests and cupboards.

Black Cross pulled the husband up by the throat. "I will not trifle any longer. *Where is the treasure?*"

"I beg you, we have no jewels." The trembling man gagged. "I trade in wool."

"You trade in wool." Black Cross nodded, glancing at the man's son. "We shall see." He took out a knife and pressed it against the boy's throat. The boy flinched, revealing a line of blood. "Show me the treasure unless you want your son to die."

"*The hearth* . . . underneath the tiles on the hearth." The father bowed his head in his hands.

In a rush, two of the knights ran to the fireplace and, using axes, crashed through the floor tiles, unearthing a secret space. From it, they raised a chest, inside of which were coins, necklaces, brooches of gold and silver. And finally, a gorgeous ruby the size of a coin, in a gilded Byzantine-style setting. It gave off a luminous glow. The knight held it aloft.

"You have no idea what you hold." The Jew blinked back tears.

"Don't I . . . ?" Black Cross grinned. "It is the seal of Paul. Your race is unworthy to even hold it. You will steal from our Lord no more."

"I did not steal it. It is you who does that. It was sold to me."

"Sold, not stolen . . . ?" Black Cross's eyes glittered. He

turned back to the son. "Then it is only a small loss, compared to what your race has taken from us."

In the same instant, he pushed his knife into the boy's gut. A gasp emerged from the boy; his eyes grew wide and blood dribbled from his mouth. All the while, Black Cross smirked.

"*Nefrem . . .*" The merchant and his wife screamed. They tried to rush to their son but were held back by other raiders.

"Burn the place," Black Cross said. "Their seed is dead. They can foul the earth no more."

Chapter 27

"IS HE DEAD?"

A voice crept through the haze. A woman's voice . . . I opened my eyes. But I couldn't make out a thing. Only a shifting blur.

"I don't know, my lady," another said, "but his wounds are grave. He doesn't look far from gone."

"Such unusual hair . . ." remarked the first.

I blinked, my brain slowly starting to clear. It was as if there were a shimmering veil reflecting my sight. *Was I dead?* There was a lovely face leaning over me. Yellow hair, braided densely, tumbling from under a brocaded purple cloak. She smiled. It warmed me like the sun.

"Sophie," I muttered. I reached to touch her face.

"You are hurt," replied the woman, her voice like the delicate trill of a bird. "I'm afraid you mistake me for someone else."

My body felt no pain. "Is this Heaven?" I asked.

The woman smiled again. "If Heaven is a world where

all wounded knights resemble vegetables, then, yes, it must be."

I felt her hands cradle my head. I blinked again. It was not Sophie, but someone lovely, speaking with the accent of the north. Paris.

"I still live," I uttered with a sigh.

"For the moment, yes. But your wounds are serious. We must get you to a physician. Are you from here? Do you have a family?"

I tried to focus on her questions. It was all too fuzzy and hurtful. I just said, "No."

"Are you an outlaw?" the second woman's voice intoned from above.

I struggled to see a lavishly robed lady, clearly royal, atop a stunning white palfrey.

"I assure you, madame," I said, doing my best to smile, "I am benign." I saw my tunic matted with blood. "Regardless of how I look." Sharp pangs of pain now lanced my stomach and thigh. I had no strength. With a gasp, I fell back once more.

"Where do you head, Monsieur Rouge?" the golden-haired maiden asked.

I had no idea where I was. Or how far I had traveled. Then I remembered the boar. "I head to Treille," I said.

"To Treille," she exclaimed. "Even if we could take you, I fear you will die before you reach Treille," the maiden said with concern.

"Take him?" the older lady questioned from above. "Look at him. He is covered with the blood of who knows whom. He smells of the forest. Leave him, child. He will be found by his own kind."

Then the young maiden winked at me. "He seems harmless. You are *harmless,* aren't you?" She looked into my eyes. A lovelier face I hadn't seen in a long time.

"Only to you." I smiled faintly.

"See?" she said. "I vouch for him."

"If you must." The grand lady sighed. She waved and the guards responded. "But he is your charge. And if your concern is so great, child, you will not mind giving up your horse."

I tried to push myself to my feet, but my strength was not there.

"Do not struggle, red hair," the blond maiden said. One of the accompanying guards, a big, hulking Moor, lifted me by the arms.

"Who saves me?" I asked her. "So I will know who to bless in Heaven should I pass on."

"Your own smile saves you, redhead." The maiden laughed. "But should the Lord not feel as favorably . . . I am called Emilie."

Chapter 28

I AWOKE, this time with a sense of peace and the warmth of a fire about me. I found myself in a comfortable bed, in a large room with stone walls. A bowl of water sat on a wooden table to my right.

Above me, a bearded man in a scarlet robe shot a satisfied grin at a portly priest at his side.

"He wakes, Louis. You can go back to the abbey now. It seems you are out of a job."

The priest lowered his flabby face in front of mine. He shrugged. "You have done well, Auguste . . . on the *body*. But there is also the matter of the soul. Perhaps there is something this blood-spotted stranger would like to confess."

I wet my lips, then answered for myself. "I am sorry, Father. If it's a confession you're looking for, you might get a better one out of the boar that attacked me. Certainly a better meal."

This made the physician laugh. "Back among us for only a second, Louis, and he's sized you up."

The priest scowled. It was clear he didn't like being the brunt of mockery. He threw on a floppy hat. "Then I'm off."

The priest left, and the kindly-looking doctor sat down beside me. "Don't mind him. We had a bet. Who got you — he or I."

I raised myself up on my elbows. "I'm glad to have been the subject of your sport. Where am I?"

"In good hands, I assure you. My reputation is that I've never lost a patient who wasn't truly sick."

"And where am I?"

He shrugged. "You, sir, I'm afraid, are truly *very* sick."

I forced a weak smile. "I meant the place, Doctor. Where am I taken?"

The physician gently patted my shoulder. "I knew that, boy. You are in Borée."

Borée . . . My eyes widened in shock. Borée was among the most powerful duchies in France. Three times the size of Treille. Borée was also a four-day ride from Treille, but north. *How had I ended up here?*

"How long . . . have I been in Borée?" I finally asked.

"Four days here. Two more along the way," the physician said. "You cried out many times."

"And what did I say?"

Auguste wrung out a cloth from the bowl and placed it across my forehead. "That your heart is not whole, though not from any boar wound. You carry a great burden."

I did not try to disagree. My Sophie lay somewhere — *at Treille*. And Treille was a week away on foot. I still felt her alive.

I pushed myself up. "You have my thanks for tending my wounds, Auguste. But I have to go."

"Whoa." The physician held me back. "You are not yet well enough to go. And do not thank me. I merely applied the salve and cauterized the wounds. It is the lady Emilie who deserves your thanks."

"*Emilie* . . . yes . . ." Through the haze of my memory I brought back her face. I had thought she was Sophie. All at once, flashes of my journey here came to me. The Moor constructed a harness for me. The lady gave up her own mount for me and walked behind.

"Without her, pilgrim," the doctor said, "you would have died."

"You are right, I truly owe her thanks. Who is this lady, Auguste?"

"A soul who cares. And a lady-in-waiting at the court."

"Court?" My eyes bolted wide. "What court do we speak of? You said you were commanded to my care. By whom? Who is it that you serve?"

"Why, the duchess Anne," he replied. "Wife of Stephen, duke of Borée, who is away on the Crusade, and second cousin to the King."

Chapter 29

I SAT UP in bed, confused and shocked.

I did not deserve this. I was no knight, no noble. Just a commoner. And a lucky one at that — fortunate not to have been ripped to shreds by a beast. My ordeal came back to me, my wife and child. It had been more than a week since I set out to find Sophie.

"Your care is most appreciated, Doctor, but I must leave. Please thank my gracious hostess for me."

I got up out of bed but managed to limp no farther than a couple of painful steps. There was a knock at the door. Auguste went to see who was there.

"You may thank the lady yourself," the doctor said. "She has come."

It was Emilie, adorned in a dress of linen gilded with golden borders. God, I had not been imagining her. She was as lovely as the vision from my dreams. Except her eyes shimmered soft and green.

"I see our patient rises," Emilie exclaimed, seemingly delighted. "How is our Red today, Auguste?"

"His ears are not injured. Nor is his tongue," the doctor said, prodding at me.

I didn't know whether to bow or kneel. I did not speak to nobles directly unless addressed. But something made me look into her eyes. I cleared my throat. "I would be dead if not for you, lady. There is no way I can express my thanks."

"I did what anyone would do. Besides, having vanquished your boar, what a shame it would've been if you had become the dinner of the next pest that stumbled by."

Auguste pushed over a stool and Emilie sat down. "If you must show gratitude, you can do so by permitting me a few questions."

"Any," I said. "Please ask."

"First, an easy one. What is your name, redhead?"

"My name is Hugh, lady." I bowed my head. "Hugh De Luc."

"And you were on your way to Treille, Hugh De Luc, when you encountered the boorish boar?"

"I was, my lady. Though the doctor has informed me that my direction was slightly askew."

"So it would seem." Lady Emilie smiled. This surprised me. I had never met a noble with a very keen sense of humor, unless it was cruel humor. "And on this journey you set out alone. With no food. Or water. Or proper clothes . . . ?"

I felt a lump in my throat — not from nerves but because of what must have seemed my enormous stupidity. "I was in a hurry," I said.

"A hurry?" Emilie nodded with polite jest. "But it seems, if I recall my mathematics, that no matter *how fast* you traveled, be it the wrong direction, it would only widen the distance to your goal, no?"

I felt like an idiot in front of this woman who had saved

me. I'm sure I blushed. "In a hurry *and confused*," I replied.

"I would say." She widened her eyes. "And the purpose of such haste . . . and confusion, if you don't mind . . . ?"

All at once, my being ill at ease shifted. This was not a game, and I was not a toy for amusement, no matter how much I owed her.

Emilie's expression shifted as well, as if she sensed my unease. "Please know I do not mock you. You cried out in anguish many times during the trip. I know you carry a heavy weight. You may be no knight, but you are surely on a mission."

I bowed my head. All the lightness of the moment fled from me. How could I speak of such horrors? To this woman who did not know me? My throat went dry. "It is true. I do have a mission, lady. But I cannot tell of it."

"Please tell, sir." (I couldn't believe it. She addressed *me* as "sir.") "You are troubled. I do not belittle you at all. Perhaps I can help."

"I am afraid you cannot help," I said and bowed my head. "You have helped too much already."

"You may trust me, sir. How can I prove it more than I already have?"

I smiled. She had me there. "Just know, then, that these are not the tales of a noble, the kind you are no doubt used to hearing."

"I do not seek entertainment," she replied, her eyes firmly on mine.

My experience with those highborn had always taught me to beware of their taxes and random killing and total indifference to our plight. But she seemed different. I could see compassion in her eyes. I'd felt it in that first glance as I lay by the road near death.

"I'll tell it to you, lady. You have earned that. I only hope it does not upset you."

"I assure you, Hugh," Lady Emilie said with a smile, "if you have not already noticed, you will find my tolerance for the upsetting to be quite high."

Chapter 30

SO I TOLD HER. *Everything.*

Of Sophie, and our village. Of my journey to the Holy Land, the terrible fighting there. Of my moment with the Turk . . . how I was saved, freed, to come back, to see Sophie again.

Then I told Emilie of the horrible truth that I'd found upon my return.

My voice cracked and my eyes filled with tears as I spoke. It was why I had been wandering the woods like a madman before they had come upon me. *Why I had to get to Treille . . .*

All the while, Emilie seemed riveted by my tale, never once interrupting. I knew that much of what I said must have brushed against the fantasies of her upbringing. Yet never once did she react as a spoiled noble. She did not question my desertion from the army, nor take offense at my ire toward Norcross and Baldwin. And when I came to why I so desperately needed to get to Treille, her eyes glistened. "Indeed, I understand, Hugh."

She leaned forward, placing a hand upon mine. "I see that you have been truly wronged. You must go to Treille and find your wife. But what do you intend to do, go there as one man? Without arms or access to the duke's circle? Baldwin is well-known here for what he is: a self-serving goat who sucks his own duchy dry. But what will you do, call him out on the field of battle? Challenge him? You will only get yourself tossed in a cell, or killed. . . ."

"You speak like Sophie would have," I said. "But even if it seems crazy, I have to try. I have no choice in this."

"Then I will help you, Hugh," Emilie whispered, "if you let me."

I looked at her, both confused and overwhelmed by her trust and resolve. "Why do you do this for me? You are highborn yourself. You attend the royal court."

"I told you the first time, Hugh De Luc. It is your smile that saves you."

"I think not," I said, and dared to hold my gaze on her. "You could have left me on the road. My troubles would have died along with me."

Emilie averted her eyes. "I will tell you, but not now."

"Yet *I* have told *you* everything."

"This is my price, Hugh. If you'd like to shop around, I can have you delivered back where I found you."

I bowed my head and smiled. She was funny when she wished to be. "Your price is agreeable, Lady Emilie. I'm truly grateful, whatever your reason."

"Good," she said. "So first we must start work on a *pretext* for you. A way for you to get in. What is it you do well, other than that keen sense of direction I saw?"

I laughed at her barb, sharp as it was. "I am one of those with skills abundant but talents none."

"We'll see," Emilie said. "What did you do in your town before the war?"

"We owned an inn. Sophie looked after the food and beds, and I . . ."

"Like most innkeepers, you poured the ale and kept the patrons entertained."

"How would you know such a thing?" I asked.

"No matter. And during the war? From what I've seen, you were certainly not a *scout*."

"I fought. I learned to fight quite well, actually. But I was told I was always able to keep my friends amused with my stories and their minds off the fighting. In the most worrisome of times, they always requested my tales." I told her how I had grown up, traveling the countryside, reciting verses and profane songs as a goliard. And how after the war I made my way home entertaining at inns as a jongleur. "Maybe I have a talent after all."

"A jongleur," Emilie repeated.

"It's a modest one, but I've always had the skill to make new friends." I smiled, to let her know of whom I was speaking.

Emilie blushed, then stood up. She straightened her dress and produced a demure look. "You must rest now, Hugh De Luc. Nothing can happen until your wounds have healed. In the meantime, I must go."

A worry shot through me. "Please, lady, I hope I have not offended you."

"Offended me?" she exclaimed. "Not at all." She broke into a most wonderful smile. "In fact, your vast talents have given me a splendid idea."

Chapter 31

THE FOLLOWING AFTERNOON, Emilie knocked on the door of the large bedchamber in the royal couple's section of the castle. The duchess Anne was at a table, overseeing a group of ladies-in-waiting at work threading a tapestry. "You called for me, my lady," said Emilie.

"Yes," Anne replied. The quintet of women stopped work and looked up for a sign to leave. "Please, stay," she said. "I will speak with Emilie in the dressing room."

The duchess motioned her into the next room, adjacent to the bedroom, where there was a large dressing table, bowls of perfumed water, and a mirror.

Anne sat on a stool. "I wish to speak of the health of your new red squire," she said.

"He recovers well," Emilie replied. "And please, he is not my squire. In fact, he is already married and seeks to find his wife."

"His wife! And that was where he was heading when we found him so neatly trussed in the woods? A curious courtship." Anne smiled. "But, now that he is well . . ."

"Not quite well," Emilie cut in.

"But now that he *recovers,* it is fitting he should be on his way. Anyway, the doctor tells me he has a will to leave."

"He has suffered great injury, madame, which he seeks to right. The owner of his offense is Baldwin of Treille."

"Baldwin." Anne grimaced as if she had swallowed spoiled wine. "Surely Baldwin is no friend to this court. But this man's affairs, lowly as they are, are no concern of ours. Your heart is admirable, Emilie. You have surpassed what anyone might expect of you. Now I want you to let him *leave.*"

"I will not shoo him away, madame." Emilie stood tall. "I want to help him right this wrong."

"Help him?" Anne looked shocked. "Help him *what?* Regain his title? His honor? A set of clothes?"

"Please, madame, every man deserves his honor, regardless of his rank in life. This man has been horribly wronged."

Anne came up to her. As she was in her living quarters and not presiding at court, her dark brown hair was combed long and over her shoulders. She was just thirty, but in many ways she was like a mother to Emilie. "My sweet Emilie, where did you get such notions?"

"You know well, my lady. You know why I came to be here, why I left Paris and my own troubles there."

Anne placed her hand tenderly on Emilie's shoulder. She *did* love the girl. "You are as caring, child, as you are rash. Nonetheless, as soon as he is ready to travel he must be off. If my husband were to hear of this, he'd come back from the Crusade and thrash me blue. This *Red,* does he have a profession? Some skill other than boar fighting?"

"I am teaching him a profession — starting today," Emilie replied.

"But not for here, I hope. We are overemployed with hangers-on as it is."

"No, not for here, my lady. Once he learns what I have to teach, he will be on his way. He has a wife to find. He loves her dearly."

Chapter 32

I RESTED FOR THREE MORE DAYS, until most of my wounds had healed.

Then Emilie knocked on the door, seeming excited. She inquired as to my health. "Are you able to walk?"

"Yes, of course." I hopped out of bed to show her, though still a bit impaired.

"That'll do." She seemed pleased. "Then come along with me."

She marched to the door and I hurried, with a slight limp, to keep up with her. She led me through the halls, wide and arched and adorned with beautiful tapestries, then down a steep flight of stone stairs.

"Where are we going?" I asked, pushing to keep up. It felt good to be out of my sickroom.

"To view your new pretext, I hope," she said.

We traveled to a different part of the castle. I had never been so close to the abode of royals before.

On the main floor there were large rooms, with long rows of tables and huge hearths, guarded by uniformed soldiers at every door. Knights milled about in their casual tunics, trading stories and rolling dice. Mounted torches lit the halls.

Then we passed the kitchen, with an inviting smell of garlic in the air, maids and porters shuffling around, casks of wine and ale.

Still we traveled, down a narrow corridor leading beneath the ground. Here the walls were of coarsely laid stone. The air grew stale and damp. We were in some sort of keep now. In the womb of the castle. Where was Emilie taking me? What did she mean by my *new pretext?*

Finally, when the halls were so ill-lit and dank that the only living thing must be some slumbering beast, Emilie stopped in front of a large wooden door.

"My new pretext is a mole," I said with a laugh.

"Do not be rude," she said, and knocked.

"Come in," groaned a voice from deep inside. "Come, come. Hurry before I change my mind."

Curious, I followed Emilie as we stepped into a cool room. It was more of a cell, or a dungeon, but large and candlelit; on the walls were shelves filled with what I took to be toys and props.

In the rear, on an ornately carved chair, sat a hunched man in a red tunic, green tights, and a patchwork skirt.

He lowered a yellowy eye toward Emilie. "Come in, auntie. May I have a lick? Just a lick would do . . ."

"Oh, *shut up,* Norbert," Emilie retorted, though not crossly. "This is the man I spoke of. His name is Hugh. Hugh, this is Norbert, the lord's fool."

"Egad." Norbert leaped out of his chair. He was squat and gnomelike, yet he moved with startling speed. He sprang up to me, almost smothering my red hair with his huge eyes, placing a hand on my head, then swiftly pulling it back. "Do you intend to burn me, ma'am? What is he, torch or man?"

"What he is, is no fool, Norbert," Emilie cautioned. "I think you'll have your work cut out for you."

I looked at Emilie with consternation. "My *pretext* is a jester, my lady?"

"And why not?" Emilie replied. "You say you have a knack for amusing people. What better role? Norbert informs me that the jester at Treille is as old as vinegar."

"And his wit even more sour," the jester croaked.

"And that he has lost the favor of your liege there, Baldwin. It should be no great feat for a youthful up-and-comer like yourself to gain his ear. Easier, I would think, than storming his castle in a fit of rage."

I started to stammer. I had just come back from the war, where I had fought as bravely as any man. I was looking to avenge a misery that cut to my core. I did not think of myself as a hero. But a *jester?* "I can't dispute your reasoning, lady, but . . . *I am no fool.*"

"Oh, you think it's a natural thing to act this way?" The gnomelike man hopped up to me. "Unpracticed, not learned . . . ? You think, carrot-top" — he stroked my face with his rough hands and batted his wide eyes — "that I was never as young and fair as you?"

He sprang back, narrowing his gaze. "Just because you play the fool, boy, doesn't mean you must be thick inside. The lady's plan is well-conceived. *If* you have the knack to carry it out."

"Nothing motivates me more than the will to find my wife," I insisted.

"I didn't say the *will*, boy. I said the *knack*. The lady says you have a way about yourself. That you fancy yourself a jongleur. *Jongleurs* . . . oh, they can soften the blood of blushing maidens and patrons drunk on ale. But the real trick is, can you walk into a room filled with scoundrels and schemers and make an ill-tempered king smile?"

I looked at Emilie. She was right. I did need some way to gain access to Baldwin's castle. Sophie, if she was alive, wouldn't be dressed up in the royal court, would she? I needed to snoop around, gain some trust. . . .

"Perhaps I can learn," I replied.

Chapter 33

"*LEARN* . . ." Norbert shook his head and bellowed laughter. "Learning would take years. How would you learn in a short time to do *this?*"

The gnome took a lit candle, waved his bare hand through the flame, not once crying out, then snapped his fingers, and the flame was snuffed as if by magic. "It's what comes natural that I need to know. So tell me, *whaddaya do?*"

"Do . . . ?" I muttered.

"*Do,*" the jester snapped. "What kind of student have you brought me, auntie? Has a rock hit his head? *What do you do?* Juggle, tumble, fall down?"

I looked around. I spotted a staff leaning against a table, roughly the same size as mine. I winked at Norbert. "I can do *this.*" I placed one end of the staff on the palm of my hand, balancing it there, then lightly transferred it to a single finger. For a full minute, it stood straight on end.

"Oh, that's *goood,*" Norbert crooned. "But can you do *this?*" He snatched the staff from me. In a flash, he balanced it, just as I had, upon his index finger. Then, with almost no hesitation, he flung it in the air and caught it as before on the same finger. Then again, on only one finger.

"Or this?" He smirked and began to twirl the staff so fast it looked as if six pairs of hands were twirling it. I could not even follow its path. Then he brought it to a stop and handed it to me in the same motion. "Let me see you do that."

"I cannot," I admitted.

"Then this, perhaps . . ." He winked at me with a bulging eye. "The lady said you were sprightly."

In a motion that defied my eyes, this squat, curved man spun into a complete forward somersault, then backward again, landing precisely where he had started.

"What about jokes, then? The lady said you could make me laugh. You must know some fabulous jokes."

"I know a few," I said.

Norbert folded his arms. "So, go ahead, boy. Bowl me over. Make me laugh until I piss myself."

Now I was eager to take the dare, eager to show the jester up. This I could surely do. I thought through my best inventory. "There's the one about the peasant who is so lazy that as he watches a gold coin drop from the money bag of a knight riding by . . ."

"Knowit," Norbert interrupted. "He says to his friend, 'If he comes back the same way, this just might be our lucky day.'"

"Then there's the one about the traveler and the whorehouse," I began. "A traveler is walking down the road. . . ."

"Knowit," the jester snapped again. "The sign says, 'Congratulations, you've just been screwed.'"

I went through two other tales that never failed to stir a laugh. *"Knowit,"* he said to both. He seemed to know them all. Emilie held back a laugh.

"So that's it? That's your entire repertoire?" The jester shook his head. "Can you at least *rhyme?* A dour king cannot ignore, *refusedly,* a spicy tale about his wife if it is told *amusedly.*

"This stuff is *easy,* right? Hump your back, hop around like an ape, everyone rolls over in stitches. C'mon, Red, you must have something decent. You want a pretext? Well, I want to be a mentor. *I want to be a mentor.*" He pranced around and whined like a spoiled child. "You know, maybe on second thought, you would have an easier time storming Baldwin's castle than making them laugh."

In a fit of vexation, I searched the room. This was no sport to me. No stupid audition. This was about the fate of my wife. Then, in the corner of the jester's cell, I spotted a ball and chain.

"That." I pointed.

"What? Wanna play catch?" Norbert asked haughtily.

"No, jester. Fetch me the chain." I remembered something I had seen on the Crusade. A captured Saracen did a trick to amuse his captors; it worked so well they kept him alive.

"Bind me with it," I said. "Wrap it all the way around, tight as you can. I will extricate myself."

This brought a worried look from Emilie. The chain was heavy. Wound too tight, it could squeeze the air out of a man.

"Your poison." Norbert shrugged.

He went over and dragged the heavy chain back to me. I took several deep breaths, as I had seen the Saracen do when he performed the trick. Then the jester began to wrap. Slowly, heavily, the chain squeezed me. I lifted my arms and he wrapped it around my shoulders. And for good luck, between my legs.

"Your rubicund friend has a knack to kill himself." Norbert chuckled.

"Please be careful," Emilie said.

I pushed out my chest as expansively as I could as the jester circled it with the chain. I had to enlarge myself. I had to hold my breath. I had seen this done. I had questioned the Turk about it myself. I only hoped I could re-create the effect now.

"Time's a-wasting," Norbert said after the chain was secure. He stood back.

The links felt heavy on my shoulders. Slowly, I released the captured air from my lungs. The slightest wiggle room developed around my chest. It was only a finger's breadth or two.

Then I was able to shift my shoulders back and forth. Then gradually my arms. Every grueling minute advanced like an hour. The weight of the chains pressed me to the floor. My hands were pinned behind my back, but finally I pulled one free. I twisted it like a snake through an opening up around my shoulders.

Emilie gasped. The jester looked on, finally interested in me.

It took all of my strength to get an arm free. My stomach and leg still ached from the boar's attack. Each exertion was grueling, but gradually, with the arm free, I was able to unwrap the chain. From between my legs, from under my arms, from around my chest. Layer after layer came off. Then I freed my other arm.

As I kicked off the final loop, Emilie screeched a happy cry.

I doubled over, drenched in sweat. I looked up at my mentor.

Norbert drummed his fingers along the side of his face. He smiled at Emilie. "I think we can work with that."

Chapter 34

I STUDIED WITH NORBERT for nearly a fortnight, until my wounds finally healed completely. My days were spent juggling, tumbling, and watching him perform in front of the court, and my nights with the telling and retelling of jokes and rhymes.

Step by step, I learned the jester's trade.

Much of it came easily to me. I had been a jongleur and was used to entertaining. And I had always been agile. We practiced forward flips and handstands; in return, I taught him the trick with the chain. A hundred times, Norbert held out his arm, like a bar, at waist height, while I strained to flip my body over it. At first, I hit my head on the straw mat again and again, and groaned in pain. "You find new ways to injure yourself, Red," my mentor would say, shaking his head.

Then slowly, surely, my confidence began to grow. I began to clear Norbert's arm, though sometimes falling to my seat. On my last day, I made it over, my feet landing in the precise spot from where I had sprung. I met his eyes. Norbert's face lit up in a monumental smile.

"You'll do all right." He nodded.

At last, my education was complete. There was an urgency to things; the image of Sophie was never far from my thoughts. If I had any hope of finding her alive, I had to go now.

At the end of our final session, Norbert dragged over a heavy wooden trunk. "Open it, Hugh. It's a gift from me."

I lifted the top and pulled out a set of folded clothes. Green leggings and red tunic. A floppy pointed cap. A colorful patchwork skirt.

"Emilie made it," the jester said proudly, "but to my design."

I looked at the jester's costume warily.

Norbert grinned. "Afraid to play the fool, eh? Your pride's your enemy, then, not Baldwin."

I hesitated. I knew I had to play the role, *for Sophie,* but it was hard to see myself wearing this outfit. I held the tunic up to me, sizing it against my chest.

"Put it on, then," Norbert insisted, smacking me on the shoulder. "You'll be a chip off the old block."

I removed a set of bells from the trunk.

"For the cap," said Norbert. "No liege wants to be snuck up on by his fool."

The uniform I suppose I had to wear, but there was no way I could see myself tinkling about. "These, I must leave with you."

"No *bells* . . . ?" the jester exclaimed. "No clubfoot, no hunch of the spine?" Again, he slapped my shoulders. "You are indeed the new breed."

I put aside my own tunic and leggings and slipped into the jester's outfit. Piece by piece, I felt a new confidence

take over my body. I had worn the robes of a young goliard, the garb of a soldier in the Crusade. Now *this* . . .

I looked at myself up and down and broke into a wide
smile. I felt a new man! I was ready.

"Brings tears to my eyes." Norbert feigned growing
misty. "The lack of limp bothers me some — a jester needs
a good strut. Oh, but you will appeal to the ladies!"

I sprang into a forward flip, stuck it, and bowed with
pride.

"You are done, then, Hugh," the jester said. He tugged
at my tunic and skirt to adjust the fit. "Just one thing
more . . . It is not enough, boy, to simply make them laugh.
Any fool can make a man laugh. Just fall on your face. The
mark of a true jester is to gain the trust of the court. You
may speak in rhyme, or in gibberish for all I care, but
somehow you must touch something true. It is not enough
to win your lord's laughter, lad. You must also win his ear."

"I'll win Baldwin's ear," I promised. "Then I'll cut it off
and bring it back to you."

"Good. We'll make a soup of it!" the jester roared. He
pulled my hand soundly, as if trying to force me off my
mark, then looked at me with some welling in his eyes.

"You are sure of this, Hugh? Of going to all this risk? It
would be a shame to waste this valuable teaching on a
corpse. You're sure your wife lives?"

"I feel it with all my heart." I looked into his eyes.

He raised his bushy brows and smiled. "So go, then,
lad. . . . He winked and stuck out his tongue. "Give her a
lick for me."

Chapter 35

IT WAS A COOL MORNING as the sun broke through the mist, low in the sky. Emilie met me on the stone road outside the castle gate. "You rise early, Hugh De Luc."

"And you, lady. I'm sorry to have brought you out so early in the morn."

She smiled bravely. "It is for a good purpose, I hope."

"I hope so too," I said.

She had on her brown cloak, which she always wore for matins. She cinched the collar against the mist. I stood before her in my ridiculous jester's outfit. I did a sprightly hop and a jump that made her laugh.

"I hear it is you I have to thank for the new duds." I bowed.

"What thanks?" She curtsied. "A jester could not do his work without looking the part. Besides, your other clothes reeked of a particular smelly beast."

I smiled, fixing on her soft green eyes. "I feel the fool in front of you, my lady."

"Not to me. You look quite dashing, if I say so."

"The dashing jester . . . Not what is normally thought of as right."

Emilie's eyes glistened. "Did I not tell you, Hugh, that I have a penchant for not doing what is considered right?"

"You did tell me." I nodded.

We stood and stared at each other for a long while, the space empty of words. A rush of feelings rose in my chest. This beautiful girl had done so much for me. If not for her, I would have been dead, a bloody mound on the side of the road. I reached my hand out to hers. There was a spark between us, a warmth against the cool of the morning.

I let my hand linger, longer than I could have dreamed. She did not pull away. "I owe you so much, Lady Emilie. I fear I owe you a debt I can never repay."

"You owe me nothing," she said, her chin raised, "but to be on your quest and to complete it safely."

I didn't know what else to say. I loved my wife, and yet, this woman had done so much. *And gotten nothing in return.* I wanted to take her in my arms and let her know how I felt. The strongest surge swelled inside me; it gave me a trembling in every bone in my body.

"I hope with all my heart your Sophie *is* alive," Emilie finally said.

"She is alive. I know it."

My hand was still cupping hers. When I finally pulled it away, I felt a loss — but also a small object pressed inside my palm, wrapped in a linen cloth.

"This was in your clothes," Emilie said, "when I first found you on the road."

I unwrapped it. The breath froze in my chest. It was the broken comb with the painted edge I had found in the cinders of our inn. *Sophie's comb.*

Emilie's eyes were liquid and courageous, her voice

strong. She took my hand. "Go find her, Hugh De Luc. I truly believe that is what you were saved for."

I nodded. I squeezed her hand back with all my might. "In all the world, I hope to see you again, my lady."

"In all the world, I hope to see you again too, Hugh De Luc. It pains me that you leave."

I let her go and tossed my sack upon my back. I picked up my staff and started south, on the true road to Treille.

Chapter 36

THE ARMORED RAIDERS SWEPT DOWN upon the sleeping manor. It was a large stone house in a neighboring duchy, miles from the nearest town.

I will make them pay, Black Cross promised. No man is bold enough to steal from God. Especially not the true relics of Christendom.

At first, there was a yip of dogs as the massive chargers thundered out of the calm night. Then torches lit up the darkness and everything went ablaze.

The horsemen set fire to the stables, horses bucking and neighing in fright. A few terrified workers who had been sleeping there ran out and were mowed down by the blades of hard metal charging by.

The manor burst alive with light. Six dark knights dismounted and two of them crashed through the heavy wooden door with their axes. Black Cross burst inside with his men.

The knight of the manor appeared in a doorway inside. His name was Adhémar. All France knew of this old man, this renowned fighter, who still stood with a strength that spoke of his past. Behind him, his wife huddled in a bed gown. The knight had donned his tunic. It bore the purple-and-gold fleur-de-lis of the King.

"Who are you?" Adhémar challenged the raiders. "What do you want here?"

"A piece of gold, old man. From your last campaign," said Black Cross.

"I am no banker, intruder. My last campaign was in service to the Pope."

"Then it should not be so hard to remember. What we seek was plundered from a tomb in Edessa."

"Edessa?" The old knight's eyes flicked from intruder to intruder. "How do you know this?"

"The noble Adhémar's fame is *well*-known," Black Cross said.

"Then you also know I fought with William at Hastings. That I wear the Gold Fleur, awarded to me by King Philip himself. That I have defended the faith at Acre and Antioch, where my blood still lies."

"We know *all* of this." Black Cross smiled. "In fact, that is why we are *here*."

He signaled to one of his men, who bound the arms of the knight's wife. Adhémar moved to defend her, but he was pinned by the blade of a sword to his neck.

"You insult me, intruder. You show no face or colors. Who are you? Who has sent you? Tell me, so I will know you when I meet you in Hell."

"Know *this*," Black Cross said, and lifted his helmet, revealing the dark cross burned into the side of his neck.

The old knight fell silent with recognition.

"Take us to the relic," Black Cross said.

His henchmen dragged the couple through their house, the knight's wife screaming futilely at her captors. They went through a stone arch leading to a rear courtyard, where there was a small chapel. Inside was a bronze altar with a crucifix hanging above.

"In Edessa, you looted the tomb of a Christian shrine. In the reliquary, there were crosses and vestments and coins. There was also a gold box. In it were ashes. That is all we came for. Just a box filled with ash . . ."

Black Cross grabbed a war ax from one of his cohorts and raised it over the knight's head. The knight closed his eyes. As the knight's wife shrieked, Black Cross swung the ax in a mighty arc, narrowly missing the knight, smashing the stone floor beneath the altar. The rock crumbled under the mighty blow.

Beneath the masonry, a hidden space came into view. Inside was a gold ark wrapped in cloth. One of Black Cross's men knelt and lifted it. He smashed the valuable chest as if it were a trinket.

He lifted out a simple wooden box. He opened the lid and gazed awestruck at the dark sand inside.

"It is blasphemy that you should hold such a thing in His name." The old knight glared.

Black Cross's eyes lit up with rage. "Then we shall let Him decide."

Black Cross scanned the broken chapel, his gaze coming to rest on the crucifix hanging on the wall. "Such a spirited faith, brave knight. We must make sure such faith is recognized for all to see."

Chapter 37

MY JOURNEY TO TREILLE took six days. The first two, the road was busy with travelers — peddlers dragging their carts, workers with tools and other belongings, pilgrims heading back home.

By the third day, the villages grew smaller, and so did the traffic.

By the fourth, at dusk, I huddled under a tree for a stingy meal of bread and cheese. I could not rest long. Treille was but a good day's walk away now, and the anticipation of reaching there and finding Sophie beat through my blood like a restless drum.

I decided to travel a bit farther, until darkness completely set in.

I heard voices up ahead. Then shouts, and a woman's cries. I came upon a merchant family — husband, wife, and son — in the midst of being attacked by two robbers.

One of the scavengers grabbed a prize, a ceramic bowl. "Look what *I* have, Shorty. A piss bowl."

"Please," the merchant begged, "we have no money. Take the wares if you must."

The one called Shorty sneered. "Let's have a trade. You can have your piss bowl back for a stab at your wife."

The blood pounded in my veins. I did not know these people. And I had my own pressing needs in Treille. But I couldn't stand by and watch them be robbed and possibly murdered.

I put down my pack and crept closer behind some brush. Finally, I stepped out from my cover.

Shorty's eyes fell upon me. He was stumpy and barrel-chested, balding on top, but very muscular. I knew I made a ridiculous sight in my leggings and skirt.

"Let them be," I said. "Leave them and go."

"What do we have here?" The fierce outlaw grinned toothlessly. "A pretty fairy come out of the woods."

"You heard the man." I came closer with my staff. "Take what you have. You can sell it in the next town. That's what I would do."

Shorty stood up, hardly about to buckle under a threat delivered by someone in a jester's suit. " '*What I would do,*' eh, big shot? What I would do is run off now. Your bad jokes aren't needed here."

"Let me try another," I said, stepping forward. "How about this one? Name the sexual position that produces the ugliest children."

Shorty and his partner shared looks, as if they could not believe what was going on.

"Don't know, Shorty?" I gripped my staff. "Well, why don't we just ask your mother."

The tall one grunted a slight laugh, but Shorty silenced him with a look. He lifted his club above his shoulders. I watched his eyes grow narrow and mean. "You really are a fool, aren't you?"

Before all the words had left his lips, I swung my staff. It cracked him firmly in the mouth and sent him reeling. He grabbed his jaw, then raised his weapon again. Before he could swing it, I sprang forward and whacked my stick across his shin, doubling him over in pain. I rapped his shin again and he screamed.

The other came at me, but as he did, the merchant rushed forward and thrust his torch into the outlaw's face. His entire head was engulfed in flames. The man howled and smacked at his head to smother the flames. Then his clothing caught fire and he fled into the woods, screaming, followed by Shorty.

The merchant and his wife came up to me. "We owe you thanks. I am Geoffrey." The merchant extended his hand. "I have a ceramics stall in Treille. This is my wife, Isabel. My son, Thomas."

"I'm Hugh." I took his hand. "A jester. Could you tell?"

"Tell us, Hugh," his wife inquired, "where do you head?"

"I head to Treille as well."

"Then we can go the rest of the way together," Geoffrey offered. "We don't have much food left, but what there is, you're welcome to share."

"Why not?" I agreed. "But I think we'd better put some space between us and the night crawlers. My pack's just over here."

Geoffrey's son asked, "Are you going to Treille to be a jester at our court?"

I smiled at the boy. "I hope to, Thomas. I've heard the one there now has grown a bit dull."

"Maybe he has." Geoffrey shrugged. "But you'll have

a difficult job in front of you. How long has it been since you have been to our town?"

"Three years," I answered.

He lifted the handles of his cart. "These days, I'm afraid you will find Treille a hard place to get a laugh."

Chapter 38

WE HAD BARELY CLEARED the forest two mornings later when Geoffrey pointed ahead. "There it is."

The town of Treille, glistening through the sun, perched atop a high hilltop. *Was Sophie truly here?* There was a cluster of ochre-colored buildings knotted on the rise, then, at its peak, the large gray castle, two towers thrust into the sky.

I had been to Treille twice before. Once to settle a claim against a knight who would not pay his bill, and the other with Sophie to go to market.

Geoffrey was right. As we approached the outlying village, I could tell that Treille had changed.

"Look how the farmers' fields lie fallow," he said, pointing, "while over there, the lord's demesne is neatly planted."

Closer to town, other serious signs of decline were everywhere. A wooden bridge over a stream had so many holes in the boards we could barely pass. Fences were broken and run-down.

We climbed the steep, windy hill that rose toward the castle. The streets stank from waste, the runoff from the castle lining the edges of the road.

The pigs were out. Each morning people got rid of their garbage by tossing it out on the streets. Then pigs were let loose to feed on the waste. Their morning meal was enough to turn my stomach.

At a crowded corner, Geoffrey announced, "Our stall is down the street. You are welcome to stay with us, Hugh, if you have no other place."

I declined. I had to get started on my quest — *which lay inside the castle*.

The merchant embraced me. "You'll always have a friend here. And by the way, my wife's cousin works in the castle. I will tell her what you did for us. She'll be sure to save you the best scraps of meat."

"Thanks." I winked at Thomas and hopped around a bit until I got a laugh. "Come visit me, if I get the job."

I waved as I left them behind, then walked through town, making my way up the hill. People stared, and I grinned and juggled my way into my new role. A new jester was like the arrival of a troupe of players, festive and gay.

A crowd of raggedy children followed me, dancing around with shouts and laughs. Yet my heart pounded with the worrisome task that lay ahead. *Sophie was here . . .* I could feel it.

It took me nearly an hour to wind through the streets and finally make my way to the castle gates. A squad of uniformed soldiers in milk-pail helmets and Baldwin's purple-and-white colors stood manning the lowered drawbridge, checking people going in.

The line had backed up. Some passed through. Others, arguing their case, were rudely pushed away.

This was it, my new pretext . . . my first test. My stomach churned. *Please, let me be up to this.*

Taking a deep breath, I stepped up to the gate.

And once again, *I could feel Sophie.*

Chapter 39

"WHAT'S THIS, jester? You have business here?" A brusque-looking captain of the guard eyed me up and down.

"I *have,* Your Grace." I bowed to the guard and smiled. "It is business I have come for and business I will do. *Important* business ... Not as important as yours, Your Grace, but the stuff of lords, I mean *laughs ...*"

"Shut your trap, fool." The guard glowered. "Who awaits you inside?"

"The lord awaits me." *And my Sophie.*

The guard scrunched his brow. "The *lord?* Awaits *you?*"

"The Lord awaits us *all.*" I grinned and winked.

Some people waiting in line began to chuckle.

"Lord *Baldwin,* then," I went on. "It is he who awaits me. He just does not know it yet."

"Lord Baldwin?" The guard screwed up one eye. "What do you take me for? *A fool?*" He roared laughter.

I bowed humbly. "You're right, sir, I am *not* needed if

such a wit as you is already here. You must truly keep the barracks up all night in stitches."

"We already have a fool, jester. His name is Palimpost. Not your lucky day, eh? It seems we're all fooled up."

I knelt down to a farmer's boy. I poked at his chin, his nose, then snapped my fingers, and a small dried plum appeared in my hand. The child squealed with delight. "It is a sad day, boy, is it not, when a laugh is barred with a sword. Don't tell me the great Lord Baldwin has something to fear from a laugh."

There was a trickle of applause from the bystanders. "C'mon, sergeant," a pretty, fat woman called. "Let the fool in. What harm can he cause?"

Even his fellow guards seemed to give in. "Let him through, Albert. The man's right. Things could use some lightening up around here."

"Yes, Albert," I added. "I mean Your Grace. Things *could* use some lightening. Here, hold this." I gave him my sack. "That's much *lighter*. Thank you." I folded my arms.

"Get your ass through," the guard growled at me, "before it ends up on the point of my lance." He thrust my sack back into my ribs.

I bowed a last time, winking thanks to the woman and the farmer as I hurried through.

A tremor of relief passed through me. *I was in.*

The drawbridge groaned under my feet; the walls of the castle loomed high above. Across the bridge, I entered a large courtyard. Busy people were scurrying to and fro.

I didn't know where to go. I didn't know if Sophie was here, or even alive. A knot tightened in my chest.

I stepped up to the castle entrance. The sun was high. It was before noon. Court would still be in session.

I had work to do. I was a jester.

Chapter 40

BALDWIN'S COURT WAS HELD in the great hall, down the main corridor through tall stone arches.

I followed the official traffic: knights dressed in casual leggings and tunics; pages scurrying at their sides, holding their helmets and arms; courtiers in colorful robes and cloaks with plumed feathers on their hats; petitioners of the court, both noble and common. And everywhere I walked I searched for Sophie.

People caught my eye and smiled. I, in turn, responded with a wink or a juggle, or a quick sleight of hand. My role was working so far. A man in a patchwork skirt and tights, juggling a set of balls . . . who would believe such a man could be up to any harm?

The din of a large crowd ushered me toward the great hall. Two tall oak doors, engraved with panels depicting the four seasons, stood at each side of the entrance. Soldiers holding halberds stood at attention, blocking the way.

My blood was pounding. *I was here*. Baldwin sat on the other side. All I had to do was talk my way in.

A herald wearing the lion shield of Baldwin seemed to be keeping track of appointments. Some were told to sit and wait; others, brimming with self-importance, were allowed in.

When it was my turn, I stepped up and announced boldly, "I am Hugh from Borée, cousin to Palimpost the Droll. I was told I could find him here."

At the herald's quizzical gaze, I whispered to him, "*Family* enterprise."

"I pray, from the funny side of the family." The herald sniffed. He gave me a quick once-over. "You'll no doubt find him snoozing with the dogs. Just keep out of the way while business is in session."

To my shock, he waved me in.

Through the wide doorway, I stepped into the great hall. The room was enormous — at least three stories tall, rectangular and long. It was filled with a throng of people, standing in line for the duke's attention or sitting idly around long tables.

A voice rang out above the din. From behind a huddle of merchants and moneylenders arguing about ledgers, I pushed to a vantage point where I could see.

It was Baldwin!

He was sitting, more like slouching, on a large, high-backed oak chair elevated above the floor. A totally uninterested look was on his face, as if these boring proceedings were all that held him from a preferred day of hunting and hawking.

Beneath him, a petitioning commoner knelt on one knee.

Baldwin . . . ! The sight of him sent a chill racing down my spine. For weeks, I had thought of little more than driving my knife through the base of his neck. His jet-black hair fell to his shoulders, and his chin was sharp, with a short black beard. He was wrapped in a purple-and-white robe over a loose-fitting blouse and tights.

I spotted my new rival, Palimpost, in similar garb to mine, reclining on a step to Baldwin's side, throwing dice.

Some formal matter was under discussion. A yellow-clad bailiff, pointing toward the kneeling serf, said, "The petitioner seeks to deny the right of patrimony, lord."

"The right of patrimony?" Baldwin turned to an adviser. "Is the right of the firstborn not the foundation of all property law?"

"It is, my lord," the adviser agreed.

"For nobles, for men of property, yes," the petitioner said, "but we are humble farmers. This flock of sheep is all we have. My older brother is a drunkard. He hasn't done a day's work at the farm in years. My wife and I . . . this farm is everything to us. It is how we pay our fief to you."

"You, farmer." Baldwin peered at him. "You are a working man at all costs? You do not drink yourself?"

"On holidays, perhaps . . ." The farmer hesitated, not knowing how to answer. "At feasts . . . when we celebrated our vows."

"So it seems I am forced to decide how to divide these sheep between *two* drunkards." Baldwin grinned. A wave of laughter echoed through the cavernous room.

"But my *lord* . . ." The farmer rose.

"Be still," the duke cautioned. "The law must be obeyed.

"And to do so, the flock must be transferred to a first-born," he continued. "Is that not right? Yet your reserve is warranted, I think, farmer. Should the flock be wasted, we will not be enriched in any way. It occurs to me that there is an option." He beamed at the room. "*I* am a first-born. . . ."

The petitioner gasped. "*You*, my lord?"

"Yes." Baldwin smiled broadly. "The *first* of the first-born, wouldn't you say so, chamberlain?"

"You are the lord, my liege." The chamberlain bowed.

"Therefore, it seems the law would be upheld nicely should these precious sheep revert to me," Baldwin declared.

The horrified farmer looked around for some support.

"So I take them," Baldwin announced, "in the name of patrimony."

"But my lord," the farmer pressed, "these sheep are all we have."

Anger swept through me. I wanted to lunge at Baldwin, plunge my dagger into his throat. This was the man who had stolen everything from me, with the same ease and indifference with which he now ruined this poor farmer. But I had to restrain myself. It was Sophie I came for, not revenge against this pig of a man.

A page leaned over to Baldwin. "Your hawks await, my lord."

"Good. Is there any more business before the court?" Baldwin asked, implying he wanted none.

I swallowed nervously. This was my chance. Why I had come. I pushed my way to the front.

"I have business, my lord!"

Chapter 41

"THERE IS THE MATTER of your western lands," I called out from the throng of petitioners.

"Who speaks?" Baldwin asked, startled. A surprised buzz worked through the crowd of petitioners.

"A knight, your lordship," I shouted. "I have taken a raiding party and sacked and burned all the villages of your enemies in the west."

Baldwin stood up. He leaned over to his seneschal. "But we don't have any enemies in the west . . ."

I took a breath and edged myself out from the crowd. "I am sorry, lord, but I fear that you do *now*."

Slowly, steadily, a trail of laughter wound through the room. As the joke became clear, it grew heartier.

"It is a *fool*," I heard someone say. "A performance."

Baldwin glared and stepped toward me. His icy stare made my blood run cold. "Who are you, fool? What has prompted you to speak?"

"I am Hugh. From Borée." I bowed. "I have studied

under Norbert, the famous jester there. I am informed that your court is greatly in need of a laugh."

"*A laugh?* My court hungers for *a laugh* . . . ?" Baldwin squinted uncomprehendingly. "You are certainly fool-born, man, I grant you that. And you have come all this way from the big city to amuse us."

"That is so, my lord." I bowed again, nerves flashing through me.

"Well, your journey is wasted," the noble said. "We already have a fool here. Don't we, Palimpost, my droll pet?"

The jester sprang up, an old, clubfooted man with white hair and thick lips who looked as if he had just been jolted awake.

"With all due respect," I said, stepping into the middle of the room and addressing the court, "I have heard that Palimpost couldn't get a laugh from a drunken sot. That he has lost his touch. I say hear me out. If you are not happy, I will be on my way."

Baldwin stepped down from his platform. He made his way across the room toward me. "Make us laugh, and we will see about your future. Fail, and you'll be practicing jokes for the rats in our keep."

"It's fair, my lord." I bowed. "I will make you laugh."

Chapter 42

I STOOD IN THE CENTER of the huge room. A hundred pairs of eyes were on me.

In a group of lounging knights, I spotted Norcross, the duke's military man, his chatelain. I eyed him tremulously, though he did not look my way. Every sense told me this was the man who had killed my son.

"You have all no doubt heard the tale of the cow from Amiens," I crowed.

People looked at one another and shook their heads. "We have not," someone yelled out. *"Tell us, jester."*

"These two peasants had a single denier between them. So to enlarge their fortune, they decided to buy a cow, and every day they would sell its milk. Now, as everyone knows, the best cows in the land come from Amiens.

"So they went there, and they traded the denier for the best cow they could find, who yielded lots of milk. And they sold the milk each morning. Soon, one of them said, 'If we can mate this fine cow, we'll have two. We can double our milk and our money.' So they searched their village and found the finest bull. Soon, they were going to be rich."

I scanned the room. Everyone seemed to hang on my words. A hundred smiles . . . knights, ladies-in-waiting, even the duke himself. *I had them. I had their ears.*

"The day of the mating, they brought in the bull. First, he tried to mount the cow from behind, but the cow wiggled away. Then, the bull came at her from the left, but the cow wiggled its rump to the right. If it came from the right, the cow wiggled left."

I spotted an attractive lady and went up to her. I smiled and wiggled my own rump. Just enough to be considered cute. The crowd *oohed* with delight.

"Finally," I said, "the peasants threw up their hands in frustration. There was no way this cow from Amiens would mate. But instead of giving up, they decided to consult the smartest person in the duchy. A knight of such rare wisdom, such vision, he knew why all things were as they were."

I noticed Norcross reclining on his elbow, following the tale. I strode up to him. "Someone like *you,* knight," I said.

The crowd cackled. "Your story errs there," said Baldwin, laughing, "if it's brains you want."

"So I've heard." I bowed to the duke. "But for the purpose of the tale, he'll do."

Norcross's amusement began to sour and he glared at me, red faced.

"So the peasants came to this *very* wise knight and they told him of their problem with the cow. They moaned, 'What must we do?'

"The wise knight replied, 'You say if the bull tries to mount it this way, it wiggles left? And from this direction, it wiggles right?'

" 'Yes!' they cried.

"The knight thought it over. 'I do not know if I can solve your dilemma,' he said, 'but I know one thing. Your cow is from *Amiens,* is it not?'

"'Yes, yes,' the peasants shouted. 'It is indeed from Amiens. How could you possibly know?'"

I turned back to Norcross. I perched on the table next to him. "'Because *my wife,*' the knight muttered, '*she* is from Amiens as well.'"

The hall burst into laughter. The knights, the duke, the ladies. All except Norcross. Then the vast room echoed with applause.

Baldwin came up and slapped me on the back. "You are indeed funny, fool. You have other jokes like this?"

"Many," I replied. To punctuate the point, I sprang into a forward flip, then one backward. The crowd oohed.

"They must laugh well in Borée. You may stay, my new companion. You are hired."

I raised my arms in triumph. The large room echoed with applause. But inside, I knew I stood inches from the very men I had sworn to kill.

"Palimpost, as of this day you are retired," Baldwin declared. "Show the new fool your spot."

"*Retired?* But I have no desire, my liege. Haven't I served you with all my wit?"

"With what little you have. So you are *un*retired, then. I grant you a new job. In the graveyard. See if you can cheer up the audience there."

Chapter 43

TWO DAYS AFTER my arrival, Baldwin announced a great feast at court, with counts, knights, and other noble-born invited from all over the region. The duke knew how to waste what had been earned by his poor serfs.

I was instructed by the lord's chamberlain that I would be a main act at the festivities. Baldwin's wife, the lady Heloise, had heard of my audition and was eager to see my act.

This would be my first real test!

The day of the gathering, the entire castle bustled with activity. An endless army of servants wearing their finest uniforms, tunics of the same purple and white, marched dishware and elaborate candelabras into the great hall. Minstrels practiced on the lawn. Giant logs were loaded into the hearths. The luscious aroma of roasting goose, pig, and sheep permeated the castle.

I spent the day polishing my routine. This was my coming out, my first real performance. I had to shine, to remain in Baldwin's good graces. I juggled, twirled my staff, practiced my flips back and forth, went over my tales and jokes.

Finally, the evening of the feast was at hand. Nervous as a groom, I made my way to the banquet hall. Four long tables filled the room, each covered in the finest linen cloth and set with candelabras engraved with the duke's lion shield.

Arriving guests were greeted with a flourish of horns. I sauntered up to each, announcing them with playful epithets. "His bawdiness, the duke of Loire, and his lovely niece, er . . . *wife,* the lady Kate." It was all meant to trump the husband and praise his wife, no matter how plain she might be. Everyone played along.

Only when the room filled did Baldwin and his lady, Heloise, make their entrance. One glance made it obvious to me that Baldwin had not married for looks. The couple waded through the room, Baldwin hugging and joking with the men, Heloise curtsying and receiving lavish praise. They took seats at the head of the largest table.

When their guests were all seated, Baldwin stood and raised a goblet. "Welcome, everyone. Tonight we have much to cheer. The court has been enriched by a new flock. And the arrival of a fool from Borée. Hugh will make us laugh, or else."

"I have heard my husband's new pet is quite the rage," Lady Heloise announced. "Perhaps he will set the tone with a few jests."

I took a deep breath, then I hopped around to the head table. "I'll do my best, my lady."

I scampered toward her but then threw myself into the lap of a fat old man seated down the row. I grinned, stroking his beard. "I would be honored to perform for you, Your Grace. I . . ."

"*Here,* fool," Lady Heloise called. "I am over *here.*"

"Gads." I shot out of the man's lap. "Of course, my lady. I must've been blinded by your beauty. So much so, I could not see."

There was a trickle of laughter.

"Surely, fool," Lady Heloise called, "you did not have the crowd shouting your name the other day with such mild flattery. Perhaps it is I who am blinded. Is that Hugh I see there or Palimpost?"

The room chuckled at the hostess's wit. Even I bowed, warming to the challenge.

At the end of the table, a potbellied priest was sucking down a mug of ale. I hopped onto the table in front of him, plates and mugs clattering. "There's *this one,* then. . . . A man went to a priest to confess his many sins. He said he had much to share."

The priest looked up. "To me?"

"We'll see, Father, how you feel about it at the end. First, the man confessed he had stolen from a friend, but added that this friend had stolen something back of equal value. 'One thing cancels out another,' the priest replied. 'You are absolved.'"

"It is true." The priest nodded.

"Next," I went on, "the fellow said he had beaten the man with a stick, but had received equal blows in return. 'Again, these both cancel each other out,' the priest replied. 'You owe God nothing.'

"Now this penitent sensed he could get away with anything. He said there was something else to confess, one more sin, but he was too ashamed. When the priest encouraged him, he said. 'Once, Father, I had your sister.'

" *'My sister!'* the priest bellowed. The man was sure he was about to feel a holy wrath. 'And I have had your mother on several occasions,' the priest said. 'Again, they cancel each other out. So we are *both* absolved.'"

The guests clapped and laughed. The embarrassed priest looked around the room and clapped as well.

"*More,* fool," Lady Heloise shouted, "in the same temper." She turned to Baldwin. "Where have you been hiding this treasure?"

The room bubbled with good cheer. Food was served — swan and goose and pig. Goblets and mugs were filled by servants scurrying about.

I leaped up to a server carrying a roast on a tray. I took a whiff of the meat. "Superb." I sighed. "Who knows the difference between medium and rare?"

Diners at the tables looked around and shrugged.

I went up to a blushing lady. "Six inches is medium, my lady. But eight is rare."

Again, they roared. I had it going. I spotted Baldwin taking congratulations, seeming delighted with the performance.

To much fanfare, a train of servers marched in from the kitchen carrying prepared plates. Baldwin stood. "Lamb, guests, from our new flock."

Baldwin stuck a knife into a slice of lamb and chewed off a piece in front of his server. "Delicious, server, wouldn't you say?"

"It is, my lord." The server bowed stiffly.

To my horror, I realized that the dejected servant was the same farmer from whom Baldwin had chiseled the flock just two days before. Suddenly my blood stirred in rage.

"Please, jester, do continue," Baldwin said with a mouthful of meat.

"I will, my lord." I bowed.

I spotted Norcross at the end of Baldwin's table, stabbing his meat among a row of other knights. "Is that my lord Norcross I see stuffing his face over there?"

Norcross looked up, then his eyes narrowed on me.

"Tell me," I asked the crowd, "who is a greater hero to our lord than the brave Norcross? Who among us could be more forgiven for conceit? In fact, I have heard this good knight is so conceited, that during climax he calls out his *own* name."

Norcross put his knife down. He stared at me, juice running through his beard. Laughter ensued, but as the knight's face tightened, it trickled away.

"And there are those who ask," I continued, "what do a holiday decoration and my lord Norcross have in common?"

This time there were no amused mutterings. A tense silence hung in the air.

"You will find," I said, "that their balls are just for decoration."

With that, the knight shot up, drawing his sword. He lunged around the crowded table toward me.

I pretended to flee. "Help me, help me, my lord. I have no sword, yet I fear I have struck too deep."

I did a flip and ran around the table toward Baldwin. Norcross pursued, weighed down and slightly drunk.

I easily avoided him, circling the table to the merriment of the crowd, who almost seemed to be making bets as to whether the knight would catch me and cut my throat. Finally, I threw myself in the protection of Baldwin's lap. "He will kill me, my lord."

"He will not," Baldwin replied. "Relax, Norcross. Our new fool has managed to get under your skin. A good laugh, not a killing, should soothe the wound."

"He insults me, my lord. I stand for that from no man."

"This is no man." Baldwin cackled. "He is but a fool. And he provides us much entertainment."

"I have served you well." The red-faced knight seethed. "I demand to fight the fool."

"You will not." Lady Heloise rose. "The fool has acted on my bidding. If anything untimely happens to him, I will know the author. You may feel safe, Hugh."

Norcross exhaled a deep, frustrated breath, the object of all eyes in the room. Slowly he let his massive sword slip back into its sheath.

"Next time, fool," he said, "the laugh will be mine." He went back to his seat, never once removing his stare from me.

"You have picked an adversary who is not one to anger." Baldwin chuckled as he ate his lamb. He tossed some bits of fat off his plate to the floor. "Here. Help your-self."

I looked across the room at Norcross. I knew I had made an enemy for life.

But so had he.

Chapter 44

I HAD NO TIME to waste. I set out to find Sophie. *She was alive. I knew it.*

My confrontation with Norcross had given me instant status among the castle staff. I was given a name, Hugh the Brave, or, I was told, with respect to Norcross's wrath, Hugh the *Brief*. People who I sensed served the duke only out of fear or obligation came and whispered their support. I was able to make a few useful friends.

There was Bette the cook, a chubby, red-faced woman with a sharp tongue who kept the kitchen running like a spotless ship. And Jacques, the upstairs valet de chambre, who took meals next to me in the kitchen. Even a cheerful sergeant at arms at the court, Henri, who chuckled at my jokes.

I questioned all of them, asking if they had heard of a fair, blond woman held captive in the castle, keeping my reasons close to the vest. No one had. "Checked the brothels?" The sergeant winked. "Once the nobles have no use for 'em, they'd be sent there." So I did. I made the rounds, pretending to be a choosy customer. But, thank God, no one fitting Sophie's description was among the poor whores at Treille.

"You look a little drawn in the face, for a jester," Bette, the cook, observed one morning as she pounded out her dough. "Your lost sweetheart again?"

I wished I could take her into my confidence. "Not mine, Bette, but a friend's," I lied. "Someone asked me to inquire."

"A *friend's,* you say." The cook eyed me skeptically. She seemed to play with me. "Is she highborn or common?"

I looked up from my bowl. "How would a rogue like me know anyone highborn?" I grinned. "Except *you,* perhaps. . . ."

"Oh yes, me . . ." Bette cackled. "I'm the duke's own blood. That's why I slave in this hearth until dark every day."

She laughed and went about her chores. But when she returned lugging a pot, she crept behind me and said confidingly, "Perhaps it's the Tavern you want, love."

I looked up. "The Tavern?"

She reached on her tiptoes for a bowl of garlic heads high on a shelf. "*The dungeons,*" she said under her breath. "They're always filled with mouths to feed. At least for a short while. We call them la Taverne. Everyone goes in on their own two feet, but usually it takes a team of four to carry them out."

I looked to thank her, but Bette quickly breezed to the other side of the kitchen, peeling the garlic for her soup.

The Tavern. For days afterward, I spied on it in the courtyard while taking my daily stroll. A heavy iron door, always guarded by at least two soldiers from Baldwin's reserve. Once or twice, I sauntered over, trying to warm up the guards. I did a little magic trick, tossed some balls in the air, twirled my staff. I never got as much as a snicker.

"Bug off, fool," one guard barked at me. "No one here even remembers how to laugh."

"You want a peek," another barked. "I'm sure Norcross'll find you a room."

I hurried away, pretending his very name had sent me trembling. But I continued plotting. *How to get in? Who could help me?* I tried the chamberlain. I even tried to play my liege, Baldwin. One day, after court, I sidled up to him. "Time for a drink, my lord. How about I buy you one . . . in la Taverne?"

Baldwin laughed and said to his coterie, "Fool wants a drink so bad, he's willing to risk the pox to get it."

One night, as I took my meal in the kitchen, Bette sat down with me. "You are a strange sort, Hugh. All day you're smiles and tricks. But at night you sulk and brood like a lost lover. Why do I think this loss you feel is not a friend's?"

I could no longer hide my sadness. I had to trust someone. "You are right, Bette. It's my wife I seek. She was taken from my village. By raiding knights. I know she is here. I can feel it in my blood."

Bette did not show surprise. She only smiled. "I knew you were no fool," she said. "And I can be a friend," she added, "if you need one."

"I need one more than you can know," I said, desperate. "But *why?*"

"Be sure, not for your silly tricks, Hugh, or your flattery." Bette's expression changed, grew warmer. "Geoffrey and Isabel, Hugh . . . They are my cousins. Why do you think I always saved you the best scraps of meat? You don't think you're that funny, do you? I owe you their lives, Hugh."

I grasped her hands. "La Taverne, Bette. I have to get in. I've tried everything, but there's no way."

"No way?" The cook stared at me a long time, searching my intentions. "For a fool, maybe. Only a fool would want to get *in*to la Taverne. But there's a saying here. The best way to end up in the soup is to ask the cook!"

Chapter 45

IT WAS CHILLY for a summer night in Borée. A breeze blew over the gardens. The lady Emilie huddled in her cloak. At her side was the jester, Norbert.

Emilie had tried to read her book of chansons de geste that night, but the pages turned emptily, her thoughts drifting into space like wisps of smoke. The rhymes of poets and the tales of imaginary heroes no longer captivated her. Her heart ached with a confusion she had never known before. It always came back to one thing. One face.

What is happening to me? she wondered. *I feel I am going mad.*

Norbert had noticed it. The jester had knocked on her door earlier that night. "I know laughter, my lady, and to know that, I must know melancholy too."

"So you are a jester and now a physician too?" She pretended to scold him.

"It takes no physician to see what ails you, lady. You miss the lad, don't you?"

With anyone else, she would have bitten her tongue. "I do miss him, jester. I cannot lie."

The jester sat across from her. "You're not alone. I miss him too."

This was something new for Emilie. She was used to feeling that men were like flies, nuisances, always buzzing around her, too concerned with their boasting and their deeds to be taken seriously. But this was different. *How had it happened?* She had only known Hugh for weeks. His life was a world apart from hers, yet she knew everything about him. Most likely, she would never see him again.

"I feel I have sent him on this quest," she told Norbert. "And now I wish I could bring him back."

"You did not send him, lady. And with all respect, he is not yours to bring back."

No, Norbert was right. Hugh was not hers. She had only stumbled upon him.

So she huddled in the garden that night. She needed to feel the air on her face. Somehow, out here, under the same moon, she felt closer to him. *I don't know if I will ever see you again, Hugh De Luc. But I pray I do. Somehow, some way.*

"You risk a lot to have such feelings," Norbert said.

"They are not planned. They just . . . *are*."

He took her hand. There was a moment between them, not as lady and servant but as friends. Emilie blushed, then smiled. "It seems my heart is owned by jesters from all around."

"Do not worry, my lady. Our Red is canny and resourceful. I taught him, you know. A chip off the old block. I'm sure he's fine. He'll find his wife."

"A jester and a physician and now a seer too?" She

hugged the jester. "Thank you, Norbert." Then she watched him go back inside.

It was late. The garden was still. She had promised the priest she would wake early for morning prayers. *"Be safe, Hugh De Luc,"* she whispered, then turned back toward the castle.

She headed along the loggia above the gardens to the living quarters. Then, out of the night, voices came to her from below.

Who could be out here at this hour? Emilie hid behind a column and peered into the deep shadows below.

A man and a woman. Voices raised.

She strained to hear. "This is not it, knight," the woman said. "This is not the treasure."

It was Anne. Out there in the dark with a man. He didn't look like a knight. More like a monk. In robes. But with a sword.

Emilie thought she had stumbled across something she should not have seen. Anne was angry. She'd never heard her mistress's tone this hard.

"You know what my husband wants," she said. *"Find it!"*

Chapter 46

A FEW DAYS LATER, as I took my evening meal, Bette the cook winked and drew me aside. "There's a way," she said. "If you still want to see the Tavern."

"How?" I asked, leaning in close. "And how soon?"

"It's not exactly a state secret, jester. People have to eat, don't they? Guards, soldiers . . . even prisoners. Every day my kitchen brings the evening meal to the dungeon. Who would mind if it was brought by the fool?"

My eyes lit up. The fool doing errands for the cook. It could work.

"I will give it a try," Bette said. "The rest is up to you. If your wife is there, Hugh, it will take more than luck to get her out. Just don't bring the duke's awful wrath down on me."

I took her hand and squeezed it. "I would bring nothing down upon you except my gratitude. I owe you much, Bette."

"I told you, I owe you my cousins' lives."

"But somehow, I think it is more than what I did for Geoffrey, Isabel, and Thomas on the road here."

She smiled and tossed a turnip into the pot. "Baldwin is our liege," she sniffed. "But he can never rule our hearts. I see why you have come. I can see you are in love. These hands may be rough and ugly, but I am not so removed from matters of the heart."

I began to blush. "Am I so transparent?"

"Don't worry, love, no one else would notice. They're too busy grabbing their sides and laughing at your silly jokes."

I raised an onion the way one would raise a mug to make a toast. "We will keep each other's trust, Bette."

She lifted a turnip. We tapped them together.

"I feel a headache coming on." She frowned. "*Tomorrow eve.* Be here at dusk.

"And something else, Hugh. You asked if a woman was being held in the cells. I checked. There *is* a lady staying in the Tavern. One who might fit your wife's description. Fair-haired. And she keeps talking about an infant."

These words . . . They were like the most exquisite magic for my soul. What was only a hope for so long now sprang free. *Sophie was here!* I knew it now. I would see her tomorrow night. At last!

I hugged Bette, almost knocking the poor woman into her pot of soup.

Chapter 47

ALL THE NEXT DAY I waited for dusk to fall. Time passed with agonizing slowness. To make things worse, Baldwin called for me to entertain him while he got new boots measured by a shoemaker. *What scum he was.* I had to keep him amused while I thought of plunging a dagger into his heart. Yet all the while I could barely count the time.

I sat on my bare mat as the afternoon wound down, watching the sun descend. Finally, the light from the slats above my space grew dim. *It was dusk.* . . . It was finally time to see Sophie.

I made my way down to the kitchen. Bette was bustling about, complaining to the staff, a damp cloth pressed to her head for effect. "I've got to lie down. I've got the duke's meals still to prepare. Who will carry over the soup to the Tavern? *Hugh,* what luck," she said, spotting me. "Will you be a dear?"

"I am but two hands," I joked to the staff, "and *one* . . ."

I wiggled a finger and sniffed with a wrinkled nose. ". . . I use for scratching."

"That's all I need." Bette led me away. "Just make sure the other stays out of the soup."

She took a covered pot from the hearth and announced, "Give it to Armand, the jailer. And give him that jug of wine. You've done me a good turn, fool." Then she gripped me conspiratorially by the arm. "I wish you luck, Hugh. Be careful. It's a bad place you go to now. It is hell."

I carried the pot and the jug of wine across the courtyard. My arms trembled a bit. Two guards stood at the door of the keep, different ones than those who had booted me away the other day.

"*Ding, ding, ding* . . . dinner bell," I announced ceremoniously.

"Who the hell are they putting to work in the kitchen now?" one of them asked.

"I do it all . . . jokes to dessert. The duke's expenses must be trimmed."

"The duke must be bankrupt if he sent you," the other guard said.

To my relief, they didn't question me. One opened the heavy door. "If you had nicer tits, I'd carry it down for you." He sniffed.

The door slammed shut behind me. I felt a tremor of relief. *I was in!*

I stood in a narrow stone corridor lit only by candles. A narrow stairway leading down.

A draft hit me, then noises — the clang of iron, someone calling out, a high-pitched wail. I stepped down cautiously, my heart nearly bounding out of my chest, my neck beaded with cold sweat.

I descended one step at a time, the pot clanging against the narrow walls, the wine jug pressed to my chest.

Finally, the passageway leveled off into a low, dungeonlike setting. The foul stink of excrement was all around. There was shouting from within, like that of mad people, terrifying moans and shrieks. I saw a hearth, and in it iron instruments, their tips white with heat.

My stomach grew hollow. Suddenly I did not know what to do — *if I found her.*

Two soldiers sat straddling a wooden tabletop, stripped down to sleeveless tunics and skirts. A swarthy one with hulking, imposing shoulders snickered at the sight of me. "We must be fucked. Look who brings our dinner."

"You're Armand?" I lugged the pot over.

He shrugged. "And if you're the new chef, the duke's really got it in for these poor bastards. Where's Bette?"

"Down with a headache. She sent me instead."

"Just set it here. There's a pot from this afternoon you can take back up."

I placed the pot on the table by a stack of wooden bowls. "How many guests tonight . . . in la Taverne?"

"What's it to you?" the other asked.

"Never been down here before." I looked around, ignoring him. "Cheery. You mind if I take a look?"

"This isn't a marketplace, fool. You've done your chore. Now bug off."

My chance was slipping away. I felt I only had a moment more to make my case. "C'mon, let me take in their food. I spend my day making silly jokes and spinning around like a top. Let me take a look. I'll bring them their bowls."

I placed the wine jug on the table in front of him. "Anyway, you guys really want to touch that slop?"

Armand slowly pulled the jug toward him. He took a swig of wine, then passed it along.

"What the hell." He shrugged and winked at his partner. "Why not give the jester's dick its rise. Take what you want in there. It's free for the asking."

Chapter 48

I TURNED A CORNER in the dungeon and then I could make out the cells. The odor here was beyond belief, nearly unbearable. *My God, Sophie . . .*

I finally set down the soup pot and started to work. These people had to be fed, and while I did the task, I would search for Sophie in every dark corner.

I began sloshing thin, murky gruel into bowls. My heart beat like a warning bell swung furiously back and forth.

I carried a bowl to the first cell. My hands were trembling. Soup splattered on the floor.

At first glance, the cell seemed to be empty. It was like a cave opening, dug out of solid rock, just a few feet deep. No light or sound, just the reek of human filth. A wet rat slithered out in front of my eyes.

Then, in the back, I saw the glow of eyes. They flickered, tremulous and afraid. From out of the shadow — a head. Hairless, gaunt, a sunken face covered with runny sores.

The prisoner crawled toward me, wild-eyed. "I mus' be dead if it's a fool come for me."

"Better a fool than Saint Peter." I knelt and shoved a bowl under the bars.

His thin, palsied hand darted out and grabbed the wooden bowl. A momentary sadness ran through me. I had no idea what he had done to put him here. In Treille, there was no reason to assume he was guilty of anything.

But I was not here for *him*. . . .

I moved on to the next cells, not even going back for more soup. As with the first, the captives looked more like hunted animals than men. They groaned, peered out at me with beaten, yellow eyes. I took a breath against the urge to violently retch.

Then, from farther along, came a wail. *A woman!* My body tensed. *Sophie?* I did not know if I could go on.

"There's your date, fool," Armand brayed from his post. "Feel free to slip inside if she suits you. She has a magical tongue."

I clenched my fists and made my way toward the woman's cries. Inside my belt, I grasped the hilt of my knife. If this was Sophie, I would surely kill the guards. Norcross too.

The woman's wail echoed again. "Go to her, fool. The bitch doesn't like to be stood up," yelled Armand.

I held my breath and stepped in front of the woman's cell. The stench was worse here. Unbearable. Why was that?

She was crouched in a tight ball deep in the cell. A beam of light slanted across her hair, which was long and straggly. She seemed to clutch a doll or toy, whimpering like an abandoned child herself. "My baby," she said, no more than a whisper. "Please . . . my baby needs milk."

I could barely see her. I could not make out her age or

her face. I gathered myself and said, "Is that you, Sophie?" Fear shot through me. My breath froze. To be kept like this — it would be better if she was dead.

The woman sputtered out nearly incoherent phrases. "Poor baby," she muttered. "Baby needs milk." Then something that sounded like . . . *Phillipe.*

Oh, God. I froze. I stepped closer to the bars. What had they done to her? "Sophie," I called. My tongue grew dry on her name. It seemed her shape, her hair. *Please, turn toward me. Let me see.*

I rammed myself up against the bars. "Baby needs milk," I heard her say again, then suddenly she emitted an ear-splitting, wrenching howl. It was like a blade running through me.

I reached out, and her eyes finally caught sight of me. The breath froze in my chest. Her strawlike hair was falling over her face. But her eyes locked on mine. Yellow. Veins running through them. The nose flat and pocked.

Oh, God! It was not her.

My legs buckled. *It was not her.* Part of me was giddy with joy; another, crestfallen and disappointed.

"My baby . . ." the woman called, pleading. She held out the doll for me to see.

Oh, God. I recoiled. It was no doll. *It was real.* A tiny newborn child, bound in a caul, clearly dead, stillborn.

"How can I help you?" I whispered. "How?"

"Can't you see?" she pushed the infant toward me. "The child needs milk."

"Let me help."

"Milk!" the woman shrieked. "Feed him."

There was nothing I could do. The poor woman was raving mad.

I stared for a moment more, then flung myself back down the corridor toward the stairs.

The jailers laughed as I went by. "Leaving so soon, fool?" cried Armand. "What, no jokes?"

I bolted out of the dungeon and up the stairs.

Chapter 49

I RAN IN A COLD SWEAT back to the castle and my alcove under the stairs. There, I threw myself on my mat. My breath raced panicked and wild.

It was not her.

My beloved Sophie must be dead after all.

I buried my head in my hands. This silly charade was over. I had clung to a hope and now that hope was dashed. I must go. I ripped off my jester's hat and threw it onto the floor. I was no jester. Just a fool! A bigger fool had never lived.

I sat there for a long time. Letting the truth sink in.

I heard footsteps near my bed, then a voice. "Is that you, Hugh?"

I raised my head . . . to see Estella, the chamberlain's wife.

She had winked at me in court. Many times. She'd grabbed at me and teased. Tonight, she had a loose shawl covering her shoulders; thick auburn hair, which I had only seen braided and pinned until now, fell all about her neck.

Her eyes were round and mischievous. And her timing — couldn't have been worse!

"The hour is late, my lady. I am not at work."

"Perhaps I did not come for work," Estella said, stepping into my bed-space. She let her shawl drop, revealing a loosely fitted bodice.

"What striking red hair," she whispered. "Now how is it such a fiery fool can look so sad?"

"Please, my lady, I am not one for jokes this night. I'll be funny again in the morning."

"I don't need to laugh right now, Hugh. Let me feel you in another way."

She sat down beside me. Close. Her body was scented with fresh lavender and lilies. She reached out and stroked my face. I moved away from her touch.

"I have never seen such hair." She seemed fixed on it. "It is the color of a flame. What are you really like, Hugh, when you are free of all those jokes?"

She pushed herself even closer. I felt the fullness of her breasts against my chest. One of her legs straddled mine.

"Please, my lady."

But Estella pressed on. She wiggled her shoulders, letting her blouse fall to her waist. Her breasts tumbled forward. Then I felt the hot tip of her tongue dance on my neck.

At that moment I felt the tip of a blade digging into my neck. I held very still. A male voice boomed, *"What mischief have I stumbled onto?"*

Chapter 50

THE KNIFE SLOWLY DREW BACK and I turned to face Norcross. The monster was grinning down at me.

Norcross dug the blade in again, and I felt the warmth of blood trickling down my neck.

"A nasty situation, fool. The lady Estella is the wife of the duke's chamberlain, a member of the court. You must be mad to wag your dick at such a lady."

Panic pumped through my chest as I realized I had been set up. "I did nothing, my lord." My heart pounded wildly.

"The little dick had no urge." Estella sighed. "It appears our fool's only ardor is in his hair."

Norcross grabbed me by the tunic and raised me, blade under my chin. Suddenly the bastard's eyes lit up with recognition.

"His *hair* . . . I do know you from somewhere else. Where, fool? Tell me."

I saw that I was doomed. I shot a glare back in his face. "My wife . . . What did you do to Sophie?"

"Your wife." The knight sniffed. "What would I do with the wife of a lowly fool? Except fuck her."

I lunged toward him, but he gripped me by the hair, and with the leverage of his arms and the blade stuck firmly under my chin, forced me down, slowly, to my knees. "Listen good, fool. I *have* seen you. But *where?* Where have I seen your face before?'

"Veille du Père." I spat out the words.

"That little shithole." Norcross snorted.

"You burned our inn. You killed my wife and child, Phillipe."

He was thinking back. The tiniest smile cracked his lips. "I *do* remember now. . . . You were the little red squirrel who tried to stop me from dunking the miller's son."

Norcross's smile widened. "And what of the vaunted Hugh? The jester of jesters who studied under Norbert at Borée?" His grin deepened into a roaring laugh. *"You?* You are an innkeeper! A fraud."

I pressed toward him again, but his blade stabbed into my neck. I felt it cut skin. "You took my wife. You hurled my son into flames."

"If I did, all the merrier, you lowly worm." Norcross shrugged. Then he winked at Estella. "I can see you are greatly offended, my lady. Go now and report the affront."

She righted her blouse and scurried away. "I will, my lord. Thank you for coming when you did." She ran out of the room. *"Guards . . ."* I heard her shout echo. "Help me! Guards!"

Norcross turned back to me. His eyes were hard-set and victorious. "What do you say, fool? It seems the laugh is mine after all."

Chapter 51

I WAS HURLED, hands bound, into a dark, empty cell on the castle's first floor. There I nervously passed the night.

I knew my fate was sealed. Lady Estella would play the offended role, just as she had played me last night. Norcross, the vindicated hero. It would be my word against that of nobles. All the laughter in the world couldn't save me now.

I was jolted by a loud rattling at the door. A sliver of light appeared beneath it. It was day. Three brawny guards in Baldwin's uniform came into the room. The captain yanked me up. "If you know any good jokes, carrot-top, now would be the time. . . ."

I was pushed roughly into the great hall. The court was buzzing with knights and courtiers just as it had been the day I arrived. A messenger was informing the court about some renowned knight who had been slaughtered by outlaws in a neighboring duchy.

Baldwin slouched in his elevated chair, chin in hand,

and beckoned the man forward. "The vaunted Adhémar . . . killed in his own home?"

"Not just killed, my lord. . . ." The messenger was clearly uncomfortable, forced to deliver such news. ". . . Impaled to the wall of his chapel by his own limbs, his wife next to him. The lord was crucified."

"*Crucified.*" Baldwin rose slowly. "You say he was roused from his own bed by bandits?"

"Marauders was more like it. They rode in armed and dressed for battle, their faces hidden behind their head-pieces. They bore no markings on their armor except for one, a black cross."

"A black cross?" Baldwin widened his eyes. I could not tell if his shock was sincere or pretended. "Nor*cross,* do you know of such a band?"

From the crowd, Norcross stepped forward. He had on a long red surcoat and his war sword hung in his belt. "I do not, my liege."

"Poor Adhémar." Baldwin swallowed. "Tell me, messenger, what treasure did these cowards seek?"

"I know not." The messenger shook his head. "Adhémar had just returned from the Holy Land, where he had been wounded. He was said to have come back bearing valuable spoils. I had heard the very ashes of Saint Matthew."

"The ashes of Matthew," Baldwin said. "Such a prize would be worth the price of a kingdom itself."

"Only one relic is holier," Norcross said.

"The lance of Longinus." Baldwin's eyes flashed. "Whose blade was dipped in the Savior's own blood."

Hidden riders, burning and slaughtering. I did not doubt Norcross was behind these murders too. How I wanted to cut his throat.

"Lord," Norcross continued, "Adhémar's fate is sealed, but there is other business to be done."

"Ah, yes, the fate of our little fool." Baldwin waved the messenger away, then sat back down and with his finger motioned me forward.

"I am told, fool, your little dick was wagging itself around where it does not belong. You seem to have offended a great many people in your short stay with us."

I glared at Norcross. "It is *I* who have suffered the greatest offense."

"You? How so?" Baldwin chuckled. "Was Briesmont's wife so unpleasant?" He picked a fistful of nuts out of a bowl and began to munch.

"I never touched the lady."

"And yet the evidence says otherwise. You contradict the testimony of a member of my own court. The offended party as well. Against the word of a fool . . . from what I am now told, not even a *true* fool."

I wrestled in my bonds toward Norcross. "This noble member of your court has killed my wife, my lord. My wife and child . . ."

There was a hush in the crowd.

Norcross shook his head. "The fool has it in his mind that I ruined him as punishment for abandoning his obligation to you when he ran off to the Crusade."

"And did you, knight?" asked Baldwin.

Norcross merely shrugged. "Truly, lord, I do not recall."

A trickle of the cruelest laughter sprinkled through the room. "The knight does not recall, ex-fool. Do you contradict again?"

"It was him, your lordship. His face was hidden, just like it was to this poor knight spoken of today."

Norcross stepped toward me, reaching for his sword. "Again, you incite me, fool. I will split you in two."

"Be still." The duke put up his hand. "You will have your chance. You make a grave charge, fool. Yet I am informed the Crusade continues, that the armies of Raymond and Bohemond are now in sight of the Holy City. Yet *you,* somehow, are *here.* Tell me, how was your service there discharged so soon?"

I was about to stammer back a reply, but to this charge I had none. I dropped my head.

A convicting silence filled the room.

Baldwin curled a smile. "You claim injury, fool, yet it seems it is *your* offenses that begin to add up. To the crimes of adultery and fraud, I must add desertion."

A rising anger swelled in my chest. I lunged, in my bonds, toward Norcross, but before I had gone a step, the duke's men kicked me to the floor.

"The fool wants at you, Norcross," Baldwin said.

"And I *him,* my lord."

"And you shall have him. But it belittles you, knight, to take him in contest. I think I have let you suffer ill from this squirrel once too often. Take him away." He waved. "At noon tomorrow you may chop off his head."

"You honor me." The knight bowed.

Baldwin shook his head sadly. "Fool, innkeeper, spy . . . whatever I should call you, it is a great shame. We will have to deal with Palimpost once more. For your stay here, you certainly provided a good laugh." He stood, wrapped his cloak around himself, and prepared to leave. Then Baldwin turned. "And *Norcross* . . ."

"Yes, my liege?"

"No need to waste a sharp blade on the fool's neck."

Chapter 52

I WAS HURLED down the stairs to the dungeon, my knees and ribs scraping against the hard rock floor.

My nostrils were forced to suck in that same repulsive stench from the night before.

I heard laughter and the clang of a heavy door as two burly guards grabbed my arms and tossed me into an open cell.

When my eyes cleared, I saw Armand, the jailer, with a mocking grin. "Back so soon, jester? You must have liked the accommodations after all."

I was about to tell him to go to Hell, but he kicked me in the stomach and the air rushed out of my lungs. "This time I'm afraid we'll be supplying the stew."

Armand's partner came in, lugging an armful of heavy chains. "So we must bind you, jester. And for such a short stay . . . But the duke has paid for the deluxe room, so chains it is."

Armand held me up, pinning my hands behind my back. "You're a lucky fool. The blade's painless. Just a little pinprick . . . *here*." He pinched my neck. "If you stayed here a while, I could show you some real fun. Ball crackers, nostril rippers, eye screws . . . red-hot pokers, right up the old ass. Sure cleans out the sinuses."

He nodded toward his partner, who slowly wound the first ring of chain around my chest.

My mind flashed to attention. "Please." I put up a hand to distract them. "Wait a minute." I took a deep breath, quietly sucking in a chest full of air.

"I know." Armand sighed. "It's a little *confining* at first. But when you get used to them, you'll be sleeping like a log."

I put my hand up for another moment, then I flashed him a smile of thanks. I took in three more deep breaths, forcing as much air as I could into my lungs. I felt my whole chest expand.

"Ready?" The jailer arched his eyebrows.

I nodded. "Ready."

Chapter 53

INSIDE THE TINY CELL, I twisted and squirmed on my back, and I ground my arms against the tight chains.

I had no idea what time it was, how long I had been here. I only knew that if I was still here when they came tomorrow, I was a dead man.

I let out all my breath. And the slightest space opened to move my arms.

Hours passed. A finger's breadth of freedom came. Then another. I felt the chains loosen some, but not enough.

I narrowed my shoulders and tucked my chin inside the chain. For the first time in hours, I took a breath with ease. I snaked an arm through the bonds. Then the other, and a loop of chain went over my head.

Then I heard the echo of voices coming down the stairs. Someone delivering dinner. Time for soup. The guards were taking their meal, laughing as they ate.

Other prisoners were grumbling, calling out. Then footsteps . . . a last meal arriving for me.

"So," a familiar voice said with a sigh, "it seems I am back in business."

I raised my eyes. It was *Palimpost,* the deposed jester, standing in front of my cell. He carried my staff.

"Come to gloat," I muttered, swallowing the bitterest taste of defeat.

"Not at all." He dangled a set of keys. "In truth, I have come to set you free."

I widened my eyes in surprise. I was sure this had to be some kind of cruel joke. *Payback* . . . I waited for the guards to come and laugh. But they did not.

"Bette and I have drugged the guards with the soup. Quick now, let's get you out of here."

"Bette . . . and you . . . !" I could not believe what he was saying. This was the man I had had sacked. Now he was dangling my freedom before my eyes. "Is this real?"

"It is real, if you can get up off your ass." He inserted a key into the lock and turned it, the door creaking open.

I still could not believe it. But it did not matter. Even if this was just a cruel joke, even if Norcross hid a few feet away, set to cut me in two, I was dead tomorrow anyway.

"Somehow we have to get you out of those chains." Palimpost exhaled.

"Not a problem," I said. I wiggled my shoulders and arms, and before his eyes, slithered through the top links. Then, I began to unwrap the chains until they fell to my ankles. I kicked them free.

The jester looked astonished. "Damn, you *are* good," he exclaimed. *"Quick . . .* come."

I held him back. *"Why* . . . why are you doing this for me?"

"Professional courtesy." The jester shrugged.

"Please, do not joke." I put my hand on his shoulder. "Tell me why. . . ."

He looked at me with pained eyes. "You saved the loved ones of a friend of mine. You think you are the only one who would risk everything for love?"

I stared at him in disbelief. "You . . . and *Bette?*"

"What's so hard to believe, man? Besides, it would have been a shame to waste you. You really weren't half bad."

He handed me my pouch of belongings, my staff, and a dark-colored cloak. I removed the knife from my pouch and put it in my belt, under my tunic. Then I donned the cloak and headed for the stairs.

"Not that way," Palimpost cautioned, taking my arm. "Follow me."

He led me deeper into the dungeon. The jagged cavern widened, then narrowed again into an opening no bigger than a small cave. At a spot he knew, Palimpost knelt and pulled a stone from the wall near the floor. A passageway appeared.

"There's a fork halfway through. When you reach it, head *left.* It empties into the moat. Head toward the forest. In the darkness you'll be safe. Go *right,* and you'll end up back at the castle. Remember — left."

I crouched down to the passage. "You are a good man. I am sorry that I caused you any harm."

"Oh, what's a little risk of one's life when there's love in the air?" He grinned. "Tell Norbert he should not sleep easy. Next time, it will be I who presses the attack."

He pushed me forward and I steadied myself with my staff. The passage was low ceilinged, narrow, and jagged. My feet struck cold water up to my shins. It smelled foul. I bumped into floating objects. I was sure they were dead rats.

I waved good-bye and, leveling my rod, hustled through. *Left,* Palimpost had said, *beyond the castle walls.* To the forest. And freedom.

But when I got to the fork, I didn't hesitate. I turned right. I headed along the dark, murky walls. Back to the castle . . .

There was one last thing I had to do.

Chapter 54

THE DARK TUNNEL LET OUT, of all places, in the hearth of the great meeting room deep inside the castle.

I pushed a stone slab out of the way of the opening and wormed my way through. Sleeping knights lay all around. If they woke, I was as good as dead.

I crept silently about the room, lifting a sword from one knight who snored dead to the world. I snatched a piece of cheese off the floor and ate the morsel furtively. Then I hurried out of the room.

I knew not what hour it was, but the castle halls were dark and completely quiet. Declining candles flickered against the walls.

I rushed toward the castle's main entrance, careful not to encounter anyone.

Outside the entryway, my heart relaxed; *I had not been seen.* Soldiers milled about the dark courtyard. Guards paced on the ramparts. A horse neighed as a rider galloped in from outside. I quickly crossed the courtyard huddled in my cloak.

I knew the room where Norcross slept, one near the barracks. It lay up a narrow stone staircase, torches lighting the walls on either side.

I made my way to the door. Then I took several deep breaths. A flash of nerves slithered down my spine. From inside the room came curious noises. Giggling and squeals. The bastard was *in,* all right.

I removed the sword from under my cloak. *This was for my wife and child.*

Chapter 55

I UNLATCHED AND PUSHED OPEN the heavy door to Norcross's room. It was dimly lit. A mound of clothes lay on the floor. Norcross's . . . and a lady's . . .

There was the sound of heavy panting and grunts.

On the heavy-posted bed, I saw a partially clad woman bracing her arms against the headboard with her legs akimbo. Norcross, wearing only his undertunic, hammered her from behind.

It took me a moment to recognize the lady Estella. Her and Norcross's ardor was so great, I wasn't spotted until I was well into the room.

The knight turned first. "Who *goes?*"

I stepped forward into the light and winked at Estella. "My lady." I bowed. "It seems you are once again offended. As often as possible, it appears."

"*You* . . ." Norcross said. His eyes lit up as if he were staring at a roasted side of beef.

"Me," I replied.

Norcross curled a smile. In no hurry, he reached for his

sword. "I might as well take your head tonight. Then I can sleep late tomorrow."

Norcross chuckled. He seemed in no great hurry as he circled away from the bed, flexing his chest muscles, looking at me contemptuously, as if I were a bug he was about to squash. "Here, fool, have your justice." Then he let out a fierce cry and swung his sword at my neck in a mighty arc.

I stood my ground and his sword clashed against mine with a loud clang. At the impact, I swung underneath, but Norcross parried as if his sword had no weight.

He was a skilled fighter. I could see that from the first blows. I had learned well in the Crusade — I was certainly frightened of no one — but it flashed through my head that he was far more experienced than I . . . a knight! And a killer of women and children.

Norcross swung the weapon in a continuous motion and charged at me again. I breached my sword to take the blow and forced his to the floor. We stood there, eye to eye, our swords pinned.

Then he butted me in the forehead and sent me reeling.

I caught myself on the bed, Estella scampering out of my way. He charged again, this time hammering his sword twice at my shoulders. Somehow I blocked both blows.

Sparks flew from the clash of steel on steel. The chilling clang of death reverberated in my ears.

I swung back. Norcross blocked it with ease. He stood up my sword almost effortlessly. Then, as he pushed it downward, it grazed across my arm, taking a slice of flesh. I let out a howl. Singeing pain sliced through me. The wound ran red on my forearm.

"Know the feel." Norcross grinned assuredly. "That will be your neck a moment from now."

He came at me, swinging his mighty sword back and

forth. I blocked it two, three times, but the weight was overpowering.

Finally, he forced me back into a corner. Frantically, I swung one last time, and he blocked me with ease. He was laughing, knowing he had me. His stale breath was in my face. The smell of his sweat tormented me. The awful sneer on his face could be the last thing I ever saw.

"Go to your grave knowing that I fucked your wife. I shot my seed into her, and when I finished, she asked for more."

My sword was slipping in my grip. His was closing on my neck, inches from slicing through the bone. With my free hand, I reached into my belt. *My knife there* . . . My last chance.

Norcross's eyes were fiery and determined. "Listen close, fool. That is the last thing you will ever hear."

"For Sophie . . . for Phillipe!" I yelled in his face.

In that instant, I shoved the knife upward into his chest. I felt sinew tear, bone crack, *but he did not move a muscle in his face.*

I pushed the knife harder and harder, but his gaze bore down on me. Incredible! He continued to press his blade into my neck.

Then Norcross opened his mouth as if to add one last thought. This time a stream of blood rushed out. I saw his hands loosen on the sword. Then he took a step backward. A stagger, actually.

I pushed him away, my knife buried deep in his chest.

Estella screamed as if the knife were sticking in her.

Norcross was trying like a drunken man to regain his balance. He wobbled, then he fell to his knees. He looked up at me, disbelief in his eyes, cupping his own vitals in his hands. Then he keeled over dead.

I felt overcome, at first with relief and then with sadness. I had avenged Sophie and Phillipe, but I realized *there was nothing for me now*.

I picked up my sword. I had to get out of here. I took Estella by the hair. She had set me up. She'd nearly cost me my life. I held her pretty head back and ran the tip of my sword across her neck. "Do not shout or call out. Do you understand?"

She nodded, terror in her round eyes.

"You are most lucky," I said, forcing a smile, "that I am a *gentle*-fool."

Chapter 56

EXHAUSTED, AND AFRAID that Estella would sound the alarm, I staggered from the fallen knight's room. I was now a murderer.

I took my staff and sword and was able to climb down the ramparts from an undetected spot near Norcross's chamber. The moat was dry, and I crossed it on foot.

From there, I ran. Ran in the shadows through the darkened streets of the surrounding village. Ran until I found the woods.

My arm hung like a roast sliced open. The wound was bleeding profusely. I came upon a stream and cleaned it as best I could and tied it with a strip of cloth from my tunic. I was an outcast again, a criminal now, not just a deserter from a far-off war but a murderer — a killer of a noble. No doubt Baldwin would come after me. I needed to put as much distance as I could between me and Treille. But where would I go?

I hid in the woods, keeping off the main roads. I was hungry and cold, but the knowledge that I had avenged Sophie and Phillipe warmed me inside. I felt vindicated, restored. I hoped God forgave me.

Just after first light, I heard a loud rumble. I hid in the brush as a posse of armed riders, dressed in Baldwin's colors, galloped by. I didn't know where they were heading. Veille du Père? Sweeping the roads and villages?

I headed east, tracking the main road, through the deepest part of the forest. I avoided any travelers I saw. I didn't know where I was going. My arm ached and throbbed.

A day out, I came to a fork in the road that I now knew well. I had passed here on my recent journey to Treille.

To the east lay my old village, Veille du Père. A day's trek. My inn was there, Matthew, my brother-in-law, what family I still had. My friends . . . Odo, Georges . . . Memories of Sophie and the grave of my poor baby son . . .

They would welcome me there. I was Hugh, spinner of tales. I made everybody laugh. Surely they would welcome back a lost son.

Then a sharp sadness came over me.

I couldn't go back there. My village lay in Baldwin's territory. They would look for me there. And it was not my home, not anymore. Just a place where memories would haunt my dreams.

I gripped my staff. I took a deep breath.

I chose the trail north, toward whatever new life lay ahead.

Toward Borée . . .

Part Three

AMONG FRIENDS

Chapter 57

THE DOOR OPENED and the jester Norbert stood there, bent over a bowl, picking his teeth with a hazel twig. His jaw dropped as if he had seen a ghost.

"Gads . . . *Hugh!* You've come back after all."

He grinned broadly, then shuffled up to me with that sideways gait of his. "What a joy to see you, lad."

"And you, Norbert," I replied, embracing him with my good arm.

"Wounded *again?* You're like a human target, son," he cried. "But come in, I'm glad to see you back. I want to hear it all."

The jester yanked out a low stool for me to sit on. Then he poured a cup of wine and sat facing me. "I can see in your eyes you've not come here with much cheer. So tell me . . . Did you find her? What is the fate of your Sophie?"

I lowered my eyes from those of my friend.

"You were right, Norbert. It was just a dream to think she had somehow survived. I am sure she is dead."

He nodded, then leaned across and squeezed me in a fatherly way. "A man's allowed to dream every once in a while. We little people live on it. I'm sorry for your loss, Hugh."

Norbert shuddered, letting out a gravelly cough.

"You're ill?" I asked with concern.

"Just under the weather." He waved me off. "Too many years of crawling around with the beetles down here." He cleared his throat again. "Tell me this — how did it go at court with Baldwin? Did you get the job?"

I finally could smile at something. "I *did,* just as we planned. In fact, I think I was a success."

"I knew it!" The jester leaped up. "I knew you would be. I taught you well, boy, didn't I? Tell me. I have to know it all."

Suddenly the weariness in my body seemed to recede; my face blushed brightly with the memories of entertaining the court. I told him everything. How I had managed my way into the castle, how I had seized upon the moment to go before the court. The jokes I had used . . . How the duke had sent away poor Palimpost.

"That old fart . . . I knew the sod was out of tricks." Norbert hopped around, cackling with delight. "It served him well to be sacked."

"No," I protested, "he turned out to be a friend. A true one . . ." I continued my tale, through my run-in with Norcross, how I'd been set up, and how Palimpost, the very fool I'd shamed, had saved my life.

"So the goon still has some virtue in him. *Good.* There's a brotherhood of us, Hugh. I guess you're part of it now." He patted my shoulder warmly, then once more doubled over in the throes of a most horrible cough.

"You *are* sick," I said, leaning over, supporting him with my arm.

"The physician says it's just the bad air down here. Tells

me I'm a miserable excuse for a man of mirth. But still, Hugh, maybe your return is well timed. Why not stand in for me until I'm well? It's a plum job."

I dragged my stool closer. "Stand in for *you?* . . . Here in Borée?"

"And why not? You're in the trade now. A professional. Just try not to do it *too* well."

I thought about the offer. I did need a place to be. Where else would I go? What else would I *do?* I did have friends here. Their trust was strong. And another aspect of the offer appealed to me, undeniably.

I had liked it. The crowds, the applause, the acclamation . . . This new *pretext* . . . I had liked it very much.

"I will stand in for you, Norbert," I said, holding his shoulder. "But only until you recover."

"That's a promise, then." We shook hands warmly. "I see you are still lugging that big stick around with you. And you still wear the garb. But you have lost your hat."

"My normal tailor was unable to dress me on such short notice."

"Not a problem." Norbert laughed. He shuffled over to his chest and tossed me a felt cap. It jingled. "Bells, I know. But, as they say, beggars can't be choosy."

I placed the cap upon my head. I felt a strange sensation, my blood warm with pride.

"You'll knock 'em dead, lad. That I know for sure." The jester grinned. "And I know for sure there is another here who will be *most* pleased to see you back."

Chapter 58

I WATCHED EMILIE FROM OUTSIDE the sitting room before she had the chance to spy me. She was amid the other ladies-in-waiting attending to their embroidery. Her blond braids spilled out from under a white hood. Her little nose seemed as soft as a bud. I saw what I had known that first day but looked beyond due to the nature of our friend-ship:

Emilie was beautiful. She was beyond compare.

I winked at her from the doorway, flashed her a smile. Her eyes stretched as wide as wildflowers blooming in July.

Emilie rose, placing her embroidery neatly down on the table, and with perfect politeness excused herself and came toward me. Her pace quickened as she did.

Only in the hall, when she rushed up to me and grasped my hands, did she show her true delight. *"Hugh De Luc . . . It's true.* Someone said they saw you. You have come back to us."

"I hope I don't wear out my welcome, my lady. And that you are not displeased."

She grinned. "I am most pleased. And look at you . . . Still in your jester's garb. You look good, Hugh."

"The same you made for me, just a bit frayed. Norbert has taken ill. I promised I would stand in for him."

Her eyes, vibrant and green, seemed to illuminate the dark hall. "I have no doubt we will all be the merrier for it. But tell me, Hugh, your quest . . . ? How did it go?"

I bowed my head, not for a moment hiding my disappointment or true feelings.

Emilie led me down the hall, where no guards were posted and we were able to sit on a bench. "Please . . . I can see you are sorely troubled, but I have to hear."

"Your plan was excellent. On the subject of my *pretext,* everything went well. I replaced the fool in Treille, gained access as we had spoken, and was able to snoop around."

"I did not mean our pretext, Hugh. I meant your quest. Your dear Sophie. What did you find? Tell me."

"As to my wife." I swallowed dryly. "I am now sure that she is dead."

The light in Emilie's hopeful eyes began to dim. She reached out for my hand. "I am most sorry, Hugh. I can see how it saddens you." We sat there silently for a while. Then she noticed my arm. "You are injured again."

"Just a bit. It's nothing. It's healing. I found the person who was responsible for Sophie and my son. I ended up having to face him off."

"Face him off . . ." A look of concern flashed in her eyes. "And the outcome?"

"The outcome?" I bowed my head again, then raised it with a slight smile. "I am *here*. He . . . is not."

Her face lit up. "And I am glad. And most glad to hear that you will stay a while too." She folded up my sleeve and studied the sword marks on my arm. "This needs treatment, Hugh."

"You are always nursing me back to health," I said. I was surprised at how easily I fell into her care again. Almost without trying. It felt good to be here. A calm spread over my face.

"But there is more I have to tell you, I'm afraid. This man I fought . . . he was a knight. More than a knight, in fact. He was Baldwin's chatelain. It ended up, in our squaring off . . . I killed him."

Emilie gazed intently at me. "I have no doubt that what you did was right."

"It *was*, Lady Emilie . . . I swear it. He murdered my wife and son. Yet the man was a noble. And *I* . . ."

"Is it not regarded as justice when one takes recompense for the loss of his property?" Emilie cut in. "Or defends the reputation of his wife?"

"For nobles, yes." I bowed my head again. "But I fear there is no justice in this world that shines on a lowborn man who kills a knight. Even if it is deserved."

"That may be." Emilie nodded. "But it will not *always* be."

Her eyes met mine. "You are always welcome here, Hugh. I will talk to Lady Anne."

"There's no way for me to thank you." I clasped her hand. Then I realized my mistake, my forwardness, my stupidity.

Her eyes drifted to my hand, but she made no move to take hers back. "The duke's chatelain, you say . . ." She smiled, finally. "You may be lowborn, as you say, Hugh De Luc, yet somehow your aim is remarkably high."

Chapter 59

EMILIE BRUSHED HER LADY'S long brown hair in front of the looking glass. Anne seemed noticeably out of sorts. In the past, Emilie had always been able to soften her with a few well-placed assurances and affable cheer. Emilie's freethinking had always been a source of discussion between them and, though her lady hid it, a bond.

But not so now. Not since the word that Anne's husband was soon back from the Crusade.

"I am no child, madame," Emilie said back.

"Yet you act like one sometimes. You urge me to look the other way for this fool who admits to killing the chatelain of a duke. Who seeks refuge here."

"He does not come to hide from justice, my lady, but because he feels among friends who understand what justice is."

"And what is this friendship worth to you, Emilie? This friendship with a common scut who always finds his way back here when he is injured. Is it worth the loss of our laws and custom?"

"The knight was killed in a fair duel, madame. The man's beloved wife was abducted by him."

"What *proof* is there? Who pledges for this man? The baker? The smith?"

"Who pledges for Baldwin, madame? Armed thugs? His cruelty and greed need no witness."

Anne met Emilie's gaze sharply in the mirror. "A *lord* needs no pledge, child." There was an awkward silence between them, then Anne seemed to soften. "Look, Emilie, you know that Baldwin is no friend to this court. But do not make me choose between your heart and what we know as the law. A lord manages his own vassals as he sees fit."

Anne held the brush and clasped Emilie's hand. "You must know, it would be my joy to shame Baldwin in my husband's absence. But your price is too high. Don't ask me to choose between *cads*, high- or lowborn."

"Showing justice on this, my lady, is how you will choose."

Anne's eyes hardened. "Don't flaunt your fancy concepts at me, Emilie. You have never had to govern. You are not *subject* to a man. You are still a guest at our court. Perhaps it is time we sent you back?"

"*Back . . .*" Emilie was startled. Fear shot through her. Anne had never threatened her before.

"So far you have not found a husband here, despite the best efforts of some of our bravest knights."

"They are trumped-up oxen, and smell like them too. Their exploits mean nothing to me. Less than nothing!"

"And yet this lowbred pup does. What makes you think you can expect more from him? You must stop this dalliance. *Now.*"

"I have given him my promise, madame." Emilie bowed her head. "Keep him here. I will not go further in the heart. If I did not press this to you, you would not be the wiser. Please, let him stay."

Anne gazed at Emilie, searching her eyes. She reached a tender hand to Emilie's face. "What has life done to you, my poor child, to have so hardened you against your own kind?"

"I am not hardened," Emilie replied, kneeling and placing her head upon Anne's arm. "I only see that there is a world beyond."

"Get up." Anne raised her gently. "Your fool can stay. At least until Baldwin inquires of him. I hope, in Norbert's absence, that we will find him a boon."

Chapter 60

THE NEXT MORNING, I made my debut in front of the lady Anne's court.

My heart was pounding. Not only for the gigantic room and the simple fact that Treille was like a village compared to this; or for my new liege and the favor that must be won. But also because of whom I was replacing. Norbert was a jester of the highest rank. To fill in for him here, in front of the court, was an honor that touched me deeply.

The arrival of the court did nothing to abate my nerves. A blast of trumpets announced the lady Anne with her long silk train and a line of ladies, Emilie among them, bringing cushions and refreshments, attending her needs.

Pages in green-and-gold overtunics announced the business of the day. Advisers flitted around, vying for Anne's ear. Scores of knights did not languish in their casual tunics as in Treille, but sat at formal tables finely dressed in her colors of green and gold.

That day there was a minor dispute before the court, a bailiff and a poor miller arguing over the levy of his fief.

As was the custom in towns everywhere, the bailiff felt the miller was holding out on him. I had seen this a hundred times in my village. *And it was always the bailiff who won.*

Anne's gaze began to wander.

"This bickering is the stuff of comedy," she said. "Jester, this is *your* domain. What say you? Come out and rule."

I stepped out from the crowd behind her chair. She seemed to regard me unexpectedly, as if surprised at the new face in the suit. "You say it is *my* rule, my lady?" I bowed.

"Unless you are as dull as they are," she replied. Mild laughter trickled through the room.

"I will not be," I said, calling to mind all the times I saw my friends cheated, "but I must answer with my own riddle. What is the boldest thing in all the world?"

"It is your stage, fool. Tell us, what is the boldest thing?"

"A bailiff's shirt, my lady. For it clasps a thief by the throat most every day."

A hush spread over the court, replacing the amused buzz. All eyes looked to the bailiff for his response.

Anne fixed on me. "Norbert informed me he was taking a leave. But he didn't inform me he was leaving his duties to such a rash wit. Come forward. I know you, do I not?"

I knelt in front of her and doffed my cap. "I am Hugh, good lady. We met once before. On the road to Treille."

"Monsieur Rouge," she exclaimed, her expression indicating she knew exactly to whom she spoke. "You seem a little better patched together than when I saw you last. And you have found a trade. When last seen you had donned your armor and ridden off on some quest."

"My armor was only this." I motioned toward my

checkered tunic. "And my sword, this staff. I hope I was not too greatly missed."

"You are *hard* to miss, monsieur," Anne said with a pinched smile, "since you do not go away."

Many of the ladies began to giggle. I bowed ceremoniously at her demonstration of wit.

"Norbert said I would find you to be a fitting replacement. And there is another at court who defends you well. And look how you perform. . . . Here, before our court, with your first step, and already soiled your boots. You take the miller's side on this?"

I bowed respectfully. "*You* are the law here, my lady. And the judge of what is right. Was it not Augustine who said, 'Remove justice, and what are kingdoms but gangs of criminals on a large scale.' "

"A jester who quotes Augustine? What sort of fool are you?"

"A fool who does not know Latin, madame, is just a greater fool." Again, a trickle of applause, some nods. And another smile from Anne.

"I was raised by goliards, Your Grace. I know a lot of useless things." I sprang onto my hands, balanced myself in a handstand, then slowly released onto one arm. From upside down, I added, "And some useful enough, I hope."

Anne gave a nod of approval. "Useful enough." She applauded. "So much so, bailiff, that I am forced to side with the fool here. If not by right, then surely by wit. Please forgive me. I am sure next time the scale will tilt to you."

The bailiff shot me an angry glance, then backed off and bowed. "I accept, my lady."

I pushed off and landed on my feet.

"So, boar-slayer." Anne turned back to me. "Your friends are right. Norbert has taught you well. You are welcome here."

"Thank you, madame. I won't disappoint."

". . . At least until my husband returns," Anne added sharply. "And I must warn you, his views of custom are quite different from my own. He is known to be much less charmed by a fool's knowledge of Latin than I."

Chapter 61

THE FOLLOWING DAYS, I worked freely at the court, entertaining Lady Anne, reciting tales and chansons from my goliard days, providing mock counsel when she called on me and needed a laugh.

A few times, I was able to poke fun at a situation and gently twist her into a certain mind, always in favor of the aggrieved party. I felt I was doing some good.

And Emilie seemed pleased. I caught her approving eye amid the other ladies-in-waiting, though I did not see her alone after that first day.

One day, at the end of court, Anne summoned me. "Do you ride, jester?"

"I do," I answered.

"Then I will set a mount. I want your presence on an outing. Be ready at dawn."

An outing . . . with the duchess . . .

The following dawn, I was ready at the stables, expecting a coterie of fancily dressed courtiers.

But it was clear from the start that this was not some

idle jaunt in the country. Anne was dressed in a riding cloak, accompanied by two other knights I recognized, her political adviser, Bernard Devas, and the captain of her guard, a blond-haired knight named Gilles. With her also was the Moor who had propped me up with a harness when they found me in the woods, and who never seemed to leave her side. The party was guarded by a detachment of a dozen additional soldiers.

The gates opened and we rode out from Borée at first light. A sliver of orange sky peeked over the hills to the east. Immediately we took the road south.

I rode behind the formation of nobles, just ahead of the rear guard. Anne was a steady rider, trotting capably atop her white palfrey. Occasionally she exchanged a few terse words with her advisers, but mostly we rode in silence, at a quick pace. We did not rest until we hit a stream, an hour south.

At a fork in the road, the party cut southwest. By midday we had entered a vast forest, with trees so dense and tall they almost blocked out the sun. Gilles led the expedition. At one point he announced, "Our domain ends here, my lady. We are now in the duchy of Treille."

Yet still we rode on. My blood quickened. I wasn't sure what was going on. I had an urge to run. But where? I would not get fifty yards if they wanted me caught.

Finally, I kicked my steed and caught up to Anne. I rode alongside her for a while, nervous, until she could see the question on my face.

"You want to know why I asked you along?"

Yes, I nodded.

She did not answer me but trotted on.

To the sides, I could now make out farms and dwellings. There was a sign scratched onto a tree: *St. Cécile*.

Our party slowed to a walk.

Finally, Anne motioned for me.

I rode up, fearing that any minute, Baldwin's soldiers might come out of the woods to murder me.

"Here is your answer, fool," she said with a taut face. "If we encounter what I am told we will in this village, I think on the way back we will all be in great need of mirth."

Chapter 62

I RELAXED, but only for an instant. The first thing that hit me was the smell. The stench of putrefaction . . . the rot of death.

Then ahead, wisps of white smoke rose above the trees. The leaves themselves were singed with the stomach-turning char of roasted flesh.

Anne rode ahead, seemingly unfazed by the repugnant stench. I felt no danger to myself now, only that this was something awful we were nearing.

The road widened. A clearing. Then a stone bridge. We were at the outskirts of a town. But there was no town. Only what had once been huts and other dwellings, their thatched roofs caved in from fire, the smoke from cinders still rising in the air.

And people sitting around numbly, blank expressions on their sooty faces, as if mimicking the still silence of the dead.

We rode into the village. Every single dwelling seemed to have been burned to the ground. Most had tall stakes driven into the ground in front of them. On them, spitted, were charred mounds, unrecognizable. The strange mix of smells turned my stomach — burned hair, flesh, blood.

"What are they?" Anne inquired as she trotted by.

Gilles, the captain of the guard, sucked in a breath. "They are children, my lady."

The color drained from her face and Anne pulled her mount to a stop. She leaned over and stared at the mounds, and for a moment I thought she would teeter. But then Anne righted herself. Her face became composed again. She called out firmly to the townspeople, "What has *happened* here?"

No one answered. The people just stared. I actually feared someone might have taken out all of their tongues.

The captain called, "Lady Anne of Borée speaks to you. *What has happened here?*"

"What has happened here? Tell me," Anne said to a gaunt, white-haired man in blackened and tattered clothes.

"They came in the night. Faceless cowards with black crosses. They hid under their masks. They said it was to purify the town for God. That we had stolen from Him."

"Stolen? Stolen what?" Anne asked.

"Something sacred, a treasure. From the Holy Land. Something that they could not find. They tore every child from its mother. Put them on spits in front of our eyes. Set them aflame . . . Their cries still ring in our ears."

"And what did they find, these killers?" Anne asked.

The man replied, ashen faced. "I do not know. They torched us and left. I am the mayor of this town. The mayor of nothing, now. Maybe you should ask Arnaud. Yes, ask Arnaud."

Anne dismounted. She walked directly up to the mayor and looked in his eyes. "Who is this Arnaud?"

The mayor snorted a disdainful blast of air. Without replying, he began to walk. Anne set off behind, accompanied by her guards, who ran ahead of her to clear the way.

At a low stone hut the mayor stopped. The entrance was smeared with blood — not randomly, but in large red crosses. A butcher-house smell came from inside.

Holding our breath, we stepped in. Anne gasped.

The place was ravaged. What scant furniture there was had been split like firewood, the ground beneath it ripped up. Two bodies hung by the arms, a man and a woman, their torsos flayed of flesh. Beneath their dangling legs lay their severed heads.

"Arnaud was born here and always called it his home. He was the bravest man any of us knew, a knight at the court of Toulouse. Yet they carved him up like a pig. He had just returned from fighting abroad."

"From fighting where?" Gilles, the captain, asked.

I knew. I had seen such horror before. I knew, but I could not answer.

"The *Crusade*," the mayor spat.

Chapter 63

I WALKED FROM THE HUT and tried to clear the repulsive sights from my mind. I had seen it all before. Men and women hung and flayed, body parts scattered as if the murders meant nothing at all.

The Crusade . . . Suddenly it resonated everywhere. Arnaud had just returned from there. Adhémar too, whose horrible death I had heard of at Baldwin's court. Their villages were ransacked and destroyed — just like my inn.

Dread shot down my spine. These faceless riders who killed with the savagery of Turks . . . Were they the same ones who murdered my wife and child?

Cold, clammy sweat clung to my back. It all began to fit.

The killers wore no crest or markings, only a black cross.

No one knew where they came from or what they sought. Then I remembered something. Matthew had said it was as if it were *my home, our inn only,* that the bastards were interested in.

What did they want with me?

During the long ride back, I kept to myself. I racked my brain. What did I have that could connect me with these killings? I had tucked a few worthless baubles into my pouch. The old scabbard with the writing I'd found in the mountains? The cross I had pilfered from the church in Antioch? It didn't make sense!

I watched Anne riding just ahead. Her face was tight and somber, as if she wrestled with some inner turmoil. Something wasn't right.

Why had we come out here? What had she needed to see?

Then a chill ran through me. Anne's husband, the duke, was returning any day. From the Crusade . . .

Anne knew.

Anne knew these atrocities were going on.

My stomach went cold. All along, I was sure it was Norcross who had done these things to me, as punishment for going on the Crusade. Was it possible it was Anne? Could it be that the answers I sought were not at Treille, but at Borée?

Chapter 64

THE NEXT FEW DAYS, I kept my eye on Anne, trying to determine what connection she might have to the murdered knights. And the killing of Sophie and Phillipe.

Her husband was returning in a matter of days, and all of Borée was in a state of anxiousness and preparation. Flags were hung from the ramparts; merchants put out their best wares; the chatelain led his troops in their welcoming formations. *Whom could I trust?*

I waited for Emilie on Sunday morning as she emerged from the chapel with the other ladies-in-waiting. I caught her eye and lingered until the others were gone.

"My lady." I took her aside. "I have no right to ask. I shouldn't ask. But I need your help."

"Here." She motioned, leading me to a prayer bench in a side chapel. She sat next to me and lowered the hood of her shawl. "What's wrong, Hugh?"

This was very hard. I sought the right words to begin. "Be certain, I would never speak to you of this unless it was of the highest need. I know you serve your mistress with all your heart."

She wrinkled her face. "Please do not hesitate with me. Haven't I proven my trust for you enough?"

"You have. Many times," I said.

I took a breath and recounted the horror of my trip to St. Cécile. I told it in detail: the charred mounds, the eviscerated knight, the most graphic images sticking in my throat like memories that did not want to come out.

I told her of Adhémar, whose similar fate I had heard of at Baldwin's court. Both knights were slaughtered, their villages razed. Both had recently returned from the Crusade. Just as I had.

"Why do you tell this to me?" she finally asked.

"You have not heard of such deeds? At court? Around the castle?"

"No. They are vile. Why should I?"

"Knights who disappear and return? Or talk of sacred relics from the Holy Land? Things more valuable than a simple fool like me would know."

"You are my only relic from the Holy Land." She smiled, trying to shift the mood.

I could see her trying to put the puzzle together. Why these horrible murders? Why now?

She took a wary breath. "I did not know of any such violence. Only that word has spread that Stephen has sent an advance guard to conduct his affairs before he returns."

My blood lit. "This guard — they are *here?* At the castle?"

"I overheard the chatelain speaking of them with some contempt. He has served the duke loyally for years, yet these men are charged with some horrid mission. He feels they are ill-trained for knights."

"Ill-trained?"

"'*Beyond honor,*' he said. Owing no allegiance. He says it is fitting that they sleep with the pigs, since they have the hearts of them. Why do you ask me this, Hugh?" Emilie looked into my eyes. I could see fear and I felt awful for causing it.

"These men are hunting for something, Emilie. I do not know what. But your mistress . . . she is not innocent in this herself. These might be Stephen's men, but Anne knows what they do."

"I cannot believe that." Emilie shot upright. "You say this is a matter more important than any in the world to you. I hear it in your voice. These things you describe . . . they are most vile, and if they are Stephen's work or Anne's, they will have to answer to God for what has been done. But why is this so urgent for you? Why do you put yourself at risk?"

"It is not for Anne or Stephen," I said, swallowing. "It is for my wife and child. I am sure, Emilie, *their killers are these same men.*"

Chapter 65

I FOUND NO TRACE of the unholy soldiers I was seeking, or anyone who knew of mysterious knights in dark robes. Nor was I able to gain access to the barracks. Time was growing short. Stephen was due back at the castle in days. Once he returned, it would be too dangerous to press my case.

Two days later, Emilie took me aside as I was playing jackstraws with Anne's son, William. She saw my demeanor was glum.

"Do not be so sad, jester," she said with a smile. "I have a job for you. And a new pretext."

There was to be a celebration that evening in the chatelain's hall, she explained. A bachelor party. Gilles, the captain of the guard, was to be married in the next few days. There would be knights, soldiers, members of the guard. Lots of speeches and drink. *Their guard would be down,* so to speak.

"I have arranged for you to be the entertainment," Emilie announced.

"You seem to have a skill at this sort of thing, my lady. Once again I owe you thanks."

"Thank me by finding what you seek," she said, and touched my hand. "And, Hugh, be careful. Please."

That night there was lots of wine and awful singing. Gilles's buddies stood and made bold and mocking speeches until they slurred their words and fell back onto their benches. I was to be the last act before they dragged Gilles down to a brothel in town.

I had to make them laugh, and yet my eyes kept searching for the rogue knights. I did sleight-of-hand tricks to warm them up, simple stuff Norbert had shown me, pulling objects out of tunics to their drunken awe.

Then it was on to the jokes. "I know this man," I announced, sliding to a stop on the tabletop in front of the groom to be, "whose cock was permanently engorged."

"You flatter me." Gilles pretended to blush. "But, joker, must you betray my secret to *all?*"

"Try as he could," I went on, "he could not get the damn thing to go down. Finally he sought out his local apothecary. There, he encountered a stunning young woman. 'I'd like to speak to your father,' the man with the problem said.

"'My father is dead,' she answered. 'I run this apothecary with my sister. Anything you can tell a man, you can tell us.' 'All right,' he agreed. In dire need, he pulled down his leggings. 'Look, I have a permanent erection. Like a fucking horse. What can you give me for it?'

"'Hmmm,' the lady apothecary replied. 'Let me go and confer with my sister.' After a minute she returned with a small pouch and said, 'How is one hundred gold coins and half the business?'"

The room roared with laughter. "Tell us more. . . ."

I had begun another — the one about the priest and

the talking crow — when from outside the walls, a terrible shout pierced the celebration. There was the clop of horses drawn to a stop. Then once again a man's scream. "Please, God help me. I am being killed!"

The drunken laughter ceased. Several of the party rushed to a window overlooking the courtyard. I followed close behind. Through the narrow opening I saw two men dragging a third by the arms across the courtyard.

I recognized them instantly! They wore slitted helmets and carried war swords strapped to their belts. It was just as Emilie had described. They wore no armor but robes. On their feet were worn sandals.

The prisoner hollered defiantly, his shouts for help echoing off the stone walls.

Then I caught a look at his face. My own twisted in horror.

It was the mayor of St. Cécile — who had stood up to Anne only a few days before.

They dragged the poor mayor toward the keep. "Who are these men?" I asked one of the soldiers at my side.

"These dogs? The duke's new business partners. *Les Retournés* . . ."

"*Retournés . . . ?*" I muttered.

My eyes followed the soldiers and the poor mayor until they dragged him through a heavy wooden door and into the keep. The dying shouts of the prisoner faded in the night.

"Not our worry." Bertrand, the chatelain, sighed. He stepped back from the window. "Come, Gilles, beauties await in town. How 'bout we get that blade of yours wiped one last time?"

Meanwhile, my heart was beating at a gallop. I had to talk to the mayor of St. Cécile. He might know why knights were being murdered and villages burned. And these awful killers . . . *Les Retournés* . . . I thought that I had seen them before.

But where?

Chapter 66

THE FOLLOWING NIGHT I waited until long after dark. Norbert lay snoring on his bed. I crept off my mat and tucked a knife under my leggings.

I sneaked out of Norbert's chamber, hurrying up the back stairs behind the kitchen to the main floor. I had to traverse the entire castle from the large rooms of the court to the military end. And talk my way past anyone who would stop me. Well, I was the jester after all.

The castle was a squared-off U shape, with a loggia of stone arches around the courtyard. Across from it were the duke's garrison, the officers' quarters, the barracks, and the keep. I successfully wound my way around the entire main floor. As I passed outside, I saw the tower above me where the mysterious knights had dragged their prisoner, lit up by the moon. I hurried that way, then slipped inside.

I was in the tower, all right, but I didn't know where to go or who might try to stop me. My stomach churned; the breath clung tight in my chest.

A draft followed me up the stairs. At each floor, the odor grew more foul. The smell of death I knew all too well.

On the third landing, two guards slouched around an open archway. One was tall and lazy looking, the other short and squat with mean eyes. Not exactly the duke's crack troops, I thought, just keeping an eye on a few cursed souls in the middle of the night.

"Are you lost, strawberry?" the mean-looking one growled at me.

"Never been up here before," I said. "Mind if I take a quick peek?"

"Tour's over." He stood up. "Go back the way you came."

I went up to him, my eyes wide. As if yanking something out of his ear, from my closed fist I produced a long silk scarf. "Come on . . . even a *damned* soul could use a last laugh."

To my delight, the oaf reached out and felt the scarf. Then he took it, my bribe for him. He looked down the hall and, finding the coast clear, stuffed it into his uniform. "One look," he said. "There's nothin' in there anyway but the pox. Then juggle your ass back where you belong."

"Thank you, sire," I clucked. "A lifetime of stiff manhood to you."

I darted through the archway behind him and up the stairs. A row of narrow stone cells stretched out before me. The putrid stench made me hold my breath. I hoped the man I was seeking was in here.

I hoped the mayor of St. Cécile was still alive.

Chapter 67

DRIVEN BY THE AWFUL SMELL and my worry that the guards would come, I hurried down the row of cells, searching for the man I had seen dragged in the night before. I prayed he was still here.

In the first cell, a man with a long dark beard, naked, barely more than a skeleton, lay on his back amid his own waste. In the next, a large dark-skinned man — swarthy as a Turk — curled under a tattered white robe. Neither raised an eye. The cells reeked. A rat licked the inside of a bowl right in front of me.

The third cell contained the person I was seeking: the mayor of St. Cécile. The poor man lay crumpled in a ball, with blotches of blood and bruises on his face and arms. To my alarm, I could not tell if he was alive or dead.

"Sir . . ." I crept close. I had to know. What did these dark knights want? What had they razed his entire village to find? What treasure was worth so many lives?

Suddenly a whimpering moan from the next cell caught my attention. I stepped over and saw a pathetic creature —

a woman, her skin as white as a ghost, her hair dry as rotted hemp, muttering under her breath like a deranged witch. Her skin was spotted with oozing sores.

I cringed. *What a sight! What heresy had she done to be left to rot away like this?*

I turned back to the mayor. Time was short. "Do you remember me, sir? I saw you in St. Cécile," I whispered.

But the witch's muttering grew louder. I shushed her to stop. Then a jolt froze my body.

The words she moaned — at first softly, almost inaudibly, into her bony hands. Then louder. My God! I could not believe what I was hearing:

"A maiden met a wandering man in the light of the moon's pure cheer."

Chapter 68

MY HEART SLAMMED against my ribs. *This could not be! Could not, could not.*

I ran to her cell and pressed against the bars, straining to distinguish her features amid the shadows.

I was staring at my wife.

"Sophie . . . ?" I whispered, the word catching in my throat.

She did not move or speak.

"Sophie!" I called, feeling my heart start to crumble. Part of me prayed she would not turn.

Then she tilted her face toward me.

"Sophie, is that you?"

She lay huddled in shadow and I still could not tell for certain if it was her. The scant light from a nearby torch traced her bony face. Her hair, which once had smelled like honey, hung wildly from her head, pulled out in spots, and white. Her sunken eyes, glazed and distant, were runny with yellow pus. Yet the nose . . . the soft line of her chin as it met her delicate neck . . . they were the same, unmistakably, though she cowered before me as a fevered wretch, pocked with sores.

"*Sophie?*" I cried, my hands reaching desperately through the bars.

She finally turned toward the sound, sallow light spreading across her face. I simply could not believe what I was seeing! How could she be here? How could she be alive after all this time?

Grateful tears welled in my eyes. I reached for her, her emaciated bones covered with a filthy rag. I tried to speak, but I was too overcome.

"Sophie . . . *look* . . . It's me, *Hugh*."

Slowly she lifted her face fully into the light. She was like an artist's disfigured re-creation of the beautiful image I held in my mind: gaunt, ghostly, covered in sores. Her eyes flickered at the sound of my voice. I could see that she was sick, that she barely clung to this rotting existence. I wasn't sure she knew who I was.

"We have to give it back to them," she finally said. "Please, I beg you. Give them back what's theirs."

"*Sophie,*" I was shouting now, "*look.* I am here . . . Hugh!" What had they done to her? Anger surged through me. I could see her suffering and I felt it too.

"*Hugh . . . ?*" She blinked. Then she almost seemed to smile. "Hugh'll be back. He's in the East, fighting. . . . But I'll see him again, my baby. He promised."

"No, I am here, Sophie." My fingers grasped at air, trying to reach her face. "Please. Come close. Let me hold you." Oh God, let me hold you, Sophie.

"He'll be sad about the inn," she continued to mutter. "But he'll forgive me; you'll see. You'll see."

"I'm going to get you out of here. I know about Phillipe, about the inn." I was bursting with heartache. "Please, come here. Let me hold you."

Sophie pulled herself toward the sound of my voice. Her cheeks were slick with fever, her eyes glassy. I could see she was terribly sick. I just wanted to hold her. God, I wanted to hold her.

She blinked like a frightened doe, hugging the wall. "Hugh . . . ?" she whispered.

"Sophie, it's me. . . . It's me, darling." I whispered the words to our song: *"A maiden once met a traveling man . . ."*

"You must give it back now," she muttered again. "They say it is theirs. I tried to tell them, *Hugh will return. He'll find me.* They said they'll give Phillipe back to us, our little son. All we have to do is give them what is theirs."

I finally knelt and wrapped my hands around her, my dear wife. I touched her face, brushed the sweat off her hollow cheeks. She was so precious to me, even more so in this misery.

"They want what belongs to God," she said, and her body rattled with a cough. "Please. Give it to them."

"Give them *what?*" I cried. What did she think I had? I did not know if it was the fever or a deeper madness talking. Or even if Sophie still recognized she was talking to me.

Suddenly she jerked out of my grasp and scampered back into shadow. It broke my heart. Her eyes bolted past me, wide with fear.

I felt as if everything I loved had slipped through my fingers one last time.

Then I saw what had driven her away. My heart nearly came to a stop.

One of the duke's rogue knights was standing over me.

Chapter 69

I RECOGNIZED HIM as one of the thugs who had dragged the mayor into the keep the previous night.

His head was covered by a dark hood, and the eyes peering out were as dark as sunken caves. He wore his sword belted over a threadbare robe and stood, hands on hips, grinning down on the two of us.

"Go ahead, have a poke." He shrugged. "The whore won't mind, fool. Anyway, she'll be dead in a week. Just be careful you don't get the pox all over your dick."

I stared at his mocking face, and the greatest rage I had ever known tightened inside me, a boiling, uncontrollable force. I reached for an iron poker lying next to me on the floor.

With a cry, I rushed at him, a wild exhalation escaping from my lungs. I swung the poker at his head before he could draw his sword. The startled knight threw up an arm to defend himself, and the rod smacked against it with a sickening crack.

He yelped and staggered back in pain, one arm hanging

at his side. I did not stop. I battered him again and again, like some mad beast, every sinew of my body concentrated on driving this piece of metal into his skull.

I shoved him against the bars of the cell. I drove my knee into his groin and felt him groan and buckle. I jammed the poker into his neck.

"Why?" I barked into his face. The soldier gagged, his eyes bulging, darting around. *"Why is she here?"*

A garbled cry emerged from his throat, but in my rage I was not waiting for his answer. I pushed the rod deeper into his neck. A force rose inside me that I could not stop. I wanted to kill this man.

"Who are you?" I screamed in his face. "Where have you come from? Why did you bring her here? Why did you kill my son?"

My thumbs pressed under his hood as I dug the poker into his throat, squeezing the breath out of him. Bit by bit, the hood fell away from his neck.

My eyes were pinned to the frightful mark I saw there.
The black Byzantine cross.

It shot me back a thousand miles. Suddenly I was in the Holy Land, revisiting the horrors I had seen there.

These bastards were *Tafurs.*

Chapter 70

I STAGGERED BACK in shock. Our eyes met, and it was as if some terrible knowledge had been passed between us.

The Tafur took my surprise as an opening and dug his hands into my face. I pressed the poker into his neck even harder. Then I heard bone crack in his neck. His eyes bulged, a final, desperate resistance. A trickle of blood seeped from his mouth. A moment later, his legs began to give way. When at last I let go, the Tafur crumpled to the filthy prison floor.

I stood over him, breathing furiously. My mind hurtled back again. *Tafurs* . . . I saw them ravaging their captives in their filthy tents. I saw them butchering the Turk who had spared me, then darting like beetles to the crypt, scavenging for spoils. *What were they doing here in Borée? What did they want with me? With Sophie?*

Suddenly I heard shouts and commotion. The prisoners were clanging the bars in their cells.

Now, with what little time we had left, I had to get Sophie out of here. I rummaged over the Tafur's body, frantically searching for a key.

I ran my eyes about the keep. Keys must be here somewhere.

I turned toward Sophie, eager to let her know that I would help her escape.

But the sight of her left me rigid as stone.

She was slumped against the bars, her face icy white. Her eyes, a moment ago mad with terror, seemed calm and far-off. I did not see her breathe.

Oh, God, no . . . !

I crawled to her, cupped her face in my hands. "Sophie, stay with me. You can't die. Not now."

She blinked, barely more than a tremor. A glimmer of life appeared in her eyes.

"Hugh . . . ?" she whispered.

"Yes, Sophie. . . . It's me." I brushed the sweat off her face. Her skin was cold.

"I knew you would come back," she said, finally seeming to know who I was.

"I'm so sorry, Sophie. I'm going to get you out of here. I promise."

"We had a son," she said, and started to cry.

"I know. I know it all." I wiped her cheek. "He was a beautiful boy. Phillipe."

I looked around, desperately searching for something to help her. "The guards will be here," I said. "I'm going to find a way out. Hold on. Please, Sophie."

Please!

I held her hands in mine through the bars. I whispered, "I'll take you home. I'll pick sunflowers for you. I'll sing you a song."

Her mouth twitched, and she took a long time to breathe again. But when she did, I also saw her smile — a faint one, unafraid. "I've never forgotten, Hugh." The words fell off her lips one at a time, so softly I could almost kiss them there: "A maiden met a wandering man . . ."

"Yes," I said. "And I've been true to you ever since we were children."

"I love you, Hugh," Sophie whispered.

Suddenly she lurched in my arms. I felt her heart starting to beat out of control. Her eyes bolted wide.

I didn't know what to do to help her. She shook terribly up and down. All I could do was hold her tight. "I love you, Sophie. I've never loved anyone else. I knew I would find you again. I'm so sorry I left you alone."

Her hand gripped me by the tunic. "Hugh . . . then don't . . ."

"Don't what, Sophie?"

A final sigh escaped her lips. *"Don't give them what they want."*

Chapter 71

AND THEN MY SWEET SOPHIE DIED in the prison cell.

She passed with a calm, far-off quiet in her eyes. Her mouth hung in the slightest smile, perhaps because I had finally come back, as I had promised.

Tears ran down my cheeks. I wanted to scream, *Why did Sophie have to die? Why her?*

I grabbed the Tafur by the collar of his robe and hurled his dead body against the bars. "Why, you bastard? Tell me, what did she mean? Why did you kill my son? Why are innocent people dying?"

Then I sank down with my head in my hands.

I wanted to take Sophie home. That's all I could think of, to bury her with her son. I owed her that. *But how?* The dead Tafur was slumped before me. Any moment, the guards would come. I couldn't even open her cell.

The truth hit me: Sophie was gone. There was nothing I could do for her now. Except maybe one thing — *"Don't give them what they want."* Whatever that could be.

I ran and found a ragged cloth, and came back and laid a corner of it under Sophie's head. I covered her body with the rest, as if she were in our bed at home, though I knew nothing could disturb her now. I took one last, loving look at Sophie, the person who had been my everything since we were ten. *I'll come back for you,* I promised. *I'll take you home.*

Then I staggered down the stone stairs and past the indifferent guards. I ran back toward my room through the castle's maze of darkened halls.

My body shook with incomprehension. *What had she been doing here?* It wasn't a dream — my wife was dead. Rotted like some diseased dog. *Here in Borée . . .* The shock tore at my brain. I shouldn't have left her. Part of me wanted to go back. To pick her up, take her home. But there was nothing I could do.

Then a new thought crawled through the haze in my brain . . . something I had to do. I had to right this wrong. I finally knew who was behind it. The blame wasn't at Treille, but here. *Anne!*

In a rage, I raced back toward the royal living quarters. No alarm had been sounded. Guards smirked at me along the way, a laughable fool who had perhaps tipped the jug too many times, staggering home to sleep it off.

Yet all the while, one thought reigned in my mind: *Anne knew.*

I bounded up the stairs toward her living quarters. Two guards stood watch on the landing. They looked at each other. *What harm could I do?* I was the lady's fool. They let me pass. Just as they always had before.

Down the hall were the lord and lady's living quarters. A new guard stepped into my way. *A Tafur.* "Whoa, fool, you are not permitted," he barked.

I didn't stop to reason. I spotted a gleaming halberd

hanging on the wall over a coat of arms. I grabbed the ax from its anchor and ran at the startled guard, taking him by surprise.

I swung with all my might, the blade catching him at the base of his neck. He let out a garbled groan, his side nearly splitting away from his body like a side of beef. He toppled to the floor, dead.

Now I had killed one of Anne's own guards.

One of her Tafurs.

Chapter 72

SHOUTS RANG OUT from behind me, deep male voices echoing in alarm.

I stormed ahead like some madman. *Where was she? Anne!* I had one single-minded desire: to hear the truth from her lips, even if I had to die for it.

Two guards from the stairs ran my way, their swords raised. I forced myself through a set of heavy doors and bolted them shut behind me. I ran deeper into the royal chambers. I had never been in here before.

I knew I would die here. At any moment I expected a blade to tear into my back, to see my own blood spilling out onto the floor. No matter. All that was important to me was to ask my lady, *Why?*

I stormed deeper into her quarters. The bedroom. An engraved wooden table with a washbasin, tapestries hung on the walls. A vast, draped oak bed, larger than I had ever seen.

But empty. No one was there.

"Goddamn you," I shouted in frustration. "Why my family? Why us? Someone tell me!"

I stood there not knowing what to do next. I saw myself in my fool's costume, blood spattered on my face. Why, why, why?

Suddenly a door opened beside me. I held my knife, expecting to face Anne, or one of her Tafur guards.

But it was neither.

For a moment, I felt as if I were back on the road to Treille, blinking out of the haze, and all the things that had happened since — Norcross, St. Cécile, Sophie's death — were just figments of a dream, terrors that could be washed away with a soft word.

I stared at Emilie's face.

She gasped, her eyes fastened on my blood-spattered clothes. "My God, what has happened to you?"

Chapter 73

"SOPHIE'S DEAD," I whispered.

She stared at me, transfixed. Then she moved forward to support me. "What has happened? Tell me."

"The duke's men have had her all along, Emilie. Sophie has been *here*. . . . Not in Treille, with my enemies, but *here,* in the tower, among my *friends*."

Shouts and pounding at the door I had bolted. What a wretched sight I must have made. My clothes torn, slick with blood, the look of madness in my eyes.

"Anne," I muttered. "I told you. . . . She is behind it all. I have to find out why she allowed these men to destroy my family. Stephen's *guard* . . ." I chortled, almost a laugh. "These are not knights, Emilie. They are scavengers, from the Holy Land. The lowest form of butcher. Even the Turks ran in fear of them. They hunt for relics, spoils. That is why the two knights were murdered. But my family . . . *We had nothing*."

The commotion outside the door grew louder. Anne's men were trying to smash it in. Emilie gripped my arm. "It doesn't matter now. Anne is not in the castle. She has gone to meet her husband at La Thanay. Come with me."

"It is too late. The time for kindness is finished. There is nothing left for me now but to face her men."

She put her face inches from my own. I could feel Emilie's breath on my cheek. "Whatever you've done, if Anne is behind this, I will do everything to see justice is given you. But you must come. I can't help you if you're dead."

Emilie hurried me out of the room, down a narrow corridor in the royal quarters. She pushed me into a small chamber and quickly barred the door. I could see she was afraid, and it touched me deeply.

Emilie searched through a drawer and found a heavy brown cloak, which upon closer inspection proved to be the robe of a monk. "Here . . . I thought at some point you might need it to gain access to the tower. Put it on."

I stared at it, confused, amazed that Emilie did this for me.

"Go now. They will search every room. Send me word. Through Norbert. You have friends here; you must believe that."

A moment later, I was no longer a jester but a monk, the hood pulled over my head.

"Your new pretext." Emilie smiled bravely.

I took a deep breath. "I fear this one will be a greater trick than before."

"Then let me add to it," Emilie said. She pulled me close by the collar and, to my surprise, pressed a quick, hard kiss upon my lips.

My blood came to a halt. The softness of her lips, the boldness of her touch. I felt my knees lock, the breath massed inside my chest. In truth, I didn't know what to feel at that moment. My head spun.

She looked into my eyes. "I know your pain is deep. I

know every part of you cries out to revenge your wife and child. But, common or noble, there is a specialness within you. I saw it the first time I looked into your eyes. And I have never seen it waver since. We will find a way to right these wrongs. Now *go*."

There was a small window above her bed. Below, it was only a short jump to the courtyard. From there, the gardens . . .

I hoisted myself up and pushed through a leg. I looked out and saw the darkened shadows of roofs in the distance. I looked back into Emilie's face. "By what luck, lady, have I earned you as a friend?"

"By *leaving*, right now. This instant."

I smiled and lifted myself through the narrow window. I turned. "I hope, in all the world, to see you again."

There was a pounding at her door. I waved at Emilie, then dropped from the window.

Chapter 74

THE AFTERNOON SUN BATHED the field. Anne stood outside her tent near La Thanay.

At her sides, two formations of Borée's infantry bearing the duke's crest stood in even rows. Banners of green and gold flapped in the breeze.

A shiver of dread went through Anne. She had brooded over this moment for weeks now: her husband's return. There were times when she had actually prayed he would be lost in the war.

She had been married to him since she was sixteen, almost half her life. She had been betrothed as a sign of alliance between her family's duchy, Normandy, and Stephen's father. But if this union had fostered trust and commerce between the two duchies, it had created only isolation for her.

Once she bore him his son, Stephen forgot her, coming only when he tired of his whores from town. When she resisted, she felt the stab of his powerful fingers on her neck or the scrape of the back of his hand.

Though she kept up the appearances of court and family that were her duty, she felt only contempt for Stephen, trapped as she was in the prison women were confined to — even duchesses and queens. She felt old, so much older than her years. The time when he was away had almost freed her. But now, knowing he was near, she felt the fears return.

Up ahead, a formation of about twenty knights appeared over a knoll, traveling slowly, their war-worn helmets barely glinting in the sun.

"Look, my lady." Bertrand Morais, the duke's chatelain, pointed. "There they are. The duke returns."

A cheer rose from the men.

So he is back. Anne sighed, pretending to smile. Fattened, she was sure, on the meat of greed and glory he had feasted on in the Crusade.

Anne nodded, and the trumpeters broke into the flourish announcing the arrival of the duke. A rider broke away from the pack and galloped toward them. Anne felt her stomach stiffen in disgust.

"God's grace to Stephen," the chatelain shouted, "duke of Borée. He has returned."

Chapter 75

THE SOLDIERS STOOD at stiff attention, swords and lances raised in salute. The duke galloped into their midst. He raised his arm to salute them, then grinned triumphantly at Bertrand and Marcel Garnier, his seneschal, the steward of his estate.

Almost as an afterthought, he turned to Anne.

Stephen then jumped off his mount. His hair had grown long and wild since she had seen him last, like a Goth's. His cheeks were hard edged and gaunt. Yet he still carried that narrow glint in his eyes. As was his duty, he came up to her. It had been almost two years.

"Welcome, my husband." Anne stepped forward. "To God's grace that He has brought you safely home."

"To God's grace," Stephen said with a smile, "that you have shined like such a beacon as to guide me back."

He kissed her on both cheeks, but the embrace was empty and without warmth. "I have missed you, Anne," he said, in the way a man might exult in seeing the health of his favorite steed.

"I have counted the days as well," she replied coldly.

"Welcome, my lord." Stephen's advisers rushed forth.

"Bertrand, Marcel." He held out his arms. "I trust the reason you have come all this way to greet me is not that we have misplaced our beautiful city."

"I assure you your beautiful city still stands." The chatelain grinned. "Stronger than ever."

"And the treasury even more filled than when you left," promised the seneschal.

"All this later." Stephen waved a hand. "We've been riding nonstop since we docked. My ass feels like it's been kicked all the way from Toulon. Tend to my men. We are all as hungry as beggars. And I . . ." He mooned his eyes at Anne. ". . . I must attend to my lovely wife."

"Come, husband," Anne said, trying to seem teasing before his men. "I will try and kick it toward Paris, so as to even it out."

All around them laughed. Anne led him to their large tent draped in green-and-gold silk. Once inside, Stephen's loving look disappeared. "You perform well, my wife."

"It was no performance. I am glad for your return. For your son's sake. And if it has brought you back a gentler man."

"War rarely has that effect," Stephen answered. He sat on a stool and removed his cloak. "Come here. Help with these boots. I will show you just what a petting pup I've become."

His hair fell over his tunic, greasy and grayed. His face was sharp and filthy from the road. He smelled like a boar.

"You look like the wars have left you no worse for wear," Anne remarked.

"And you, Anne," Stephen said, reaching out to pull her down to him, "you look like a dream from which I am not yet willing to awaken."

"Then awaken now." She pulled herself away. It was her duty to tend to him. Remove his boots, rinse out the damp cloth around his neck. But there was no way in hell she would let him touch her. "I have not sat alone for two years to be mounted by a pig."

"So hand me the bowl and I will wash, then." Stephen grinned. "I will make myself fresh as a doe."

"I did not mean your stench," she said.

Stephen still smiled at her. He slowly removed his gloves.

A servant stepped in, carrying a bowl of fruit. He placed it on the bench and then, feeling the stiffness in the air, hurried out.

"I have seen your new interests," Anne said derisively. "The dark troops you have sent from the Holy Land. Your *noble* men of the black cross who kill and slaughter women and children like curs, innocents and nobles alike."

He got up, slowly sauntered over to her. Her skin felt like an insect was crawling up her back. He walked around her as if he were inspecting a steed. She did not look at him.

Then Anne felt his hands caress her neck, icy and loveless. She felt his lips close to her.

"I may be your wife," she said, turning away, "and for that, Stephen, I will tend to your health and welfare, for the sake of my son. I will stand for you, as is my duty, in our court. But *know*, husband, you will not touch me, ever again. Not in my weakest moment or in your most urgent need. Your hands shall never soil me again."

Stephen grinned and nodded, as if impressed. He stroked her cheek and she pulled away, trembling. "How long, lovely Anne, have you been working on that little speech?"

Before she even knew it was happening, he tightened

his caressing grip on the nape of her neck. Pain flashed through her. Slowly, he increased the pressure, all the while fondly smiling at her.

The air shot out of her lungs. She tried to cry out, but to no avail. No one would come. Her cries would be misunderstood as pleasure. Her pulse echoed like a drum in her ears.

Stephen pushed her down to the ground. He followed, all the while pinning his thumb and forefinger into her neck and forcing her thighs apart with just the power of his legs.

She felt him erect and hideous, the detestable hardness she had grown to loathe. "Come," he whispered, "my bold, headstrong Anne. . . . After all this time, would you deny me what I want?"

Anne swallowed back an urge to vomit. *No, this cannot be happening.* Her heart beat in panic. *I swore, not again . . .*

"Do not misunderstand me, wife," he hissed in her ear. "I did not mean I desire your cunt. . . . *I meant the relic.*"

Part Four

TREASURE

Chapter 76

THE HULKING MAN in the sheepskin overvest pounded in the fence post with well-timed strokes of his heavy mallet.

I crept from the woods, still in the torn remnants of my jester's garb, carrying Emilie's cloak. I had clung to the forest for a week now. Hungry, avoiding pursuit. I had nothing. Not a denier or a possession.

"You'll never mend a fence by lazing away like a fat cow," I said boldly.

The burly man put down his mallet and arched his thick, bushy eyebrows. He stepped forward to the challenge. "Look what's crawled out of the woods . . . some scrawny squirrel in a fairy's costume. You look like you wouldn't know a day's work if it jumped up and strummed your dick."

"I could say the same for you, Odo, if it wasn't always in your hand."

The big smith eyed me closely. "Do I know you, malt-worm?"

"Aye," I answered. "Unless, since I've seen you last, your brains have grown as soft as your gut."

"Hugh . . . ?" the smith exclaimed.

We embraced, Odo lifting me high off the ground. He shook his head in astonishment.

"We heard you were dead, Hugh. Then in Treille, wearing the costume of a fool. Then word that you were in Borée. That you killed that prick Norcross. *Which of these are true?*"

"All true, Odo. Except for rumors of my demise."

"Look at me, old friend. You killed the duke's chatelain?"

I took a breath and smiled, like a little brother embarrassed by praise. "I did."

"Ha, I knew you'd outfox them." The smith laughed.

"I have much to tell, Odo. And much to regret, I feel."

"We too, Hugh. Come, sit down. All I can offer you is this rickety fence. Not as fine as Baldwin's cushions . . ." We leaned against it. Odo shook his head. "Last we saw you, you ran into the woods like a devil, chasing the ghost of your wife."

"She was no ghost, Odo. I knew that she lived, and she did."

Odo's eyes widened. "Sophie *lives?*"

"I found her. In a cell in Borée. I found her, Odo, but only long enough for her to die in my arms. They held her as a hostage, thinking that we had something of theirs, something of great value. I've come back to tell her brother, Matthew, of her fate."

Odo shook his head. "I'm sorry, Hugh. That won't be possible."

"Why? What's happened, Odo?"

"Baldwin's men were here again. For you . . . They said you were a murderer and a coward. They said you ran from the Crusade and killed the lord's chatelain. Then they ransacked the village. They said any who harbored you would be tried on pain of death. . . .

"Matthew said you had been wronged. That the chatelain had burned your house and child, and taken your wife, and if Norcross was dead, it was justly deserved for what he had done. He showed them the inn, which he was starting to rebuild. These men were horrible, Hugh. They hung Matthew up. Then they stretched him. His neck in a noose and his legs tied to their mounts. They whipped the horses . . . until his body split in two."

"No!" A pain shot through my chest. Another weight seemed to crush my heart. Poor Matthew. Why him? Now another was dead . . . because of me. This nightmare had to end!

I raised my head. A terrible fear pulsed up in my gut. "What is that smell?"

Odo shook his head. "They burned the town, Hugh."

Chapter 77

I WALKED WITH ODO into the desolate village, the place that only two years before I had called my home.

All around, fields, cottages, and grain holds were no more than mounds of cinder and stone. Dwellings were either caved in and reduced to rubble, or in some beginning stage of being rebuilt.

People put down their hammers, stopped chopping wood.

A group of children shouted and pointed. "Look, it's Hugh. He's come back. It's Hugh!"

Everyone looked up in disbelief. People rushed up to me. "Is it you, Hugh? Have you truly come back?"

A clamor built up, some crying, "Glory to God, it's Hugh. He's back," while others spat in my path. "Go away, Hugh. You're the devil. Look what you've done."

By the time I reached the square, maybe seventy people, most everyone in town, had formed a ring around me.

I gazed at our inn. Two new walls of rough logs had been erected, supported by columns of stone. Matthew had been rebuilding it, better and sturdier than it was before. A flood of anger rushed through me. God damn them!

A rush of tears streamed down my cheeks. I began to weep in a way I hadn't done since I was a small child.

God damn you, Baldwin. And God damn me, for my stupid pride.

I fell to my knees. My wife, my son . . . Matthew . . . Everything was ruined. So many had died.

The ring of townspeople stood there and let me weep. Then I felt a hand on my shoulder. I choked back sobs and looked up. It was Father Leo. I had never paid much heed to him, with his little domed head, his sermons. Now I prayed he would not remove his hand, for it was all that kept me from keeling over in a ball of shame and grief.

The priest lovingly squeezed my shoulder. "This is Baldwin's doing, Hugh, not yours."

"Aye, it *is* Baldwin's work," someone shouted from the crowd. "Hugh meant us no harm. It is not his fault."

"We pay our shares, and this is how the bastard repays us," a woman wailed.

"Hugh must go," another said. "He killed Norcross. He will cause us all to burn."

"Yes, he *did* kill Norcross," echoed another. "God's praise to him! Who among us has stood up like that?"

Voices rose. The shouting built into a clamor — some for me, some against. A few, including Odo and the priest, begged for reason while others started throwing pebbles and stones at me.

"Have pity on us, Hugh," someone wailed. "Please, go, before the knights return!"

In the midst of the clamor, a woman's voice shouted above the din. Everyone turned and grew quiet.

It was Marie, the miller's wife. I remembered her kind

face. She and Sophie were best friends; they had been to the well together the day her son was drowned.

"We've lost more than any of you." She scanned the crowd. "Two sons. One to Baldwin. One to the war. Plus our mill . . . But Hugh has suffered more than we have! You point your scorn at him because we are all too frightened to point it toward the one who deserves it. It is *Baldwin* who deserves our rage, not Hugh."

"Marie's right," said her husband, Georges, the miller. "It is Hugh who killed Norcross and avenged my son." He helped me to my feet and put out his hand. "I'm grateful you're back, Hugh."

"And I," said Odo, his voice booming. "I'm sick of quaking every time I hear horsemen come near town."

"You're right." Martin the tailor hung his head. "It is our own liege who is responsible, not Hugh. But what can we do? We are pledged to him."

It hit me there, in that moment, as I observed my neighbors' helplessness and fear. I knew what we must do. *"Then break the pledge,"* I said.

There was a moment of stunned silence.

"Break the pledge?" the tailor gasped.

People turned to one another and shook their heads, as if my words were a sign that I was mad. "If we break the pledge, Baldwin will come back. This time it won't be just our houses that he burns."

"Then next time, friends, we'll be ready for him," I said, turning to catch every eye.

A wary silence filled the square. These people looked at me as if the words I uttered were heresy that damned us all.

I knew that these words, and this idea, could set us free.

I stared out at them and shouted, *"Break the pledge!"*

Chapter 78

EMILIE STORMED PAST the guards to Anne's bed-chamber. "Please, ma'am." One guard went to restrain her. "The lady is resting."

Emilie's blood was surging. The duke had returned the night before, yet it was not Stephen who was in her mind but Anne, her mistress, the person she served, *who had lost touch with right.*

She pushed open the large wooden door to Anne's chamber.

Anne was in bed at this late hour, still wrapped in bed-clothes.

"You are ill, madame?" Emilie asked.

"You storm into my chambers," Anne said, turning her face away, "as if concern were not the issue at all."

"On the contrary, I have much to take issue with you," Emilie said.

"Take issue, child. . . . No doubt this, as all things, concerns your protégé, the fool."

"You are right, madame, he is a fool. But only to have trusted you. As am I."

"So, this is no longer about him, I see. But you and me . . ."

"You have wronged him in a great way, my lady, and by doing so, wronged me."

"Wronged you?" Anne laughed coldly. "Your Hugh is a wanted man now. A murderer, a deserter as well. He is sought in two duchies and will be caught. And once he is, he'll be hanged in the square."

Emilie stared, aghast. "I am hearing your voice, lady," she said, "but the words do not seem as if they could come from you. What has become of the woman who was like a mother to me? Where is the Anne who stood up against her husband? Who ruled in his absence with even temper and grace."

"Go away, child. Please go. Do not lecture me on things you do not know."

"I know *this*. Your men raided his village. They killed his son, stole and imprisoned his wife. She is dead now. In your prison. You knew."

"How would I know?" Anne shot back. "How would I know some worthless harlot thrown in our dungeon was in fact this man's wife. I do not govern these Tafurs. They are my husband's. I do not know whom they rouse and what insane deeds they do."

"These deeds, lady." Emilie met her eyes. "They are now imprinted on you."

"Go." Anne waved her away. "Do you think that if I knew the person we sought all along was here, at Borée, in our court, your jester would still be running around, pained and aggrieved, but *alive?* He'd be as dead as his wife."

"You sought Hugh?" Emilie blinked. "For God's sake — why?"

"Because the fool holds the greatest prize in Christendom, and he does not know it."

"What prize? He has nothing. You have taken everything from him."

"Just go." Anne sank back in bed. "And take with you your mighty sense of what is right and just. All that propelled you to run away from your father and your destiny. Go, Emilie!" In her anger, Anne turned to face Emilie, exposing for the first time what she had concealed.

There was a large red welt. And much worse.

"What is that?" Emilie moved forward.

"Stay away," Anne snapped, shrinking into her pillows.

"Please, my lady, do not turn from me. What is the bruise on your face?"

Anne took a sharp breath. She dropped her head. "It is my *own* prison, child. You want to see it — well, look!"

Emilie let out a gasp. She rushed over and, against Anne's efforts, gently stroked the wound. "Stephen did that to you?"

"You should know it, child, for it is the very *truth* that you claim to know so well. A woman's truth."

Emilie recoiled in horror. The side of Anne's face was swollen to twice its normal size.

Chapter 79

THE FIRST THING I DID was go up to the hill overlooking town where my infant son, Phillipe, lay buried.

I knelt by his grave and crossed myself. "Your mother spoke of you in her last breath." There I sat, on the hard earth. "Dear, sweet Phillipe."

I still did not know what these sons of bitches wanted with me. What they thought I possessed, which clearly I didn't. Why my wife and son had to die.

I dug up the objects I had brought back from the Crusade and spilled them onto the grass.

The gilded perfume box I had bought for Sophie in Constantinople . . . How sure I had been that I would bring it back to her with pride. Just thinking of all that had happened — Nico, Robert, Sophie — I felt my eyes fill up.

I looked at the inlaid scabbard with the writing I had found crossing the mountains. Then the gold cross I had taken from the church. Were these the treasures? The things that cursed me? If I gave them back, would they leave me, and the town, alone?

A wave of anger swept over me, mixed with grief and tears. *"Which are you?"* I screamed at the pieces. "Which is the thing that caused my wife and son to die?"

I picked up the cross and went to hurl it into the trees. *Trinkets! Baubles! None of it worth the lives of my wife and son!*

Then I held back, remembering Sophie's last words: "Don't give them what they want."

Don't give them what, Sophie? Don't give them what?

I sat by my Phillipe's grave and cried, my fingers digging into my scalp. "Don't give them what?" I whispered over and over again.

Finally, I pulled myself up, spent and exhausted. I gathered the things and laid them in the hole, replacing the displaced earth. I took a deep breath and said good-bye.

Don't give them what they want.

All right, Sophie. I won't.

Because I don't know what in God's name it could be.

Chapter 80

SUMMER GAVE WAY to autumn, and bit by bit, I fell back into the life of the village.

Rebuilding.

I picked up the work Matthew had begun on the inn. All day, I lugged heavy logs, hoisted them into place, and notched them together in joints to form walls. At night I slept in Odo's hut, his wife and two kids and I curled up by the hearth in a single room, until I had rebuilt my quarters behind the inn.

Piece by piece, the town came back to life. Farmers prepared for the harvest. Crumbled homes were patched together with mortar and stone. Harvest time would bring travelers to market; travelers meant money. Money bought food and clothes. People began to laugh once more, and to look forward.

And I became a bit of a hero in town. In no time at all, my stories of how I had dazzled the court at Treille and fought the knight Norcross became part of the local lore. Children clung to my side. *"Show us a flip, Hugh. And how you got out of the chains.*" I amused them with my tricks, removed beads or stones from their ears, told stories of the war. I felt my soul being restored by the sound of their laughter. Yes, laughter truly heals. This was the great lesson I'd learned as a jester.

And I mourned my sweet Sophie. Each day before sunset, I climbed the knoll outside town and sat at my son's grave. I spoke to Sophie as if she rested there too. I told her of the progress on the inn. How the town had banded together around me.

And sometimes I spoke to her of Emilie. What a gift it had been to have her as a friend. How she saw something special in me as no other noble had, from that very first day. I recounted the times she had saved me. How I would have been a lifeless mound had she not come upon me after my fight with the boar.

Each time I talked of Emilie, I could not fail to notice the flame that stirred in my blood. I found myself thinking of our kiss. I did not know if it was meant to bring back my wits in a frantic moment or just as the last good-bye of a true friend. What had she seen in me to risk so much? *A specialness . . . a specialness, Sophie!* Sometimes I even felt myself blush.

One such afternoon as I was heading back to town from the gravesite, Odo ran up the path toward me. "Quick, Hugh, you can't go back there now. *You have to hide!*"

I gazed beyond him. Four riders were approaching over the stone bridge. One an official, colorfully robed and wearing a plumed hat. The other soldiers, wearing the purple and white of Treille.

My heart stood still.

"It's Baldwin's bailiff," Odo said. "If he sees you here, we will all be dead."

I ducked behind a copse of trees, my mind flashing

through options. Odo was right; I could not go back there. But what if someone gave me up? It would not be enough just to run. The town would be held accountable.

"Bring me a sword," I said to Odo.

"A sword? Do you see those soldiers, Hugh? You must *go*. Run as if a beggar had your purse."

I crouched, hidden from sight, and headed toward the eastern woods. A few people saw me scurry away. I crossed the stream at a low point and thrashed my way into the brush.

I found a spot near the square and watched the bailiff clip-clop his way forward like Caesar on a stallion.

An anxious crowd formed around him, buzzing. A bailiff never brought good news: only higher taxes and harsh decrees.

He took out two official-looking documents. "Good citizens of Veille du Père." He cleared his throat. "Your lord, Baldwin, sends his greetings.

"'In compliance,'" he began, "'with the laws of the land, in the reign of Philip Capet, king of France, Baldwin, duke of Treille, decrees all subjects known to give aid or shelter to the fugitive known as Hugh De Luc, a cowardly *murderer,* shall be treated as accomplices to the above-mentioned fugitive and receive the full and swift measure of the law.' Which, for you sow-addled farmers who may not fully understand, means hanged by the neck until dead.

"'Additionally,'" he went on, "'all lands, property, and belongings owned or leased from the duchy by such persons shall be immediately forfeited, confiscated, and returned to the demesne, and all spouses, siblings, and descendents, free or indentured, shall be sworn into life-long service to his liege.'"

My blood almost burst through my veins. The town was being punished for my crimes. All personal property handed over, worked lands returned, families ripped apart. I waited, holding my breath, for a voice to cry out against me. A wife, at wit's end, afraid to lose any more. An unknowing child . . .

The bailiff took a long, measuring look around. He was an obscenity. "Thoughts, townspeople . . . ? A sudden change of heart?" There was a tense, drawn-out silence. But no one spoke up. *Not one of them.*

Then Father Leo stepped forward. "Once again, bailiff, our lord, Baldwin, shows he is a wise and charitable liege."

The bailiff shrugged. "Appropriate measures, Father. Word has it the scum is back in these parts."

"So what *good* news have you brought in your other decree?" someone called out.

"Almost forgot . . ." He smiled and rapped his head. He unfurled the parchment and, without reading, nailed it to the church wall. "General increase in taxes. All raised ten percent."

"What!" A gasp escaped from the crowd. "That's not fair. It cannot be."

"Sorry." The bailiff shrugged. "You know the reasons . . . Dry summer, stocks are low. . . ."

Then, all at once, the bailiff stopped talking. Something had caught his eye. He stood there, motionless. *It was the inn.* My heart clenched in my throat.

"Is this not the inn that only weeks ago was burned to the ground? The one belonging to the person we seek?" No one answered. "Who is rebuilding it? If my memory serves me, the last of its proprietors was, shall we say . . . torn apart by grief."

A few eyes traveled about uneasily.

"Who rebuilds it, I say?" The bailiff picked up one of the stones.

I began to tremble. *This was surely it! The end of me.*

Then a voice rang out of the crowd. "The town rebuilds it, bailiff." It was Father Leo. "The town needs an inn."

The bailiff's eyes lit up. "Most charitable, Father. And most assuring to hear this from you, a man whose word is above refute. So tell me, who will run this establishment?"

Another silence.

"I will," shouted a voice. Marie, the miller's wife. "I will tend to the inn while my husband mans the mill."

"You are most enterprising, madame. A good choice, I think, since you seem to have no heirs to run your mill."

The bailiff held her gaze. I could see he was unsure whether to believe a word. Then he tossed the stone he still held aside and made his way to his mount.

"I hope this is all true." He sniffed and pulled the reins. "Perhaps on my next visit I will stay longer, madame. I look forward to the chance to test your hospitality for myself."

Chapter 81

AS SOON AS THE HATED BAILIFF was out of sight, panic spread through town. I marched back out of the woods, grateful that no one had spoken against me. But I saw the mood had changed.

"What do we do now?" A frightened Martin the tailor shook his head. "You heard him; the prick suspects. How long can we keep up this ruse?"

Jean Dueux, a farmer, looked ashen. "The land we work returned to the demesne? We'd be ruined. Our entire lives lie in this land."

People crowded around me, shouting and afraid. I was the cause of their misery. "If you want me to leave, I will." I bowed my head.

"It's not you," the tailor said, looking around for support. "Everyone's afraid. We've finally picked ourselves up from the ruins. If Baldwin's men come back . . ."

"They *will* come back, Martin," I said to his worried face. "They will come back again and again. Whether I stay or go."

"We took you in," the baker's wife shouted. "What is it you expect us to do now?"

I went over to the inn, and I felt my wife's soul stirring in the rubble. "Do you think I drag these rocks every day and sweat building these walls so that this inn I promised my dead wife I would rebuild can be brought down once again?"

"We all feel that way, Hugh," the tailor said. "We've all rebuilt. But what can we do to stop it?"

"We can defend ourselves," I shouted.

"Defend?" The word was whispered through the crowd.

"Yes, *defend*. Draw the line. Fight them. Show them they can never take away our lives again."

"Fight? Our liege?" People looked stunned. "But we are all pledged to him, Hugh."

"I told you before. . . . *Break the pledge.*"

The gravity of these words silenced the buzzing crowd. "Break it," I said again.

"If we did, that would be *treason*," the tailor objected.

I turned to the miller. "Any more *treason*, Georges, than the murder of your son? Or you, Marte — your husband lies not far from my son. Was it any less treason when he was struck down defending your home? Or my own boy, who did not even know the word when he was tossed into the flames."

"Baldwin's a ruddy prick," the miller replied. "But these obligations you want to throw down, they are the law. Baldwin would come at us with everything he has. He would crush us like moths."

"It can be done, Georges. I've seen how a small, able detachment can defend themselves for months against a greater force. I'm not trying to stoke up fire like the little hermit, then have you follow me to ruin. But we can beat him if we stand up."

"The duke has trained men." Odo stepped forward. "Weapons. We are just farmers and smiths. One town. Fifty men."

"Yes, and in each town between here and Treille there are another fifty men who hate Baldwin just as you do. Hundreds who have suffered the same misery and oppression. We beat them back just once, these men will join us. What can Baldwin do, fight us all?"

Some were nodding in agreement; for others, the thought of standing up against the liege was almost impossible to conceive.

"Hugh's right," Marie, the miller's wife, said. "We have all lost husbands and children. Our homes have been ruined. I'm tired of quaking in my bed every time we hear the sound of riders."

"I too," Odo shouted out. "We've pandered to that bastard our whole lives. What comes of it? A load of shit and death." He stepped over to me and shrugged. "I'm a smith. I know smelting, not soldiering. But if you need me, I can wield a hell of a fucking hammer. *Count me in!*"

One by one, other voices were raised in agreement. Farmers, carters, shoemakers . . . people who had simply reached the end of their tether.

"What say *you*, priest?" the tailor begged, hoping for an ally. "Even if we beat Baldwin back, will we survive one hell only to be damned to another?"

"I cannot say." Father Leo shrugged. "What I can promise, though, is that the next time Baldwin's riders come to town, you can count on me to throw a stone or two."

There were shouts of acquiescence all around. But the town was still divided. The tailor, the tanner, and some farmers who were petrified to lose their lands.

I went up to the tailor. "One thing I *can* promise . . . Baldwin's men will come. You'll rebuild your homes and pay to the bone every year until your hands blister or your will dies. But they will always come. Until we tell them *they cannot*."

The tailor shook his head. "You wear a patchwork skirt and a bell upon your cap, and *you're* going to show us how to fight?"

"I will." I looked him in the eye.

The tailor seemed to measure me up and down. He fingered the hem of my tunic. "Whoever did this, it's a nice job." Then he took my hand and clasped it wearily. "God help us," he declared.

Chapter 82

"MOVE IT HERE!" I called to Jean Dueux, on his perch atop a tree. "A little to the right. Where the road narrows."

High above the road, Jean hoisted a heavy wheat sack bulging with rocks and gravel. He tied off the sack with a long rope and double knotted the other end to a sturdy branch.

"I'll send the horse," I said to him. "When it reaches my position, let the rocks go."

Since the bailiff's visit, we had begun the task of fitting the town for its defenses. Woodsmen sheared off wooden barriers to be placed in rows along the town's western edge. Stakes were sharpened and driven into the ground at jutting angles that even the bravest warhorse would not advance upon. Large stones were half buried in the road.

And we began to make weapons. A few old-timers brought out their swords, rusty things. Odo polished and sharpened them on his lathe. The rest of our arsenal consisted of clubs and mallets, a few spears and billhooks, iron tools. From these we made arrows that could pierce armor. We were a town of Davids preparing for Goliath.

I backed off and signaled down the road. Apples, the baker's son, slapped the horse and sent him coming. Jean braced himself on his perch, tipping the weighted sack to the edge. When the horse passed my spot, I shouted, *"Release!"*

Jean let it go. In a sweeping arc, it hurtled out of the sky like a boulder, picking up speed. As the horse passed, it swung across the road with a loud whoosh, at exactly the height of a man atop his mount. It might as well have been hurled by a catapult. Even the staunchest rider would not withstand its force.

Jean and Apples cheered.

"Now it's your turn, Alphonse." I turned to the tanner's oldest boy, who had a slight stutter. He was a strapping fifteen, muscles beginning to bulge. I placed a club in his hands. "The fallen knight will be stunned. For a few moments, he'll be pinned to the earth by his armor. You cannot hesitate." I looked him in the eye and swung the club hard into an imaginary shape on the ground. "You have to be prepared to do the deed."

"I w-will." The boy nodded. He was big and strong but had never been in as much as a tussle. Yet he had seen his brother sliced in half by Baldwin's men. He took the club and sent it crashing down. "D-don't worry about m-me," he said.

I nodded approvingly.

It felt so good to see the town come together. Everyone could do something useful. Woodsmen could shoot; children could throw stones; the elderly could sew leather armor and sharpen arrows.

But when it came down to it, it would take more than high spirits and eagerness to ward off Baldwin's raiders.

The townspeople would have to fight. I prayed to God we were up to this. That I was not, like Peter the Hermit, leading them into a murderous rout.

"Hugh!" I heard an urgent voice call from the direction of town. Pipo, Odo's little son, was running toward me. His face was ruddy with importance. I felt a shudder of alarm.

"Someone's here," he gasped, out of breath.

"Who?" For a moment, my heart clenched. *Who knew I was here?*

"A visitor," the boy said. "And a pretty one." He nodded. "She says she came all the way from Borée."

Chapter 83

EMILIE!

I ran the dusty road back to the village, my heart bounding with excitement and surprise. I had thought of her so much, yet I always felt it was just another stupid dream to actually believe that I would ever see Emilie again!

I took a shortcut through the stables and blacksmith stalls, and saw her in the square — with her maid. She wore a simple linen dress, her hair pinned up under a cap, and a plain brown riding cloak about her shoulders. And yet she was lovely, so beautiful. I had to tell myself this was no dream. She was here!

I came out from behind the barn and let her see me. I did not know whether to run and sweep Emilie up into the air or just stand there. "In all the world, my lady," I finally said, "you have no idea what joy this brings me."

" 'In all the world' is *right*, Hugh De Luc." She smiled, her eyes twinkling. "For it feels as though I have traveled it to find you."

"I'm sorry for your trouble." I shook my head. "But you are a sight for dreaming eyes no matter how far you've come. But *how* . . . ? How did you find me here?"

"You said you were from the south." Emilie picked up her satchel and walked up to me. "So I merely went to the spot where we found you on the road and continued south. And south. And *south* even more. Every village we passed, I asked, 'Is there a very strange person here who has come from Borée, who wears a jester's suit?' I had gone so far south I thought I would hear Spanish, when this nice boy answered, 'Yes, ma'am. You must mean Hugh.' I thanked God to hear that word, since we could not drag ourselves one more mile. This is Elena." She waved her attendant forward. "She accompanied me on the trip."

"Elena." I bowed. "I have seen you at Borée."

The servant curtsied wearily, clearly delighted their journey had come to an end.

I turned back to Emilie. "So tell me, how have you come here?" I shook my head. "And *why?*"

"Because I promised I would see you again. Because I told you I would do what I could do to find you the answers you sought. I will explain later."

"And you came all this way alone? The two of you? Do you not know the risk you took?"

"I told Anne that I had arranged a visit to my aunt Isabel in Toulon. There was such commotion in Borée with Stephen's return, I am sure she was happy to be rid of me. We were escorted on our way by a party of priests headed south on a pilgrimage."

"But your aunt? When you fail to arrive in Toulon, you will be missed."

Emilie bit her lip guiltily. "My aunt Isabel does not know. There never was any visit. I made it up."

I broke into a wide grin. "You have taken on the worl
to visit me. But enough questions. You and Elena must b
tired. And hungry. I'm afraid we have no castles in thes
parts." I smiled. "But there is no shortage of hospitality
Come, I know just the place."

Chapter 84

THERE WAS A BIG CELEBRATION in town that night.

We ate at Odo's table, which filled most of his hut. His wife, Lisette, cooked, helped by Marie, the miller's wife. There were Odo and Georges, my closest friends, and Father Leo. And, of course, Emilie.

A special meal was prepared, a goose roasted in the hearth. With carrots and turnips and peas, a soup of vegetables in a garlicky broth, and fresh bread that we dipped in the soup. There was no wine, but the priest brought along a cask of Belgian ale he'd been saving for the bishop's visit. By our standards, it was a rare feast.

Odo played the flute, and we all pitched in with chansons. The children danced as if it were Mid-summer's Eve. And I performed a few tricks, a flip or two. Everyone laughed and danced, Emilie too. For a few hours, we forgot the past.

All the while I could not keep my gaze far from the brightness of Emilie's eyes. They were as light as the moon, and just as genuine. She clapped and laughed as

Odo's kids tried to reproduce my flips, as if this were the most natural role in the world for her. She told them of life in the castle. It was a golden evening, free from all barriers and stations in life.

Afterward, I walked with her back to the inn. There was a chill in the air, and Emilie huddled tightly in her cloak. Part of me wanted to put my arm around her; another part quivered with nerves.

We walked amid the noises of the night — owls hooting, other birds fluttering in the trees. A bright round moon peeked through the clouds. I asked her, "How is Norbert? His health?"

"He is fine again," Emilie said, "except he is still unable to do that trick with the chains. But things have changed since Stephen's return. The Tafurs are everywhere, and the duke is behind them."

"Stephen and *Anne*," I replied.

"Anne . . ." Emilie stopped, hesitating. "I believe with all my heart she did not act of her own accord."

"You mean the raids she directed in her husband's absence, the slaughter and mayhem, these were not hers?"

"I only meant that she behaved from fear. I do not justify it. She said something to me, Hugh, that I did not understand. I pressed her on why she allowed these things to occur, and she said, 'If I knew the person we sought all along was at Borée, your jester would be as dead as his wife.'"

I shook my head in confusion.

"She called you the *innkeeper* from the Crusade. It was why they took your wife. But she claimed she did not know this was you."

"Why? Why in God's name would they want me?"

"Because you hold 'the greatest prize in Christendom.'"

Emilie tilted her head to me. "And do not know. That is what Anne says."

"The greatest prize in Christendom . . ." I started to laugh. "Are they mad? Look around you. I have nothing. All that I had they've already taken."

"I told her the same. But you were there, Hugh, in the Crusade. Perhaps they confuse you with someone else."

We had arrived at the inn. Emilie shivered in the cold night air, and I ached to hold her, just for a moment. I would have given anything to have her in my arms. Even "the greatest prize in Christendom."

"I brought something for you, Hugh. I have it here." We ducked inside the door. By the fiery hearth, Elena was already asleep on her mat. Emilie went over to her satchel.

She came back with a calfskin pouch cinched at the top, and from it removed a wooden box the size of my two palms. It was finely engraved, the mark of a craftsman, with an ornate letter *C* on its lid.

She placed the box in my hands and stepped back. "This belongs to you, Hugh. It's why I came."

I stood there examining the box a moment, then lifted the tiny latch and opened the lid.

Burning tears welled in my eyes. Immediately I knew what the box contained.

Ashes.

Sophie's ashes . . .

"Her body was cremated the following day," Emilie said softly. "I went and gathered these. The priests say her soul will not reach Heaven unless she is buried."

A knot rose in my chest and throat. I took the deepest breath, as if sucking air into every fiber in my body. "You cannot know how much I treasure this gift, Emilie."

"As I said, Hugh, it belongs to you."

I wrapped my arms around her and drew her close. I felt her heart beating against mine.

I whispered beneath my breath, so only I could hear. "I meant you."

Chapter 85

THE FOLLOWING MORNING, I rose before the sun. I took the calfskin pouch that was next to my bed and slipped out of the inn.

Next to the woodshed, I found a few scattered tools. I took a shovel. The cocks had not yet crowed.

A few other early risers fluttered about their chores. A carter was heading out with his mule. By the baker's hut, the smell of fresh baking bread perfumed the air.

I headed for the knoll overlooking our village.

I had dreamed of this so many times since Sophie had died in my arms. Bringing her home. The thought that her soul was incomplete, with no rites or blessings, tormented me. Now her life would be complete. She would rest here forever.

By the ford in the stream I began to climb a steep hill. The morning was alive with birds chirping in the soft light. The sun tried to burn through the mist. I climbed for a few minutes; soon I was above the town. I looked back over the

waking valley. The little huts had begun to show life. I saw
the square and the inn. Emilie was sleeping there.

On top of the hill, I went to a spot near a spreading elm
where my son's grave was.

I knelt and put the calfskin pouch down. Then I began
to dig. I made a space in the ground next to Phillipe. Tears
gathered in my eyes as a heavy drum pounded inside my
chest.

"At last you're home, Sophie," I whispered. "You and
Phillipe."

I opened the pouch and held the box with the *C*. Then I
scattered her ashes into the dug-up earth and covered them
up again. I stood there at her grave and looked back over
the awakening town.

You are finally home, Sophie. Your soul can rest.

Chapter 86

STEPHEN OF BORÉE SAT STOLIDLY on the high-backed chair in his court. A crowd of toadying favor-seekers stood in line as his bailiff brought him up to date on a new tax. Behind him, the seneschal readied a report on the status of his demesne. His thoughts were a thousand miles away.

The prize. The treasure.

It haunted him, invaded his dreams. This holy relic miraculously preserved for centuries in the tombs of the Holy Land. He longed for it with an avarice he had felt for no woman. Something that had touched Him. He woke in the night dreaming about it, his body covered in sweat. His lips grew dry just thinking of its touch.

With such a prize in hand, Borée would be among the most powerful duchies in Europe. What a cathedral he would build to house its glory. What was the worth of the meager bones of his own patron saint, resting in his reliquary? It was nothing compared to this prize. People would come from all over the world to make pilgrimages to Borée. No cleric would be greater than him, or closer to God.

And he knew who had it.

A furor built in Stephen's chest. His underlings were lathering on, blabbering about his holdings, his wealth. It was all rubbish — insignificant. He felt as if he were about to explode.

"*Get out,*" he stood and screamed. The bailiff and the seneschal looked at him, surprised. "Get out! Leave me be! You go on about this new tax, or a new flock of sheep. Your eyes are fixed on the ground. I am dreaming of everlasting life."

He swept his hand across the table in front of him, and a tray of wine goblets clattered to the floor. Everybody scurried, fleeing their places as if the whole structure were about to collapse.

A servant nervously approached to clear the mess. Stephen waved him away. His eyes followed the trail of spilled wine until they came to rest upon someone's boot.

Who is so presumptuous as to approach? Stephen thought. He looked up at the face of Morgaine, the leader of his Tafur guard. *Black Cross.*

"Have you come to taunt me, Morgaine, with news of another village laid waste without my prize?"

"No, I have come to cheer you, my lord, with news that I know where the treasure is."

Stephen's eyes widened. "Where?"

"Your cousin, the lady Emilie, has led me right to it," Black Cross said with a pinched smile.

"Emilie?" Stephen's face twitched. "What has Emilie to do with this prize? She is in Toulon."

"She is not in Toulon," Black Cross said. He whispered close. "But in a little pisshole in the duchy of Treille, Veille du Père."

"Veille du Père? I know that name. I thought you had already sacked —"

"Yes." Morgaine nodded, seeing Stephen come to understand. "She is with the innkeeper as we speak. And so is the treasure."

Chapter 87

TO MY AMAZEMENT AND DELIGHT, Emilie did not leave as soon as she had delivered her gift. She stayed on for the next few days. I was in heaven.

I showed her the work we were doing to fortify the town. The perimeter defenses of sharpened stakes, strong enough to repel a sudden charge; the battle stations high in the trees, from where we could rain arrows and stones on any attackers. She saw the passion with which I urged my friends and neighbors to resist. And she heartily approved.

In between, I treated her to the best sights of our village. The lily pond in the woods where I liked to swim. A field high in the hills where sunflowers ran wild in the summer. And she helped me at the inn. I showed her how to fit logs into a support column with pegs and joints. She helped me hoist up a log as a support beam. Then we carved her initials into the wood: *Em. C.*

I knew this fantasy would have to come to an end. Soon she would leave. Yet she seemed comfortable. So I allowed myself to pretend. That Emilie would not be missed and looked for. That it was safe here, free from attack. That something unthinkable was happening between us.

It was on a warm afternoon a few days later that I tossed down my tools before noon. "Come." I took Emilie by the hand. "It's not a day to be working. I want to show you a beautiful place. Please, my lady."

I took her up into the hills, past the knoll where Sophie and Phillipe lay. The sun beat deliciously against our skin. High above town, an open meadow stretched out, the tall grass golden under the blue sky.

"It's gorgeous," Emilie exclaimed, her eyes soaking in every burst of blue and flash of gold.

She flung herself down in the field and fanned her arms and legs into the shape of a star. "Come here, Hugh, this is heaven." She patted the grass next to her.

I lay down beside her. Her soft blond hair fell off her shoulders, and I could see the hint of breasts peeking from the neckline of her dress. My blood was running wild, and it terrified me for obvious reasons.

"Tell me," I said, propping myself up on my elbow, "what does the *C* stand for?"

"The *C?*"

"Your family name . . . It was on the box you gave me, and the initials we carved into the inn. I know nothing about you. Who you are. Where you are from. Your family."

"Are you concerned," she said with a laugh, "that I may not be a high enough match for you?"

"Of course not, I just . . ."

"I was born in Paris, if you must know. I am the fourth child, with two brothers and a sister, all older. My father is remarkable, but not for the reasons you may suspect."

"He is a noble, that much I know. A member of the royal court?"

"He is important; leave it at that. And educated. But sometimes his vision is as narrow as a fly's."

"You are the baby." I winked. "And yet you have wandered away from the nest."

"The nest is not always a welcome place." Emilie looked away. "At least not for a woman down the pecking order. What is there for me except to be educated in lofty arts and concepts I will never use? Or to be married off for gain to some old sod twice my age. Can you see me entertaining and receiving gifts from gassy old coots?"

"I have met only two duchesses," I said, beaming, "and you outshine them in both beauty and heart."

She put her palm against mine, and we held it there, for a moment, in silence. Then Emilie pushed me away. "Make me laugh, will you?"

"Make you laugh?"

"Yes. You were a jester. Quite a decent one." Her eyes shined. "Come on. It shouldn't be hard for you."

"It's not so easy," I protested. "I mean, you just don't blurt out a joke, in a place like this, and have it succeed."

"Are you embarrassed, then? With *me* . . . ? Come." She pinched my arm. "It is only us. I will close my eyes. In all the world, it should not be so hard to know what will make me smile."

Emilie closed her eyes with her chin raised. I stared at her face, the delicate yellow hair falling off her shoulder.

I felt my breath come to a halt.

She was incredibly lovely. . . . And kind, generous, smart as a whip.

All of a sudden, there was nothing between us: no words, no barriers, just our two beating hearts. I placed my hand on her hip. Nervously — I prayed she would not take offense — I moved it up her side, over the curve of her waist.

She made no move to resist. I felt the strangest urge come over me. My breath was tight, my spine tingling. Had I felt this from the start? From the first moment I opened my eyes and saw her face?

I moved my hand over her shoulder and let it fall gently against the round of her breast. I felt her heart quiver. I had felt this only once before. Yet here it was again.

Slowly I placed my mouth upon her lips.

Emilie did not resist, only moved closer, her mouth softly parting. Our tongues seemed to merge and dance as softly as clouds meeting in the sky.

She put her hand on my cheek, her breath as heavy as my own. Her skin smelled of lavender and balsam. In the warm rush of our kiss, I felt a new world open to me.

In a breath, we pulled away. She smiled. "You take advantage of me. I was warned of such country boys."

"Tell me to wake up," I said. "I know I am in a dream."

"Wake up, then." She placed my hand upon her heart. "And know that this is real."

My own heart almost exploded with joy. I could not believe what was happening.

Then I heard the loud peal of church bells coming from town.

Chapter 88

MY MIND JOLTED BACK to reality. I frantically rose to my knees and looked down toward the village. I saw no riders. No sign of panic yet. But a crowd was forming in the square. *Something had happened.*

"Come." I pulled Emilie up. "We have to get back."

We ran down the hill as fast as we could. As soon as I came within earshot of town I heard my name shouted.

Georges ran up to me. "Hugh, they're coming. Men from Borée are on the way."

I looked at Emilie, then back at Georges. "How do you know this?"

"Someone is here to warn us. Come, quick, in the church. He looks for you."

Georges ran with me into the main square. The town had assembled there, and voices rang out, panicked and afraid.

I pushed through the crowd around the church and came upon a young man resting on the steps. No more than six-

een, panting, clearly out of breath. When he saw me, he
tood up and eyed me.

"You are Hugh," the boy said. "I can tell by your red
air."

"I am," I answered. He looked vaguely familiar. "You
come from Borée?"

"Yes." The boy nodded. "I have run the whole way. I am
sent by your friend Norbert, the jester. He said to tell you
hey are coming. For everyone to prepare."

"I must try and go back," Emilie said, clutching my
arm. "I must tell them it's a mistake."

"You cannot." The boy shook his head, alarmed. "Norbert said you *must not return*. That Stephen knows you are
here. You were followed. The duke's guard is on the way.
They will be here tonight, perhaps. Latest tomorrow."

Frantic cries rose in the crowd. Martin the tailor pointed
at me. "Now what? This is your work, Hugh. What are we
to do?"

"Fight," I shouted back. "This is what we expected."

There was whimpering and worried faces. Wives sought
out their husbands and clutched children to their bosoms.

"We are prepared," I said. "These men come to take
away what is ours. We will not bow down to them."

Dread hung over the crowd. Then Odo stepped forward.
He looked around, tapped the head of his hammer on the
ground. "I'm with you. So is my hammer!"

"I-I'm with you too," said Alphonse. "And my sharpened
ax."

"And I," cried Apples.

They ran toward their positions as the rest of the crowd
remained still. Then others followed, one by one.

I turned back to the messenger. "How do I know you are
who you say? That you've come from Norbert? You say
the lady Emilie was followed. This could be a trick."

"You know my face, Hugh. I am Lucien, the bake
boy. I sought to apprentice with Norbert."

"Apprentices can be bought," I challenged him furth

"Norbert said you would press me. So he sent pro
Something of value to you that could come from no o
other than him."

He reached behind him on the church steps and u
wound a woolen blanket.

A smile curled on my face. Norbert was right. What t
boy had brought was of great value to me. I had not seen
since I left Borée in the middle of the night.

Lucien was holding my staff.

Chapter 89

IN THE NEXT FEW HOURS, the town bustled with a purpose I had not seen before.

Bales of sharpened stakes were dragged to positions just inside the stone bridge and driven into the ground. Sacks filled with rocks were readied in the trees. Those who could shoot sharpened their arrows and stocked their quivers; those who could not sat with hoes and mallets in their hands.

By the time night fell, everyone was nervous but prepared.

The plan was for old folk and some of the women and young children to flee to the woods before the first sign of trouble. I told Emilie she had to go too. But when the time came, no one would leave.

"I'm staying with you." Emilie shook her head. She had torn her dress at the hem and sleeves to move about more easily. "I can stack arrows. I can distribute arms."

"These men are killers," I said, trying to reason with

her. "They'll make no distinction between noble and co
mon. This is not your fight."

"You are wrong. The distinction between noble a
common is clear here today," she replied with that sa
unbending resolve as when she rescued me at Borée. "A
it has become my fight."

I left her stacking rocks and ran to the first defenses
the bridge. Alphonse and Apples were tightening the ro

"How many will come?" Alphonse asked.

"I do not know," I said. "Twelve, twenty, maybe mo
Enough to do what it takes."

I took my station on the second floor of the tailo
house, near the entrance to town. From there I could ov
see the defense. I had a sword, an old clunker sharpened
a tee.

My stomach was in knots. Now all that was left to
was wait.

Emilie met me toward evening. We sat against a wa
her head resting on my shoulder. I felt what I had alwa
known about her. *She gave me strength.*

"Whatever happens," she said, tightening against me,
am glad to be here with you. I don't know how to explai
but I feel you have a destiny in front of you."

"When the Turk spared me, I thought it was just to ma
people laugh." I chuckled.

"And you became a jester."

"Yes. Thanks to you."

"Not me." Emilie pulled away and looked at me. "*You.*
is you who had the court at Borée eating out of your han
But now I think God has found you a higher purpose. I thi
this is it."

I pressed her tightly to my body, feeling her breas
against my ribs, the cadence of her heart. In my loins, I fe
desire spark. We looked at each other, and something to

e, unspoken, that this was right. She was where she be-nged. And so was I.

"I do not want to die," Emilie said, "and never know hat it is like to be with you."

"I won't let you die." I cupped her fist.

She lowered herself onto me and we kissed. Not as be-ore, with the thrill of friendship turning into something nore, but deeper, more forcefully. The tempo of Emilie's reath began to quicken.

I put my hands under her dress and felt the smoothness f her stomach. My skin jumped alive all over.

She raised herself on my lap. We looked in each other's yes and there was no hesitation. "I love you," I told her. From the first. There was no doubt."

"There was doubt," she whispered, "but I loved you oo."

She lowered herself on top of me and gasped as I came in-ide her. Soon she was calm and at ease. I held her by the hips nd we rocked. Her eyes lit with pleasure, and my skin grew eated and damp as we increased the pace. We were eye to ye, rocking against time, a smile and a sheen of ardor on her ace. "Oh, Hugh." She squeezed her pelvis into me. "I do ove you."

At last she cried out, a body-tremoring moan. I held her lose to me and squeezed her shoulders as if I would never et go. She tremored once more in my arms.

"Do not wake me," she said with a sigh, "for I am in the nidst of the most marvelous dream."

She buried her face in my chest, and I could have stayed ke that forever. I looked out at the moon and thought, What a miracle it is that I have found this woman. I wanted o hold her and protect her with all my heart, as she had isked everything to protect me.

Is this why I had been saved? I could ask no better p
pose.

Then I heard a shout, and an alarmed cry. A chilling, f
off rumble came from the earth.

I ran to the window. A fiery arrow arced toward
across the sky. The lookout's signal.

I looked at Emilie, the calm of a moment ago replac
by a stabbing dread. *"They are here!"*

Chapter 90

BLACK CROSS'S MEN STOOD just outside the sleeping town. The moonless night covered their approach. They had ridden for the better part of two days, barreling at full speed, knocking people and carts out of their way as they charged through tiny forest towns. He knew that the hard journey only heightened their eagerness for blood.

Morgaine chuckled. This would be child's play. Babes slaughtered in their sleep. He had sought this beetle all the way from Antioch. Now he was only minutes from holding his prize. The greatest of all of them. This insect would not get away again.

Morgaine said to his men, "Whoever finds the prize will have a castle waiting for him on his return. Kill who you have to, fuck who you like, just find the redhead. Run a blade up his ass and bring the worm to me."

His men's eyes lit up. Senses eager for battle, they chose their arms — maces and pikes and heavy swords. They donned their steel-beaded gloves. In a few moments they would turn this sleepy mound of dung into a slop of blood.

They fitted on their helmets. Bright eyes glinted throu
the slits.

Morgaine's lieutenant signaled him. "What orders, si

"Level it," Morgaine said evenly. "Every home, ev
child. Other than the innkeeper, nothing lives. I want no
ing left, and that includes the lady Emilie."

The Tafur nodded. At Morgaine's nod, he gave the s
nal to charge.

Chapter 91

THE FLOOR SHOOK beneath my feet. The rumble of hooves grew louder and louder, like an avalanche approaching fast.

I ran into the street. People stuck out their heads from their positions, looks of terror building in their eyes.

"Do not panic," I urged them. "They think this will be child's play. Everyone remember the plan."

Inside, I felt the grinding fist of fear that must now be intensifying in everybody's gut. I hurried toward Alphonse and Apples, bracing the rope on both sides of the bridge. I told them, "Remember what they did to your friends and family the last time they were here. Remember what you swore in your heart you would do to them if you ever had the chance. Now is that chance!"

The thundering noise had risen to a terrifying level. I could not tell if the noise crashing through me was the drum of approaching hooves or my heart beating out of control.

Finally we saw them — a black cloud bearing down on

us from out of the woods, torches in hand. Twelve to four-teen, howling cries of death.

A spark of hope flared in me. The town was dark. I knew they could not see our defenses.

"Hold tight," I hollered as the horses neared, but my words were drowned in the advancing roar.

The first line of horsemen galloped over the bridge, straight into the tautness of the rope. The horses came down in a tangle. The lead riders were pitched into the air. With a scream, one was hurled headlong into the sharp-ened stakes and impaled through the chest, his limbs out-stretched and twitching. The other catapulted off his mount, landing on his neck, his body trampled under the advancing hooves.

Seeing the ambush, the next line of marauders at-tempted to stop, but their speed was too great. A third rider fell, screaming. Then another.

I saw Odo leap out from under the bridge and, as one struggled to right himself, swing his heavy club down-ward, smashing it into the man's head. His helmet caved in like tin. Buoyed by the sight, Apples dashed out as well, thrusting his sword through the other raider's neck.

The torches carried by the fallen riders sent the wooden defenses up in flames. Horses whined and bucked. Arrows shot out from the trees, and two other riders hit the ground, pierced through the neck and head. The other marauders, seeing what had happened, regrouped on the bridge. Then they darted single file through the burning defenses into town.

Now Tafurs on horseback were in the streets, flinging torches into our homes. I waved my sword at the trees. "Now, Jean, *now!*"

A dark shape fell out of the sky, hurtling across the road and crashing into one of the riders, knocking him off his mount with a loud groan. He remained there, stunned, pinned to the ground by the weight of his armor. I raised my sword and screamed into the slits of his helmet, "This is for Sophie, you bastard. See what it's like to be killed by a fool." I crashed the sword down, penetrating cleanly through the seam above the chest plate. There, it remained embedded. I couldn't pull the sword free.

For a moment, and even without a weapon, I felt exultant. This was working. People were fighting. Seven of the invaders were down, perhaps slain. Two more were off their horses, surrounded by townsmen.

I watched as Alphonse climbed onto the back of one of the attackers and pushed a knife through the eye slit in his helmet. The Tafur pitched forward. Alphonse jerked the blade across the bastard's neck and soon he rolled over, dead.

A few riders made their way through town, hurling torches onto the thatched roofs, which shot into yellow flame. I counted only five invaders left, but five armed and deadly, still on their mounts. If we backed down now, they were enough to take the town.

I started to run — weaponless — toward the square. *"Here,"* Emilie yelled, and tossed me my staff.

Across the road, I saw poor Jacqui, the ruddy-faced milk woman, hurling stones at one attacker while another galloped up from behind and knocked her to the ground with a mace. Arrows shot out of the trees, and the second attacker fell.

Suddenly the square lit up in flames.

Aimée, the miller's daughter, and Father Leo had set fire to the line of brush ringing the square. The horses of the invaders reared. One rider was immediately thrown, landing in the flames. The others darted and circled, unable to break through.

The fallen rider stood up, engulfed in flames. He thrashed about crazily, smoke pouring through the slits in his armor.

Two other attackers remained trapped inside the ring of flame. One forced his mount through, but Martin ran up and whacked the horse's legs. The rider clubbed at him but was thrown from his mount. He flailed on the ground, struggling to right himself, his weapon out of reach. Then, from out of the darkness, Aimée ran out. She raised an ax and crashed it solidly into the man's head.

We were winning! The town continued to battle as only people clinging to their last hope can do. Still, two or three invaders remained.

Then, to my horror, the last Tafur who'd been contained within the ring of fire burst free. He reared his steed and made his way, ax whirling, toward Aimée, who still stood staring at the man she had killed.

"Look out, Aimée," I yelled. I started toward her, helplessly screaming at the top of my lungs. I couldn't bear to see the miller lose his last child. The girl did not move, oblivious to the death descending upon her. I was twenty yards away, not thinking, running as fast as my feet would fly. The rider crouched in the saddle and raised his ax.

Twenty feet away . . . I shrieked, *"No . . ."*

I reached her at a cross angle just as the Tafur swung his ax. I swept Aimée to the ground and covered her, expecting at any moment to feel the blade of the ax buried in my back. But no blow came.

The Tafur galloped by, then reversed. He stood for a moment, tightening his reins, surveying the rout of his fellows.

I knew his mind; I had seen it many times in the Crusade. It was the time of the battle when one knows all is lost; the only thing left is to fight whatever comes into your path and cause as much death and mayhem as possible until you too are taken down.

I pushed Aimée out of the square and raised myself to my feet. I stood there facing the attacker, nothing to defend myself with but my wooden staff.

I didn't want to die here. But I would not run.

The raider reared his giant horse and galloped into a charge. I stood my ground as the thundering shape barreled toward me.

I braced myself and raised the staff.

Chapter 92

AS THE CHARGING HORSEMAN raised his ax, I darted to the side opposite his weapon. I swung my staff as hard as I could at his mount's legs. The animal neighed in pain, buckled, then threw its rider. The Tafur hit the earth with a mighty crash and rolled over several times until he came to a stop ten feet from where I stood.

His giant war ax had fallen to the side. I ran to grab the weapon. In the time it took to arm myself, the Tafur had managed to right himself and draw his sword.

He charged at me with a ferocious roar.

I could see him go high with his blade and met his blow, our weapons colliding with a loud clang. We stood there eye to eye, each trying to drive his blade into the other's neck, muscles straining to the limit. All of a sudden the Tafur jerked his knee into my groin. The air rushed out of me. I gasped and bent in two. In the same instant, he swept his sword toward my knees, and I summoned every sliver of strength to counter with the ax.

Again we faced each other, eyes blazing. He tried to

head-butt me with the crown of his helmet, but I threw myself back. I stumbled, and the Tafur leaped at me, swinging his blade back and forth with a maniacal fury.

The Tafur saw that I was slowed. He laughed. "Come here, fairy. You look like you might want to feel a set of real balls."

I crouched back warily. His sword was too quick. In this form of fighting, I was no match for him. The ax was clumsy and heavy in my weakened grasp.

"Come . . ." He blew me a kiss.

I looked him in the eye, panting heavily. I knew I would not be able to ward off the blows much longer. I searched my mind for any form of skill or trickery I had seen in the wars. Then one clicked in. It was crazy, desperate, not a soldier's but a jester's trick.

"Why wait?" I said, lowering the ax, pretending to be beaten, out of fight. "What's wrong with now?"

I turned my back to him. I hoped I wasn't insane.

I bent into a deep crouch, flipped up my tunic, and let him see my rear. *"C'mon . . ."* I said. "I'd wait for a real man, but you're the only one here." I tossed the ax about four feet ahead of me.

In my crouch, I saw him raise his sword and come. Just as he was set to run me through, I sprang into a forward flip. The Tafur sliced at the air where suddenly there was no person. His sword stuck in the soggy earth.

I landed on my feet and in the same movement pivoted and grabbed the handle of the ax. I sprang back around as the surprised Tafur struggled to free his sword.

A look of panic spread over his face. This time it was I who laughed and blew *him* a kiss.

I swung with all my might and sent the Tafur's head hurtling like a kicked ball.

I sank to my knees, out of breath. Every muscle in my

body felt as if it were about to explode. I dropped the ax, sucking precious air into my lungs.

Then I rose and picked up my staff. As I did so, a snickering voice intoned, "Well done, *innkeeper*. But you must conserve your kisses. You may need one or two over here. . . ."

I turned. There was another Tafur. He had a black cross painted on his helmet, but his visor was up, revealing a cold, scarred face that I thought I had seen before.

But it was not the face I was focused on.

The bastard was holding Emilie.

Chapter 93

"LET HER GO," I told him. "This isn't her fight."

The Tafur was large and strong, and he twisted Emilie roughly by the hair with his sword edged into her neck. His dark hair was long and greasy and fell over his scarred face. A cross was burned into his neck.

"Let her go?" He laughed. The Tafur twisted Emilie harder. "But she is so pretty and sweet. What a treat she'll make for me." He inhaled her hair. "Like you, I am not used to sifting my pole through such highborn trash."

I took a step toward him. "What is it you want from me?"

"I think you know, *innkeeper.* . . . I think you know where we have met once before too."

I focused on his hard, laughing eyes. Suddenly the past rocketed through me. The church in Antioch.

He was the bastard who had killed the Turk.

"You are the one doing these terrible deeds?"

The Tafur grinned in recognition. He forced Emilie to

her knees. "I would be happy to let her go. You only have to hand over what is mine."

"Tell me what you want!" I shouted. "You've already taken everything I have."

"Not all, innkeeper." He forced Emilie's chin up and edged his silvery blade along her neck. She sucked in a gasp. "Where is it? Her future awaits."

"Where is what?" I screamed. I looked at Emilie, so helpless there. Anger flared in my blood.

"Do not toy with me, Red." The Tafur glared. "You were there in Antioch, the church. I saw you. You were no more praying than I was. Quick now, or I will ram my blade through her pretty skull."

I was there . . . Suddenly it came clear to me. The cross. The gold cross I had stolen from the church. That is what this was all about. Why so many people had died. "It is buried on the hill," I said. "Let her go. It is yours."

"I will not barter with you." The Tafur's face began to twitch with rage. "Hand me what I want, or she will be pig slop, and you next."

"Then take it. I stole it from the church. It was just a trinket to me. I don't even know what it is, what it signifies. Just let her go and I will bring the gold cross to you. Just let her go."

"Cross . . . ?" I could not tell if it was confusion or rage that shook his lips. He dug the blade into Emilie and spat, "I do not want your fucking cross, not if you took it from Saint Peter's ass. You know very well what prize you hold."

"I *don't* know!" My head was spinning. Panic shot through me. "I do not have anything else."

"You must." He jerked Emilie's head back.

"No!" I cried. *What else could it be?* I looked at this monster. Black Cross. He had killed Sophie. He had tossed my son into the flames. He had taken from me everything I loved. And now he would do it again. For what? *For a thing I did not have!*

"Whatever it is, is it worth following me all the way back from the Holy Land? Slaughtering innocent villages and children? My wife and child?"

"It is!" His eyes lit up. "Those souls are meaningless compared to it, and a thousand more like your wife and seed. *Now,* innkeeper!" he yelled. "Or I will rid the world of yet another you claim to love."

"No." I shook my head, at first numbly, then with rage. "You will not take anything else from me."

I looked at Emilie. Her eyes bravely met mine.

I knew if I charged him, he would *not* kill her. It was me the Tafur needed. I was the path to his precious prize, not her. He would not risk leaving himself unguarded. I gripped my staff firmly in my palms. It was all I had, this stick against his sword. And my hands. And my will.

In the next breath, I screamed and charged the bastard.

Chapter 94

I SWUNG MY STAFF at him with everything I had.

In the same instant, Black Cross flung Emilie aside and readied himself for my blow. He was huge and agile, and blocked it easily with his sword.

"What is this prize," I screamed, smashing and flailing my staff at all angles, "that you would murder people who had never even heard of it?" I swung at him again and again. For Sophie. For Phillipe. Each blow crashed harmlessly against his sword. I thought my staff would surely split, or that at any moment I would feel the sword run through my gut.

He forced me backward and began advancing, swinging his sword with half strength and forcing me to block the blows with the staff, the wood rattling in my grasp.

"I do not have it," I shouted. "I never have. You are mistaken."

He swung at my legs and I darted back. His sword chipped slivers of wood off my staff. "You were there, jester. The church in Antioch. We all sought it out. Do you think these nobles were fighting for the souls of a few nuns? You were there for what, jester, mass? You try to tell me you don't know that the relic you fought the infidel for, which lay for centuries in that vault, was not the same used to sacrifice our Lord, and stained with His holy blood?"

I had no idea what he was talking about. He cut at my torso. I blocked it again, the blade slicing against my hand, but it was only a matter of time before he landed the blow that would do me in.

"Did you sell it? If you have, your death will only be more warranted." He swung again, this time knocking me backward to the ground, shattering another piece of my staff, which I barely held up now in defense.

My knuckles bled. My mind ricocheted back and forth. "I do not have it. I swear!"

He swung again, the brute force of his blow almost breaking the staff in two. I knew it could sustain only a few more hits.

I heard shouts behind me. Emilie was screaming.

The Tafur's eyes flashed. "Give it to me, thief, *now*. For in another minute you will surely be in Hell."

"If I am," I said, whacking my stick at him, "it will only be to welcome you."

I was done. Out of breath and strength. I blocked his blows, but each one hacked a little farther into the staff. I wanted with all my heart to kill this man — for Sophie, for Phillipe — but I didn't have the strength.

He kicked me into a ditch off the road. I looked about for a weapon, anything to fight him. He raised his sword above my head. "I give you this final chance," he grunted. "Produce it. You can still go free."

"I have nothing," I yelled at him. "Can't you see that?"

He came down with his sword. I think I closed my eyes, for I knew this last, desperate defense would not hold. A chunk of my staff shattered. To my astonishment, *a patch of metal showed through.*

Black Cross slashed at me again and again, yet each time, the staff miraculously held. The wooden rod split open like a casing, revealing something underneath.

Iron.

My eyes clung to it. I was staring at the long, rusted shaft of an ancient spear.

The Tafur stopped, his gaze transfixed. The spear shaft led to a molding in the shape of an eagle, a *Roman* eagle. The blade that came from it — dark, blunt, rusted — was encrusted with a bloodlike stain.

Good Lord in Heaven. I heard myself gasp. I blinked, twice, to make sure I wasn't in Heaven already.

My staff . . . the wooden staff I had taken from the church in Antioch, from the dying priest's hands . . . It wasn't a staff at all.

It was a lance.

Chapter 95

I DO NOT KNOW how to describe what happened next.

Time seemed to stand still. Neither of us moved, held by the incredible sight. Whatever this was, I could tell by the Tafur's stupefied amazement that the lance was what he had sought all along. Now, miraculously, it was in front of him. His eyes were as large as moons. Though it was rusted and dulled, just a common thing, a glow seemed to emanate from it.

Suddenly he lunged for it! I yanked it out of his reach. He was still above me, with all the advantage. He reared back his sword. I had no defenses. He would surely split my chest this time.

I thrust with the only thing I had — the lance. The blade split his mail and pierced his ribs. Black Cross cried out, his dark eyes open wide, but even with the lance in him, he did not stop. He went to raise his sword again. I pushed the lance in deeper. This time his eyes rolled back in his head. He tried to lift the sword once more, his arms reaching the height of his head, hands squeezing the hilt.

But his arms suddenly dropped. He gasped, opened his mouth as if to speak, and blood leaked out.

I pushed hard on the lance again and he froze, upright, disbelieving, as if he could not lose now, not with his prize in sight, so close. Then with a final grunt, Black Cross crumpled and fell onto his back.

I lay there for a second, stunned that I was alive. I forced myself to my knees and crawled to the dying man, his hands wrapped around the shaft of the lance. *"What is it?"* I asked.

He did not answer. Only coughed: blood and bile.

"What is it?" I cried. "What is this thing? My wife and son died for it."

I pulled the spear out of his body and held it close to the dying man's face. He coughed again, but this time it wasn't blood — he was laughing. "Do you not know?" His chest wheezed — and then, a thin smile. "All along . . . you were blind?"

"Tell me." I pulled him by the mail. "Before you die."

"You *are* a fool." He coughed again and smiled. "You are the richest man in Christendom and do not know it. Do you not understand what lay in those tombs for a thousand years? Do you not recognize your own Savior's blood?"

I stared at the ancient, bloodstained spear, my eyes almost bulging out of my head. The spear of Longinus, the centurion who had stabbed Christ while He was dying on the cross.

A numbness was in my chest. My hands began to tremble.

I was holding the holy lance.

Chapter 96

I STAGGERED to my feet, cradling the precious relic in my hands. Emilie rushed up first and threw her arms around my neck. The battle had ended and we had won. Georges, Odo, and Father Leo came running toward me.

Other people approached, cheering, dancing with joy, but I could not take my eyes from the lance. "My staff . . ." I was barely able to speak. "All along, it was the holy lance."

Everyone stopped, converged. A hush fell over the crowd.

"The holy lance . . . ?" someone repeated. A ring formed around us. Murmurs of exclamation and joy. All eyes fell on the rusted blade, the tip slightly broken.

"Mother of God." Georges stepped forward, his tunic splattered with blood. "Hugh has the holy lance."

Finally everyone knelt, myself included.

Father Leo examined the lance without touching it, fixing on the old, hardened blood upon the blade. "God's grace." He shook his head with a look of wonderment in his eyes. He recited scripture from memory: "But one of the soldiers with a spear pierced His side, and forthwith came there out blood and water."

"It's a miracle," someone shouted.

"It's a sign," I said.

Odo spoke, his coarse voice on the verge of laughter. "Jesus, Hugh, were you trying to save this thing until we really needed it?"

I could not speak. People were shouting my name. Stephen's henchmen were dead. I did not know whether it was our will or the lance that was responsible, but either way, we had beaten them back.

I looked at Emilie. What a knowing smile she had, as if to say, *I knew, I knew.* . . . I reached for her hand.

Everyone whooped and shouted. "Hugh. *Lancea Dei.*" Lance of God.

I had been saved. Not once but many times. Who could understand it? What had been entrusted to me? What did God want with an innkeeper? With a jester?

"The holy lance!" everyone shouted, and I finally threw my fist in the air.

Chapter 97

OUR VICTORY WAS COMPLETE, but it came at a great cost. Thirteen of Stephen's mercenaries lay on the ground, but we had lost four of our own: Apples; Jacqui, the stout and cheery milk woman; a farmer, Henri; and Martin, the tailor. Many others, like Georges and Alphonse, nursed messy wounds.

When the smoke cleared, the body of the Tafur I had fought with the lance was nowhere to be found. He had not died after all.

In the ensuing days, we extinguished the fires and bade good-bye to our brave fallen friends. For the first time in anyone's memory, bondmen had stood up to a noble. And to the fear that we could not defend ourselves simply because they were rightly born and we weren't.

Word spread fast. Of the fight *and* the lance. People from neighboring towns came to see. No one could believe it at first. Farmers and tradesmen had stood up against a noble and his men.

Yet I did not join much in the celebration. I spent the

next several days in a troubled state atop the hill. I couldn't work on the inn. I had to make sense of what had happened. That I had picked up the lance from the dying priest's hand in Antioch. That, penniless, I now held a prize worth kingdoms. *Why had I been chosen? What did God want of me?*

And a deeper dread hung over me. What would happen next — when news of the battle reached Stephen's ears? When he learned that we possessed the prize he so desperately coveted. Or when word reached Baldwin in Treille.

Had the poor tailor been right? *Had I saved them from one slaughter only to lead them to another?*

Emilie stayed with me the whole while. I looked at the lance and did not know what to do, but to her, the answer was clear. She understood what I resisted. "You have to lead them, Hugh."

"Lead them? Lead them *where?*" I asked.

"I think you know where. When Stephen hears of this he will send more men. And Baldwin . . . your village is pledged to him. He will not permit such rebellion in his domain. The stone has been pushed, Hugh. You've sought a higher destiny. Here it is. It's in your hands."

"I'm just a lucky fool," I said, "who picked up a silly antique, a souvenir. I'll end up the biggest fool of all time."

"I saw you in that costume many times, Hugh De Luc." Emilie's eyes shone brightly. "And never once thought you a fool. A while back, you left this town on a quest to make yourself free. Now, leave it again and free them all."

I picked up the lance, weighed it like a measure in my hands.

Lead them against Baldwin? Would anyone follow? Emilie was right on one thing. We could not remain here. Baldwin would burst a vein when he heard the news.

Stephen would send more troops, this time hundreds. Something had been started that could not be drawn back.

"You will be by me?" I took her hand, searched her eyes. "You will not change your mind when we are standing against Baldwin's army and it is just us two?"

"It will not just be us two," she said, crouching beside me. "I think you know that, Hugh."

Chapter 98

THAT DAY, I called the town together in the church. I stood at the front, in the same bloody rags I had worn in the fight, holding the lance. I took a sweeping look around the room. The place was full — the miller, Odo, even people who never went to church.

"Where have you been, Hugh?" Georges stood up in his place. "We've all been celebrating."

"Yes, that lance *must* be holy." Odo stood too. "Since it found you, it's been hard to even buy you an ale."

Everyone laughed.

"I do owe you an ale," I said, acknowledging Odo. "I owe you all an ale, for your courage. We did a great thing the other day. But the ale must wait. We are not done."

"Damn right we are not done." Marie, the miller's wife, stood up. "I have an inn to run, and when that fat bailiff comes back, I intend to stuff him so full of squirrel droppings he pukes himself dead."

"And I'll be happy to serve it to him." I smiled at Marie. "But the inn . . . it has to wait too."

Suddenly everyone noticed the look on my face. The laughter settled into a hush.

"I pray I have not drawn you in against your will, but we cannot stay here. Life will not return to what it was. Baldwin has made a promise to all of you, and he will keep it. We have to march."

"March?" Voices rang out, skeptical. "To where?"

"To Treille," I answered. "Baldwin will come at us with everything now. We must march against *him*."

The church went silent. Then, one by one, people shouted up to the front.

"But this is our home," the farmer Jean Dueux protested. "All we want is for things to go back to the way they were."

"Things will never go back, Jean," I said. "When Baldwin hears of this, he'll send his henchmen to ride down upon us with the full fury of his will. He will raze the town."

"You talk of marching against Treille," Jocelyn, the tanner's wife, declared. "Do you see any war horses or artillery? We're just farmers and widows. "

"No, you are not." I shook my head. "You're fighters now. And in every town there are others, who have farmed and toiled their entire lives only to hand over what their liege demands."

"And they will join us?" Jocelyn sniffed. "These others? Or will they just cheer and cross themselves as we march by?"

"Hugh is right," Odo's deep voice cut in. "Baldwin will make us pay, just like the bailiff promised. It's too late to back down."

"He will surely take my lands anyway," Jean moaned, "after what's happened here."

"H-Hugh has the lance," Alphonse said. "It is a greater weapon than all the arrows in Treille."

Shouts and murmurs rose around the church. Some stood in agreement, but most were afraid. I could see it in their faces. Am I a soldier? Am I fit to fight? If we march, will others follow?

Suddenly a pounding was heard from the church steps outside. People froze. *Everyone in town was already inside.*

Then three men stepped into the doorway. They were dressed in working hides and tunics. They knelt, made the sign of the cross. "We seek Hugh," a large one said, taking off his hat. "The one with the lance."

"I am Hugh," I said from the front.

The man grinned at his companions, seemingly from relief. "I am glad you truly exist. You sounded more like a fable. I'm Alois, a woodsman. We've come from Morrisaey."

Morrisaey? Morrisaey was halfway between here and Treille.

"We heard about your fight," one of the others said. "Farmers, bondsmen fighting like devils. Against our liege. We wanted to know if it was true."

"Look around. *These* are your devils," I said. Then I showed him the lance. "Here is their pitchfork."

Alois's eyes grew wide. "The holy lance. Word is that it changes things for us. That it's a sign. We couldn't just sit by and twiddle our thumbs if there was going to be a fight."

My chest expanded. "This is good news, Alois. How many men do you have?" I was hoping it was more than these three.

"Sixty-two," the woodsman shouted proudly. "Sixty-six if the fucking Freemasons don't back down."

I looked around the church. "Go back and tell your townsmen you are now one hundred and ten. A hundred *fourteen* if the fucking Masons take part."

The man from Morrisaey grinned at his companions again. Then he turned back. "Too late for that . . ." he said.

He swung the church doors open wide. I saw a crowd in the square. Everyone rushed out of their seats to look and saw woodsmen carrying axes, farmers with hoes and spades, ragged-looking peasants carting hens and geese. Alois smiled. "Already brought 'em."

Chapter 99

THAT WAS HOW IT BEGAN, that first day.

Barely a hundred of us, farmers, tailors, and shepherds, makeshift weapons in hand, food and other supplies carted behind. We started on the road toward Treille.

But by the next town we were two hundred, people kneeling before the lance, grabbing their belongings. By Sur le Gavre we were *three* hundred, and at the crossroad between north and south, a hundred more were waiting, clubs and hoes and wooden shields in hand.

I marched at the front, carrying the lance. I could not believe these folk had come to follow me, in a fool's suit, yet at every corner, more joined us.

They knelt — husbands, wives — kissing the lance, and Christ's blood, singing praise and vowing the nobles would crush them no longer. Banners were hoisted, with the purple-and-white lions of Treille upside down or with the crest slashed and tattered.

It was like the hermit's march all over again. The hope and promise that had captured my soul more than two

years before. Simple men — farmers and serfs and bondmen — banded together to raise up their lives. Believing
that the time had finally come. That if we stood up with the
might of numbers, no matter how long the odds, we could
be free.

"Are you tired of being shat on?" went the refrain as we
wound past a watching goatherd.

"Aye," came the reply. "I've been tired my whole life."

"And what would you risk," another would shout, "to
gain your freedom?"

"All I have. Which is nothing. Why do you think I'm
here?"

The ranks swelled with people from all corners of the
forest. *"Follow the lance"* was the cri de coeur. *"The lance
held by the fool."*

By St. Felix, we had grown to seven hundred strong. By
Montres, we had lost count. We could no longer feed them;
we had no more stocks or provisions. I knew we could not
stand a drawn-out siege, yet people continually joined.

Near Moulin Vieux, Odo edged his way up to the front.
Behind us was a column of peasants at least a thousand
strong.

The big smith grinned, walking alongside me. "You
have a plan, don't you, Hugh?" He eyed me warily.

"Of course I have a plan. You think I brought all these
folks along for a picnic in the woods?"

"Good." He sighed. He dropped back into the ranks.
"Never doubted . . ."

"Of course Hugh has a plan," I heard him whisper to
Georges the miller, a row behind.

From Moulin Vieux, Treille was two days' march
away. That night, I curled up at our fire with Emilie. Behind us, the glow from hundreds of others lit up the night.
I stroked her hair. She nestled close. "I told you this was

no accident," she said. "I told you if you stood up to lead they would follow."

"You did." I held her. "Yet the real miracle is not them, but you. That you have followed."

"For me there was no choice." She rolled her tongue and toyed with my jester's tassel. "I always had a thing for a man in uniform."

I laughed. "But now comes the real miracle. Treille is two days away. I have a thousand men and only fifty swords."

"I overheard you had a plan," Emilie said.

"The outline of one," I admitted. "Father Leo says we should draw up our demands: that taxes must be reduced immediately, that all fiefs should apply toward purchase of a parcel of land, that any nobles who take part in raids must be brought before the court."

"Look at the numbers." Emilie nodded optimistically. "Baldwin will have to sue for peace. He cannot fight us all."

"He won't fight us." I shook my head. "At least not right away. He knows we cannot provision such an army for a long siege. He will wait us out. He'll stall, and let the songs subside, until the food runs out and people lose patience and start to go home. Then he will open the gates and send out his dogs to slaughter us. He will chase us down and burn our towns so thoroughly even the scavengers will not think anything was once alive there. I've seen Baldwin's diplomacy. He will never submit."

"You have known this from the start, haven't you? That the duke would never comply. It was what was troubling you back at Veille du Père."

I nodded.

"So if you know this, Hugh, what then? All these people, they've given you their hope, their very lives."

"What it means . . ." I tucked my head onto her lap, begging to drift off to sleep. ". . . is that we must *take* him."

Emilie raised herself up. "Take him? In order to take Baldwin you must seize his castle too."

"Yes." I yawned. "That is usually the case."

Emilie shook me. "Do not jest with me, Hugh. This requires weapons and provisions. For this you have a plan?"

"The outline of one, I told you. It lacks but one thing." I curled myself into her warmth. "Fortunately, it is the thing you are best at."

"And what is that, Hugh?" She pounded my shoulder.

"A *pretext,* my lady." I glanced up and winked.

Chapter 100

DANIEL GUI'S SWORD CLATTERED as he rushed into the duke's sitting room. He was Baldwin's new chatelain, having taken over for Norcross.

"You can't go in there," said a page, flashing a cynical wink. "The duke's in council."

"The duke will find this news more urgent than any meeting," Daniel said, and pushed by the page.

His lord was upright against a wall, his leggings down, fucking a young chambermaid.

Daniel cleared his throat. "Liege."

The maid gasped and fixed her skirt, running out through another door.

"I am sorry to interrupt," the chatelain said, "but I have news you must hear."

Baldwin pulled up his leggings as if it were the most natural thing in the world and tied his tunic. "I hope this news is crucial, chatelain, for it has taken me months to back that little sow up against a wall." He wiped his hand across his mouth.

Baldwin disgusted the young chatelain. Daniel looked at his position as a chance to serve his native town, not plunder and slaughter defenseless subjects. He told himself that being in the duke's pen was not tantamount to being a pig.

"It is news of the redhead you seek. The jester who escaped after killing Norcross."

"Hugh. That little canker." Baldwin sprang alive. "What of him? Speak!"

"He has turned up. In his own town, after all. It seems he has led an uprising there against a raiding party from Borée."

"Uprising? What do you mean, *uprising?* There's nothing but field mice and manure out there."

"Apparently these field mice defended their nest quite well. Our messengers report all of Stephen's men were killed."

Baldwin shot up out of his seat. "You tell me this little maw-worm has led a bunch of farmers and hayseeds against Stephen's crack troops?"

"It is so, but it is only the tip of it, my lord." A tremor of enjoyment rippled through Daniel, as he knew the next piece of news would send Baldwin into a rage. "The thing Stephen's men sought . . . this will amuse you . . . was apparently a relic stolen from the Crusade. Some kind of lance . . ."

"The holy lance?" The duke pursed his lips skeptically. "The holy lance belongs to a jester? You must be mistaken, chatelain. The holy lance, if it even exists, exceeds in value everything I own. It is a child's fancy to conceive it could be in the hands of that kitchen-rot."

"Then apparently it is a tale children from all over seem to believe. And grown men too. For they flock to him as to a crusade. The whole region is up in revolt."

"Revolt!" Baldwin's eyes were ablaze. "There is no revolt in my domain. Rouse the men, chatelain. We'll ride tonight and nail the little bastard to a cross if he's so holy."

"I do not think that is wise, sir."

"Not wise . . . ?" Baldwin stepped up, eyes twitching. "And why is it not *wise?*"

"Because," said the chatelain, "this little maw-worm, as you call him, commands an army of these worms over a thousand strong."

The color drained from Baldwin's face. "*A thousand . . .* That cannot be. That is all the towns in the forest. That is three times the size of our own garrison."

"Perhaps more," Daniel said. "This news is days old. Every peasant in the duchy seems to have joined him."

Baldwin sat down on a bench. His face was taut, the color of spoiled fruit. "Ready the men anyway, chatelain. I will call to my cousin in Nîmes for additional troops. Together we will cut them down in the forest like saplings."

"Then I think you must hurry," Daniel said. "For these cowherds are in Moulin Vieux as we speak. It appears they are coming *to you.*"

Chapter 101

WE CAME TO THE EDGE of the forest only a half day's march from Treille.

There it was, in the distance — many towered, seemingly hung in the clouds, the sun glinting off its ochre walls. The good mood of our march dimmed, replaced by a troubled silence. There would be no deceiving them now. All of Treille — including Baldwin — now knew we were here.

I called the people closest to me together: Odo, Georges, Emilie, Father Leo, and Alois, the woodsman from Morrisaey. I had constructed a plan, but it depended on help from within. "I have to go into Treille," I told them.

"I do too," Odo chortled. "And Georges. And Alois here. I want to open Baldwin's eyes. With an eye wrench."

"No." I smiled at his joke. "I meant alone. In Treille, I have friends who will help."

"Just how do you intend to get in there?" Georges asked. "Sneak past the guards while Odo here juggles balls? They'll never let you through the gates."

"Listen, if we are to take this castle, it can only be through trickery, not force of arms. Baldwin has few friends, even within his own walls. I have to gauge the mood inside."

"All right, but it's a huge risk," Alois agreed. "So what's your big plan?"

I pointed toward the town. "Father, your eyes are best. Are those riders coming from there now?"

Everyone spun their heads to see.

"Where?" Father Leo said. "I don't see anyone."

When the priest turned back, I handed him his prayer beads, which I had lifted out of his robe. His eyes widened with surprise. Emilie smiled. Everyone started to laugh.

"I'm a jester. You don't think I would go in there without a trick or two?"

Odo grunted skeptically. "Your tricks may be artful enough here, but if you drop the ball in there, the rest of us are left plowing the north field with our God-given hoe, if you catch my drift. Send someone else."

"I don't see another way." I shrugged. "Except to surround the castle with our shovels and picks and storm Baldwin's army in one massive charge."

Odo and Georges swallowed uneasily at each other, considering that unseemly prospect.

The smith glanced around, weighing my suggestion, then slapped me on the back. "So, Hugh, when do you go?"

Chapter 102

THAT NIGHT, I LAY with Emilie by a fire. I felt her nervousness as I wrapped my arm tightly around her.

"Don't be worried for me," I said.

"How could I not? You are walking into a lion's den. . . . And there are other things on my mind."

"What things? The stars are out. We are here. I can feel the beating of your heart. . . ."

"Please, do not mock me, Hugh." Emilie turned in my arms. "I cannot help myself. My mind has been returning to Borée."

"Borée . . . ?"

"Anne." Emilie rose up on an elbow. "Stephen's wrath will be great now that his men have failed. He'll want this lance more than ever. I am worried for her."

"I don't share your concern."

"I know you have no love for her." She stroked my face. "But Anne is a prisoner too, just as surely as if she were behind bars. You must understand that. I am pledged to her,

Hugh. It is a bond I simply cannot run away from and break."

"You are pledged to me now." I tickled Emilie's ribs. "Can you break that one?"

"No." She sighed and kissed me on the forehead. "That I will never break."

Emilie rested with her head on my chest, the distant campfires lighting up the night. She sighed, so I knew she was happy, but then a shiver rippled across her shoulders. "What happens," she said warily, "once Baldwin is defeated? Things cannot just go back. These lands have been in his family for generations."

"I have been thinking that too," I said. "I have no wish to govern. Only to right this wrong. I was thinking I would write to the King. I have heard he is a fair man."

I turned her face to me. "You said you know the King. You said your father was a member of his court."

"Well, yes . . . I have met him, but . . ."

"Then you could intercede," I said. "You could tell him we are only humble men who want to return to their lives and work in peace. We have no thought to stealing anyone's title or territory. He will have to see."

I felt Emilie nod, her chin upon my chest, but distantly, as if she was not convinced.

"Do not be so worried for me." I held her tightly. "You have made me strong."

"I do not worry just for you, but for all that will follow. For you, I have a secret charm."

"And what is this charm that will protect me?" I laughed, stroking her hair.

"I'm coming along."

"What?" I raised her up. "There is no way, Emilie. I can't allow it."

"There is *every* way," she said, her eyes unwavering.

"I am in this as deeply as you, Hugh De Luc. I told you, we are together, our fates entwined. I am going with you. That is all."

I moved to argue, but she stopped me with a finger to my lips. Then she put her head back on my chest and held me as if she would never let go.

Chapter 103

DANIEL GUI BOLTED into the planning room.

"My lord, your jester's army has been sighted. It lies half a day from the city, at the edge of the forest."

"You mean the rabble." Baldwin sniffed. His advisers, the bailiff and chamberlain, seemed delighted with the news.

"You must attack, then," the bailiff wheezed. "I know these peasants. Their courage will crumble at the first sign of a fight. Their resolve is only as strong as their last ale."

"It appears their resolve has stiffened," Daniel observed. "This jester has given them hope. They outnumber us three to one."

"But we have horses and crossbows," Baldwin said. "They have only tools and wooden shields."

"If we go after them in the woods," Daniel said, "all our horses and crossbows would be reduced to nothing. Your men would be slaughtered just like Stephen's. The jester has this lance. It emboldens them."

"The chatelain is right, my lord," said the chamberlain.

"Even if you won, you would turn each carcass into a hero's grave. You must hear their demands. Consider them, even disingenuously. Promise them the slightest gain if they return to their fields."

"You are wise, chamberlain." Baldwin grinned. "These peasants have no means for a long siege. They will grow bored and tired as soon as their bellies start to ache."

The bailiff and the chamberlain puffed back their agreement.

"Do not forget, my lord," Daniel cut in, "the jester has this lance. They believe it makes them right."

"This lance will rest in Treille before the negotiation is done," said Baldwin. "They will give it up for a bag of wheat. And they will give *him* up too. I will have the fool's head upon his precious lance and place it before my bath."

"I merely meant," Daniel pressed on, "that you take a risk by inviting this siege."

Baldwin slowly rose. He walked around the table and put his arm across Daniel's shoulders. "Come," Baldwin motioned him toward the fire. "A word with you, by the light."

A lump grew in Daniel's throat. *Had he gone too far? Had he angered his liege, whom he was pledged to serve?*

The duke wrapped his arm around Daniel tighter, drew him close to the flames, then smiled. "Do you for a moment think I have any intention of handing over even a cup of grain to this traitorous puke? I would be the laughingstock of France. I have contacted my cousin. He sends a thousand troops.

"Let the idiots begin their siege. We will eat meat while they boil roots. When the reinforcements arrive, we will open the gates and crush them. You and I, Daniel, we will make sure not a single gray-haired grandfather among this rabble leaves Treille alive."

Baldwin brought Daniel's hand so close to the flames that he had to restrain himself from crying out.

"No one threatens my rule, least of all these miserable spawn. So how does that plan sound, *chatelain?*"

Daniel's heart pounded furiously. His mouth was dry as dust. He looked into his liege's eyes and saw nothing but dark holes. "Most wise, my lord."

Chapter 104

THE FOLLOWING NIGHT, outside the gates of Treille, a Hebrew merchant, carrying his sack of wares across his back, approached the gates as they began to close.

He wore the dark wool robe and the fringed shawl of the Sephardim, a skullcap upon his head, and held a rusted staff. With him was his young wife, dressed in modest clothes, her hair pinned under a black scarf.

"Move it along, Jews," growled the guard. The checkpoint was manned by a team of pail-helmeted soldiers, hurrying the travelers along like oxen into a pen. The guard stopped the merchant when he reached the gate. "Where do you come from?"

"From the south." I peeked from under my hood. "Roussillon."

"And what is in the sack?" He poked at it.

"Wares for the kitchen. Olive oil, pans, a new utensil called a fork. You stab your meat with it. Want to see?"

"What if we stab *you* with it, you little pests? You say

you came from Roussillon? What have you seen? We've heard the forests are teeming with rebels."

"In the east, perhaps, but in the south there are only squirrels. And Italians. Anyway, it's no concern to us."

"No, nothing's a concern to your lot, except a fee. C'mon." He pushed us roughly. "Get your tick-bitten asses in."

Emilie and I hurried through the gates. Inside the thick limestone walls heavy beams were braced against the ground to bolster the gates against assault. I glanced around. The towers and ramparts were manned by dozens of troops. They were heavily armed with crossbows and lances, gazing eastward.

From under my hood, I flashed Emilie a wink. "Come."

We climbed the hill leading to the center of town and Baldwin's castle. Soldiers on horseback shot about, clattering over the rough stone. Carts dragged rocks and shields down to the outer walls. The defenses were being readied. The air was sharp with the sulfurous smell from vats of burning pitch.

"Here . . . this way," I said. It was the market street. Stalls of bakers and butchers were still open for business, and swarming with flies. Others, which sold tin and tools and cloth, were closed for the night.

Emilie and I hurried through a neighborhood that seemed to be home to these merchants. There were not only huts, but stone houses, some with iron gates guarding small courtyards. The smell of burning lard was everywhere.

I stopped before a two-story dwelling with a tin scroll-like ornament hammered next to the doorway. "Emilie, we're here."

I knocked on the door. A voice called out from inside,

some shuffling, then the door cracked open. A familiar face looked out from under a skullcap.

"We've traveled a long way," I said. "We were told we would find friends here."

"If you are in need, we are friends," the man replied. "But who told you this?"

"Two men in the forest," I said.

The man arched his brow, confused.

"One named Shorty. I asked him what position makes the ugliest children. When he could not say, I told him: 'Ask your mother!'"

The man's eyes grew wide, then his beard parted into a smile.

"So, Geoffrey." I grinned, removing my hood. "Can it be you do not remember your jester?"

Chapter 105

THE MERCHANT WHOSE LIFE I had saved on the road to Treille broke into a hearty smile. He held me by the shoulders, then hugged me, and hustled Emilie and me through the door. I took off my skullcap and shook out my red hair.

Geoffrey laughed. "I said to myself, you look like no Jew I had ever seen before."

I laid down my staff and unfastened my robe. "This is Emilie. She's a close friend. This is Geoffrey, who once helped save my life."

Isabel and Thomas came in from another room. We were led to a sitting room lined with weavings and old scrolls and tracts. Geoffrey offered us his bench.

"What is the mood of the city?" I asked.

He frowned. "Foul. What used to be a thriving city is now just a pigpen that feeds the duke. And it will only get worse. There is talk of an uprising somewhere, an army of peasants in the forest who took up arms, headed here. Farmers, shepherds, woodsmen, led by a fool with some kind of relic gotten from the Crusade. . . . A lance with their Savior's blood on it."

"You mean *this?*" I took out my staff and let his eyes travel over it. I smiled. "I have heard of such an uprising."

The merchant's eyes grew wide. "This is *you.* . . . You are the jester. . . . *Hugh.*"

I nodded. Then I told Geoffrey my plan.

Chapter 106

THE FOLLOWING MORNING, my work was done and it was time to head back to the forest.

Emilie agreed to stay behind in town. It was safer for her there, with the terrible battle that was to come. She fought me gamely, but this time I would not back down. When it was time to leave, I hugged her close and promised I would see her in a couple of days.

She leaned up and kissed me. "God bless you, Hugh." Tears welled in her eyes. "In all the world, I hope to see you again."

I hoisted my sack and headed down the lane, waving a final farewell at the end of the street. I buried my head in my hood and hunched under my shawl, avoiding any eyes in uniform. As I wound back down the hill, I turned, watching the town recede. A tremor of panic ripped through me that I might never see Emilie again.

When I got back to the forest, I found the men waiting and ready for a fight. We marched at the break of dawn.

Farmers, woodsmen, tanners, and smiths, in every form of clothing imaginable, carrying homemade bows and wooden shields, stretched out as far as I could see.

At the head of the procession, I felt my blood surge with pride. Whatever the outcome, these men had stood tall. They were people of courage and character. To me, they were all highborn.

Every settlement we came to, a crowd formed, cheering us on. "Look, it is the jester," they would exclaim. They would bring out their children too. "See, child, you will always say you saw the lance."

Word spread like a brushfire. More joined us all the time.

All the while, Treille grew closer, the color of an amber sunset. Its formidable towers reached high into the sky. The nearer we got, the more the mood stiffened; the ranks grew worried and quiet.

The sun was high when we reached the outskirts of town. No force had charged out to confront us yet.

Instead, downtrodden townspeople stood aside, exhorting us on. "It is the jester. *See,* he exists! *He is real!*"

The massive limestone walls of the outer city rose above us with their crenellated battlements. At each opening, I could see teams of soldiers, their helmets gleaming.

They did not attack, though. They let us come. They allowed us to march within a hundred yards of the outer walls.

Just out of arrow-shot, I signaled the column to a halt.

I ordered the ranks to fan out around the perimeter, forming a massing ring twenty men deep. No one knew what to do, to shout or charge.

"Go on, Hugh," Georges said with a smile. "Go on and tell 'em why we're here."

I stepped out, trying to calm the thumping in my chest. I shouted to the defenders above the gate.

"We are from Veille du Père, and Morrisaey, and St. Felix, and every town in the duchy. We have business before Lord Baldwin."

Chapter 107

FOR A MOMENT there was no answer. I thought, *What do I do now? Say the same words again?*

Then a brightly clad figure whom I recognized from my stay here as Baldwin's chamberlain leaned out. "The lord is napping," he yelled back. "He knows no business before him today. Go back to your wives and farms."

Curses and taunts began to rise from the crowd. "The pig is napping?" someone growled. "Let us be careful not to wake him up, friends."

A thunderous jeer rose. Weapons rattled, shouts rang out.

Someone rushed forward and pulled down his leggings. "Come on, Baldwin. Here's my ass. Try and fuck me now."

A few rash ones charged up to the walls, spitting curses and insults. "Stay back," I yelled. But it was too late.

From the ramparts came the blood-chilling whine of arrows in reply. One man gagged, an arrow piercing his neck. Another clutched his head. A young boy sprinted up and hurled a stone, which fell halfway up the wall.

A wave of burning black pitch rained down on him. The boy fell, rolling on the ground, his skin sizzling with flame.

"Go home, you stinking filth," spat a soldier from the top.

Now everyone moved forward in a rush. Some of us shot off fire arrows, which streaked across the sky and died harmlessly against the massive walls.

Volleys of arrows whooshed down on us in return, so heavy and strong they tore through flimsy shields and pierced men in two. The volley sounded like a thunderstorm.

Images from the Crusade burned in my brain.

I waved frantically for everyone to move back. Some were angry and wanted to charge. They had followed me for days with little food. All they had thought of was striking their picks and hammers against the walls of Treille, tearing it down chunk by chunk. Others, seeing blood and death for the first time swarmed back, afraid.

This is what Baldwin wanted. To show that our makeshift weapons were useless. Anger was setting in, and we hadn't even begun the siege. My blood was racing. I had brought a thousand men here. We had the town surrounded. We had the will to fight but not the weapons to break through. All Baldwin had to do was open the gates and I knew all but the most hardened fighters would turn and flee.

But the gates did not open. No warhorses thundered out. He was probably amused at our spineless lack of resolve.

The commitment of this entire army hung in the balance. All eyes looked toward me.

A farmer carrying a broken hoe came up to me. "You have brought us here, jester. How will we take this castle?

With *this*?" He threw the hoe down as if it were a useless twig.

"No." I tapped my chest where my heart was. "We will take their castle with *this*.

"Get the raiding party together," I told Odo. My spine stiffened with resolve. "We go tonight."

Chapter 108

THAT NIGHT, as most of our ranks dozed, I got together the twenty brave men who would sneak into the castle.

There was Odo and Alphonse from our town, Alois and four of his best from Morrisaey. For the rest, we chose strong-hearted men we could trust, who would not back down from killing with their bare hands.

One by one, they arrived before my fire, wondering, *why were they here?*

"How do you intend to take this castle with *us*," Alois asked, "when you can't make a dent in it with a thousand men?"

"We'll have to take it without a dent," I said. "I know a way inside. Come with me now or go back to sleep."

We armed ourselves with swords and knives. Father Leo blessed us with a prayer. I handed him the lance. "On the chance that I don't return."

"Are you ready, then?" I looked around at the men. I clasped each of their hands. "Say good-bye to your friends. Pray we see them on the other side."

"Are we talking about Heaven?" Odo asked.

"I was speaking of the wall," I said, and faked a laugh.

Under the cover of night, we crept away from the campsites and out behind the hutted settlements and narrow streets that clung to the city walls. Torches lit up the defenses above us, lookouts peering for signs of life. We crouched in the shadow of the wall.

Odo tapped my shoulder. "So, Hugh, this ever been done before?"

"What?"

"People like us, bondmen, rising against their liege."

"A group of farmers rose against the duke of Bourges," I said.

The smith seemed satisfied. We crept a little farther. He tapped me again. "So, how'd it turn out for them?"

I pressed my back against the wall. "I think they were slaughtered to a man."

"Oh." The big smith grunted. His face turned white.

I mussed his shaggy hair. "They were discovered talking under the walls. Now shush!"

We continued, creeping along the east edge of town. In the crook of a ravine, we came across a shallow moat. It reeked, stagnant with putrid water and sewage. It was more of a large ditch; we could cross it with a jump.

At each point, I scanned the base of the wall for a sign of the tunnel once shown to me by Palimpost. *None* . . . As we moved along, the terrain grew tougher to traverse and the walls rose high above us, too tall for any kind of assault. That was good; no lookouts would be manning the walls here.

But where was the blasted passageway?

I began to get worried. Soon it would be light. Another day. There was the chance Baldwin would unleash his warriors to break our will.

"You're sure you know what you're doing, Hugh?" Odo muttered.

"Hell of a time to ask," I snapped.

Then I spotted it: a formation of piled rocks concealed behind some brush on the bank of the moat. I sighed with relief. *"There!"*

We scurried down the embankment and straddled the moat. Then I pulled my way up the other side. I ripped through the dense brush and began to tear apart the pile of rocks.

The declining pile revealed the entrance to a tunnel.

"Never doubted you for an instant." Odo laughed.

Chapter 109

THE CRAWL SPACE WAS AS I REMEMBERED —
dark, narrow, barely enough room for a man to pass. And
shin-deep with murky, foul-smelling water trickling down
to the moat.

There were no torches to light our way. I had to trust my
instincts against the dark, feeling along the cold, rocky
walls. I knew each one in my party had his heart in his
throat too. It was like crawling into Hell — cold, pitch-
black, odiferous. Floating shit and other refuse lapped
against our feet. Moments stretched along like hours. With
every step, I grew less sure of the way. After countless
prayers, I came upon a fork in the tunnel. One path continued up, the other went left. I decided to follow the path upward, since the castle stood at the top of the hill.

Suddenly a blast of air hit me from ahead. I noticed light
slanting onto the wall. I quickened my pace and came to a
spot I vaguely remembered. *The dungeon.* Where Palimpost
had sneaked me into the tunnel.

I passed the word, *"Ready your weapons."* Then, with a deep breath, I pressed at the stone in the cave where the light trickled in.

It moved. I pushed it a little more. The slab gave way.

Soon, all twenty men had pulled themselves out of the tunnel. By my reckoning, it was still before dawn. The relief detail had not come.

Two guards were asleep, their feet up on a table. A third guard snoozed on the stairs.

I signaled Odo and Alois, and each silently crept behind one of the guards. We had to take them quickly. Any sound would be as good as an alarm.

At my nod, we were on them. Odo took the one on the stairs, and as he gagged on a loud snore, wrapped his thick, muscular arms around the man's throat.

Alois cupped his hand over the mouth of one sleeping at the table. His eyes flew open. As he strained to scream, the woodsman slid a sharp blade across his neck. The guard's legs stiffened and shook, more of a spasm than a fight.

The third was mine. At the sound of commotion, he blinked himself awake, befuddled. I bashed him in the face with the hilt of my sword. He toppled backward, kicking the table aside, and landed, mouth bloody, on his back.

He reached behind him for an iron stake leaning on the wall. François, one of the Morrisaey woodsmen, stepped up.

"No need to be so civilized." The woodsman shrugged and hammered him to the floor with his club, stepping on his throat and pinning the struggling jailer's airway with his huge foot. In a minute, the man's arms relaxed.

"Quick," I said to Odo and Alois, "into their uniforms."

We stripped the guards and donned their purple-and-white tunics. Then we put on their helmets and armed ourselves with their swords. We dragged the bodies back down the corridor.

Suddenly there was the creaking of a door opening above. Voices coming down the stairs.

"Time to wake up, sleepyheads," someone called. "It's almost light. Hey, what's going on?"

Chapter 110

IN AN HOUR'S TIME, fourteen of our men stood about the courtyard, dressed as Baldwin's own brigade.

The rest kept from sight, concealed behind the dungeon door. Three of Geoffrey's friends had helped lure soldiers into our trap.

Odo and I stood guard at the dungeon door, looking for a sign that the duke was conducting business. Across the courtyard, two guards stood with halberds on either side of the castle entrance. Others crossed back and forth at a crisp pace, wheeling weapons and armaments down to the ramparts.

From down the road, we could hear our own men massing at the city walls — shouting and taunting, just as I had ordered them.

Finally I spotted Geoffrey entering the courtyard. He scratched his head, then flashed me a purposeful nod.

"It's time," I said, rapping at the dungeon door.

Odo slid it open. The balance of our party, some still in their own clothes, headed out. In the hubbub of people moving about, no one noticed. We made our way across the courtyard. We were joined by the rest of our ranks in Baldwin's uniforms, loitering about.

As we approached the castle guards, one of them lowered his halberd in our path. "Only military personnel in the castle today."

"These men have business before the duke," I said, indicating those not wearing guards' uniforms. "They have come from the woods and know of the jester."

The guards hesitated. They eyed us up and down. My heart beat wildly. "We've come from the wall," I said in a firmer voice. "Do you have the time to conduct an investigation when there's important news to deliver to the duke?" Finally, eyeing our uniforms, the guard retracted the halberd and let us by.

We were inside the castle. I boldly led the group through the main vestibule toward the great hall.

To my surprise, the halls were not as busy as I expected. Most of the duke's manpower was defending the walls. The times I had been here before, these same halls were crowded with petitioners and favor-seekers.

I led the way to the great hall. Two more guards stood at attention before the large doorway. The duke's voice bellowed inside. My stomach churned.

"We are wanted within." I snapped a nod to the guards. I wore the purple and white. We'd made it this far. No one made a move to block us.

Our ranks sifted into the duke's large meeting room. It was just as I remembered when I had been a jester here, except that then, it had been packed with people conducting business; today, I saw mostly Baldwin's retinue and knights.

Baldwin was slouched in his chair. He wore a military

tunic with his crest and high leather boots. His sword was sheathed in an ornate scabbard.

The pig!

A high-ranking officer was concluding a report on the scene outside the walls. Two of my men remained behind, near the guards at the doorway.

"My lord," the chamberlain said, "the rabble has made a petition for you to consider."

"A petition?" Baldwin shrugged.

"A list of demands," the new chatelain, who had presumably taken over for Norcross, explained.

My men circulated around the room. Odo and Alphonse took positions behind the duke. Alois and two others from Morrisaey edged near the chamberlain and the chatelain.

"Who brings these demands?" Baldwin perked up. *"Our fucking jester?"*

"No, my lord," the chamberlain replied. "Your jester is nowhere in sight. Perhaps he is afraid to get out of bed. But it is as we spoke. Let them deliver their complaints. And you give them the impression that you will seriously take them into account."

"Into account." Baldwin stroked his beard. He turned to the chatelain. "Chatelain, choose your lowest, most unfit soldier, prop him up on a mule, and send him out to receive these grievances. Have him convey to the filth that they have his assurance it will receive our most urgent review."

A few of the knights snickered.

The chatelain stepped up. "I beg you, sir, not to mock these men."

"Your protest is heard. Now, hurry off and find this latrine-cleaner. And Gui, when your man is safely back, kill a few of them. Just to assure them we are placing their petition under our most urgent review."

"But my lord, they will be protected, under truce," the chatelain said hesitantly.

"Are you whining again? *Chamberlain,* do you think *you* could head to the walls and carry out this decree? My military man seems to have come down with a case of cold dick."

"I can, my lord." The fat weasel scrambled away.

About the room, everyone stood aghast at the chatelain's rebuke.

"Now." Baldwin stood, staring around the room. "Is there anyone else in here who has a similar plan?"

"Yes," I shouted from the back of the room. "I think we should *attack.* Attack your enemies in the west."

Chapter 111

BALDWIN POUNDED his fist. "We don't *have* any fucking enemies in the . . ." Then he fixed perfectly still. His eyes bulged like dark plums. "Who said that? Who is that man? Come forward."

I stepped out from the crowd and let the military tunic fall off my shoulders. I stood in my checkerboard tunic and leggings. I removed my helmet. I watched his eyes home in on my face.

"You do *now*. . . ." I winked at him.

Baldwin's face drained of color. Then he stood and pointed at me, saying, "It's him. The jester!"

Soldiers went for their arms but were immediately intercepted by men in their own uniform, *my men,* pressing swords to their throats.

The chatelain made a move toward me, but Alois subdued him before he drew his sword.

"Seize him. Do you hear?" Baldwin ordered the guards behind his chair.

They moved toward me but in almost the same motion

took hold of the duke. Odo was one of them. He placed a knife against Baldwin's throat; Alphonse dug his sword into the middle of Baldwin's back.

The duke's eyes grew wide with disbelief. He looked at his knights, many of whom had scrambled for their arms.

"If they charge, you're a dead bastard," I said to him. "It would give me much pleasure."

Baldwin looked about, his neck muscles twitching. Outrage smoldered in his eyes. All around, men loyal to the duke were held at knifepoint. Some knights drew their swords, looking to Baldwin for the word.

"Tell them, arms *down*," I said. Odo pressed his knife and finally drew a trickle of noble blood.

Baldwin's eyes flitted desperately from side to side as he estimated the probable outcome of any resistance.

"Trust me, liege, these men who hold you hate you more than I do," I said. "I do not know if they will even heed me, they want to spill your guts so badly. But on the assumption that they want their children to live in peace more than they want your steaming entrails on the floor, I beg you, tell the knights to put down their arms. Otherwise, when I drop my hand, *you are dead*."

Baldwin did not answer but continued to look about. Then he nodded almost imperceptibly. One by one, the knights' blades clattered to the floor.

My chest heaved a sigh of relief. "Now we go outside, my liege. You'll tell your men on the walls to lay down their arms."

The duke swallowed, a lump slowly traveling down his throat. "You are insane," he spat.

"And you seem to be a little *foolstruck* as well, my lord, if you don't mind me saying."

An amused snicker traveled across the room.

"You will be dead by nightfall." Baldwin burned his

gaze into my face. "Towns will come to my defense. To rise against a lord this way, you could only be the biggest fool in history."

I looked slowly around the room. Odo curled back a smile, then Alphonse, then Alois.

"Perhaps the second biggest," I replied.

Chapter 112

WE DRAGGED THE LORD BALDWIN outside, forcing him at sword point to the castle gates.

Each soldier we passed looked on with dumbfounded shock. Some, no doubt eager to resist, looked to their liege for a sign, but at the sight of Baldwin's beaten eyes, and the bailiff, chamberlain, and chatelain trailing submissively behind, they held their weapons at their sides.

As we marched, stunned townspeople rushed to line the streets. A few began to jeer. *"Look at Baldwin. It's what you deserve, you greedy hog."* There was laughing, and scraps of food and debris began to be thrown.

As we approached the walls, I saw that word must have traveled ahead. Soldiers were just staring at us, lances and bows held at their sides.

"Tell them the battle is over." I pushed Baldwin forward. "Tell them to lay down their arms and open the gate."

"You can't expect them to stand by and let in that mob," Baldwin sniffed. "They will be ripped to shreds."

"Not a soul will be harmed; you have my word on it. Except, of course, *you*," I continued, pressing the sword in deeper, "if you fail to comply. My guess is, not one of them would mind the sight of that very much."

Baldwin swallowed. "Put down your arms," he said through gritted teeth.

"Louder." I prodded him.

"Put down your arms," Baldwin shouted. "The castle is lost. Open the gates."

Everyone remained still. In disbelief. Then two of my men ran and threw off the heavy beams that secured the gates. They flung the doors open, and a band of our men, Georges the miller at the lead, burst in.

"What took you so long?" the miller said, coming up to me.

"Our liege was so thoroughly set on hearing each last grievance, we lost track of time." I grinned.

Georges ran his eyes over the captured duke. No doubt he had been thinking of this moment for a long time. "My apologies, lord. You raised our taxes. I think I owe you my last installment."

With that, he spat a thick yellow wad all over the duke's face. Georges's eyes remained on him while the spit slowly trickled its way down Baldwin's chin. "Now here's *my grievance*." He put his face close to the duke's. "I am Georges, miller of Veille du Père. I want my son back."

All around us, farmers and peasants spilled into the streets and climbed up the ramparts. Hesitant soldiers climbed out of the towers and ran terrified off the walls.

A few people started to shout my name, *"Hugh, Hugh, Hugh . . ."* I looked with pride at the miller and Odo, and we thrust our arms victoriously into the air.

Chapter 113

WE TOSSED BALDWIN into his own dungeon — into the dark, cramped cell where I was once held myself.

There was much in those first hours that needed my attention. With the duke under lock and key, his soldiers had to be disarmed, and the plotting chamberlain and bailiff put under guard. The chatelain too, though, strangely, I did not feel him an enemy. Order had to be maintained in our ranks as well if we intended to press our case in a peaceful way before the King.

My mind ran to Emilie.

Where was she? I needed to share this with her. Our victory was as much hers as mine. A flash of worry went through me.

I hurried out of the castle and down the narrow streets in the direction of Geoffrey's home. People tried to stop and cheer me, but I pushed through, keeping up a brave face but inwardly beseeching them to let me pass. *Something was wrong!*

My pace quickened as I neared the market. Some of the

merchants shouted my name, but I ignored them and finally turned down the street to Geoffrey's house.

I pounded on the door. Something now terrified me. I slammed my fist against the door, my heart galloping with each desperate knock.

Finally the door creaked open. Isabel was there! She had a look on her face that was first pleased to find me well, then all at once serious and alarmed. I knew that something was wrong.

"She's gone, Hugh," she muttered.

"Gone?" *Gone where . . ? How?* All the strength in my body seemed to drain away.

"At first I thought she went to find you, but just a while ago I saw this."

Isabel handed me a note, scribbled in a hurried hand.

My brave Hugh,

Do not fear as you read this, for my heart is yours — always. But I must go.

By now, your victory is complete. I was not wrong, was I? What once was will not always be. You have climbed a rung to your own destiny. To see you do this, confirm the specialness I saw in you from the first, nothing in the world could make me more proud.

But now I must return to Borée. Don't be angry. Anne is like a mother to me. I cannot abandon her and be joyous in the glow of your triumph.

Please, do not worry. There are some things I have not shared with you, and even Stephen would not dare do me any harm. Write the King, Hugh. Make your triumph true. I will do my part.

This was so cruel. My eyes welled with stinging tears.

I could not lose her. Not now, after so much had happened. I swallowed hard, struggling to read the end:

> *You have been my true love since I saw you that very first day. I know I shall say that to you when we see each other again. I hold up my palm. Remember the words,*
> *In all the world . . .*
> *Emilie*

Chapter 114

"WHO IS THERE?" a cranky voice barked from behind the door. "Speak to me!"

Emilie hunched inside her dark hood. The familiar testiness was like an old friend, and it made her smile. "Have your wits become as dull as your jokes, Norbert?" she called back.

Slowly the door to the jester's chamber cracked open. Norbert peeked out, his tunic open to his chest and his hair tousled and awry.

At first, he regarded the huddled shape suspiciously. Then, as she removed the hood, his eyes opened wide. *"Lady Emilie!"*

Norbert glanced down the corridor to make sure she was alone, then spread his arms and embraced her. "It's a beautiful sight to see you."

Emilie squeezed him back. "It's good to see you too, jester."

Norbert hurried her inside his room. He shut the door, then frowned. "It's a beautiful sight, my lady, but not necessarily to see you *here*. You've taken a great risk to come back. But tell me quick — you've been with Hugh?"

Emilie brought him up to date. First, on the raid on Veille du Père and the existence of the lance. *"The very staff you sent to Hugh."* Then, of the incredible events that followed. The townspeople who had risen up with him. Treille. With each piece of news, the jester's eyes grew more incredulous, his cackles of delight more unrestrained.

When she told him of Baldwin's capture, he danced around and fell back on his mat, kicking his legs with glee. "I knew that boy was a gift from God, but *this* . . ."

He lifted himself back up, his laughter subsiding. He studied her face, the rosy cast of her cheeks. "But tell me, my lady . . . why are you here now?"

Emilie lowered her eyes. "For my mistress. It is my duty."

"Your mistress! Then you have traveled a long way and at much risk for no end. Things are much changed here. The duke dreams of killing Hugh with the zeal of a dog slobbering over a cooking roast. Does anyone know you have arrived?"

"I mingled with a party of monks returning from pilgrimage. I came to you first."

"That is wise. Your last running off is exposed. It is assumed you were with Hugh. If not for Lady Anne's protest, Stephen's guards would be looking for you too."

Emilie's face lit up. "I *knew* she would be true. I was right about Anne."

Chapter 115

IT TOOK SEVERAL DAYS to completely secure Treille. There were a few stubborn knights still loyal to Baldwin. And word of a purported reprisal from one of the duke's supposed allies. But no reprisal came.

Treille was ours.

Now there was the matter of what to do with it.

There was the issue of the duke's treasury, which had been fattened on the backs of those who now occupied his city. And vast stores of grain and livestock had to be redistributed fairly.

A debate raged between those who had been with us from the start and those who joined later about what to do. Georges said give out the keys to the grain holds. Let each man leave with a sack and a hen. Alois said why stop there. *Raid the treasury. Redistribute all the money. Put a noose to the bastard!*

I wished Emilie were there. I had no skill to govern, nor the urge. I did not know exactly what to do, or what was right.

It was only a matter of time before I would lose my army. The ranks were growing impatient. They wanted to go back to their homes. *"It's harvest time,"* they said. *"When do we get what we were promised?"*

And not just food and money. They needed laws to protect them. The right to choose: where to live, whom they would serve. If a man was pledged to a lord, need his children and their children be bound by the same pledge? Someone had to rule on such things.

One night, I found a sheaf of paper, Baldwin's seal, and a vial of viscous, red-tinged ink. I sat down and started to write the most important letter of my life.

To His Majesty, Philip Capet, Ruler of France,

I pray God grants me the words by which to write this, for I am a humble townsman. A bondman, in fact, thrust into a larger role.

I am said to be the leader of a group of brave men who have risen up against our liege lord after repeated cruel and unnecessary attacks.

I write from Treille, Your Majesty, where I sit at Duke Baldwin's own table, his lordship held prisoner, while I await word from you as to what to do next.

We are not traitors, far from it. We bound together to fight cruel injustice, and only when it threatened our safety and well-being. We bound together to demand laws, so that rape and murder could not be committed on us freely, and property destroyed without cause. We bound together to free ourselves from a servitude without end.

Is it such an incredible dream, Sire, that all God's men, common and noble alike, should be governed by just laws?

We have done all this with little bloodshed. We have

acted in peace and respect. But our ranks grow weary. Please send us word, Your Majesty, of your conviction on such matters.

In return for your judgment, I offer you the only tribute I have — but, I think, a worthy one: the most holy treasure in all of Christendom, thrust into my possession in Antioch.

The very Lance that pierced the Lord Jesus Christ upon the Cross.

It is a treasure worth having, yet, amazing as it is, it is not nearly as great as the hearts of these men who serve you.

We await your answer,

In faith, Your humble servant,

Hugh De Luc, Innkeeper, Veille du Père.

The lance was leaning against the table. What if I had died in that church at the hands of the Turk? I thought. What if none of this had taken place?

I folded the parchment and bound it with the duke's own seal. I saw that my hands trembled.

A most miraculous thing had just taken place. I, a bondman, a jester by trade, a man without a home, without a denier to his name . . .

I had just addressed a letter to the King of France.

Part Five

SIEGE

Chapter 116

"YOUR GRACE!" Stephen knelt to kiss the ruby ring of Barthelme, bishop of Borée, even though he thought him the most air-filled, well-fed functionary in France. "So good of you to join me on such short notice."

Bishop Barthelme was a corpulent, owl-eyed man with a sagging jowl that seemed to sink almost undetectably into his massive purple robe. Stephen wondered how such a man could take a step, or climb a stair, or even perform his sacraments.

"You have taken me from my sext for this?" the bishop wheezed.

At Stephen's nod, a young page filled two silver cups with ale.

"It's called alembic." Stephen raised his goblet. "It is brewed by monks near Flanders."

The bishop managed a smile. "If it's God's work, then I feel I have not strayed too far."

They both took a deep draft. "Aaah." The cleric licked

his lips. "It is most sweet. Tastes of apples and mead. Yet I feel you did not call me to hear my opinion of your ale."

"I have asked you here today," Stephen said, "because there is a hole torn in my soul which you can help mend." He leaned close. "You have heard of this uprising in the south, where a jester has led a rabble of peasants."

Barthelme smirked. "I know a stupider man does not exist than Baldwin, so it is not so far-fetched that he was outfoxed by a fool."

Stephen put down his cup and glared through the bishop's haughty smile. "Let me get to the point, Your Grace. Do you know what this jester carries with him, that is the source of his appeal?"

"The message of a better life. The freedom from bondage," the bishop said.

"It is not his *message* that I speak of, but his *staff*."

The cleric nodded. "I have heard that he parades around with a spear purported to be the holy lance. But these petty prophets are always claiming this or that . . . holy water from the baptism of Saint John, burial shrouds of the Virgin Mary."

"So this does not concern you?" Stephen asked. "That a trumped-up country boy uses the name of our Lord to incite rebellion?"

"These local prophets." The bishop sighed. "They come and go like the frost, every year."

Stephen leaned forward. "And it does not concern you that this peasant marches around with the word of Christ, inciting the rabble to overthrow their lieges?"

A smile etched onto the cleric's face, the smile of a gambling man with knowledge of the outcome. "What do you want, Stephen, for the church to fight your battles? Shall we contact Rome and declare a holy crusade against a fool?"

"What I want, Your Grace, is to strike these ignorant puppets where they most ache. More than their bellies or their desires, or their silly dreams of this precious freedom they long to taste."

Barthelme waited for him, quizzically.

"Their *souls,* Your Grace. I want to *crush their souls*."

Chapter 117

NO REPLY CAME from the King, and day by day, the ranks grew more tired and impatient. These were not soldiers, prepared to occupy a city like Treille. They were farmers, tradesmen, husbands, and fathers.

Lookouts were scattered along the road to the north, but each day, no answer came.

Why? If Emilie had contacted him? If she was able. And what if she was not?

Then one day the lookouts did spot a party traveling south toward the castle. I was in the great room. Alphonse burst in. "H-Hugh, a party of riders is approaching. It looks like it could be from the King!"

We rushed to the city walls as fast as our legs would carry us. I climbed the ramparts and watched the party approach. Knights, carrying a banner, but not in the purple and gold of the royal flag.

But with a cross upon it. Knights pledged to the Church.

They escorted a rider in the center of their group, in the dark robes of a cleric.

We drew open the outer gates, and the party rode into the courtyard. A crowd gathered in the square.

"Is this good or bad?" Alphonse asked.

"I think it's good," Father Leo said. "The King wouldn't send a priest to rebuke us."

The gaunt, clear-eyed priest slowly dismounted. He wasted no time and faced the crowd. "I am Father Julian, emissary to his eminence Bishop Barthelme."

"I am Hugh," I said. I bowed and made the sign of the cross to show respect.

"My message is for all to hear," the priest said, passing his eyes right over me.

"'Occupiers of Treille,'" the cleric began in a loud, clear voice. "'Farmers, woodsmen, tradesmen, bondmen and free, all followers of the man known as Hugh De Luc . . . a *deserter* from the Army of the Cross, which still valiantly fights to free the Holy Land . . .'"

A flash of worry chilled my blood. The crowd grew still.

"'His eminence the Bishop Barthelme Abreau rebukes you for your false rebellion and urges you, this day, the seventeenth of October, 1098, to disband at once, and to return to your villages at once or face the full consequence of your actions: immediate and total excommunication from the Church of Rome and the separation from Grace, *forever, for your eternal souls.'"

The priest paused to observe the look of shock that was on every face, including mine.

"'His eminence insists,'" he continued, "'that you repudiate all teachings and promises of the heretic, Hugh De Luc; deny the legitimacy of and confiscate any relics or symbols claimed to be of holy origin in his possession.'"

"No." People shook their heads. "This cannot be. . . ."

The young priest shouted over them, "In the hopes that you will adhere to this decree immediately and that your souls may be made available to once again receive the Holy Sacrament, a two-day period of enforcement is declared. This edict is signed His Eminence, Barthelme Abreau, bishop of Borée, representative of the Holy See.'

Borée! I thought. *Stephen had done this!*

A frightened hush hung over the crowd.

"This is madness." Father Leo spoke. "These people are not heretics. They only fought for food in their mouths."

"Then I suggest they chew quickly," the young priest said, "and return to their farms before their souls remain hungry forever."

"This is Stephen's blackmail," I shouted to all around. "It is the lance he wants."

"Then give it to him," someone yelled, "if it buys back our immortal souls."

All around, our army looked terrified and overwhelmed. Some climbed down from the walls and meandered slowly toward the city gates.

"That's right." The priest nodded. "The Church welcomes you, but only if you act now. Go back to your farms and wives."

How could I fight against this poisonous assault? These brave men thought they were doing something good when they followed me. Something that God would shine on.

I watched as a steady stream of friends and fighters passed dejectedly by me and toward the city gates. A tightening anger burrowed deep into my chest.

We had just lost the war.

Chapter 118

THAT NIGHT, ODO FOUND ME huddled by myself in the chapel. I was actually praying. Praying about what to do. If there was indeed a God.

"I know we're deep in shit," Odo said with a snort, "if we've got *you* praying."

"How many of our men are still left?" I asked.

"Half, maybe less. By tomorrow, who knows? We still have some good ones. Georges, Alphonse, the Morrisaey boys ... Most of those who've been with us from the start."

I gave him a weak smile. "Still trusting me?"

"No, I wouldn't say that. Let's just say, if they're making their bet with God, they trust the holy lance more than they trust that slimy church mouse."

I pulled the lance from the bench next to me and cradled it in my palms.

"So ... ?" Odo said. "That thing providing any answers? What is next?"

"What is next," I replied, "is that it's me Stephen wants,

or at least *this* . . . not your souls. This edict is a challenge. 'Come face me if you have the will.' I've no choice but to go."

"Go?" Odo laughed. "You're going to march on Borée with what we've got left?"

"No, my friend." I shook my head. "I'm going to march on Borée *alone*."

It seemed to take Odo a second to decide whether to object or roll his eyes. "You're going to Borée?"

"You see what he's telling me, Odo? He has burned villages to get this lance. He killed my wife and child. He has Emilie now. What else can I do?"

"We can wait. Keep Baldwin under guard until word comes. The King will surely stop this lunacy."

"This *is* the King's word." I shook my head. "The King will side with Baldwin and Stephen without even hearing our claims. These men are pledged to him. They raise armies to fight his wars. *We* . . . what do we raise, hens?"

"Even a king can be swayed by a good omelet." The big smith chuckled. Then he looked at me plainly. "I am with you, Hugh, until the end."

I grabbed his wrist. "No more, Odo. You've trusted me more than any fool could ever ask for." I shot him a smile. "But now I have to face this. This *thing* . . . it has brought me mostly pain. But some things — seeing the town stand up, feeling the pride as we marched on Treille, Baldwin's face — they've been a joy."

"You've become quite a bad philosopher since you put on that skirt," Odo commented.

"Maybe . . . but I go alone."

Odo didn't answer, just took a deep breath and smiled. Then he looked around. "So this is what it's like on the inside of a church. The seats are hard and there's nothing to eat. I don't see the attraction."

"That makes two of us." I grinned in reply. We sat a moment, draped in silence.

"So where would we be," I asked, "if I hadn't wandered off that day on the Crusade? If I had never left, and Sophie and Phillipe were still alive. And Father Leo was preaching dull sermons. And you still put in an honest day's work."

Odo checked the window for the angle of the sun. "I figure, hoisting an ale. Listening to your stupid jokes."

I stood up, patted him on the back. "Then let's do that, friend. I'm sure there's a cellar here. And I still know a few you haven't heard."

Chapter **119**

AT DAWN THE NEXT MORNING, I pulled on my tattered jester's tunic, said good-bye to my old friends who had been with me from the start, put the sacred lance under my arm, and left.

Georges, Odo, Father Leo, and Alphonse met me by the city gates. I urged them not to buckle, but to remain and hold the city. That what we had done was right and would one day be honored.

But what *I* had to do now was right too. And I had to face it, alone, whatever the cost.

As I prepared to mount my horse, I gave Georges and Odo heartfelt hugs. "God bless you both," I said. I thanked them for following me, for believing. For taking the chance. In their strong, silent embraces and held-back tears, I felt the grip of a sadness that we might never see one another again.

Then I mounted the horse and, glancing back with a wink and a smile, headed down the hill. I vowed not to look back again.

At the base of the hill, with the gates closed and Treille rising behind me, I broke the promise to myself. I stared back at the tall, foreboding walls, the high, unscalable towers. The town that could not be taken. I couldn't help but utter a laugh. A spark of pride warmed my blood. Serfs and bondmen had seized their liege's castle without even fighting a battle. Baldwin's apoplectic face rose up in my mind — and for that single moment, it had all been worth it.

But now Baldwin was behind me. One final challenge lay ahead. It was with the person who had burned our village, who had killed my wife and child. Who now held the one I loved. I knew this battle was no longer simply about rights and freedom. It had narrowed to something deeper, personal.

I turned my back on Treille a final time and kicked my mount upon its way.

My mind was set on Borée.

Chapter 120

STEPHEN'S BOOT HEELS sounded loudly as he pushed into a small, squalid room near the rear of the barracks. Hunched silently in a dark corner, its occupant turned, a man who was filthy and covered with sores.

"Come, Morgaine." Stephen threw the door wide open. "Your moment is here again. I need to make use of your talents. You are still a knight, are you not?"

The dishonored knight slowly lifted his muscular frame off the floor. Tattered, soiled cloth still hid the spot where the lance had pierced his side, and the tiny cubicle reeked of putrefaction.

"I am here to serve you, my liege."

"Good," Stephen said. "You must air this place out. Your hygiene is odious anyway, Morgaine, but these days a latrine would smell less foul."

"It is unavoidable, my liege. The stench keeps the memory of my wound awake in my mind, and the lowly bastard who gave it to me."

"I'm glad your memory is fresh," Stephen said. "For if God grants, you will have a second chance for vengeance."

The Tafur's eyes lit up. "Each breath I force myself to take is in hope of such a moment. How?"

"Events, larger than you can contemplate, bring the fool back to me."

"The fool! He comes to Borée? You know this?"

"Do you think I would soil these boots in this pit of infection for any other reason? Now, get up. I will have the physician mask that stench."

The Tafur pulled his war tunic off the floor, still torn and bloodstained at the spot where the jester's lance had ripped through. He moistened his lips the way a famished man would awaiting, impatiently, a fresh roast.

"The thought of vengeance has made you alive again, warrior." Stephen grinned. His instincts had been good. He'd been right to save this drooling beast and not lop off his head when he crawled back without the lance.

"I will gut him," the Tafur said, grinding his teeth, "and let my sores drip in his wound so that he may die knowing the contagion that he inflicted on me."

"That's the spirit." Stephen slapped him on the shoulder, then looked at his own hand with distaste. He leaned close to the wounded warrior, as if they were drinking mates, then dug the hilt of his own sword sharply into Morgaine's side. He gasped.

"This time make sure you come away with the lance," Stephen sniffed.

"But first, there is other work to be done," he went on, returning to his earlier tone. "In your absence, all sorts of scum have come to Borée. That is why I need you. Whom else am I to trust?"

"Just tell me what you need done."

"Good." Stephen's look brightened. "That's what I

hoped to hear. You seem like a man who could use some entertainment, Morgaine. How about we order some up? Let us call upon the jester, Norbert. You know Norbert, don't you, Morgaine? Why don't we see if we can prod him to make us laugh?"

Morgaine nodded, and Stephen knew he understood perfectly. It wouldn't matter whose blood was on his blade, as long as it led to the fool.

"And Morgaine . . ." Stephen said as he departed the filthy room. "As long as it's a party, why don't we ask along the lady Emilie?"

Chapter 121

I HAD TRAVELED in the forest for two days, riding during light until my back ached, then, once it was dark, curling up in the brush, my mind racing as I drifted off to a troubled sleep.

I had just finished a few bites of bread and cheese that morning and was preparing to go on my way when I became aware of the slow advance of a rider approaching from behind.

I ducked behind a tree and took out my knife.

Gradually a single rider clip-clopped into view. A churchman, a friar, perhaps.

I relaxed and stepped out from my cover. "You must be either foolishly brave to chance these woods alone, Father," I called to the advancing shape, "or just as foolishly drunk."

The churchman stopped. "That's an unusual warning," he replied from under his hood, "coming from a man in a patchwork skirt."

To my shock, the voice was familiar!

He lifted his hood, and I saw it was Father Leo, with a smile the width of his face. "What are you doing here?" I exclaimed.

"I knew it was a risk," the priest said, brushing dust off his robe. "Truth is, it's taken me so long to find a true sign from God, I couldn't bear being separated from the lance."

I laughed and helped him brush off the road dirt. "You look tired, Father. Drink."

I handed Father Leo my calfskin and he tilted it back. "We will make quite an army when we get to Borée." I smiled. "The fool and the priest."

"Yes," the priest said and wiped his mouth, "very imposing. I knew we would frighten no one, so I hope you don't mind that I asked along a friend."

"A friend . . . ?"

From down the road, the hoofbeats of another rider could be heard, and as he came close, I blinked twice and realized it was Alphonse. The lad trotted up to me dressed for battle.

"You two are crazy," I said.

"Dressed as you are, marching to attack the castle at Borée alone, and you call us *crazy?*" muttered Father Leo.

"Well, now we are three fools." I grinned, my heart warmed.

"No." Alphonse sniffed and shook his head. "No, we are not."

"Got anything good to eat?" another voice called from the forest. "Anything sounds good after these squirrels and lizards I've been chasing."

Odo!

I looked at the smith, dressed in his leather armor, carrying his mallet, one of Baldwin's purple-and-white cloaks slung around him. "I knew you must be behind this," I said, attempting to look stern.

"Nah." Odo grinned. He indicated with his head. "It was *him*."

Behind him, the miller thrashed his way out of the woods.

I faltered. "I put you in charge, Georges. I left you with Baldwin. And four hundred men."

"So you did, didn't you?" The miller winked.

From down the road, the heavy rumble of footsteps now rose in my ears. Many people, marching. From around a bend, the first of them came into view. It was Alois, from Morrisaey, and three of his townsmen.

The column grew. Alois's four turned into forty. Then forty more. Faces I recognized. From Morrisaey, Moulin Vieux, Sur le Gavre. Some on horses, others on foot. A lump caught in my throat. I didn't speak. They kept coming, line after line, men who still believed in me. Who had nothing left but their souls.

Then, on a pale stallion, bound like a sack of wheat, *I saw Baldwin*. And his chatelain close behind.

I could not believe what I was seeing!

"They all came? All four hundred?" I asked Alois.

He shook his head. "Four hundred and *four*." He grinned. "If the Freemasons came along."

My heart almost exploded with pride. I stood there watching the column grow and grow. Feeling the common heart of these men. Some called out to say hello, "Hey, General, good to see you again." When the end of the column came in sight, it was trailed by four scruffy men hurrying to keep up, hoisting a white banner with an eye painted on it — the sign of the Freemason society.

I mouthed "Thank you" to Odo and Georges, the words sticking in my throat.

I put my hand on the miller's shoulder.

"Guess we're going to Borée," Odo said with a shrug,

and I nodded, watching the column as it stretched down the road.

"You better have a real plan if you want to take *this* place," he muttered.

Chapter 122

JUST AS IT HAD HAPPENED weeks before when we marched on Treille, at every village we came to, every crossroad, people joined our ranks. Our fame had spread, and it was embarrassing. Certainly it was humbling.

Farmers in their fields, carpenters, goatherds with their flocks, ran to their fences to see a lord like Baldwin bound behind a fool.

"How can you continue on?" people asked in wonder. "Stephen has damned your very souls."

"He might as well," we called back, "since that's all we have left."

Once again I marched at the front in my tattered jester's suit, carrying the holy lance. But this time the army was properly outfitted. We had real swords and newly minted shields taken from Baldwin's men and painted in the green-and-red checkerboard that had become our crest. We also had crossbows and catapults to mount a siege, oxen and stores of food to sustain an entire army.

"You cannot take Borée," some mocked us. "A thousand men could not take Borée."

"We could not take *Treille,* either," Odo replied huffily.

"We trust the lance," Alphonse would say. "It is truer than any b-bishop's judgment."

New recruits fell constantly into line. *"I'll come. This is a new world if a lord is dragged by a fool!"* Young and old knelt before the lance and fell in.

Yet even as we marched, I knew this new battle would not be as easy as the last. Stephen would never let our ragtag army approach without a fight. He had a much larger and fiercer army than Baldwin. Better trained. He himself was known to be a formidable fighter.

And to be sure, *I was no general.* The only military skills I had were those I had picked up in the Crusade. Nor did Georges, or Odo, or any of my other men have any tactical training. They were farmers and woodsmen. An old worry began to consume me: that I could be leading innocent men, who believed in my call, to slaughter.

I needed a leader, but where could I get one?

The third night out, I wandered over to where Baldwin and his men were being held. The duke glared at me belligerently. I merely shook my head and laughed.

I knelt beside his chatelain, Daniel Gui. He was handsome and held himself with a strong bearing. He'd never complained of being a captive, unlike Baldwin, who spat curses and threats at anyone who met his eye. I'd heard other good things about him.

"I have a dilemma," I said as I sat on the ground next to him. I looked Daniel Gui in the eye, man to man.

"You have a dilemma?" The chatelain laughed, showing me his bonds.

"Mine first." I smiled. "I am at the head of an army, but I know little of how to fight a great battle."

"Is this a riddle, jester? If it is, let me play. I *know* how to fight, yet my army is disarmed and scattered."

I offered him a sip of ale. "It seems we are aligned yet opposite. But you command the duke's forces."

"I command Treille's forces," he responded firmly. "My job was to lead them in defense of my city, not slaughter innocent subjects that our lordship did not trust."

"Treille *is* Baldwin, though. You try and separate them, but you cannot."

"My *dilemma*." The chatelain smiled. He showed me his wrists. "By which I am now unfortunately bound."

"I need a general, chatelain. If we march on Borée, we will not overcome it with sleight of hand."

He took another sip of ale, seemed to think this over. "What do I get if I help you take this city?"

I smiled. "Mostly a lot of trouble with your old boss."

Daniel Gui grinned. "I'm not exactly sure I can return to that job now anyway."

Indeed, Baldwin would be already savoring the taste of someone to blame. "Only a chance," I answered. "The same chance any of us have. To sue for peace and go back and live our lives as free men."

"There's an irony here somewhere." The chatelain chuckled. "So far, you have taken my castle and put my liege in chains. You don't seem too bad a soldier for a man in a checkerboard suit."

"I was at Antioch and Civetot," I said, "in the Crusade. . . ."

The chatelain nodded in a deep and acknowledging way.

"So, will you help us? I know it will mean breaking your pledge to Baldwin. Your career may not be the brighter for it. Yet we are not such a bad bunch, for heretics and rebels and fools."

Daniel took in a deep breath and smiled. "I think I will fit in just fine."

Chapter 123

WE CAME OUT OF THE FOREST the next day facing a river. A truly terrifying sight stood before us.

On the high ground, directly in our path, waited an ominous horde of warriors. Maybe three hundred of them.

They wore no colors, just rough skins and high boots, swords and shields gleaming in the noonday sun. They were long-haired and filthy, and regarded us with no particular alarm. They looked ready for a fight.

Panic shot through our troops, and through me as well. The ferocious-looking horde just stood there, watching us assemble out of the trees. As though battle were an ordinary thing for them.

Horns blew. Horses whinnied. A few carts toppled over. At any moment, I expected them to charge.

I ordered our column to a halt. The rabble ahead of us looked restless. *Shit, had I led us into a trap?*

Odo and Daniel ran up to me. I had never seen Odo this scared.

"They growl like Saxons," Odo muttered. "These ugly

bastards are meaner than shit. I heard they live in caves and
when food is scarce, they eat their young."

"They are not Saxon." Daniel shook his head. "They are
from Languedoc. From the south. Mountain men. But they
are known to eat their young even when the harvest is
good."

His depiction gave me chills. "Are they from Stephen?"
I asked.

"Could be." He shrugged. We watched them watching
us, showing no concern about our larger ranks. "Mercenaries. He has used them before."

"Have the men fan along the ravine," I said. I hoped to
make a show of strength. This threat had come upon us so
suddenly. "Lances to the front in case they charge."

"Keep the horses in reserve," Daniel said. "If these bastards come at us, they'll do so on foot. To a Languedocian,
it's a sign of cowardice not to."

Everyone rushed into formation. Then we stood there,
hearts tense, holding our shields. The field was silent.

"Seems a good enough day to meet my maker." Odo
strapped on his mallet. "If you're still *listening*, God."

All of a sudden, there was movement in the Languedocian camp. *Get ready*. I gripped my lance.

Then two riders rode out from the pack and galloped toward us.

"They wish to talk," Daniel said.

"I'll go," I said. "Here." I turned to Odo. "Hold the
lance."

"I'll go with you," Daniel said.

Daniel and I rode out between the armies. The two
Languedocians sat there indifferently, eyeing us as we
came up to them. One was large and stout, built like an ox.
The other was leaner but just as mean looking. For a moment, no one spoke. We just regarded one another, circling.

Finally, the ox grunted a few words in a French I could barely make out. "You are the jester *Hugh?* The one with the lance?"

"I am," I replied.

"*You're* the little fart who has led the peasants and bond-men against their lords?" the other growled.

"We've risen up in the face of murder and oppression," I replied.

Ox snickered. "You don't look so big. We were told you were eight fucking feet tall."

"If we have to fight, it will seem that," I said.

The Languedocians looked me up and down in a way I could not read. Then they looked at each other and started to laugh. "*Fight* you?" The big one chortled. "We've come to *join* you, fool. Word reached us you intend to march on Treille. We are sworn enemies of that prick Baldwin. We've been enemies of Treille for two hundred years."

I looked at Daniel and we broke into grins. "This is good news . . . but you're too late. Treille is already taken. We are marching on Borée."

"*Borée?*" the thinner one said. "You mean against that prick Stephen?"

I nodded. "The same."

For a moment, the two Languedocians drew their horses close and huddled together. I could hardly understand the tongue they were speaking in. Then Ox looked back to me and shrugged. "All right, we march on Borée."

He raised his sword to his ranks and they erupted — lifting their swords and spears in a riotous cheer.

"You're lucky." Ox grinned through his beard. "We've been enemies of Borée for *three* hundred years."

Chapter 124

STEPHEN WAS IN his dressing room when Anne stormed in and found him, in a chair, peeling an apple. Annabella, a lady of the court, was bent over his waist, swallowing his cock.

At the sight of Anne, Annabella gagged. She jumped, frantically replacing Stephen's leggings as if to hide the evidence. Stephen looked on, seeming not to care.

"Oh, do not bother, Annabella." Anne sighed. "When the lord hears what news I bear, we shall all be amused to see to what size his manhood shrinks."

The lady smoothed her ruffled tresses, curtsied, then scurried out of the room.

"These are my private quarters, not your parlor," Stephen said, hitching himself up. "And do not feign offense, dear wife, since you obviously knew what business you would find here."

"I do not feign offense." Anne eyed him sharply. "Only regret, to have interrupted you from such pressing work."

"So." Stephen rose. "By all means, let me know. What's the big surprise?"

"A runner has arrived from Sardoney. He's brought word that your little jester is on the way. Two days out. With his lance."

"*This* is the news you thought would disarm me?" Stephen seemed to yawn, taking another deep bite from his apple. "That this poor fool marches on us? Why should this mean any more to me than a bite of this fruit, I say? But come," he said, eyeing the bulge in his hose, "as long as the table is set, why not put the little weasel to some work?"

Anne crept behind him and smoothed her hands across his chest, even though the pretense of such affection was as repulsive to her as kissing a snake. She bent down to his ear and whispered, "It is not the fool that I thought would concern you, my husband." She rubbed her hand near his cock. "But the thousand men who march along with him."

"*What?*" Stephen twisted around. He screwed up his face in disbelief.

"Oh, has the weasel crept back in his little cave?" Anne laughed. "Yes, my liege, apparently an army follows him that is even greater than before. An army of lost souls, *heretics,* thanks to you. And thanks to Baldwin, fully armed."

Stephen jumped out of his seat, hot with rage. "Impossible! They damn their souls to follow him."

"No, husband, it is *your* soul that is damned."

"Get out of my way." Stephen shot out his hand. It slashed across Anne's face, knocking her to the floor. "If you have any hope for that little brat you call your cousin, you will mock me no more."

"If you harm her, Stephen . . ." Anne forced herself up to her palms.

Stephen burned his gaze right through her. He moved as if to strike again. She did not flinch. Then the color came back into his face, and he softened and knelt, cupping her quivering face in the palm of his hand.

"Why would I want to hurt her, my precious wife? She is a part of you." He raised himself, smoothing his tunic, the veins in his forehead now calm. "I have merely detained her for her own protection. There are dangerous conspirators about who plan us harm, even within these very walls. *Haven't you heard?*"

Chapter 125

"LOOK." Men began to point. *"Up on the hill. There it is. Borée!"*

Above the rolling hills of vineyards and farms, its limestone towers rose with roofs of blue, like lapis etched into the sky. There was the facade of the famous cathedral, gleaming white; and the castle that I had stayed in, its donjons reaching to the sky — where Emilie was.

As we neared, the exhilaration spread: "I'm gonna take Stephen in one arm and his largest hen in the other, and squeeze them till they both lay a fucking egg," a boastful farmer yelled.

Behind me, my new army stretched for nearly a mile. In every row, men marched in different clothing: tailors, woodsmen, and farmers in their own garb, but with thrown-together mail and helmets they had swiped from Baldwin. They carried pennants from their towns, pikes and clubs and bows on their backs. Some even spoke different dialects.

The vast line included men and horses, carts drawn by

heavy oxen, and catapults, mangonels, and trebuchets with their loads of heavy stone. All beat a cloud of dust that seemed to smother the sky.

But the giddy boasts and dares began to fade the closer we got to Borée. This was no ant's nest in the middle of nowhere with a pompous duke who did not want to dirty his hands with combat. This was a city, the largest many of us had ever seen. We had to take this place! It was protected by rings of walls, each manned with archers and artillery. Its reserve of knights was twice our number, many of them emboldened by bloody victories in the Crusade. The closer we got, the higher the walls loomed over us. I knew the same reality drummed through every soul: *Many of us would die here.*

All around, farms close to the city were shuttered and abandoned, livestock nowhere to be seen. Plumes of smoke trickled into the sky, from bales of hay and grain carts set afire. Stephen was giving us no sustenance or quarter. He was preparing for a siege.

People we passed did not cheer us as at Treille. They spat at us or averted their eyes. "Go home, rebels, heretics. You're God's curse!"

"Look at what you've brought on us," a woman wailed, scavenging for food. "Go on, your welcoming committee lies just ahead."

Welcoming committee . . . ? What did she mean by that?

As we neared the city, men at the front pointed to what seemed a row of crosses lining the road. A few ran ahead.

As they did, their faces lost some color. A silence came over the ranks, which only moments before had been boasting of what they would do when they reached Borée.

The welcoming committee.

These were not crosses but bodies, some still alive, muttering, moving their limbs feebly, impaled on long shafts that split their torsos.

Some through the anus. Others, even worse, upside down. Men, young and old, farmers, tradesmen in common garb. Women too, stripped naked like whores, moaning, choking for breath, eyes glazed over in agony. There was a row of thirty of them.

"Get them down," I shouted. My heart sank as at Civetot, or riding into the damned village of St. Cécile. What had these poor people done? I rode by, barely able to look.

Then I stopped at one of the bodies. My blood came to a halt. My eyes actually rolled back in my head.

It was Elena, Emilie's maidservant.

I jumped off my horse and with my sword started to hack at the stake until it sheared, then I gently eased her down.

I lifted Elena's head in my hands and stared at her chafed white face, peeking through tufts of bloodied hair. She was in torn, soiled rags, desecrated like some shameless murderess. All the poor soul had done was serve her lady.

Anger dug into my ribs, sharp as a knife. If this was Elena, what had happened to Emilie?

What kind of warning was this monster giving me?

My breath stuck in my chest. I turned to the man behind me. "Bury her as well."

Chapter 126

FARTHER AHEAD, we came to a fieldstone bridge that crossed the river along the outskirts of the city.

It was guarded by a stone tower. I drew the ranks to a halt about sixty yards away. Three or four of Stephen's knights were waiting there, mounted on horseback, draped in their lordship's green-and-gold colors.

The first sign of the enemy.

They began to taunt us, questioning the size of our balls. "You call this rabble an army?" one yelled. He lifted his leg as a dog pees. "It's a bunch of peasants who wouldn't know a fight from a good fart."

"They are only trying to bait us into something stupid," Daniel cautioned. "Stay your ground. They will fall back as soon as we advance."

A few of the men, fueled by the horrific sight they had just seen, ignored him and ran toward the taunting soldiers, ready to do battle with their clubs and swords.

When they were about twenty yards away, archers appeared in the tower armed with crossbows. They sent a volley of arrows whooshing down. Four men dropped immediately, clutching their chests. The rest peeled back out of range.

Behind me, I heard Alphonse yell out, "They want their fight, they'll g-get it!"

"No," I called, "we can't lose more." But against my futile shout, he took off. He and his group ran bravely toward the tower.

Then one of our fire arrows struck the wooden roof of the guard tower. Chaos broke out among the archers as the flames caught. Our ranks began to cheer. For a second the enemy archers disappeared, then we caught sight of them on the ground, scampering back with their heavy bows toward the city walls.

Our men set after them, Alphonse leading.

At first, they were met by knights on horseback, who fought bravely. But soon there were too many of us to fight. Stephen's knights were pulled down from their mounts, their bodies bludgeoned with swords and clubs. Several of us went after the retreating archers, overtaking them in a gully by the river. One knelt, ready to fire into the back of one of our men, but Alphonse leaped and clubbed him into a heap.

To a man, the archers were hacked to bits. A chorus of cheers rose in our ranks. Our party of rescuers returned, dragging the wounded and dead, raising aloft captured crossbows.

It was our first engagement, and we had shown Stephen we were here to fight.

Chapter 127

EMILIE PULLED HER COVERS UP to warm herself in the dark, drafty tower room that had been her cell over the past days. The narrow slit of a window high up on the wall barely let in an angle of outside light. She was not sure if it was day or night.

For the past few hours, she had heard the rumble outside of troops and heavy carts being dragged down to the walls. Something was happening. A flicker in her heart told her it had to do with Hugh.

A pitcher of drinking water and a plate of half-eaten food rested on a table by her side with a few of her books and embroideries. But she had no appetite and no mind to read or weave.

Stephen was a dog, foaming with the madness of greed. All honor and law had been set aside to detain her. All reason too.

But it was fear for Hugh that gnawed at her, festered in her heart through the dark, isolated nights.

Hugh . . . Stephen would not dare harm her, but he

would see Hugh dead with the relish of a cruel child picking the wings off a fly. Now he prepared his army, his awful Tafurs, his archers, and his death-dealing machines of war.

"Do not come," she prayed, whispering herself back to sleep. "Please, Hugh . . . do not come."

But something was different this day. There was a far-off rumble. And a sharpness to the voices nearby. The tremor of large machines being wheeled into place.

Battle machines!

Emilie threw the covers from her bed. She wrapped herself in her bedclothes and dragged a table beneath the high window. Then she hoisted a sitting bench and placed it on top of the table. High above the floor, she balanced herself on the bench and craned her neck to see over the lip of the narrow ledge.

Below, on the inner walls of Borée, soldiers in pail helmets and green-and-gold tunics were bustling along the ramparts.

What was beyond was a sight that stole away her breath.

A vast gathering of men, beyond the walls, as far as the eye could see.

In peasant clothes, with weapons and oxen and mangonels.

An army of them. Stephen's edict be damned! She began to laugh. She could not help herself. It was as if everyone who had ever marched alongside Hugh were here. Every peasant in the forest!

Then something else caught her eye.

She raised herself on her toes as high as she could.

Her heart almost exploded. She wanted to scream at the top of her lungs, but she knew he was too far away and could not possibly hear her. She waved and shouted and whooped anyway. She heard herself giggling uncontrollably.

Standing there — in the very tunic she had sewn for him herself, facing Borée as if he knew *precisely* where she was — she saw Hugh.

Chapter 128

THE FOLLOWING MORNING, we pushed our siege engines forward under the watchful eyes of Stephen's men. Mangonels, their baskets stretched, followed by wheeled carts filled with giant stones, massive rams hewn from tree trunks and ladders stacked in piles.

We began the construction of wooden towers as tall as the outer walls, as well as smaller platforms called "cats" covered in moist, bloody hides to protect our charging ranks from the rain of burning pitch.

I was in Daniel's tent, running through the siege plans, when a shouting was heard outside. I rushed out and saw that everyone was running for their weapons and pointing toward the city gates. The drawbridge was lowering. *This was it!*

At any moment, I was certain, a formation of green-and-gold-clad knights would come swarming out.

As the portcullis opened, two priests clad in sacramental robes slowly rode out under the banner of the Church.

After a pause, Bertrand Morais, Stephen's chatelain, followed. And behind him, as if his presence alone would cause the field to kneel, a noble in full battle gear on a white charger.

Stephen himself.

Chapter 129

"HE WISHES TO TALK," Daniel said. "He hides behind the priests as a flag of truce."

"He wishes to trap you, more like it," Odo said. "You'd be a fool."

I couldn't wait to put my vengeful eyes on the bastard. "Don't forget." I put on my cap. "I *am* a fool."

I rushed to the front, found my horse, and called for Father Leo. "Come, here's your chance to be an equal to the highest priests in Borée." We fetched him a horse. "And Daniel?" I slapped him. "Want a chance to see a duke piss in his pants?"

We mounted our horses and rode halfway out into the rutted no-man's-land separating our camp from Borée.

Stephen waited for us to reach a spot. Then, gauging his distance from our archers, he trotted his own entourage to meet me. My blood was racing just to see this reptile. His look sent chills through me. He wore no helmet; his jet-black hair hung long and greasy. His elaborate chain mail had his dragon crest displayed on the chest. His hands were covered in studded gauntlets, and a heavy sword, befitting a Crusader, was strapped to his side.

As he reached us, he did not stay his horse. He circled us, his glance darting from my face to the lance.

Then Stephen drew his mount to a halt. He smiled quite amiably. "*So,* you are the deserting coward who rouses men against their lords in the name of heresy."

"And you are the prick," I said, unheeding, "who killed my wife and child. With all respect." I bowed to the priests.

"What a shame, then," Stephen said, "if a similar fate befell another whom you prize."

Fury tightened in my chest. "If any harm comes to her, it will take more than a delegation of priests to save you. Lady Emilie returned here of her own will, out of loyalty and concern for her mistress. She has no conflict with you."

"And do *you?* Jester, rebel, heretic . . . *How* is it I should address you?"

"Hugh," I said, fixing on his cold, superior eyes. "I am Hugh De Luc. My wife was Sophie. My son, who never saw his second year, was Phillipe."

"I'm sure all of us are delighted to hear your family tree, but what is it you want here, *Hugh?*"

"What do I want?" Part of me wanted to pull him off his mount right there and end this thing, just he and I. I directed my horse one step closer to him. "I want your admission of the wrongs you have done. I want restitution paid for each man, woman, and child killed in pursuit of *this.*" I put forward the lance. "I want the lady Emilie sent to me at once."

"And what if I said the lady Emilie was here of her own mind," Stephen snapped. "That it is her choice to stay, even upon my demand."

"Then I would call you a liar, Stephen. Or a hopeless fool."

"Again, jester," he said, yanking his horse, "you waste precious time on jokes. Your new chatelain will tell you, you are on the verge of a bloodbath."

"We are ready, my lord. This battle has your handprint on it, if it occurs, not mine."

Stephen ran his eyes over the lance. "You know, should I return with that, all I described could be avoided. You could have the little slut and ride off to the far corner of the earth for all I care. As for your men, I will see that we restore their souls."

"Most tempting," I replied, pretending to ponder his offer for a moment. "Problem is, my men have not assembled here for Lady Emilie, but for the single purpose of seeing the offenses of your rule brought to justice. They're here to demand recompense for your crimes. To see you bow down, lord, nothing less. Then I will give you the lance. That is *my* offer. In the meantime, with all respect to the bishop, we'll take our chances on our souls."

"I could simply take it, you know. My archers could cut you in half with just a nod."

"And mine too, my lord. Then God would have to decide."

A tiny twitch tremored on Stephen's nose. "You think I would trade the dignity of my name even for a vault of such lances?"

"It should not be so hard," I said, holding it close to his face, "since you have traded most of it already just to be *this* close."

Stephen reared his horse and smiled. "I can see why the court grew fond of you. Get prepared, jester. I will reply. Within an hour." He yanked his horse around and started to head back toward the gate.

Chapter 130

OUR ARMY WAITED just two hundred yards from the towering walls of Borée in a broad and teeming line.

Archers tensed their bows, fire arrows tipped in oil. Foot soldiers, some holding ladders like crosses, focused on the walls, on the line of silent green-and-gold defenders.

A thousand men, cradling their weapons, muttering last prayers, awaited my sign.

"What are you thinking now?" Odo asked.

I took a breath. "That Emilie is in there . . . And you?"

"That those are the biggest fucking walls I've ever seen." The smith shrugged.

I fixed on the impressive main gate, waiting for Stephen's reply. Odo to my left, Georges, Daniel, and Alphonse flanked to my right. The tension beat around like a drum of war.

Stephen's defenders crowded the walls, crossbows tilted down at us. There were no taunts or curses rattling back and forth, only a heavy silence hanging like a fog between the two armies. In the distance, the chirp of birds could be heard. Any moment, the tense calm would be shattered like a club smashing through glass.

All at once, from behind the walls, the *ping* of a catapult releasing pierced the air and a black projectile shot high into the sky. Murmurs rippled through the ranks, men pointing as the object descended toward our front line.

"Brace yourselves! Here it comes," someone yelled.

The projectile struck the ground and rolled to a stop only a few yards from where I stood. My stomach fell.

The mound had features — hair, charred and singed; startled, round eyes bulging out of their sockets.

I let out a sickened cry.

The face seemed to be staring at me. It had a grin that was both impish and impudent. The eyes spat back in their moment of death, familiar, unmistakable.

Norbert!

His eyes looked at me as they had that first day, when Emilie brought me to his chamber. I almost expected him to wink: *Had you fooled, didn't I, boy? That is the best you can do . . . ? Watch this!*

I rushed out of formation and knelt over the remains. My ears were filled with a deafening ringing. Countless images of things that had transpired since I first set out from home flashed before me.

The ringing finally subsided. I raised the holy lance and, perhaps for the first time, I believed in it. I looked at my men, who in their readiness reminded me of horses unwilling to be held back.

"Your freedom lies within those walls. Now," I shouted. *"Now is the time!"*

Then the cry from my lungs was drowned by the stampede of a thousand men hurling themselves at the walls of Borée.

Chapter 131

THE FIRST SOUND of battle was a belching groan from one of the mangonels, as a massive rock was launched high into the sky and crashed with a thunderous blast into the wall above the main gate. Fragments of stone and sparks and dirt exploded everywhere. But when the dust cleared, the wall still held.

Then another boulder whistled into the sky. Followed by a third, both striking high on the wall, shattering guard posts, sending bodies and battlements flying like debris. Then a volley of flaming arrows. *Whoosh.* Some struck against the walls, sticking in wooden battlements, where small fires ignited; others clattered harmlessly to the ground.

I raised my arm. "Now, men. What is yours is within those walls. *Charge!*"

Our men raced toward the walls in a mountainous wave of steel, spears, and ladders. Eighty yards. The closer we got, the larger the walls grew. Sixty yards . . .

I could see the faces of the defenders — ready for our charge, holding fast, waiting for us to come within range.

Fifty yards . . .

Then, all of a sudden, the cry of, *"Tirez!"* Fire!

Arrows whooshed down from above. Our warriors stopped in their tracks, arrowheads ripping viciously through their chests and necks. Hands clutched the exposed tips.

"Don't stop," I heard Daniel shouting. "Get behind your shields. You *must* make the wall."

The sweeping advance, narrowed to a crawl, continued. I saw Odo and Daniel and Georges in the first charge. *Twenty yards from the wall.*

Above us, soldiers stood and fired. Lances were flung in reply. Some defenders clutched at their chests with a yelp and fell over screaming, dropping from the walls.

Dozens of ladders were thrown against the walls, the men climbing up. Defenders reached over to push them off.

"Bring in the cats," I shouted, as waves of boiling tar splattered down on us, followed by screams and the smell of sizzling flesh.

The tall cats were pushed up to the front. For a moment, they provided a refuge from the smoldering pitch, which sizzled on the moist, stretched skins. Under this protection, men with a ram backed up and battered the gate over and over. Crossbows were fired from directly above. A man next to me, not wearing a helmet, had an arrow pierce the top of his scalp. From behind, the mangonels continued, and an enormous boulder crashed into a tower. A cloud of smoke shot up and when it cleared, the top of the tower was caved in and mangled body parts fell away from it like branches.

The once-shiny walls of Borée were soaked with mud,

pitch, and blood. I had no idea if we were winning or in the midst of being routed.

Many yards away, I spotted Odo leading a charge up a ladder. He wrestled in a tug-of-war with the lance of a defender, then Odo won, pulling his opponent over the edge.

Then another defender reared up and ran the point of his lance into the smith's leg. I *screamed*. Odo arched back in pain. He wrenched the lance out of the defender's grasp and frantically tried to pull the blade out of his leg.

"Odo!" I yelled, but the roar of battle made every shout indistinguishable from the others.

I watched him take two Borée soldiers by the tunics, then fall back against the wall, swarmed over by a wave of men. I tried vainly to fight my way along the wall to get to him, but the line would not yield.

Arrows rained down from above with terrifying force. Men were huddling under shields, starting to cry, realizing they were trapped. *Where was Odo?*

Those of our men who made it up the ladders were hurled backward or run through as they tried to fight their way forward. I realized we were losing. I could see the will in the men begin to bend.

Then a voice cried, *"Look out!"* A huge wave of rocks crashed down on us from above. One of the cats collapsed under the weight, pinning the men with the ram.

"The towers themselves are coming down," someone yelled. "Get back or be crushed."

But it was not the towers. Stephen's soldiers were toppling bins of heavy stone over the edge.

"Go back, go back!" I heard panic rippling down our line.

"Stay!" I yelled at the top of my voice, and so did Daniel. "Don't quit the fight now! Don't give up ground!"

But I realized we had lost. The rear of our line finally broke, men heading away from the walls at a dead run.

Nausea rose in my gut as the men peeled away, running for their lives. They were farmers and cobblers and woodsmen, not trained soldiers.

I trailed the field and scanned for Odo, arrows whizzing by my head. But the smith was nowhere to be found. The ground was piled with bodies. I could not believe our losses. I staggered back, finally out of arrow range.

I saw Georges limping on the shoulder of Daniel, both men as white as ghosts.

"Have you seen Odo?" I asked them. They shook their heads and stumbled on.

I turned back toward the castle. Men on the walls were cheering. They were shooting arrows at anything that moved. My best friend was still out there. What was once a blossoming field was now a swamp of blood.

Not a single man had made it over the walls alive.

Not one.

Not Odo.

Chapter 132

WE HAD LOST!

Alphonse hurled down his sword, unable to speak, as were so many others. Georges threw himself onto the ground, spent and drained. Father Leo did his best to comfort everyone, but his face was as desolate as any.

"You men must not let down your guard," Daniel yelled. "Stephen may send his horsemen to finish the job tonight."

His warning, however real, seemed a million miles away. Darkness was falling. Mercifully, as if its black cloak offered some reprieve. Our soldiers sat down around fires, exhausted, rubbing salve on their burns and other wounds. Some wept for their friends; others thanked God that they were still alive.

"Did anyone see Odo?" I looked around. I had known Odo since I was a boy. Alois and Georges merely shook their heads.

"He's a wily sort," Georges finally said. "If anyone could make it back, it's him."

"Many died today." Daniel sighed, spreading out a map of Borée. "We can't spend time on one more."

"The chatelain is right." Ox nodded. "Thirty of my men are dead, maybe more."

I looked in the Languedocian's eyes. "Your men were brave to join us. But this is not your fight. I release you from your pledge. Go, take the rest home."

Ox stared back as if insulted. "Who said anything about going home?" He cracked a toothy smile through his beard. "In Languedoc, we say a good fight doesn't even begin until some blood is on the floor."

Around the fire, we all started to laugh. Then the din subsided. Georges shrugged. "So, what do we do now?"

I looked at the men, face by face.

"Continue the fight," Alphonse said. "Stephen massacred our town. That's why we came here, no?"

"You've grown a lot of spunk, lad," Georges sniffed. "But tomorrow it could be you who's left moaning out there."

"Keep pounding the walls," Daniel insisted. "By the river, they are not as fortified. We can hit them with our mangonels all day. Sooner or later, they'll cave."

Father Leo cut in, "Maybe soon, word from the King will come?"

"It is autumn," Daniel pressed. "You were in Antioch, Hugh. You've seen that a siege is not determined in one day. Stephen has scorched his own earth. They couldn't have stockpiled food and water for the entire winter."

I had to ask: "Is anyone for meeting Stephen's terms?" I looked around, awaiting their reply. There was only silence.

Finally, Georges picked himself up off of the ground. "I was raised to grind grain, not to soldier. But we've all made our choice here. We've each lost loved ones. My boy

Alo. Your friends, Ox . . . Odo. What would any of their deaths mean if we turned it in now?"

"*Whose* death are you speaking of?" a voice barked in the darkness.

We looked up. A huge, hulking shape came forward. At first, I thought it was an apparition.

The big smith limped stiffly toward our fire. Odo's skins were torn and smeared with blood. His bushy brown beard was matted with who knew what.

I met Odo's eyes, which showed the horror that he had faced. I was so exhausted, I could not even get up to give him a hug. "What the hell took you so long?"

"Fucking hard to claw your way out with all those green-and-gold shits piled on top." He sighed with an exhausted grin. "So, anything to drink?"

I finally got up, wrapped my arms around his shoulders in an adoring hug, and slapped his back. I felt his broad shoulders tense. Someone put a mug in his hand and he drained it in a single swallow. A nod from Odo said, *One more*.

Then he looked up at us, our incredulous smiles. "It was a bad day today, huh?"

We stared back.

"*Well . . .*" Odo swung his bloody leg up, the gash in his thigh causing even Ox to cringe. He took the second mug and poured it all over the wound, sucking back pain. "No mind." He shrugged at our blank stares. "We'll kick their asses tomorrow."

Chapter 133

WE PUMMELED BORÉE again and again over the next few days. Our catapults battered the walls with heavy rocks. Our sturdiest rams pounded at the gates. Charge after charge, ladders were pitched against the walls, only to be thrown aside, and the men on them killed.

The bodies of our fallen comrades piled high outside the walls. I feared we could not take the city. It was too strong, too well fortified. With each repelled charge, the hope of victory faded. Food and drinking water were growing scarce. No answer was received from the King. Our will began to crack.

This was what Stephen had relied on, I realized. All it would take was one mounted strike by his knights against our depleted ranks, and we would be finished.

I called our leaders to the dilapidated grain tower we used for strategy sessions. The mood inside was anxious. Many friends had been left on the field. A somber look was etched on every face, even Daniel's.

I went up to the hearty Languedocian. "Ox, how many men do you have left?"

"Two hundred," he said grimly, "of what was once three."

"I want you to take them, then . . . *tonight,* and leave camp. And the Morrisaeys . . . You, Alois, I want you to take your men too."

Ox and Alois were stunned. "Give up? Let that bastard win?"

I did not reply. I stood in the center of the group, catching Odo and Alphonse's eyes, taking in their looks of disappointment and anger.

The Languedocian shook his head. "We came a long way to fight, Hugh, not to run."

"We too, Hugh," Alois protested. "We've earned our place."

"Yes, you have." I nodded. "All of you have." I turned and faced each one to convey my thanks.

"And you shall have it," I declared, my voice coming alive. "You shall have the chance that each of your friends sought as they were cut down."

They stared at me, lost between alarm and confusion. "Oh, shit." Odo's jaw dropped. "It's another of those fucking *pretexts.*" He looked at me as if he were trying to gauge the weather inside. "We have Emilie to blame for this. What is the plan, Hugh?"

My face gave away nothing.

"We're going to take this city," I finally said, "but not as soldiers. I have tried to fight this as a military man, and as a general, but I'm really a fool. . . . And as a fool, even the great Charlemagne would have no advantage over me."

"I'm not sure this is a revelation I'm pleased to trust my life to." Ox sent a skeptical gaze my way. "But I'm all ears. Tell us about this pretext of yours."

Chapter 134

STEPHEN WAS IN THE MIDST of stabbing a piece of breakfast ham, the morning light tumbling into his quarters, when his page called out, "Look, your lordship, to the window, quick. The rabble has fled."

Just minutes before, the duke had woken in a sour mood. These rebels had proven more resistant than he'd imagined. In wave after wave they came at him; he could not understand their zeal to die. Plus, two weeks ago, Anne had moved to the ladies' quarters. He'd been sleeping alone.

At his page's call, he hurried to the window. His empty stomach filled with glee. The boy was right! The rebel ranks had thinned, cut by more than half.

Those fucking Languedocians, with their arms as thick as ox legs and their horsehair vests, had fled. All that remained was a measly little force, standing around like chickens waiting to lose their heads.

And there, at the head of them, the green-and-red rooster himself, in full view. *With the lance!* This decimated rabble of woodchoppers and farmers was no more than mop-up work for his men.

From behind, his aides burst in. Bertrand, the chatelain, followed by Morgaine.

"Look," Stephen cackled, "the gutless bastards have given up. Look at that stupid prancing cock, standing about as if he still had something to command."

"You said, when the opportunity arose, the little fool was mine," Morgaine rasped.

"So I did." Stephen beamed a gloating grin. "I did promise you that. Tell me, Bertrand, what strength do you estimate they still have?"

The chatelain scanned the field. "Barely three hundred, my liege. All on foot, with limited weapons. It should be no feat to round them up with our horsemen and achieve a quick surrender."

"Surrender?" Stephen's eyes widened. "I hadn't thought of that. Yes, it might be good to extend a hand and save these poor, misguided fools a bit more blood. How does that word sound to you, Morgaine? Surrender?"

"These men are soulless, my liege. We'd be doing God a service by removing their heads."

"So what are you waiting for?" Stephen jabbed him in the chest. "The little bastard's lance still makes an ache in your side, does it not? You heard the chatelain's advice. Let the knights ride with you."

"Liege, those are my men," Bertrand interrupted. "They are our castle's reserve."

"You know, Bertrand," Stephen interrupted. "That surrender thing . . . I've never been particularly keen on it. Morgaine makes a case. These men have already forfeited their souls. No reason to keep them fluttering around in this world."

The chatelain's stomach sank.

"The holy lance or my dignity — that was his choice, was it not?" Stephen's eyes lit up. "Now it seems that I will have them both. Won't I, chatelain? And Morgaine . . . one more thing. I know how you enjoy your work, but do not forget your real purpose out there."

"The holy lance, my lord. My thoughts have never strayed from the prize."

Chapter 135

"LOOK!" A cry of alarm spread among the troops. Several men pointed toward the castle.

The gates of Borée had suddenly opened. We watched, all eyes fixed on the sight, not knowing what would emerge. Then, we heard the rumble of heavy hooves clattering over the lowered drawbridge and saw armored men atop massive crested chargers, trotting in rows of two.

Silently, we watched the deadly battle formation assemble.

No one moved. I knew even the strongest among us debated whether to fight or throw down our arms.

"Positions, men," I called. The troops remained, eyeing the ever-growing enemy force massing on the ridge. *"Positions!"* I called again.

Then, slowly, Odo picked up his gigantic club. And Alphonse, taking a deep breath, strapped on his sword. Then Georges and Daniel too armed themselves.

They took their places without saying much. One by one the rest began to fall in. We gathered into a tight formation, like a Roman phalanx, covered by shields. I prayed this final pretext would work.

Alphonse took a breath. "How many of them do you count?"

"Two hundred. All armed to the teeth." Daniel shrugged. He continued to count as they steadily poured out of the gate and took their places on the field. "Make that three."

"And how m-many are we?" the boy asked.

"Never mind," Daniel sniffed, raising his weapon. "What are warhorses and pikes against a good hoe, anyway?"

A stream of grim laughter trickled around the ranks.

"What is this city, just one big fucking garrison?" Odo shook his head.

On the walls, green-and-gold defenders of Borée stood silently, gaining confidence as the ranks of their horsemen grew. Chargers blew and snorted, held back from the charge as knights adjusted their armor and weapons.

When the force was finally set, a sole rider walked his horse out of the gate and took his place at the head of the formation. I expected Bertrand, the chatelain, but it was not.

On his helmet, I saw the outline of a dark Byzantine cross. My blood went still. Once again, I was facing the man who had killed my wife and baby son.

Odo swallowed dryly. He leaned close to me. "Hugh, I know I've asked this before . . ."

"Yes, I think it'll work," I told him. "But if it doesn't . . . what's the cost? I always thought you made a better soldier than a smith."

"And you were a better jester than a general," he shot back.

I started to laugh, but suddenly my voice was drowned out by a terrifying rumble from across the field.

"Here they come!" Daniel cried. "Shields!"

There was a harried, desperate murmuring. People could be heard muttering their last prayers. I slung the holy lance through a strap across my back and took hold of a heavy sword.

The ground had started to shake. Shouting and cheers erupted from the castle walls.

We linked together in tight formation, our perimeter protected by a wall of shields. The drum of heavy hooves grew closer and closer, like an advancing landslide.

"Hold together," I yelled. Forty yards . . . thirty . . . Then they were on us!

Chapter 136

THE WAVE OF HORSEMEN crashed into our formation with the impact of a hundred-foot crest swallowing up a ship. Sparks and shields and armor flew into the air.

Our ranks staggered backward from the force, shields raised over our heads. Steel came crashing down on us. But the men did not break.

A knight barreled into me, chopping furiously at my shield with an enormous pike. My legs buckled under the heavy blows. All around were the sounds of groans and terror, the chilling clang of iron, shields splitting against the weight of steel, horses neighing, soldiers crying out.

Fighting back, I managed to pin the face of my attacker's pike against the dressings of an adjacent mount. Then I lashed upward with my sword, praying it would strike something. It pierced the armor just above his knee plate. The knight howled, and his mount bucked. I was able to drag him from the saddle and throw him under the hooves of his own horse.

Our ranks were already two-thirds encircled. Men

groaned and dropped in place; the ranks thinned. We could not withstand much more of this onslaught.

"Back," I shouted. "Now!"

Slowly we started to retreat, still fighting in formation, making our way toward the cover of the woods.

Across the way, I saw Black Cross fighting with fury and rage, cutting down men with a single strike, pushing his own knights out of the way. I knew he was trying to get to me.

We made our way back toward the trees. Stephen's horsemen closed for the kill. We continued to resist in formation. Someone's blade slashed across my arm. All around, we were being encircled, a noose strangling our ranks. I saw Black Cross steadily approaching, watching me as he came.

Suddenly a roar rose from the woods. The trees themselves seemed to come alive with hide-clad horsemen and club-wielding warriors springing forth out of the green. The knights between us and the woods spun around. All of a sudden they faced a charging enemy *from behind*. Their horses, caught in the squeeze, tripped and reared, tossing riders off. We began to strike at them, using our swords like battering rams, crumpling armor until it gave and then running the knights through.

Now Stephen's horsemen were pinched, fighting a renewed foe from all sides. You could see in their darting eyes the terror of this unanticipated shift of fortune. More knights began to be stripped from their mounts, their heavy weapons useless in the closeness of battle among the trees. It was a massacre. A massacre — but not the one they had planned.

Soon, barely half of Stephen's knights were standing. Many were off their horses, fighting two or three of us at a time in their cumbersome suits of armor. Shouts of exhortation were replaced by pleas for mercy. Some began to cease fighting and put up their hands. Weapons dropped to the ground.

Relief rippled through me. I could not believe it. I was so tired I wanted to sink to my knees.

Then a fearsome voice pierced through me, sharp as any lance. "You rejoice too soon, jester. Before we call it a day, let us see how much power that little stick of yours really has."

Chapter 137

HIS VISOR WAS UP, a cold expression on his scarred face. I fastened on the hard-set eyes of Black Cross, the man I hated more than any other in this world.

"*Twice,*" I spat at him.

"*Twice what,* innkeeper?"

"Twice I have to rid the world of the scum who killed my wife and child."

I rushed toward him, hurtling my sword at his neck.

The Tafur put his visor down and stood his ground, pinning back my strongest thrust with ease. I hacked at him again and again. Each time he parried my blade.

"You have caused me *shame,*" Black Cross said. Through his visor's narrow slits I could see his pupils darting from side to side.

With a ferocious howl, he leaped and swung his blade down on me with the power of a mangonel. I darted backward, the wind from his blade only inches from my face.

The Tafur did not even stop to regain his breath. He swung again, backhanded, aiming to slice through my legs.

The mighty force of his blow almost drove my own blade into my thigh.

Slowly I forced his blade upward, but it took all of my strength. I felt like a boy straining against the power of a fully grown man.

He sliced at me again, each blow harder to fend off. I darted to the left, trying to catch my breath. Only my speed prevented me from being cut in half. But my quickness was waning. I couldn't beat Black Cross, I realized.

He butted me, helmet into my forehead. I staggered back, the crash reverberating through my skull. The breath was heavy in my chest. A voice inside me pleaded, *Please, God, show me the way.*

The Tafur pressed closer and I stumbled, trying to scamper away. I crawled along the bank of the river, knowing my death was only seconds away. Stephen would end up with the holy lance after all.

Black Cross stood in front of me. There was no escaping him now. He put up his visor and let me see his awful, scarred face.

He sniffed. "Your soul is already lost. I only do God's dirty work by delivering your corpse to Him."

For a moment I blinked, disoriented, the sun glinting off his armor. I felt in another place, Antioch, staring up at the Turk, sucking in the last, precious breaths of my life.

Once again, the craziest urge took hold of me.

I began to laugh. I did not know at what. That I had come full circle, back to the moment of my death? That despite all my hope, life in the duchy would remain as it was? That I would die in the patchwork clothing of a fool?

Something crazy had come into my head. A line from a stupid joke. I don't know why it seemed funny to me, but I could not help myself. I was a fool, wasn't I?

"It sure is deep," I said. Then I started to laugh again, twisting up my legs and rolling on my side.

"You die witless, jester. Tell me, what image is so funny that you will carry it to your grave?"

"Oldest joke in the book." I caught my breath. I did not know if it was cunning or total lunacy that was in control. "Two men pissing off a bridge. Each trying to prove to the other who's bigger. One rolls out his pecker. '*Bbrrr . . .* this water's cold,' he says. 'Yeah,' goes the other, 'and it sure is *deep.*'"

Black Cross looked blank, not understanding. He stood on the bank of the river, ready to dispatch me to Hell.

"It sure is deep," I said again, this time a renewed certainty in my voice.

It was only a flash, but I was sure I saw on his face the subtle recognition that *all was not what it seemed,* that he had misjudged something.

Before he could figure it out, I kicked my legs and struck him squarely in the midsection. The blow sent him stumbling to the very edge of the riverbank.

Black Cross struggled to keep his balance. And he did! He smiled disdainfully, as if to say, *You little man. That's all you have?*

Then his boots could not hold the ground. He teetered, his armor dragging him backward. And still his look was not of peril but merely annoyance. *Little man, little problems.*

But then he began to fall. A clang of metal, the armor dragging him, picking up speed like a boulder until he rolled, grasping at rocks and weeds, all the way down the embankment and tumbled into the river.

He slid under the surface. I am certain that what flashed through his mind was that he would pick himself up and climb back and finish me off. Moments passed. I could not

No cheering . . . *Could Hugh have won? Was it possible?*

Suddenly the bolt jangled and the door was flung open. Stephen was there, his eyes fierce. Two soldiers followed him into the cell.

She forced a smile. "I hear no cheers coming from the walls, my lord. Why do I think the battle has not gone your way?"

"For *both* of us." Stephen snorted and seized her arm. "There's a noose in the courtyard that awaits your pretty neck. Tomorrow morning, you traitorous bitch!"

"You have no right to pass such judgment." Emilie tried to twist away. "You sentence me to death on what charge?"

"Sedition, abetting the rebels, fucking a heretic . . ." Stephen listed them with a shrug.

"Have you lost your mind? Is there no honor left in you? Have you bargained everything with the Devil for a piece of metal? That lance?"

"The lance," Stephen said, his eyes flashing, "is worth more to me than you *and* your fool, and all the pitiful *'honorable'* souls left in France."

Emilie shouted, "You will not beat him, Stephen, whether you hang me or not. He came for you as one man; now an army stands behind him. You cannot stop him, not with all your titles and mercenaries, no matter how many men."

"Yes, yes, your ruddy little fool. Oh, now you've really got my knees knocking." Stephen laughed.

"He *will* come for me."

Stephen shook his head and sighed. "Sometimes I think the two of you actually deserve each other. Of course the fool will come for you, my pathetic girl. That's precisely what I'm counting on."

Chapter 139

THE REALIZATION SETTLED over the men that the battle was finally over. No more fighting. No more blood.

They looked around, stunned and elated. Those who had lived sought out friends and embraced them. Georges and the Languedocians, Odo and Father Leo, Alphonse and Alois, farmers and Freemasons, jubilant just to be alive.

I led our men back to the castle walls, exhausted, out of fight. But as *conquerors!*

The same defenders who had pushed aside our attacks now sullenly watched us, arms at rest. Stephen's captured knights were pushed to the front, stripped of their armor, and forced to kneel. A cry rose up. Not a cry of victory but a single, steady voice that grew in power until all joined in.

"Submit, submit," they chanted.

Finally, from a parapet above the front gate, Stephen appeared, dressed in a ceremonial purple cloak. He surveyed our ranks contemptuously, as if he could not believe this ragtag rabble had beaten back his troops.

"What happens now?" I asked Daniel.

"You must talk with him. Stephen has to comply or his knights will lose their heads. He is bound by honor."

"Go on." Odo pushed me forward. "Tell the bastard he can keep his fucking grain. See if there's any ale in there."

I grabbed the lance. Someone hitched up a mount for me.

"I'll go with you," Daniel said.

"I'll come too," the miller said.

I looked at Stephen. I didn't trust this bastard, no matter how deeply he was bound by honor. "I think not." I shook my head. I had someone else in mind.

We brought up Baldwin. He had long been stripped of his fancy clothes and was dressed in a burlap tunic like any common man. His wrists were bound, his haggard face badly in need of a shave.

"It is your lucky day," I said, plopping a plumed hat upon his head. "If all goes well, you'll soon be back in silk."

"You do not need to dress me up." He threw off the hat. "You can be sure Stephen will recognize one of his own."

"Suit yourself." I nodded solemnly.

We headed forward out of the ranks, Baldwin's mount tethered to mine. Soldiers on the walls watched us silently approach.

We stopped, out of arrow-shot, forty yards from the wall. Stephen gazed down, barely acknowledging me, as if he had been called away from a meal.

"Black Cross is dead," I announced. "The fate of your best knights, what's left of them, awaits your word. We have no more urge for blood. Submit!"

"I commend you, carrot-top," the duke replied. "You have proven to be as worthy a fighter as you are a fool. I have taken you too lightly. Come, ride forth where I can see your face. I will present my terms."

"*Your* terms? It is our terms you are bound to hear."

"What do I detect, jester? Do you not think me a man c honor? Ride forth and claim your prize."

"I think you bargain freely, lord, with something you ar short of. Do not be offended if I send out my man instead.

A smile curled on Stephen's face. "Your man, ther jester. And I will send mine."

"Shall I go?" Daniel offered.

I shook my head and glanced toward Baldwin. "No . . *him*."

Baldwin's eyes bolted wide. A film of sweat broke ou on his forehead.

"Here's your chance." I pulled his hood over his head "Show us how your fellow lord recognizes you."

I untied his horse and gave it a hard slap to the rump and it bolted forward. The duke, hands bound, tried t gather it under control. As he crossed over into no-man's land, he began to shout, "I am Baldwin, duke of Treille!"

A few guards on the wall began to point and laugh.

The duke's voice became more agitated. "I am Baldwin you fools. Disregard these clothes. Look at me, Stephen Do you not see?"

All that could be seen was a lowly-clad figure galloping toward the gates on his horse.

"Here, jester," Stephen called from the wall. "Here are *my* terms."

A chilling whoosh was heard and an arrow struck Baldwin's chest. The duke keeled back. Then another, and a third arrow cut into him. Baldwin's body slumped in the saddle. The horse, sensing something was wrong, reversed its course and drifted back toward our ranks.

"There are my terms, fool," Stephen called from the wall. "Enjoy your victory. You have *one day*." Then he wrapped his purple cloak about his shoulders and left, without even waiting for a response.

Daniel rode out to meet the returning horse. Baldwin's lifeless body crumpled to the ground.

A parchment was rolled onto one of the arrows in his chest.

Daniel leaped off his horse and, without pulling out the arrow, unfastened the paper bound to its shaft. He read, then looked up. I saw the bitterness in his eyes.

"Lady Emilie is decreed a traitor. We have the day to lay down our arms. Unless *we* submit, and turn the lance over to Stephen, she will be hanged."

Chapter 140

THAT NIGHT, I went out into the fields behind our camp, my chest exploding with rage.

I needed to be alone. I headed past the sentries manning our perimeter. What did I care if I was in danger? I wanted to hurl the blasted lance against the castle walls. *Keep it, Stephen. My life has been sorrow and misery since I found it!*

Behind me, the flames of a hundred fires sparkled in the night, my men dozing or making bets on what tomorrow would bring: fight or surrender.

I began to feel heartened, my shoulders free of strain. Maybe I would see Emilie if I walked close to the walls. Just for a moment, as I passed by the gates. The thought lifted me — that I might see her beautiful face one more time.

I let out a breath, cradling the lance in my palms, staring at the massive walls.

Suddenly I felt a muscular arm around my neck. I

gulped for air, the grip tightening. The tip of a blade was pressed into my back.

"Most accommodating, jester," hissed a voice in my ear.

"You've picked a daring place for a murder. If I shout out, you will be meat for our dogs."

"And if you shout, you would be out a very dear friend, boar-slayer."

I slowly turned and was face-to-face with the Moor who always guarded Anne.

"What are you doing here, Moor? Your mistress, Anne, is no friend of mine. You're not welcome either."

"I come with a message," he said. "You must listen, just listen."

"I have already seen your lady's message, but my wife died in her dungeon."

"A message not from my lady," the Moor said with a smile, "but from *yours*. Emilie. She bids you come with me tonight. I told her no sane man would come back with me through these walls. She said to tell you, '*That may be, but it will not always be.*'"

The sound of those words took my breath away. I could hear Emilie's voice, see her as I set off that day in the jester's suit to Treille. My spirits lifted at the thought of the brave twinkle in her eyes.

"Do not smile yet," warned the Moor. "It will be a long shot to save her. Choose two men. Your best. Two whom you would be happy to die with. Then we must go. Inside. Now."

Chapter 141

I CHOSE ODO and Ox. Who else? They were the two bravest, and they had gotten me this far.

Around midnight, we left, snaking our way through the camp and into the woods without attracting attention. Then we followed the river to where it neared the city walls, away from the main gates.

Through the darkness, I saw the outline of the great cathedral, lit by the flames of sentry fires. We could even hear Stephen's men talking while manning the walls.

We kept close to the river, approaching a part of the city I did not know. We forded the river at a low point the Moor knew.

Creeping along the wall, we finally reached a spot that seemed to be the exterior of a large stone building many stories high. Narrow window slits were carved in the wall. I had no idea where I was.

The Moor climbed up to one of the narrow slits. He scratched at the opening. A voice whispered back, *"Who is there, fool or king?"*

In his broken accent, the Moor said, "If fools wore crowns, we'd all be kings. Quick, let us in — or we'll all be hanging tomorrow."

Suddenly chunks of the wall began to shift. The slit grew larger, a block at a time, and I could see it was not a window but a tunnel.

"What the hell is this?" I asked.

"*La porte du fou,*" the Moor said, hurrying us through. The fool's gate. "It was dug during the wars with Anjou as an escape route, but the Anjevins found out and they were waiting there. They slaughtered all who came out. Anyone who went through was said to be a fool. Thought you'd appreciate the touch."

"Very reassuring." Odo swallowed uneasily.

"My apologies," the Moor said. "I would have suggested the main gate, but all these men in green-and-gold surcoats with big swords were standing around guarding it." He pushed Odo forward.

We crept through the narrow opening. A dim light appeared up ahead. "Come, quick," I heard a voice say on the other end. I did not know where I was or whom I was heading toward. I prayed this was not an ambush.

The tunnel was not long, only the length of a building. We came out into a torch-lit room, arms assisting us as we jumped.

Those arms belonged to a man in a deep blue robe with a white beard. I immediately recognized him: Auguste, the physician who had healed me after I was attacked by the boar. This was his hospital. People in the throes of disease reclined on mats or leaned half-naked against stone walls.

Auguste led us down a hall into a large adjoining chamber. A study. The walls were lined with heavy manuscripts, scrolls all about.

I had barely enough time to thank Auguste for his help

before the physician scurried off, shutting us in. My heart beat nervously.

"What is next?" I turned to the Moor.

"What's *next*," said a voice from the shadows, "is to pray that holy lance of yours has a fraction of the powers it's said to — if you intend to save the life of the woman you love."

I spun to see a shape in a hood emerge from a corner. I did not know whether to raise my knife or bow.

I was staring at Lady Anne.

Part Six

LAST RIGHTS

Chapter 142

A DRUM BEAT SOLEMNLY in the courtyard outside the castle. An anxious crowd had begun to form, eager to see what was happening.

Usually, before a thief or a murderer took the rope, people gathered around laughing and gossiping as if they were going to a feast. Peddlers hawked cakes and candles; children played hide-and-seek through the crowd.

But today the mood was different. Everyone knew they were going to see something they had never seen before.

A noble was going to be hanged.

A noble woman.

High above the courtyard, I hid on a castle ledge, crouched in a nook the Moor had found for me. In the square, I spotted Odo in the crowd near the gallows. And Ox, balancing two pails on his shoulders, making his way in the direction of the main gate.

On the walls, soldiers lined the ramparts, poised in case the rebels charged. A bonfire burned in the square, its flames fanned by a whipping wind. The fire was for Emilie's body, once she was dead.

A flourish of horns shattered the restive quiet. Murmurs buzzed through the crowd. It was time! The door to the donjon opened.

A detachment of soldiers marched out, Emilie at their center.

"There she is," someone shrieked.

"I beg you, pray, lady," a woman wailed. "God's Heaven is great. If he finds room for us, he will for you."

My heart was pounding against my ribs just to see Emilie after such a long time.

She wore a plain cotton smock and a shawl wrapped tightly around her shoulders. Her blond hair was pinned and fell about her neck. She didn't look noble, just as brave as I had ever seen her.

"Let her go," someone finally yelled. "We have no fight with her."

Emilie stopped for a moment, a smile of kindness on her face, but a soldier pushed her toward the scaffold.

The crowd hollered to save her life, even as a masked hangman pulled her by the arms up the stairs and led her to the noose. I knew how frightened she must be; I knew how her heart must be fluttering. I glanced at Odo: *Hold!*

Then the horns sounded again — this time the duke's flourish. From the entrance to the castle Stephen appeared, flanked by his lackeys, the bailiff and the chamberlain.

The bailiff pulled out a scroll and began to read: "'In accordance with the laws of the Duchy of Borée and sanctioned, heretofore, by the Archbishop of the Diocese, it is willed that all known abettors and caregivers to the heretic rebels will be deemed agents of corruption, and therefor be hanged by the neck until dead, and their body burned, as is the law.'"

"Let her live," a voice shouted from the crowd. "It's Stephen's neck that fits the noose, not hers."

Stephen's face reddened. "Where is your jester now, lady?" He stepped up to the gallows and said to all, "I have given him a chance to spare her life, to spare the city more blood, and yet he does not appear. Lady Emilie, you have only these weak-willed women to speak for you."

"Your deeds speak for me," Emilie said. "I pray he does not come."

Odo looked at me with readiness. *Now,* his eyes said. *We must strike now.* I gave him no signal.

Suddenly a lookout called from the walls, "My lord, it is the jester's army. Their arms are down. They *submit.*"

Stephen's face lit with joy. "Be sure, sergeant. Submit or attack? There must be no tricks."

"No, the sergeant is right," confirmed the chatelain from the ramparts. "They carry their banners down. They do submit. *And the jester,* he is at the head of them."

From my perch, I could make out rows of my men approaching with their arms at bay. And Alphonse, in my patchwork skirt and cap, at the head.

"The fool's stupidity amazes even me." Stephen smirked, bounding up the steps and peering over the wall. "He lays down everything for a woman."

He signaled to his gatekeepers to draw up the portcullis. Two men hoisted the heavy metal gate skyward.

At the same time, Stephen ordered, "Hangman, secure the noose."

The crowd gasped in protest. Something vile was about to occur. The masked executioner fitted the rope around Emilie's neck and positioned her body over the trap.

I could no longer restrain myself. I looked to Odo in the crowd, and to Ox hovering by the opening gate. Across the way, I spotted the Moor on a balcony above the square.

I signaled them. *Now!*

But suddenly Stephen shouted, *"It is not him!"* He strained over the wall, his eyes bulging. "It's a trick! The jester is not there! Close the gates!"

Chapter 143

THE MOOR'S ARROW streaked across the square, striking one of the gatekeepers in the back. He slumped to his knees.

Ox threw off his pails and jammed a rod in the pulley, bringing the heavy portcullis to a stop. He ran his knife into the back of the other gatekeeper, who was struggling to bring the gate down.

A swarm of my men, Alphonse in the lead, rushed inside. They overwhelmed the soldiers at the gate as arrows rained down on them. Soon they were battling Stephen's men hand-to-hand.

Stephen leaped down from the walls and ran toward the scaffold and Emilie. "Where is your fool?" he asked her. "He lets you die? He does not come for you?"

He gave the nod to his hangman. Then Odo pushed his way past two guards. He plunged his knife into the hangman's gut, hurling him off the scaffold. He went to Emilie.

"He *does* come, Stephen," I called. I held up the lance.

Our eyes locked in a hateful exchange. "I am here, my lord. Norbert told me you were a jester short."

The thrill of victory twisted into rage on Stephen's face. *"Get him!"* he screamed. "A hundred gold pieces for the man who brings me that lance. *Five* hundred!"

His guards started to move toward me. I raised the lance.

"You threw my son into the flames," I said, fixed on Stephen. "Here, fetch your lance."

I hurled it with all my might into the center of the bonfire. To everyone's horror, it stuck firmly amid the flames.

"No . . . !" Stephen hollered.

He ran like a madman to the fire, desperately pulling at branches and wood, flames biting at his flesh. He hurled sticks toward the lance, trying to dislodge it. Then he backed off, driven away by the raging heat. He stared at the lance fixed in the center, red-hot and starting to lose its shape.

Then he turned toward me, murderous hatred in his eyes. "You!" he screamed. "You incredible *fool!*"

Chapter 144

STEPHEN BOUNDED UP the stone stairs two at a time and onto a parapet, climbing to my level with great speed and agility for such a large man. His eyes burned.

I took my sword and leaped from my ledge to a second-floor balcony of the castle. One of Stephen's soldiers moved to stop me, and I slashed him across the chest, sending him flying.

The duke hurdled another ledge, racing toward me in a frenzy. He came to face me on the same balcony — ten paces away.

"Your wit has never been in doubt, carrot-head," he said, leering at me. "Now we'll see if you have fight."

He leaped upon me, bringing down his blade. A bone-chilling clang reverberated through my arms as I parried the blow. Stephen pivoted deftly and swung his sword, two handed, at my chest. The blade cut my side.

I buckled, stung with terrible pain.

"Come on, fool," he taunted.

He struck with his sword again, forcing mine back inches

from my neck. His eyes were ablaze; hot breath fumed i
my face.

With the last of my strength, I kneed him. Stephe
groaned and buckled. I pushed him away and swung m
blade, knocking the sword from his hand. His eyes widene
as it toppled over the ledge. He stood there, defenseless, ye
still glaring.

Then he jumped up onto a ledge overlooking the square
He laughed. "Just know that if I get to her first, she i
dead!"

He leaped across to the next balcony. Then he darted in
side the castle.

I ran to the edge of the balcony, scanning the courtyard
looking for Emilie. I didn't see her anywhere. Odo eithe
Blood was seeping from my side.

I ran into the castle, expecting Stephen and a fight to th
death. I was in the living quarters. No sign of the bastar
anywhere.

"Where are you?" I hollered down the halls. Onl
echoes answered.

I smashed through a door and into Stephen and Anne'
private quarters. I looked around madly. I had been here tha
night when I hunted for Anne after finding Sophie in the dun
geon.

I looked down at my side. A damp patch of blood wa
spreading on my tunic. *"Stephen,"* I yelled. *"God damn i
come fight with me."*

His voice came from behind me. "You want me, I an
here, jester. Tell me a joke."

Stephen emerged from a corner smirking, a loade
crossbow aimed at my chest. "I may *be* a jester short, a
you say," he said, "but you, it seems, are the one who is ou
of tricks."

A chill went down my spine. I backed up to the wall. There was nowhere to run.

"What do you say? Our little fool is out of tricks? He dreams of being noble, but he has only fucked one. Shame about the lance, though," he said with a grin. "Don't you agree, wife?"

Wife . . . ? Anne?

Chapter 145

ANNE STEPPED into the light, remaining behind Stephen. My legs grew weak. A hollowness was in my gut.

In her hand she held the lance. *The holy lance . . . not* the ordinary one I had cast so theatrically into the fire. The lance I had entrusted to her last night! Entrusted.

"I *am* a fool," I said, seeking out her eyes. How could Emilie have been so wrong about Anne? How could I?

I looked at the crossbow leveled at my chest. And Stephen's mocking grin. For the first time, I felt ready to die.

"One last word, jester." Stephen smirked. "Your death is trivial to me, serf. All that mattered was the lance. But what would *you* do with such a thing, anyway? You could not possibly know the power it holds. I hunted the world for it. By all God's justice, it is mine." He tensed his finger on the trigger of the crossbow.

"Then *have* it, Stephen." Anne's voice rang from behind him.

Suddenly Stephen lurched and his eyes wrenched open.

I stiffened, expecting my guts to fall into my hands. But no arrow came from his crossbow.

I heard the most horrible sound — the splitting of ribs and sinew, the tearing of flesh. An awful gasp came from Stephen's mouth. But instead of words, a river of blood followed.

Anne pushed forward strongly. This time, the blade of the lance pierced the base of his neck and came out before his very eyes. *"Have it, husband."*

Then Anne put her mouth close to his ear and whispered, "But know how worthless it is now, our Savior's blood having mingled with your own."

Stephen looked down. He stared disbelievingly at the Roman eagle and the bloody tip of the holy lance's blade protruding from his neck.

Then he fell to the floor.

I stared at Anne, dumbstruck. She merely stared in return. Neither of us spoke. Then I saw a softening in her eyes and she nodded, as if we shared some kind of understanding, one that would never be put into words.

"I think it's safe to say," she said, "that when we pulled you from the ditch that day, such an ending would not have entered our minds."

"Very safe, madame."

I heard footsteps from down the hall. Emilie burst into the room, breathless. Our eyes met and my heart nearly exploded with joy. She looked at Stephen crumpled on the floor. Then at Anne standing over him. Then at me again, her eyes darting to the blood leaking from my side.

She gasped. "You are wounded."

"And you are always nursing me back to health," I said. "Oh God, Emilie, you cannot know how it feels to see you now."

"I do know," she said.

Emilie ran to me and flung herself into my arms. I lifted her off her feet and squeezed her as tightly as I have ever held anything in my life. I kissed her over and over, kisses of hope and gratefulness. For the first time, *I actually realized that she was mine.*

My eyes were moist as I thought of all that had taken place since I first set out from Veille du Père. All who had died. "I have nothing. Not a denier to my name," I muttered. "Not even a career. How is it possible that I feel like the richest man in all the world?"

Emilie took my hand and whispered, "Because you are free."

Chapter 146

THE LANGUEDOCIANS WERE THE FIRST to leave, early the following morning. Ox told me there was a saying in their part of the woods: No sense hanging around the wine cask when the party's over.

He and his men assembled at the gates at dawn, their horses loaded with sacks of grain, a few pigs, and hens fluttering behind. I went out in the early light to bid them farewell.

"You should stay," I told him. "Anne has promised to address all your claims. You deserve a lot more."

"*More?* We are farmers," Ox said. "What else do we need? If we came back laden with gold chalices, our people would think they were to piss in."

"In that case . . ." I patted him on the shoulder and flashed him a glimpse of a plate of gold engraved with Stephen's crest that I intended to give him as a memento. "No need to leave with *this*."

Ox looked around and then tucked it in his saddle pouch.

"I guess I'll have to teach them some proper manners." He grinned.

I embraced him, patting the warrior warmly on his broad back.

"Look us up, jester, if you ever have the urge to return that lance." He winked. He slapped his horse and signaled his men forward.

I watched until the last of them had disappeared through the city gates. Stephen was being buried later that day. That was one last thing I had to do.

A few of my men were there as the coffin was brought to the cathedral. It was not a service befitting a duke who had died in battle. Only Anne, their son, Emilie, and I were inside the church with the bishop.

The duke's coffin was carried into a crypt deep inside the castle and placed in a marble sarcophagus. In this dark, narrow space, well below ground, lay the remains of past bishops and members of the ruling family. There was barely enough air to fuel a torch.

The blessing was simple and quick. What was there to say?

That Stephen had bargained his honor away for greed and power. That he had been a shit to his wife and an indifferent father to his son. That he had plundered the Holy Land in search of loot.

The bishop of Borée, the same who had excommunicated us, muttered through a quick prayer, his eyes darting toward the lance. Emilie looked on, holding my hand. When the blessing was done, Anne bent over the casket and planted a dry kiss upon Stephen's cheek.

Then a final blessing was said. Anne led her son out of the crypt, the bishop stumbling close behind.

"Give me a moment," I said to Emilie.

She seemed not to understand.

"I need to say something for my wife and son."

She finally nodded and left me. *Just Stephen and I.*

I looked at his deep-set eyes, his turned-down hawk nose. "If there ever was a bastard in this world, you are it," I said. "May you rest in Hell, you prick." I closed the coffin.

I held the holy lance in my palms. It brought back memories of all those whose lives had been changed by it. Maybe years from now someone would find it, I thought. In a different time, when it would be celebrated for what it was. Something miraculous, close to God.

You were a hell of a good walking stick. I smiled. *But as a relic, you brought more blood than peace.*

I placed the holy lance inside the sarcophagus. Then I moved the heavy lid into place and looked away.

The crypt attendant came back and I nodded for him to go about his duty. I stayed and watched, saying good-bye to Sophie, Phillipe, and the Turk who had spared me in Antioch.

The sarcophagus was sealed for good and pushed into the wall, where it fitted almost seamlessly into the stone, then mortar was smoothed in the cracks.

It would lie there forever.

Or until it was needed again.

Chapter 147

CHURCH BELLS WERE RINGING.

As I came out of the crypt, Emilie rushed up, excite
"We have visitors, Hugh! Archbishop Velloux is arriving
the gates."

"Velloux . . . ?" I did not know the name.

"From Paris."

Paris! I did not know if this was good or bad. T
Church had excommunicated us. If this was upheld, all
had fought for could be lost. No matter what Anne vow
to rectify, without the Church we were outcasts, more de
than alive.

I hobbled into the courtyard. Anne stood by expectant
Bishop Barthelme too. From all about, my men gathe
around the courtyard: Odo, Georges, Alphonse, Fath
Leo.

The archbishop of Paris! This was a humbling thing.

As the portcullis was raised, a column of soldiers
crimson surcoats galloped two by two into the courtyar

Behind them, an ornate carriage drawn by six strong
eeds.

It bore the cross of Rome, insignia of the Holy See.

My heart was leaping out of my chest. Emilie squeezed
y hand. "I have a good feeling," she whispered.

I wished I could say I did as well.

A captain of the guard jumped off his mount and placed
stool in front of the carriage door. When it opened, two
iests wearing scarlet skullcaps emerged. Then, a moment
hind them, the archbishop, about sixty by my estimate,
s hair gray and thinned, wearing a crimson robe and a
rge gold cross around his neck.

"Your Eminence," Bishop Barthelme exclaimed. He
d his priests dropped to one knee. Slowly, everyone
ound them did the same. "This is a great honor. I pray
u did not have too unsettling a trip."

"We would not have," the archbishop curtly replied,
vere it not that on your word we went first to Treille, ex-
cting to find a rebellion there, 'heretics and thieves.' Yet
stead we found only peace and order. And, remarkably,
lord. I am told there was a battle fought here."

"There was, Your Grace," the bishop said.

"Well, you look no worse for wear, Barthelme," the
chbishop observed. "Obviously the Church still func-
ons. Show me, where are all these dreaded lost souls?"

"Why, they are *here*," the bishop said, stabbing his fin-
r toward my men. *"And here."* He pointed at me.

The archbishop looked closely at us. "These men seem
ite benign, for apostates and heretics."

The bishop's face turned white. A few snickers were
ard around the square.

"The duke felt . . ."

"The duke obviously felt," Velloux interrupted, "that

the Church's laws were available, as were you, to enact h
personal bidding."

For the first time, the tightened bowstring that was n
chest began to relax.

"Your Grace." Anne stepped forward and knelt. "Yo
presence is most welcome, but there are matters of ci
law that also need to be addressed."

A voice called from out of the carriage. "That is why
came along, my dear."

A stately figure emerged, wrapped in a purple cloak e
broidered with gold fleurs-de-lis. Each of the soldiers in
mediately dropped to a knee.

"Your Majesty," Anne exclaimed, her face blanche
She immediately rose and curtsied, eyes fastened to t
ground. Gasps rippled through the crowd. Words I cou
scarcely believe.

"The King . . ."

The entire square dropped to one knee. *The King!* I
had answered my call. I had to blink twice to make sur
wasn't dreaming.

Then I heard something that stunned me even more.

"Father!" Emilie exclaimed.

Chapter 148

FATHER! Did I hear right? My body slammed to a halt. I know that my jaw hung wide.

The King's eyes were drawn to Emilie. I could not tell if he was pleased or stern. "Has your absence from the court made you forget, child, whom it is you address?"

"No, my lord," Emilie replied. She knelt and averted her eyes. Then she lifted them, twinkling with amusement. "Father . . ." She exhaled and smiled.

"So." The King signaled for us to rise. "Show me the misguided fool who I am told is responsible for this unrest."

Emilie shot forward, clasping my arm. "You are mistaken, Father. It is not Hugh who is responsible but —"

"Quiet," the King interrupted, his voice raised. "I was referring to *Stephen,* the supposed duke, not your damned jester," he said.

Emilie, her eyes moist, broke into a blushing smile. She took my hand.

"The duke is dead, my lord." Anne came forward. "H died, realizing his shame, by his own hand."

"By his own hand . . ." The King glanced at the arch bishop and snorted. "Then it is *he,* after all is done, who withheld from God's grace. As for the rest of yo heretics . . ." He turned and faced my men. "Conside yourselves restored. I speak for Archbishop Velloux whe I give you back your souls."

A joyous cheer rose up. The men hugged one anothe and threw their fists in the air.

"Now, as for *you,* jester . . ." The King turned back me. "You have made demands that if granted would thro half the country into disarray."

"No demands." I bowed my head. "Only the hope to r turn to our homes in peace, and some manner of law to r dress ills perpetrated on us."

The King sucked in a breath. For a moment I thoug he would go into a rage. Then he relaxed. "My daughte has been talking about this very thing for years. . . . Pe haps it is time."

The courtyard exploded in cheers, but he immediatel put up his hand to stop them. "The fact remains, you ha risen up against your lords. Against those you wer pledged to. The law of liege and serf is not at issue her Some justice must be meted out."

Emilie pushed me down. I knelt.

"You must be educated in the manner of the noble said the King.

"My lord. I was a jongleur and an innkeeper. I am as f from highborn as one can be."

"Yet you will *have* to be educated." The King cocke his eye. "If you intend to marry my daughter."

I slowly raised my head. I looked about, a smile sprea ing on my face.

"Father!" Emilie gasped and pulled me to my feet. Then she ran to the King and without so much as a curtsy, threw her arms around him.

"I know, I know. Fools are everywhere, even those who wear the royal robe. But first, I need a word with your boy."

He came to me, evaluating me. Then he placed an arm around my shoulder and ushered me away. I felt some rebuke about to come.

"Not to seem ungrateful, son, for I know Emilie is in your debt . . . but in your letter you mentioned a lance."

I took a breath, then spoke.

"It was destroyed, Your Highness. Hurled into flames in the fighting here. I'm afraid there is nothing left."

The King sighed deeply. "It was the lance that pierced our Savior's side? Such a relic was more valuable than my own crown. You are sure of it, lad?"

"Only sure that it has produced the most miraculous of outcomes. Look around you, Sire."

He looked — at the ebullient men, at his daughter's eyes wet with joy — then nodded wistfully. "What a treasure that would have made. But perhaps it is just as well. . . . In my experience, such things are better left the stuff of legends and myths."

EPILOGUE

"GRAND-PÈRE!"

My little grandson Jack came up to me in the gardens. It was a bright late-summer morning. I had just returned from the hill with a handful of sunflowers, as I did every morning in the summer. Though climbing to the spot was a little harder for me now.

Little Jack, my daughter Sophie's son, who was five, threw himself into my arms and almost toppled me over. He pointed to the checkerboard crest that hung above the entrance to our inn. (Of course, the inn was slightly larger than my first one. We now owned a quarter of the land that had once belonged to Baldwin. Some things do come with being married to the daughter of a king.)

"Mother told me you would tell me what our crest means. She said you were once a jester."

"She said that?" I pretended to be surprised. "Well, if she said that, then it must be true."

"Show me," Jack insisted, his blue eyes twinkling.

"Show you?" I took his hand. "Then first you must hea the tale."

I took him to the bench that overlooked the town where we had lived these forty years, near where Sophie and Phillipe were buried. Around us, the fields exploded with sunflowers galore.

I took Jack back to the time when all I had was a tiny inn. When an army marched through here, an army led by a hermit. To the battles near and far, and the holiest prize in the world, which for a short while was in my hands. To the fight of men to make themselves free, forty years before.

My little blond-haired grandson listened without so much as a breath. "That was you, Grand-père? You did these things?"

"Me and Odo and Alphonse. When Uncle Odo was just a smith in town, and not our seneschal."

"Let me see." He screwed up an eye as if I were joking "Show me what you learned."

"What I learned?" I touched his tiny freckled nose Then a thought flashed into my head. I got up off the bench and winked at him as if to say, *"This is our secret. What ever happens, don't tell your grandmother."*

I sucked in my stomach and held my breath. I hadn' done this in thirty years. I tucked myself into a deep crouch. I prayed to God I would not kill myself. *"Watch this!"*

And I sprang. Through the air into a forward flip. And in that fleeting instant, a thousand memories flashed through my mind: Sophie. Norbert. And the Turk. I sprang for all of them. One last time.

With a thump, I landed on my feet. Every bone in my body seemed to rattle. But I had nailed it! I was in one piece. Norbert would've been proud!

I looked at Jack. His eyes glistened bright as the summer sun. I saw my beautiful Emilie in those eyes. Then all at once he started to laugh. A true child's laugh, like water rushing in a brook. It almost choked me as I watched him. *Laughter,* the most beautiful sound in all the world.

"*That's* what I learned." I tousled his long blond hair and smiled. "To make people laugh. That's what this crest is all about. That is *everything.*"

I took my little grandson by the hand and led him back to the inn. Emilie, my queen, was waiting for me there. The hearth was roaring.

And I had sunflowers for her.

Sources

The following books on the Crusades and the Middle Ages have been sources of information and background for both setting and characters in this book:

Armstrong, Karen. *Holy War: The Crusades and Their Impact on Today's World.* New York: Anchor Books, 2001.

W. B. Bartlett. *God Wills It! An Illustrated History of the Crusades.* Gloucestershire: Sutton Publishing, 2000.

Bishop, Morris. *The Middle Ages.* Boston: Houghton Mifflin, 1968.

Cantor, Norman, F. *The Medieval Reader.* New York: HarperCollins, 1994. Including original works of: Song of Roland, William of Tyre, Peter Abelard, the Magna Carta, Goliardic Verse, St. Ambrose, Gregory of Tours, Marie de France, Bernard Gui.

Cohn, Norman. *The Pursuit of the Millennium.* New York: Oxford University Press, 1974.

Connell, Evans. *Deus lo Volt! Chronicle of the Crusades.* New York: Counterpoint Press, 2000.

Goetz, Hans-Werner. *Life in the Middle Ages: From the Seventh to the Thirteenth Century.* Translated by Albert Wimmer. Notre Dame, Indiana: University of Notre Dame Press, 1993.

Holmes, George. *The Oxford Illustrated History of Medieval Europe.* New York: Oxford University Press, 1988.

Keen, Maurice, editor. *Medieval Warfare: A History.* New York: Oxford University Press, 1999.

Konstram, Angus. *Atlas of Medieval Europe.* New York: Checkmark Books, 2000.

Lacey, Robert, and Danny Danziger. *The Year 1000.* New York: Little, Brown and Co., 1999.

Ladurie, Emmanuel Le Roy. *Montaillou: The Promised Land of Error.* New York: Vintage Books, 1979.

Read, Piers Paul. *The Templars.* New York: St. Martin's Press, 1999.

Tuchman, Barbara. *A Distant Mirror: The Calamitous 14th Century.* New York: Ballantine Books, 1978.

Villehardouin, Geoffroi de, et al. *Memoirs of the Crusades.* London: Penguin Books, 1963.

Acknowledgments

he authors would like to acknowledge that *The Jester* is,
all ways, a work of fiction, an entertainment, and while
ainstaking care has been paid to historical detail and
mes, now and then a fact has been stretched or a truth
ent for the sake of the story.

Thanks to H. D. Miller of Yale University for his schol-
ly, yet always anecdotal, reading of the manuscript. And
so to Mary Jordan, who kept this project on the right
ack at all times.

And most of all, thanks to Sue and Lynn, whose warmth
d laughter and spirit found its way onto many pages of
is book. And to our kids, Kristen and Matt and Nick
d Jack, in the hope that the sound of laughter will never
il to be a guiding companion and a cherished friend in
eir lives.

About the Authors

JAMES PATTERSON is the author of many international best-sellers, including *Along Came a Spider, Roses Are Red, Violets Are Blue,* and *1st to Die*. He lives in Florida.

ANDREW GROSS coauthored *2nd Chance* with James Patterson. He lives in New York.

More
James Patterson!

Please turn this page
for an excerpt from

3RD
DEGREE

a new
Little, Brown
hardcover available
wherever books are sold.

Chapter 1

It was a clear, calm, lazy April morning, the day the worst week of my life began.

I was jogging down by the Bay with my border collie, Martha. It's my thing Sunday mornings. Get up early, and cram my meaningful co-other into the front seat of the Explorer. I try and huff out three miles—from Fort Mason down to the bridge and back. Just enough to convince me I'm bordering on something called *shape* at thirty-six.

That morning, my buddy Jill came along. To give her baby Lab, Otis, a run, or so she claimed. More likely, to warm herself up for a bike sprint up Mount Tamalpais or whatever Jill would do for *real* exercise later in the day.

It was hard to believe it had been only five months since Jill had lost her baby. Now here she was, her body toned and lean again.

"So, how did it go last night?" She shuffled sideways. "Word on the street is, Lindsay had a date."

"You could call it a date . . ." I said, focusing on the heights of Fort Mason, which weren't getting closer fast enough for me. "You could call Baghdad a vacation spot too."

She winced. "Sorry I brought it up."

All run long, my head had been filled with the annoying recollection of Franklin Fratelli, "asset remarketing" mogul (which was a fancy way of saying he sent goons after the dot-com busts who could no longer make the payments on their Beemers and Frank Muellers). For two months Fratelli had stuck his face in my office every time I was in the Hall, until he wore me down enough to ask him up for a meal on Saturday night (which turned out to be a fancy way of describing the short ribs braised in port

wine I had to pack into the fridge after he bailed on me
the last minute).

"I got stood up," I said mid-stride. "Don't ask, I wo
tell the details."

We pulled up at the end of Marina Green, with a lur
clearing bray from me, while Mary Decker over the
bobbed on her toes like she could go another loop. "I do
know how you do it," I said, hands on hips, trying to cat
my breath.

"My grandmother." She shrugged, stretching out a ha
string. "She started walking five miles a day when she w
sixty. She s ninety now. We have no idea where she is."

We both started to laugh. It was good to see the old J
trying to peek through. It was good to hear the laugh
back in her voice.

"You up for a mochachino?" I asked. "Martha's buyin
"Can't. Steve's flying in from Chicago. He wants
bike up to see the Dean Freidlich exhibit at the Legion
Honor as soon as he can get in and change. You know wh
the puppy's like when he doesn't get his exercise."

I frowned. "Somehow it's hard for me to think of Ste
as a puppy . . ."

Jill nodded and pulled off her sweatshirt, lifting her arr
"Jill," I gasped. What the hell is *that?*"

Peeking out through the strap of her jog bra were a co
ple of small, dark bruises, like finger marks.

She tossed her sweatshirt over her shoulder, seemin
caught off guard. "Mashed myself getting out of t
shower," she said. "You should get a load of how *it* look
She winked.

I nodded, but something about the bruise didn't sit w
with me. "You sure you don't want that coffee?" I aske
"Sorry . . . You know El Exigente. If I'm five minu
late, he starts to see it as a pattern." She whistled for O

and started to jog back toward her car. She waved. "See you at work."

"So how about you?" I knelt down to Martha. "You look like a mochachino would do the trick." I snapped on her leash and started to trot off toward the Starbucks on Chestnut.

The Marina was always one of my favorite places. Curling streets of colorful, restored townhouses. Families, the sound of gulls, the sea air off the Bay.

I crossed Alhambra, my eye drifting to a beautiful three-story townhouse I always passed and admired. Hand-carved wood shutters and a terra-cotta the roof like on the Grand Canal. I held Martha as a car passed by.

That's what I remembered about the moment. The neighborhood just waking up. A kid in a FUBU sweatshirt practicing tricks on his Razor. A woman in overalls carrying a bundle of clothes hurrying around the corner.

"C'mon, Martha." I tugged on her leash. "I can taste that mochachino."

Then the townhouse with the terra-cotta roof exploded into flames. I mean, it was like San Francisco was suddenly Beirut.

Chapter 2

"Oh my God!" I gasped, as a flash of heat and debris nearly knocked me to the ground.

I turned away and shielded Martha as the oven-like shock waves from the explosion passed over us. A few seconds later, I turned to pull myself up. *Mother of God . . .* couldn't believe my eyes. The townhouse I had just admired was now a gorged-out crater. Fire ripped through what used to be the second floor.

In that instant, I realized, *People could be inside.*

I strung Martha to a lamppost. Flames gusted just fifty feet away. I ran across the street to the blazing home. The second floor was gone. If anyone was up there, they didn't have a chance.

I flailed at my fanny pack and fumbled for the cell phone. Frantically, I punched in 911. "This is Lieutenant Lindsay Boxer, San Francisco Police Department, Shield 2721. There's been an explosion at the corner of Alhambra and Pierce. A residence. Casualties likely. Need full medical and fire support. Get them moving!"

I cut off the dispatcher. Procedure told me to wait, but if anyone was in the house, there was no time. I ripped off my sweatshirt and wrapped it loosely around my face. *Oh Jesus Christ, Lindsay,* I said and held my breath.

Then I pushed my way into the flaming house.

"Is anyone there?" I shouted, choking immediately on the gray smoke. The intense heat bit at my eyes and face and it hurt just to peek out from the protective cloth. A wall of burning Sheetrock and plaster hung above me.

"Police," I shouted. "Is anyone there?"

The smoke felt like sharp razors slicing into my lungs. It was impossible to hear above the roar of the flames. suddenly understood how people trapped in fires on high floors would leap to their deaths rather than bear the intolerable heat.

I shielded my eyes, pushing my way through the bil

lowing smoke. I hollered a last time, "Is anyone alive in here?"

I couldn't go any farther. My eyes were singed. *I realized I could die in here.*

I turned and headed for the light and cool that I knew were behind me. Suddenly, I spotted two disfigured shapes, the bodies of a woman and man. Clearly dead, clothes on fire.

I stopped, feeling my stomach turn. But there was nothing I could do for them now.

Then I heard a muffled noise. I didn't know if it was real. I stopped, tried to listen above the rumble of the flames. I could hardly bear the pain of the blistering heat on my face.

There it was again. *It was real all right.*

Someone was crying.

Chapter 3

I gulped air and headed deeper into the collapsing house. "Where are you?" I called. I stumbled over flaming rubble. I was scared now, not only for whoever had cried, but for myself.

I heard it again! A low whimpering from somewhere in the house. I headed for it. "I'm coming," I shouted. To my left, a wooden beam crashed. The deeper I got, the more trouble I was in. I spotted a hallway where I thought the sounds came from, the second story teetering where the ceiling used to be.

"Police," I yelled. "Where are you?"

Nothing came back.

Then I heard the crying again. Closer, this time. *Someone was alive!* This time I stumbled down the hallway blanketing my face. *C'mon, Lindsay . . . Just a few feet more.*

I pushed through a smoking doorway. *Jesus, it was a kid's bedroom.* What was left of it.

A bed was overturned on its side up against a wall. I was smothered in thick dust. I shouted, then heard the noise again. A muffled, coughing sound.

The frame of the bed was hot to my touch, but I managed to pry it from the wall. *Oh my God . . .* saw the shadowy outline of a child's face.

It was a small boy. Maybe ten years old.

The child was coughing and crying. He could barely speak. His room was buried under an avalanche of debris. I couldn't wait. Any more time, the fumes alone would kill him.

"I'm gonna get you out of here," I promised. Then I wedged myself between the wall and the bed and, with all my strength, pried it away from the wall. I took the boy by the shoulders, praying I wasn't doing him harm.

I stumbled through the flames, carrying the boy. Fumes were everywhere, searing and noxious. I saw a light where I thought I had come in, but I didn't know for sure.

I was coughing, the boy clinging to me with his tiny petrified grip. "Mommy, Mommy," he was crying. I squeezed him back, to let him know I wasn't going to let him die.

I screamed ahead, praying someone would answer. "Please, is anyone there?"

"Here," I heard a voice through the blackness.

I stumbled over debris, avoiding new hot spots flaming up. Now I saw the entrance. Sirens, voices. The shape of a man. A fireman. He gently took the boy out of my arms. Another fireman wrapped his arms around me. We headed outside.

Then I was out, dropping to my knees, sucking in mouthfuls of precious air. An EMS tech carefully wrapped me in a blanket. Everyone was being so good, so professional. I collapsed against a fire truck up on the sidewalk. I almost threw up, then I did.

Someone put an oxygen mask over my mouth and I took several deep gulps. A fireman bent over me. "Were you inside when it went?"

"No." I shook my head. "I went in to help." I could barely talk or think. I opened my fanny pack and let my badge drop open. "Lieutenant Boxer," I coughed. "Homicide."

Carnival Elation

7 Day Exotic Western Caribbean Itinerary

DAY	PORT	ARRIVE	DEPART
Sun	Galveston		4:00 P.M.
Mon	"Fun Day" at Sea		
Tue	Progreso/Merida	8:00 A.M.	4:00 P.M.
Wed	Cozumel	9:00 A.M.	5:00 P.M.
Thu	Belize	8:00 A.M.	6:00 P.M.
Fri	"Fun Day" at Sea		
Sat	"Fun Day" at Sea		
Sun	Galveston	8:00 A.M.	

TERMS AND CONDITIONS

PAYMENT SCHEDULE:
50% due upon booking
Full and final payment due by July 26, 2004

Acceptable forms of payment are Visa, MasterCard, American Express, Discover and checks. The card-holder must be one of the passengers traveling. A fee of $25 will apply for all returned checks. Check payments must be made payable to **Advantage International, LLC** and sent to: Advantage International, LLC, 195 North Harbor Drive, Suite 4206, Chicago, IL 60601

CHANGE/CANCELLATION:
Notice of change/cancellation must be made in writing to Advantage International, LLC.

Change:
Changes in cabin category may be requested and can result in increased rate and penalties. A name change is permitted 60 days or more prior to departure and will incur a penalty of $50 per name change. Deviation from the group schedule and package is a cancellation.

Cancellation:

181 days or more prior to departure	$250 per person
121 - 180 days or more prior to departure	50% of the package price
120 - 61 days prior to departure	75% of the package price
60 days or less prior to departure	100% of the package price (nonrefundable)

US and Canadian citizens are required to present a valid passport or the original birth certificate and state issued photo ID (drivers license). All other nationalities must contact the consulate of the various ports that are visited for verification of documentation.

We strongly recommend trip cancellation insurance!

For further details call 1-877-ADV-NTGE or visit www.GetCaughtReadingatSea.com

For booking form and complete information
go to **www.getcaughtreadingatsea.com** or call **1-877-ADV-NTGE**

Complete coupon and booking form and mail both to:
**Advantage International, LLC,
195 North Harbor Drive, Suite 4206, Chicago, IL 60601**

**Warner Books is not responsible for
any portion of the Get Caught Reading
at Sea promotion.**

more...

VIOLETS ARE BLUE

"ANOTHER PAGE-TURNER...YOU WON'T BE ABLE TO PUT 'VIOLETS' DOWN UNTIL YOU'VE REACHED THE BACK COVER."
                    —*New York Times*

"PARTICULARLY JUICY . . . ENJOYABLY SPOOKY . . . BOTTOM LINE: BLOODY GOOD CREEPFEST."
                    —*People*

"AS ADDICTIVE AS ALL OF PATTERSON'S BOOKS. . . . YOU HAVE NO CHOICE: YOU MUST READ IT."
                    —*Denver Rocky Mountain News*

"EERILY BELIEVABLE . . . FRIGHTENING . . . VINTAGE PATTERSON, the latest in a series of thrillers featuring the eminently admirable and likable Detective Alex Cross. . . . Keeps you guessing until the end . . . will keep Patterson readers in suspense until his next book. We can only hope it comes out soon."
                    —*Providence Sunday Journal*